Whickering Place

Legacy of Darkness, Volume 2

London Clarke

Published by Carfax Abbey Publishing, 2019.

This is a work of fiction. Similarities to real people, places, or events are entirely coincidental.

WHICKERING PLACE

First edition. July 30, 2019.

Written by London Clarke.

For Donna
The best teacher in the world
My best friend and confidante
The world is a darker place without you.

"Ah, it is the fault of our science that it wants to explain all; and if it explain not, then it says there is nothing to explain."
— **Bram Stoker,** *Dracula*[1]

"The desire for safety stands against every great and noble enterprise."
— **Tacitus**

---

1. *https://www.goodreads.com/work/quotes/3165724*

Charlotte, North Carolina
Ten Years Ago

Avery looked down at her arms, her hands. They were covered in blood.

Vermilion rivulets dripped from her fingertips. Deep slashes bisected the skin of her forearms.

A woman from the crowd prodded the onlookers to move away, stand back while a man pulled off his T-shirt and tried to press it to Avery's arms. Then the woman turned to her, reaching out as though she wanted to touch her but wasn't sure if she should.

"Come on, honey," she said, her voice shaking. "Hold on. Ambulance is on the way. Can you hear the sirens?"

A minute before, Avery had been standing beside Vince, her boyfriend, while they waited for the 4th of July parade to start. Later they would have been going to a party, celebrating her acceptance into the criminal justice program at UNC. There would've been a lot of smiling people.

Not the screaming people who surrounded her now.

Avery shifted her gaze to the ground where Vince lay. Several people squatted around him. His legs jutted out from their huddle—but only from the knees down. He wasn't moving. He'd been wearing shorts, and his summer-tanned skin was slick and stained red.

Something had happened. Avery tried to compose her thoughts to remember what. A girl had sprung out of the crowds, slashing at them with something sharp. A knife?

"Vince!" Avery called out.

Vince didn't answer.

People spoke rapidly, frantically—to her, to each other—their voices fading in and out ... just like her vision.

"She's losing a lot of blood."

"Tie the tourniquet tighter."

"It doesn't seem to be working." A man breathed. "At this rate, she's gonna bleed to death."

"Ambulance is here. They'll help."

Were they talking about her? Bleed to death. But she couldn't die. She'd just turned eighteen. She was going to be the best police officer in North Carolina. Just yesterday, she'd won her division in an archery competition. Bull's eye. Every time.

But that moment seemed like years ago as she stared at her arms, fixated on the blood. The sunny day slowly dimmed, the edges of her vision framed by a black haze that narrowed to a small circle of sight. Her knees buckled, and she barely felt the grip of hands around her waist as she started to sink.

"They were stabbed. Both of them."

The whir of lights around her.

More sirens.

And then darkness.

Chapter One
North Carolina
Present Day
Tuesday, January 7

"This will be our last session for a while. Maybe for a long while."

Dr. Murphy sat across from me, dressed as always in slacks and flats. Her brown hair flipped up at the ends—probably newly styled from a trip to the salon.

Dr. Murphy and I had been sitting across from each other once a week for the past five years. Now, it struck me that I might never see her again.

A hard lump materialized in my throat. "It's starting again."

"What's starting again?"

I toyed with the ends of my hair. It was so long I could keep my hands in my lap while twisting it around my fingers. "I woke in the middle of the night and couldn't move. Just like before. Like something was lying on top of me, holding me down, breathing in my face."

"You haven't had that happen in a few years." Her eyes remained steady on mine. "Was there any particular formation to what held you down?"

"No. I never see anything. And I can't scream."

"How long did it last this time?"

"About five minutes. Then it lifted off of me. And everything went back to normal. Except I couldn't go to sleep."

She breathed in through her nose. "It sounds like more sleep paralysis. You're experiencing a natural reaction to a big life change."

But there was more to it. "And then I didn't want to go outside again today. I feel like I'm right back to where I started."

She nodded.

I waited for her to say something. When she didn't, I filled in the blanks. "Maybe it's not the right time for me to do this."

Dr. Murphy shifted her position in the mauve armchair that looked like a leftover from someone's garage sale and crossed her legs. "Avery, moving is stressful for anyone, and for someone who has recently walked through some of the challenges you've had—your mother moving back to Italy, your father's suicide—this is doubly hard."

Tell me I don't have to do this now. Tell me I should give it more time, wait a while before making such a big decision. The lump in my throat swelled.

"Agoraphobia is hard enough to overcome on its own, but you've made some great strides this past year. Facing a move to a new house and a new town is bound to cause you fear. Give it time."

I looked down at my hands, defeated.

"You're twenty-seven. It's been nearly ten years since the stabbing. And you've made progress. But this is your chance to really step out and try your wings, so to speak."

I nodded.

"You've refilled your meds?"

"Yes."

"You have your daily schedule made out—the one we've talked about?"

"Yes."

She clasped her fingers together and settled them in her lap. "You can always call me if you need me."

"What about the sleep paralysis?"

"Get settled in. Then we'll reassess."

Chapter Two
Friday, January 17

D r. Murphy told me this move was critical. It would change my life, possibly for the better. But I'd only ever lived in small apartments, and she thought moving directly into a mansion in a new town might be too much.

So we'd worked out a transition.

I would stay in a hotel in Asheville, one on the outskirts of town—a less busy, less populated area—with a coffee shop just across the street. For a week before moving into my new home, I would acclimate to the new city by venturing out to the coffee shop, where I could take my laptop and possibly work for an hour or two.

Then, it was essential I stick to a regular daily schedule.

Wake at 7:00. Breakfast at 7:30. Yoga at 8:00. Check emails at 9:00. Walk one block to the coffee shop by 9:15. Start work on my laptop by 9:30.

And remember to take my meds.

And for the first few days, it had gone like clockwork.

But this morning, I left the hotel later than usual. Even that small deviation in timing had thrown me off.

More people milled around at this time of day. One might even call them crowds. People hurrying off to work. Bustling into the coffee shop for their latte on the way to a business meeting.

But I forced my legs to move. If I was going to make this work, I had to meet challenges head-on. That's what Dr. Murphy said.

Come Monday, my schedule would change again anyway. I'd be leaving the hotel for Whickering Place, my father's old home—the one I'd somehow inherited.

My father, Ace Tullinger, a well-known painter, had committed suicide last summer. I hadn't seen him in close to twenty years, but I was his only living relative.

Maris Manners, my father's attorney, told me she'd take me on the tour of Whickering Place whenever I was ready. She'd been handling everything for me. All the paperwork, all the legal documents. Tenants currently lived in the house, and she offered to manage their leases as well. And if I wanted to sell, she knew willing buyers.

I was grateful. A huge learning curve loomed ahead. Maybe more than I was ready for.

But as I stepped into the coffee shop that morning and joined the line, I glanced at my usual table in my safe corner.

Someone was already sitting there.

Damn.

This was why I *had* to stay on schedule.

I scanned the room for alternative seats while twisting a fistful of my hair around my fingers. The only seats available were the ones lining the window, and I'd have to sit beside someone. My chest tightened. My hands started to sweat. Preliminary signs of an attack.

I just want to go back to the hotel.

Sam, the barista who usually took my order, stood at the register. Her bright orange vest was covered in awareness ribbons of all different colors. Yesterday I'd asked about them, and she'd told me what they were for. I only remembered the purple and turquoise one. Suicide prevention.

She rang up my order—didn't even ask what I wanted. I'd ordered the same thing all week. Almond milk latte. Blueberry scone.

"No mug, though," I specified. "Just a to-go cup."

She cocked her head. "No? Not staying with us this morning?"

I glanced over my shoulder at the full room behind me. "I don't know. I don't think so."

"It should clear out soon." She pushed the paper cup toward me.

I shouldered my laptop bag and carried my latte toward the seats by the window. Now for the big decision. I started to follow two other ladies out the door but hung back. Completely flustered, I veered toward the window seats and went for the last stool by the wall. At least I'd only have to sit by one other person.

Simultaneously, a man reached for the same stool.

I looked up at him. Maple-brown eyes framed by long, dark lashes.

"Oh, sorry." He motioned to the stool. "Please. Take it."

I stood back. "No, you take it. I think I'll just go."

He motioned more emphatically toward the stool. "No, I insist. Really. I don't have a lot of time. I don't need to sit."

A woman one seat over slid off her stool and left.

The man smiled, gave a little laugh.

We both sat.

I cringed. I probably couldn't work with a stranger sitting next to me. Without removing my bag from my shoulder, I awkwardly pulled out my laptop, bumping my elbow against the man's arm. "Sorry."

"You're fine. It's close quarters here."

I tucked my elbows into my sides. The ledge was barely wide enough to fit a laptop, and the front of the computer hung off. It was hard to maneuver the mouse without brushing the man's hand.

Scrolling through my emails, I mentally planned my escape.

"Is this your office?" he asked.

I tried not to look at the guy as I responded. "Most mornings, yeah."

"That's great—you get to work wherever you want." He had an accent. But I couldn't tell from where.

I nodded.

"What do you do?"

"Website designer."

"Cool."

I stared at my emails without reading them.

"How did you get involved with doing that? Making websites?"

My first conversation in the coffee shop with anyone other than Sam, the barista. Dr. Murphy would be proud. *Make conversation with new people. Daily, if possible.*

My heart sped. I wiped my hands on my jeans. "Well, I was a criminal justice major, but then I sort of had an accident and couldn't become a police officer like I wanted, so..." I motioned toward the computer. "Website design." *A great stay-at-home career for agoraphobics.*

I stole a glance at the guy. He wasn't bad looking if you liked the rough-around-the-edges type. Longish hair. Unshaven. Leather jacket. Still, he was a stranger. Even if his accent was intriguing.

Dr. Murphy's voice again: *It doesn't have to be a long conversation. It's good practice to participate in small talk.*

"What about you? What do you do? You sound like you're from … somewhere else."

He looked out the window as he answered. "I am, yeah. New *Awlens.*"

"Oh. I would've said New York."

"Yeah, I get that a lot." He nodded. "I guess there are some similarities in the accent."

"So, you live here now?"

"Yeah, I've been up here a few months. For a job. I'm sort of in the medical profession." He glanced at his watch. "Working at the Asheville Medical Center."

"That's great." And that was about all I had.

He picked up his cup and slid off the stool. "Speaking of, I need to get over there now."

I forced a tight smile. Relief. "Okay."

"Nice talkin' to you."

After he'd gone, I glanced over my shoulder. My regular table was empty.

I made a dash for the corner and threw myself into the chair, slamming my laptop hard against the tabletop. I looked down at my hands—covered in sweat. But the inside of my mouth was dry like I'd sucked on felt.

How was I ever going to survive this transition?

Chapter Three
Whickering Place

S omeone new is coming to Whickering Place.

Over the years, there have been many. Some more beneficial than others as they carried out the legacy of those who came before. Most are unaware of what is here—the power that hides behind these walls. Of what awaits them.

We have been here for nearly a century—receiving what is offered and sometimes taking what is not. We feed on ignorance, unbelief, and bitterness. Still, our favorite flavors lie in the recesses of the human body that secrete emotions of fear, terror, and despair.

At first glance, this new inhabitant appears no different from the others. She's a skeptic of the supernatural but fears humanity's dangers and has known them. Therefore, she looks at that man dragging his garbage out to the curb and wonders if he is a threat. She does not glance off to the right, to the shadows that lurk outside the house, stretching out their arms and beckoning her inside. She cannot see the yellow eyes that watch her from the windows and the roof, although she stares up, surveying the stone gargoyles that perch high above her head.

She does not hear the voices as she mounts the stairs, as we whisper and position ourselves in readiness for her entrance.

But they all hear us eventually. They all believe in time. Some of them even come to know us by name. A few join us in our quest. Every one of them participates in our game.

Willingly or not.

Chapter Four
Tuesday, January 21

So this was it. Whickering Place.

Staring up at the hulking, stone structure and its massive, castle-like turret, I felt small and out of place.

I'm really going to live here.

I needed to tell myself and repeat, remind myself that this was real.

A shiver ripped through me as I approached the front door, past the perfectly manicured hedgerows, up ten steps, and under the yawning archway leading to the front door.

Maris Manners and I had talked several times on the phone about legal issues and paperwork, but now, meeting her for the first time, she didn't look anything like I'd imagined. She was attractive, on the skinny side, with a swan neck and long arms that made her look like a dancer. Her blonde hair was swept away from her face in a tight bun, completing the ballerina image.

She extended her hand to me. "Avery. Finally, we meet. Maris."

I shook her hand before following her inside.

Standing in the foyer and looking up at the curving staircase and high ceilings, I tried to remember being here. I'd only visited the house a couple of times as a child.

Had my father's house always been this dark?

Maris quickly flipped on lights, and I looked up at the chandelier hanging overhead.

"The floors are all original." She pointed to the polished hardwood floors and briskly led me into a room off to the right, her heels click-clacking.

I glanced down at my jeans and tennis shoes and my old, white wool coat with the gray stain on the sleeve from brushing up against wet paint in my old apartment building. Living alone and rarely venturing out, I'd had little reason for any other kind of clothing.

"This is the great room—or the ballroom, I like to call it." Maris held out her arms on either side as if she might do a pirouette. "This is where your father held his art receptions. Did you ever go to any of those?"

I shook my head. The room was massive. Gold columns. Three chandeliers hung in a line down the middle of the ceiling. A raised stage at one end was flanked by mullioned windows partially covered in heavy drapery. "No, but as a little kid, I remember this room being locked, off-limits."

Maris held up a finger. "Let me show you something really cool about this room." We walked to the opposite end where a mythological mural covered the wall—imps and fairies dancing naked and playing lutes and harps. Other figures wore togas and held up gold chalices. Maris pressed her hands against the wall. She winked at me and then pushed.

The panel opened.

As we entered, a sconce illuminated the space. We wound up the circular stairs. At the top, another door led us into a bedroom.

"This was your father's room. It's the master bedroom, so you'll probably want to sleep in here."

"Is that the only way to get in here? Through the ballroom?" I really hoped not.

She giggled and playfully smacked my arm. "No, sweetie." She walked to a door opposite and pushed it open. You can come through this door, from the hallway."

"Oh, that's good. So the other way's kind of a secret?"

Maris nodded. "Don't know how often Ace used it, but I've always thought there was a good reason why the architect built it. Quick escape from the ball without anyone noticing? Or easy way to sneak young ladies into the master's bedroom?" She shrugged. "Anyway, it offers another route to the downstairs if needed. There's also a fire escape off of the attic roof."

I made a revolution, taking in the surroundings. Dark colors. The walls were a deep gray with a pattern of charcoal spades. The bed looked like something Dracula might have slept in—a gothic headboard of liver-colored wood with sharp, triangular edges.

I suppressed a shudder. I couldn't imagine sleeping in here.

As we returned to the ballroom via the secret passage, I fought the compression in my chest. The house already overwhelmed me.

Maris touched my arm. "Are you all right, sweetie?"

I forced a weak smile. "It's a lot to take in."

"I understand." Maris compressed her lips. "And I know you've been through a lot."

How much did she know? Although my father had stopped calling me long before the stabbing, my mother had contacted him after the fact, told him I was in the hospital. He'd sent flowers.

From what I'd heard, at the end of his life, Ace was a recluse. Like father like daughter.

Maris lifted her eyes and scanned the room. "Your father and I were close, but Ace was an intensely private man. As you know, he was a well-known figure here in Asheville. His death has hit a lot of people hard. Including me."

My hands were sweating. The medication must have started to wear off. I took deep breaths, hearing Dr. Murphy's voice in my head. *Hold it together. You just got here. Give it time.*

Snapping out of her reverie, Maris turned back to the room. "Your father rented out parts of the house for community purposes like weddings and social gatherings. The room itself measures fifteen hundred square feet, so you can fit a lot of people in here." She pivoted toward me. "*You* might even consider renting out the space. To help with the utilities and upkeep. I'm already receiving calls about rentals for this year. I can set up the events if you like."

I tried to imagine living in a house with people coming in and out all of the time, holding parties, banquets, weddings. It was bad enough that I'd have to deal with tenants. "No. I don't think so. At least, not right now. That would be too stressful."

"Well, think about it," Maris exhaled. "You may find the expense and upkeep of this place drive you to reconsider." Her perfectly outlined lips downturned. "Or, have you considered selling?"

Blowing out air, I pinched my temples between my thumb and forefinger. "I did consider it. Yeah."

Maris straightened. "Sold."

"What?"

Her lips pulled back from teeth that looked too perfect. "I'll be happy to buy it from you. You can name your price."

My mouth fell open. I didn't know what to say. Was she joking? "I—I don't know if—"

"Your father would've completely understood. I can take care of all the paperwork, the closing costs, any expenses you may have incurred."

She gave me a sidelong glance.

I shook my head, my chest constricting. She wasn't joking. "Well, I ... just got here, so ... I mean, where would I go?"

"Wherever you like—with the money you'd make off of this place!" She beamed.

"No, no, I couldn't."

"Or don't you have some friends you could stay with until you find the right living situation?"

Panic poured into my gut at the thought of arriving here only to uproot again. "Not really."

Her mouth sank at the edges, her ice-blue eyes narrowed.

"I need to settle in one place for a while before I think about selling."

She raised her chin, nodded. "I understand." Then she pivoted on her heel, motioning for me to follow her.

I moved behind her into the hallway, trailing in the wake of her floral perfume. "But two tenants are living here now?"

"Yes," she called over her shoulder. "Two brothers. One is a doctor—an internist or something like that. The other brother works at the medical center too, I think."

"Are they here right now?"

"No, at work. But I'm sure you'll meet them tonight."

The idea of tenants both comforted and terrified me. I hadn't lived with anyone in years. Another lifetime ago. And I'd never lived with men. Not even my father.

We walked across the hall and into a large room arranged with couches, tables, and chairs that looked faithful to the time period—streamlined, symmetrical. A flat-screen television was positioned on one end of the room near the couches. The other end was mostly taken up by the fireplace with its mantel of dark, polished marble with inlaid lines and angles.

Maris turned to me. "Here in the south, we call this the front parlor. It's part of the common area, and the tenants use this room. You'll have your separate living space upstairs. Other than sharing the kitchen, you needn't run into them at all if you don't wish to. The house is roughly ten thousand square feet."

We swept quickly through the front parlor and into a billiard room, where the pool table was positioned in the middle, and smaller game tables for chess and cards sat in the corners.

"A lot of famous people have spent time in this room. F. Scott Fitzgerald and his wife. The Vanderbilts, musicians, painters, writers." She pointed to a door at the back of the room. "File cabinets are in there—documents date all the way back to the original owners. It's locked now, but I can get you a key."

Files, paperwork, tenants. A ten-thousand-square-foot house. More responsibility than I'd ever had in my life.

How would I manage this place and its legacy? My father's legacy...

Maris seemed to read my mind. "Don't worry, sweetie." She put her arm around me and squeezed. "I'm going to help you run this place. I'll be with you every step of the way." With her arm still firmly around my shoulders, she led me out of the room. "I still talk to Ace, you know. And sometimes, I think he talks back to me. I've promised him I'll look after you. I'll be your mentor—your advisor. Didn't your mother just move to Europe or something?"

"She moved back to Milan. That's where she's from originally."

"I think your father mentioned that."

"I'd like to see my father's studio," I said.

Maris nodded. "Of course. It's this way."

She continued to hold my shoulders in the vice of her arm. I hadn't encountered this much physical contact in years.

We migrated up one set of stairs and down another, entering a hallway lined with Ace's paintings. Canvas after canvas narrated his tell-tale style—abstract, bright clashing colors, wild and whimsical brushstrokes.

"This part of the house is off-limits to the tenants," Maris said. "Your father's studios and the rooms down this hall were used only by him."

I stopped in front of one of the paintings—mesmerized by its dark red background and black, frantic lines. I dabbed a finger to the canvas. My father had encouraged people to touch his paintings. "As long as the paint's dry." His artwork was meant to be touched, seen, and felt. "Through the eyes, under the hand, and in the heart."

Maris unlocked a door, and we stepped inside.

No doubt my visits had fulfilled a custody agreement or perhaps assuaged my father's own guilt. Still, I remembered the few times I'd visited him—when I'd watched him paint and tried to copy his brushstrokes.

I remembered this studio.

Canvases perched atop easels. Half-filled jars of discolored water littered one table. On the other side, palettes of paints and wadded-up cloths with streaks of color cluttered a bench. Paintings, finished and unfinished, hung from the walls.

It was as though my father had just gotten up and left it all.

"The paintings are yours now, of course," said Maris. "You may do with them as you please. Keep them, sell them."

I approached an easel and stared at the unfinished canvas. Purple strokes halfway down the surface gave way to a deeper violet and finally black.

Maris glided over to stand beside me. "When was the last time you were here?"

Had I been eight? Nine? No, not so old—more like six.

"It's been like, twenty years."

"Ace loved you, you know."

Maris's words slashed at my heart. It was hard to believe. "Well, he didn't try very hard to have a relationship with me."

"He wanted to. He really did."

A familiar knot of anger hardened in my chest. "He's the one who stopped all contact. Not me." My throat constricted. "And we have these things called phones and computers. Lots of ways to communicate—text, email, an old-fashioned telephone call." I shrugged. My eyes burned.

Maris looked down at the floor, her mouth moving side to side. "Ace was a complex man. He kept his emotions in a back pocket, definitely not on his sleeve."

"It seems like you knew him pretty well." Maris was probably in her mid-forties—about twenty years younger than my dad. But a relationship between them wasn't unrealistic.

Maris met my gaze. "We shared similar interests and friends."

I scanned the cluttered state of the room. "How am I going to keep this place clean?"

"Not to worry. Housecleaners come in once a week on Friday. Your father had a standing contract with them. And it's paid up through next year."

That was a relief. One less anxiety.

Maris grabbed my hand and squeezed. "And you know, if this all gets to be too much for you, I meant what I said about buying Whickering Place. You could make a lot of money on it. I have a feeling that may have been what your father intended for you all along."

"I might decide to do that. Eventually. Not now. It all depends on how things go."

A coin sitting on the edge of one of the tables caught my eye. It was the size of a silver dollar but copper with a deep patina. It looked familiar. As soon as I picked it up, the memory clicked.

"I have one of these." I held it up to the light and turned it over. A likeness of the house and the name Whickering Place was minted onto the backside. On the front, the writing had worn away. "One time when I visited, I found one upstairs. I just took it, but then I felt guilty and showed it to Dad. He said I could keep it. I've hung onto it all of these years." I laughed a little. "Up until now, it was really the only thing he ever gave me."

"Hm," Maris said absently.

"Do you know what they are? These coins?"

She shook her head.

I set the coin back on the table and followed Maris out of the studio.

She locked the door behind us. "Avery, there's something you should probably be aware of."

"Okay."

"From time to time, you might see or hear some things that seem scary to you. But your father learned not to be frightened."

"What do you mean? Like what?"

"Ace always said there was something else here—another spirit, or entity if you will."

I shook off the suggestion. "What—like the house is haunted or something?"

"Something like that."

"I don't believe in that kind of thing."

Maris's hand floated down to rest gracefully on my shoulder. "Good for you. I'm sure it's fine." She stopped when we reached the foyer. "I didn't want to alarm you. But I also didn't want you to be scared if you did experience something."

"I'm not worried about ghosts. Real people are a lot scarier."

I was tired and ready for her to leave. I hadn't done this much talking since the last time I saw Dr. Murphy.

As I opened the front door, cold air blew across the threshold. "Thanks for your help."

"If you need anything at all, please call me." She pointed to a side table where the card was wedged under the base of an urn.

"Oh, and I forgot to bring the tenants' paperwork, but I'll bring it by later in the week." She put her hand on my shoulder again. "Just give it a little time. I know you're nervous about having tenants, but you may find living in this huge house by yourself gets a bit nerve-wracking. It'll be nice to have company. A friend, even."

Maris was the only person I knew in Asheville. Whether I liked it or not, I couldn't afford to shrug off offers of friendship. "Thank you."

After I'd shut the door and locked it, I stood in the foyer and breathed slowly and deeply, just as Dr. Murray had told me to do, pretending I heard her soothing voice advising me. *Everything will be fine. This your home now. It's a new life.*

Even so, my heart didn't slow.

My medication. I reached into the side pocket of my purse for a pill container. My fingers rushed over the steel of my Glock 9mm. I'd almost forgotten that I'd stuffed it into my purse. Usually, it was inside the portable safe.

I took my medicine and waited for it to kick in.

Remember, you can always call Dr. Murray if you need to. She said to call her anytime.

The room Maris called the front parlor had a large bay window, which offered a wide-angle view of the street. A truck pulled up to the curb, and several burly men hopped out and opened the back. My stuff had arrived. One of the men carried my couch, slung it on his back as though he were Atlas with the world on his shoulders. The other man wore my kitchen table chairs over his wrists like bracelets while helping the first guy hoist the furniture.

My couch wouldn't fit in here.

I didn't fit in here.

But here I was. Committed to this. Determined to conquer this illness once and for all.

Any second the men would ring the doorbell, and I'd have to let them in.

You'll be trapped inside with them.

The naked, unchecked thought ran through my brain like a streaker.

I peered out at the street—at the houses across from Whickering Place where normal people probably lived. Or maybe not so normal.

There were dangers out there.

Murderers.

Accidents.

Sometimes people bled to death.

Chapter Five

Our attachment to Whickering Place is fluid. Although many of us remain here most of the time, it is easy to attach to something, or someone, and be carried from the house, out into the world, where we may settle in another location. Objects—ones prepared in advance for these occasions—facilitate travel. Willing persons, often unaware of the vessel-like void inside of them, are easily fashioned into vehicles of change.

This new inhabitant is blissfully unaware of us or any of our intentions, making her easy prey. Just like her father. She tries to mask her sheltered existence—the fact that she has hardly set foot outside in a decade. The notion of this new life and all of its unknowns terrifies her to the core. She likes to think of herself as she once was—physically and mentally strong—a fighter. But humans love to cling to the delusion that they are immutable overcomers. They like the idea of justice and happiness above all things. When in fact, they are fragile, brittle ... easily bent, broken. Mere dust.

She will have to pretend. She will have to hide her insecurities and fears from those around her. She will not see us immediately—her refusal to believe in anything outside her limited scope may blind her at first.

But eventually, her physical senses will take over.

That's part of why she's here. She's desperate for change. Hungry to feel.

Something.

Anything.

Even if the feeling destroys her.

Chapter Six
Wednesday, January 22

I didn't sleep at all my first night in Whickering Place. As Maris suggested, I stayed in my father's part of the house—what she'd referred to as the east wing. And the whole night, I'd endured the sensation of ants crawling over my skin.

Finally, exhausted, I'd slept once the sun came up. Had the tenants come home last night? Even if they had, by the time I rose, it was after ten in the morning, and I was once again alone in the house.

I spent the day exploring, wandering the halls, opening doors to bedrooms, thrusting my head inside and withdrawing again. Each room was similar to the one next to it. Empty. Creepy. Beds stripped of sheets, mattresses covered in plastic, curtains drawn.

The upstairs of the house needed updates and repairs—a feat I wasn't ready to take on. Only one room located just outside the attic looked freshly painted. But there wasn't a stitch of furniture within. Only a red Oriental rug. And the space was freezing.

I approached one of the walls and ran my fingernail against a crack where the paint was flaking, picking at it until a shard of white fluttered to the ground. Underneath, a strip of deep vermilion suggested the room must have had red walls at one time.

The room had one window. Through the iced-over panes, I could see the dentals of the rooftop, and beyond that, the neighborhood and the mountains behind it. Metal construction stuck up a few inches above the stone—the fire escape. Just like Maris had said.

A crushing sense of loneliness pressed into me. I'd lived alone for years and never worried about it. Maybe I was only experiencing it now because Whickering Place didn't feel like my house at all. I doubted it ever would.

Despite my prior concern about living with people, I actually wanted to meet the tenants. Two brothers. Maybe old bachelors or widowers.

For the rest of the afternoon, I caught up on client projects. Even though Maris had said the front room was common area, I set up my laptop at the small desk in the corner by the bay window, where at least some sunlight streamed in.

Late that evening, the front door creaked open. Footfall followed. After a day of feeling like I was stranded in the catacombs, hearing other life entering the house was a relief. I watched the door leading into the front room, expecting to see the kindly gray-haired doctor who lived here.

"Hello?" I forced the word from my throat and then flinched at the echo.

"Hello." The reply sounded deep-voiced, resonant.

I remained at the edge of the wall and waited.

The dim hall light silhouetted the outline of the man.

"Are you Avery?" He stepped into the light.

Not a grandfather. Tall. Dark hair. This was the tenant? Was he even old enough to be a doctor?

He extended his hand. "Colin Gallagher."

I met his hand with my cold, clammy one. *Act like you're normal.* "I—I'm sorry, I expected someone older."

He smiled down at me and rested his left shoulder against the wall. "Sorry to disappoint."

"Oh, well, no, I'm sorry. I didn't mean that you should be older, only that I expected..." I shook my head. "Never mind."

His eyes fixed on mine. "Did you just arrive?"

"Yesterday, actually."

This was terrible. Why hadn't Maris warned me? But why would she? Maris *was* normal. She didn't consider this a problem.

"Sorry for the loss of your father," he said. "I never had the chance to meet him, but I understand he was a fascinating man."

"Thank you. I barely knew him myself."

"Where were you living before?"

I unstuck my tongue from the roof of my mouth. "In a little town called Morganton. About sixty miles east of here."

A dark lock of hair slid across his eyes, and he pushed it away before repositioning his shoulder against the wall. "Hey, thanks for letting us stay on, by the way. I'm looking for a house to buy but haven't found the right one yet."

I shrugged. "It's too big a house to live in on my own."

He shifted his weight from the entryway and began to turn. "Well, I won't keep you."

"Nice to meet you, Dr. Gallagher."

"Call me Colin."

Chapter Seven

I stared at my reflection in the ebony-framed mirror hanging on the wall in my bedroom. I'd really let myself go. My hair had grown so long it nearly touched my waist, and I couldn't remember the last time I'd worn any makeup.

Moving closer to the mirror, I pulled gently at my lower eyelids. In a little over two years, I'd be thirty. Where had my twenties gone? "They slid down the drain of Morganton Psychiatric," I informed my reflection.

I no longer considered myself eligible for any sort of life outside the one I had. Relationship, marriage, children—those events happened to someone else, not me. Anyone who knew my history would run a mile.

I lifted my hair up and off my face. Supposedly, I'd inherited Francesca Bodini's dark Italian eyes and thick hair. I'd been told more than once that I looked like my mother. But my mother was beautiful and vibrant, and it was hard to believe that I resembled her now as I stared into the tired planes of my face and dark circles under my eyes.

But you haven't always been like this.

Right. I used to be in stellar psychological and physical shape. Senior year in high school, I was voted Most Likely to Survive *The Hunger Games*. Because of my archery awards, of course. I was just glad none of my old classmates could see me now.

I resumed unpacking. It shouldn't have taken me long. I hadn't brought that much, but putting my clothes in the dresser that had once been my father's seemed wrong, too permanent.

My compound bow rested against the wall—a gift from my mom after my last archery tournament. It had probably been five years since I'd shot a bow and arrow ... or my gun. For now, my 9mm was stowed in the safe beside my bed. I carried the bow and quiver full of brand-new, unused carbon-shaft arrows and placed them in the walk-in closet.

I checked the time on my phone. 10:20. Usually, by this time, I was in bed asleep. But my stomach growled, and the familiar gnawing sensation of hunger wouldn't let me rest. The notion of dinner had escaped me.

As I stepped out of the confines of the master bedroom, a blast of frigid air sliced through me. Was a window open somewhere? A prolonged creak stopped me, and I whipped my head around. Supposedly, tenants weren't allowed up here. I groped the edge of the wall and located a light switch. Wall sconces cast a yellow gleam across the floor. I scanned the corridor. Empty.

I hurried through the hall and down the stairs into the common area.

Downstairs was warmer, and the tenants had left a light on in the front room. At least I could see my way.

An antique phone sat on one of the hall tables, which looked straight out of the 1920s. The ornate brass receiver rested atop an upright base with a wooden body and rotary dial. I ran my finger over it. It was a beautiful piece and probably original to the house.

A metallic bell vibrated through the hallway, propelling me backward with its unexpected ring. "Crap."

The metal ringer beat out another blare. I snatched up the receiver. "Hello?"

Silence.

My eyes trailed down the wall in search of a cord. There was none—nothing attached to a wall or a phone jack.

Turning the phone upside down, I searched its underbelly for signs that it might be wireless or reconfigured to receive calls without aid of a cord. But nothing about it looked unusual beyond its age.

I replaced the receiver, let out a shaky stream of air, and moved into the kitchen.

The kitchen was dark except for a few shiny reflections off of the industrial stainless steel. On the other side of the room, only the silver sink glowed under the cast of moonlight through the window. I felt along the wall for a switch, found one, and flipped it on. The room remained unlit.

"Light's burned out."

I jumped at the low voice. "Shit!" I grasped at the neckline of my shirt. "First the phone and now... You scared me."

"Sorry. I just got home and realized the light was out. I can fix it for you if you want." The man stepped into the direct cast of the moonlight, his form silhouetted against the window. Definitely not Colin. This man was taller, his curly hair touching his shoulders. "I don't know what to tell you about the phone. Just rings on its own. Figure it's haunted."

I flipped on the light over the stove. A section of the room was illuminated, allowing me to see the man's face. He looked familiar.

"You must be Avery," he said.

And he sounded familiar. That accent.

"Yes."

"I'm your tenant. Well, one of them. Pearse." He held out his hand.

I shook his hand and did a double-take. Wait. The guy from the coffee shop...

"Colin's brother," he added.

He obviously didn't remember me. "Yeah, I met Colin earlier."

Silence followed. I clenched and unclenched my fists.

The light above the stove flickered and went out.

"This place needs massive rewiring," I said.

Pearse gave a short laugh. "I don't mind standing in the dark, but you might find it kind of awkward, so I think I'll just..."

His leather jacket rustled as he swept by me and out of the open doorway, allowing me a glimpse of his profile. Definitely the guy from the coffee shop. He looked similar to his brother—same nose and facial structure—but a totally different vibe. Ripped jeans, combat boots. He slouched slightly.

"I'll fix those lights for you tomorrow," he called over his shoulder.

I should have told him we'd already met, but the moment had passed.

I returned to the upstairs—still having eaten nothing. Appetite gone. After locking the door, I lay in bed, my heart thrashing in my ears. What had I done? Maybe I wasn't ready for this. Maybe I should have stayed in Morganton and just allowed the Gallagher brothers to continue on as tenants.

You said a decade was long enough. Remember?

"Yes, I remember," I said aloud.

Then I heard it again—the creaking noise—like footsteps just outside my door.

I sat up—every fiber and sinew tautly suspended, every hair on my body raised like antennae. What was that?

Creak. Creeeak. Creak. Creeak. A heavy shuffling, slithering sound followed—leather against hardwood, bringing to mind the image of an alligator snaking down the hall.

Had one of the two men come upstairs? Then another thought struck me. Who were these guys? Could I even trust them?

I rushed to my small gun safe positioned on the second shelf of my bedside table and quickly typed in the code. My hands shook as I held the steel against my forefinger and waited. I wouldn't rack the slide unless someone actually entered my room.

A minute ticked by.

Then another.

A rivulet of sweat glided down my back and settled at the elastic of my underwear.

After that, the hall outside my door was silent.

I let a few minutes pass before replacing the gun in the safe. Then I relaxed back onto my pillows.

Slow and deep.

Sleep hovered over me like a mist. I was so tired. So tired...

But outside, the wind blew, and as the drafts rattled the window panes, it seemed voices stirred all around me.

Chapter Eight

C onfusion. Chaos. Discord.

Uncertainty takes many forms and holds many possible outcomes. When confusion is the result of the unknown, a multitude of emotions spawns from it. Fear, of course, and then self-doubt, and often outright panic—that's our favorite. What really brings us joy is when confusion is brought on by humans themselves. That makes our job so much easier.

Ace Tullinger was an unbalanced man. He had no idea what he wanted out of life, and before he met us, his paintings were unremarkable. If he sold one during a street festival for a hundred dollars, he was having a good night.

When he first came to Whickering Place, he was optimistic, hopeful that his career would take off, that he would find peace.

But he soon found loneliness, and it took its toll. He drank to excess. He entertained women far too young to be considered appropriate relationships. Then he stopped painting and slept all day. All of these elements primed the pump for the voices.

And he began to listen.

We taunted him, settled into his inner ear until he was demented with fatigue and fear and confusion.

And where confusion lives, many other vices lurk. Lust, for one. Only for sex at first, but once satisfied, different, stranger appetites manifest. All Ace needed was a little push in that direction.

His daughter does not realize it yet, but there are parts of her that are like her father—soft and weak. Like rotting drywall that only needs the slightest pressure from a fingertip before it breaks through.

She already shows signs of vulnerable trigger points. More will be found. Now, we assemble, prepare, and position ourselves to exploit each and every one of them.

Chapter Nine
Thursday, January 23

Whickering Place was quiet during the day, but at night the house seemed to pulsate, breathe.

It was my third evening, and I sat in the front room watching TV. I already hated living here.

Thump, slither, creak, creak.

I muted the television, stared up at the ceiling, and expected to see it vibrate. It sounded like footsteps. Except I was the only one in the house. But what else could make a noise like that?

The sound continued—as though someone paced the floors in the room above.

The doorbell chimed. I caught my breath, held it. Then I checked the time on my cell phone—9:28. Slowly, I rose from the chair and took careful steps toward the door, stopping several feet in front of it. "Who is it?"

The voice on the other side was muffled. "Avery? It's Maris."

Thank God. I relaxed my shoulders, exhaled, and opened the door.

Maris beamed. "I know it's really late, but I texted you before I came over and didn't hear back. Then I saw your light on and thought you might still be up, so..." She stepped inside.

"Oh, I didn't see the text."

She waved her free hand. The other one held a manila envelope. "No worries. I didn't wake you, did I?"

I shook my head. "No. I was awake."

"Oh, good."

I admired her outfit. Even though she was dressed casually in jeans and faux-fur-lined boots, she still looked stylish. She always did.

"I'm just watching some TV." I looked down at my sweatshirt and jeans, pretty sure I'd been wearing the same thing the first day we'd met. "Do you want to come in?" I pointed my thumbs behind me.

Her face brightened. "Thanks." She followed me into the front room, craning her head to the ceiling, side to side. "I can't stay but a minute, but I wanted to bring you these." She held the envelope out to me. "The tenant agreements and some other odds and ends. Oh, and the key for the files in the billiard room."

I took them from her and looked at the outside of the envelope—its smooth, tan exterior as blank as my mind. "Okay. What am I supposed to do with these?"

"Just hold onto them. If you decide to renew the tenants' lease next fall, you can do it yourself. Or I can help if you want."

She must have seen the shake in my hand as I brought it to my forehead.

"Everything all right, sweetie?"

"Yes. Fine, thank you."

Maris moved past me and grabbed the remote off the coffee table, muting the flashing and flickering television. "How are you managing? Everything going okay?"

I swallowed. "Sort of. I guess. I mean, I'm just trying to settle in."

She walked to the other side of the room and stared at the three-paneled painting on the far wall—one of my father's abstract works.

"Your father loved this painting. He thought it was one of his best."

I trailed over to stand beside her and stared up at it, noting the broad brushes of vermilion and flecks of black that started on the far-left canvas and extended to the third canvas on the right. "He was colorblind. I don't get how he knew what colors to use."

Maris turned to me and smiled. "Oh, he could actually see a lot of colors."

"But nothing on the red-green spectrum from what I understand. It always seemed so ironic to me that he became a painter."

Maris backed up and lowered herself onto the arm of the sofa. "Yes. Ace often asked me what colors I'd like him to use. Red's my favorite. When he painted that big triptych up there, he said the background looked gray to him—but to the rest of us, it's crimson."

Standing in front of the mantel, I spotted something round and copper on the top. It nearly blended with the dark marble. "It's another one of those coins." I picked it up, held it out to Maris. "I keep finding them all over this house. I found a little bag of them in one of the upstairs bedrooms."

The scrape of a key rattled in the lock, and Maris and I both turned toward the entryway.

Colin did a double-take as he passed the room and paused, shrugging out of his long, wool coat. "Hey. Everything all right?" He smoothed his ruffled hair.

"Um, yeah." I turned toward Maris. "Have you met Dr. Gallagher?"

"No," she said, sweeping toward him. "Maris Manners. I was Ace Tullinger's attorney. It's a pleasure to finally meet you, Dr. Gallagher."

"Colin," he corrected.

Maris's eyes widened, and a smile pulled at the corners of her mouth. "You look a lot like your younger brother."

"People tell us that all the time, and we're only half-brothers. Otherwise, we're really nothing alike." He gave a slight wave. "Anyway, nice to meet you. I'm going to grab something to eat."

As his footsteps receded down the hall, Maris turned to me and raised an eyebrow. "He's not bad, is he?"

Heat rushed into my face. "I guess."

"But what did you think of his brother?"

An involuntary smile brushed my lips. "He. Seems. Nice. They both do."

Maris patted my shoulder. "Lucky girl. Anyway, I'm going. Call me if you need anything. Or just call me if you want to go out for a drink this week." Her sky-blue eyes stared into mine, seemingly reading my fear. "Or if you want me to come over here for a drink."

A much more likely scenario. "Thanks."

Once she'd gone, I returned to my chair in the front room and unmuted the television. The movie on the women's channel was the usual, mind-numbing variety. A couple rolled around in a bed, panting and covered in sweat.

It actually looked unrealistic.

Probably.

Not that I'd know.

The only sexual contact I'd had was with Vince, which had consisted of a few stolen make-out sessions in his car. We hadn't dated long enough for anything else to happen ... before he'd been murdered.

"Looks like a great movie."

I swiveled around. Once again, Colin stood in the entryway, leaning his shoulder against the wall.

"Um, I don't know. It's mindless TV. Just turned it on for background noise." My cheeks burned as the actress moaned loudly.

Colin moved into the room and sat on the couch beside me. He rested his head against the cushions. "What a day."

I muted the sound of the heavy breathing. "What happened?"

He rocked his head back and forth. "I don't even know where to start."

I drew my legs up under me and stared down at my Orlando sweatshirt—a faded picture of a palm tree on the front. My mother had brought it back after her trip to Florida eight years ago. Couldn't believe I still had it—complete with its moth-eaten holes in the fabric.

Colin stared up at the ceiling for several silent moments. Then he inhaled sharply and raised his head. "I saw something really disturbing today."

"What?" I breathed.

"Had a teenager come into the clinic. His mother brought him because he's been fainting, sleeping all the time."

"Mono or something?"

"Acute anemia." He sat up, clasped his hands between his knees. "This might sound weird, but have you ever heard of kids—teenagers—or anybody ... drinking blood? For fun? Or whatever."

"Like a vampire?"

"Yeah. So, apparently, this is the new thing now. This kid—his arms were covered in bruises and lacerations. Anyway, he said he and his friends are into these bloodletting rituals."

"Could he be cutting—you know, like people sometimes do when they're trying to relieve emotional pain?"

"No, that's what I thought at first. But he said the cuts were specifically for drawing blood—to get enough to fill a container so they could drink it."

I wrinkled my nose. "Ew. That's disgusting."

"Yeah, well, I looked it up." He raised his eyebrows. "It's a thing. I guess sneaking vodka from their parents' liquor cabinets and smoking pot gets boring after a while, so they have to do something else to top that." He sat back, crossed his ankle over his knee. "Anyway, the articles talked about how medical professionals are starting to see more blood fetishists and sanguinarians."

I shrugged. "It's gross, but I knew kids in high school who were into goth dress and read all the vampire novels. I could see where some might take it to the next level."

Colin rubbed his temples. "Yeah, maybe." He closed his eyes. "I can't stop thinking about it. I've just never... You know, I'm an internist. I deal in blood all the time, but I just can't process it. Why would anybody want to do that?"

This was obviously really bothering him. He had the look of someone who'd witnessed a car accident and had seen bodies of children carried from the wreckage.

"I can't imagine ever wanting to do it. I don't even let anyone..." I shifted, resettled myself on the couch. "Well, I'm supposed to make an appointment to see a hematologist. My doctor in Morganton made me promise to do that when I left, but I'm terrified of having blood drawn. So I just keep putting it off."

"Why do you need to see a hematologist?"

I tore at a hangnail with my teeth, and a sharp pain shot through my cuticle. "I was born with this blood disorder called von Willebrand disease. Ever heard of it?"

He nodded. "Von Willebrand. Your blood has trouble clotting. That's because of an abnormal gene. You have low levels of the protein that promotes clotting. Your platelets don't stick together like they should. It's not uncommon."

"Right. Lucky me. I've had a few scary episodes of uncontrollable bleeding."

He ran his hands through his dark hair. Suddenly, I imagined doing the same. Shaking the image from my mind, I continued. "So, I've been stalling on going to see a hematologist because I kind of have a hard time giving up any blood voluntarily."

"When were you diagnosed?"

"When I was eighteen. After... well, I was stabbed." *Geez, could my life sound any more bizarre?*

"Stabbed?" Colin looked at me, narrowed his eyes. "What happened? I mean, if you don't mind me asking."

"No, it's fine." I'd told the story over the years so many times to so many doctors that it felt like I was talking about someone else's life. "My boyfriend and I were both attacked at a Fourth of July parade. Vince—my boyfriend—well, he died."

"That's terrible. I'm sorry."

"This woman just came out of the crowds." I made the classic *Psycho* stabbing motion. "I didn't even know what was happening at first—until I looked down at my arms—but she knifed Vince in the throat."

His eyes widened. "That's horrible. Was she a random lunatic or what?"

"She was a jealous lunatic. Vince's ex-girlfriend." I swallowed. "Some guys in the crowd were finally able to take her down, but it took several of them."

"Was she on drugs?"

"No. That's what everyone thought at first. But during the trial, it came out she was just 'possessed with rage.'" I made air quotes with my fingers. "That's what the headlines said."

"Rage can be a powerful emotion."

"Yep." I jerked my head, shaking the stray images from my mind. "Anyway, Vince died before they got him to the hospital. They charged her with first-degree murder and intent to commit murder."

"What about you? Your wounds?"

"My wrists, hands, and forearms. But I mean, I was covered in blood. The EMTs couldn't stop the bleeding. That's when the doctors realized I had von Willebrand."

"Is the girl that attacked you in jail now?"

"Yep. To the best of my knowledge, she's still in jail."

He leveled his gaze. "That may be the most horrifying story I've heard this year." He sat forward in his chair. "And how about you? I mean, that must've really affected you. The trauma."

"Yeah. Too bad you didn't know me before it happened. I was a totally different person. I'd just graduated, wasn't afraid of anything. I did archery and competitive shooting. I was on my way to getting a degree in criminal justice to be a police officer. And then blam," I deadpanned. "All over."

"You must have suffered massive PTSD."

"You could say that." I stared at my hands. The scars were there—along my palms, up my arms.

"Were you treated? For the von Willebrand disease, I mean."

"For a few months, I think. I remember some kind of nasal spray."

He nodded. "Desmopressin. Very common treatment. Why didn't you continue it?"

"It gave me headaches."

He inhaled sharply. "Okay, look. You *should* see a hematologist. Von Willebrand is a totally treatable disease. Don't procrastinate."

I nearly laughed. "I'm not procrastinating, I'm just..." *Scared to leave the house.* My shoulders dropped. "Okay, I am procrastinating."

"I'll give you the name of a hematologist I know. Dr. Darnell. His office is right next to the medical center where I work. He's really good."

I clenched my teeth. "I'll think about it."

Colin stared at the TV, a smile creeping over his lips. I followed his gaze. The couple was finally finished. They lounged in the bed, basking in the afterglow.

"I'm interrupting your show," he said.

"I'm really not watching it." I grabbed the remote and flipped to another station.

Colin pushed himself off the couch. "I'm gonna turn in."

"Good night."

"Yeah, you too."

Hopefully, my night wouldn't be like the last one. As Colin turned to leave, I asked, "Have you heard any strange noises since you've been living here?"

"What kind of strange noises?"

"Footsteps. Slithering."

"Slithering?"

"Yeah, sort of."

The blank expression on his face told me he hadn't.

I shook my head. "Never mind."

But then he stood there, staring.

I looked away.

He gave a short huff of a laugh. "Sorry. I didn't mean to stare. You just remind me of someone."

I blinked. "Oh."

Then he was gone. Relief. Making conversation exhausted me.

I lifted a lock of my hair and twisted it around my fist, covering my fingers. How long until I felt comfortable sitting on this couch, watching television, not jumping at every noise or cringing every time I encountered Colin or his brother?

I sat back and breathed out a long stream of air, settling my focus on a breaking news segment.

The blonde reporter seemed flustered, as though she'd been covering some other story and suddenly had to take this one instead.

"We're here at the skatepark tonight where the body of a teenager has been found." The reporter stood in front of the glass doors of the skatepark. Yellow caution tape stretched behind her. "The body was discovered around five o'clock this evening. Police are trying to identify the youth, and preliminary reports suggest the victim was between fifteen and eighteen years old. Although autopsy results are pending, police believe he may have been murdered as part of a ritual and ask that if anyone has information that they contact Crime Solvers at—"

I flipped off the television.

Just another reason not to set foot outside.

Chapter Ten

Over the years, many have come to Whickering Place. Some are sent for; many come to pay homage. Others seek favors so that their greatest desires may come to pass. After all, we are the originators of their yearning. It is from us that their new and powerful gifts emerge. Those looking for wealth, luck, prestige, sex, or talent do not leave wanting.

A blood pact is all we require. A drop of their blood on the wall of sacrifice seals the agreement and sets everything in motion.

But nothing is free. To receive these gifts, there's a price.

A few must die. Sometimes, an early death is necessary for the receiver of the gifts. Always, a sacrifice must be made.

Often, the person does not know they are required to reimburse us—at least not until the voices whisper in their ear, fill their heads with nonstop instructions—telling them to kill their mother, sister, boyfriend, or themselves. Yes, of course, those with an ounce of morality will fight it, insist they cannot kill anyone. They will attempt to renegotiate the terms. But there are no renegotiations. The agreement is binding and final.

The blood lust will intensify until our will has been done.

The young are particularly desirable for this arrangement. Their underdeveloped, or, in some cases, complete lack of moral matter, makes them easy prey. They will destroy others or themselves without a thought. They have little to lose. Everything to gain. Once they've tasted of what we have to offer them, they rarely ever want to leave.

Even unto death.

Equally satisfying is the feckless adult, the unwitting victim who drifts hopelessly, carelessly into the arms of a person under our control. Their fall is especially sweet.

Chapter Eleven
Friday, January 24

I hadn't meant to eavesdrop. I was simply passing through the hall, by their bedrooms, when I heard the Gallagher brothers.

The door to Pearse's room was partially open, and although Colin's form blocked most of my line of vision, I could see Pearse sitting up in bed. Only a dim bedside light revealed the curve of his bare shoulders, his hair tousled. He looked like he'd just woken up.

He gazed up at his brother, his mouth slightly open. "Well, anyway, what did you want?"

"Look at you," Colin said. "You're twenty-six years old, but you look ten years older."

I slipped further into my hiding place in the shadows. Pearse fell back on the pillows. "Just leave me alone." He groaned and covered his eyes with his hand.

"You look like shit—your coloring's bad, your eyes are all sunken in."

"Thanks, bro."

"Are you doing drugs?"

Pearse pushed himself up and rested his back against the headboard. "What the hell are you talking about? No, I'm not doing drugs."

"Look at your arm—the bruises in the crease. Yeah, the purple and yellow ones. Needle marks. You're shooting up, aren't you?"

Pearse shook his head. "You don't know what you're talking about."

"If I'd known this is what I'd have to deal with, I'd never have agreed to live with you."

"This is always the way it is with you," Pearse said in a low voice. "You were always Dad's golden child. I was just the bastard son no one wanted to claim."

"That's a load of bullshit."

"Is it?"

"Anything negative anyone might say about you you've brought on yourself."

"Oh, yeah. That's it."

"Well, look at you. You're sleeping all the time. Bringing home strange women. Hanging out with weird people. What else am I supposed to believe?"

Pearse shoved out of bed.

I took another step back. Then Colin moved and completely blocked my view.

"Like I said," Pearse growled, "you don't know what you're talking about, so you need to shut the hell up. Stop interrogating me."

The swish of denim against skin—Pearse sliding on his jeans.

"And you need to cut Lacey loose," Colin said. "Since you changed your work schedule, she's coming to me all the time, asking about you, where you are, why you haven't called—"

"I don't know anything about that."

"Just tell her you're seeing someone else or something, so I don't have to keep running interference."

The door suddenly jutted open, and I took a step forward, trying to look like I was just casually walking down the hall.

Pearse roared out of the room, thrusting his arms through a white T-shirt while pulling it over his head. I nearly collided with him and caught a glimpse of his eyes—eclipsed suns, with only the tiniest rim of light around them.

"Sorry." He grasped my shoulders, the heat of his hands burning through my shirt, and shifted me out of the way.

"N-no. My fault," I stammered.

As he traipsed down the hall, I noted his lithe form, tapered waist, muscled back. He didn't look like a drug addict to me. But then, I couldn't say I knew any.

Colin came out of the room, his mouth compressed. "Sorry about that."

"Everything all right?"

He leaned against the wall and raked a hand through his hair. "Who knows?" He motioned toward the hallway where Pearse had just disappeared. "My brother. He's just being an idiot right now."

I nodded and pushed at the cuticle on my thumbnail.

"Don't worry about it. It's just something he's gotta deal with. Consequently, *I* now have to deal with it." Colin's gaze lowered to meet my eyes, and his face softened. "Anyway, going to work now." He continued down the hall, pulling his coat over his shoulders.

I trailed into the foyer just as the front door closed behind him. The telephone on the table yodeled its metallic call.

I stared at it. It rang twice more, and I approached slowly, eyeing the receiver as it rattled against its holder.

Why was it ringing? Pearse had confirmed it wasn't connected to anything. No way anyone could call in on it.

Instinctively, I picked up the receiver and stared down at it. Echoey static quaked from the earpiece as I placed it to the side of my head. Lightning-fast electricity bolted through me as I heard a whispery and distant voice rasp.

It was another language. Latin? *Noctem ... periculum ... mortalia.* The tones faded in and out like a radio station losing reception. I slammed the receiver against the base and then picked it up again to listen.

Silence.

Was someone playing a prank? There had to be an explanation for it. Something logical.

Chapter Twelve

The housekeepers came in to clean, just as Maris had said they would. Headed up by a team leader named Ada, three women worked downstairs and then moved upstairs.

I sat in the front room and listened to their footsteps overhead. It was a comfort to know where the noises were coming from. But the women weren't up there long.

Soon their voices echoed in the foyer.

"Did you dust the hall table?" Ada asked.

"Which one?" her teammate asked. "I cleaned the one by the door."

"No, that one. The one against the wall."

"I don't touch that one. That phone ... ugh. It makes me crazy."

I made my way into the hall.

Ada was a middle-aged woman with a stern face and a deep crease between her eyebrows. She drew a rag from her box of cleaning supplies and circled it over the table's surface, carefully avoiding the phone.

"You guys have been plagued by the mysterious ringing phone too, huh?"

Ada glanced up at me, the line deepening between her brows, even as a smile twitched at her lips. "It scares my girls."

One of the other three stood by and watched Ada clean the table. She shot me an apologetic glance and a shrug.

"It scares me too," I said. "I can't figure out how it's ringing. It's not connected to anything."

Ada picked up a vase of dried flowers and pushed the rag under it. "Why don't you get rid of it?"

Fair question. Why hadn't I? Probably because I still didn't feel like this was my house, and it seemed wrong to throw anything out. "I probably will."

Ada nodded, her gaze resting on the phone. "I don't touch it. And I don't touch none of those coins around here neither, so I apologize if you find a little dust on the fireplace mantel."

"What's wrong with the coins?"

Ada finished her dusting, shook out the rag, and put it back into her bucket. "May, you and Trina take the stuff out to the truck." After the other two had carried out the buckets and equipment, Ada straightened. "It's the demons in this house. They're connected to the phone, and they're connected to the coins." She pulled a chain from her neck with a large wooden cross and lowered her voice. "I'm not afraid of them. I'm a Christian woman. I just tell 'em where to go. So they don't bother me. But I've lost several teams of girls to this house. Good ones."

A prickly feeling worked its way over my shoulders and up my neck. "I don't believe in that kind of stuff."

Ada raised her graying eyebrows. "It doesn't matter if you believe in them or not. If they here, they here. And *they* here." She reached down and grasped the handle on her blue tray of cleaning supplies. "I've seen 'em, and I've heard 'em, and I guarantee you will too." She walked toward the door and then turned. "They got to your father, you know. I cleaned for him for fifteen years, and I watched him change. I begged him to get this house exorcised, but he wouldn't do it." She shook her head. "It's a crying shame. Them things's what took him in the end."

As the door closed behind her, an involuntary shudder ripped through me.

Thankfully, you don't believe in that stuff, I reminded myself.

A belief in the supernatural would be all I'd need. My wellbeing already balanced precariously on a mixture of anti-anxiety medication and a will to survive. Having to worry about demons floating around in the halls would probably send me over the edge.

But her words had unnerved me.

And I still didn't have an explanation for the phone.

THE DAY WORE ON. THE sun sank low in the sky and the deep evening chill crept in.

I was still working in the front room when I heard Pearse's distinctive shuffle in the foyer. He gave me a brief wave as he passed by. "Hey."

Ada's words hung heavy in my mind. But the house had been quiet today after the cleaning team left. No ringing phone, no footsteps, no thump-slither.

The doorbell's chime reverberated through the entry. I'd been expecting a grocery delivery, but it had come later than I thought. I opened the front door, eyeing the young man standing on the other side wearing a white Krueger's Grocery baseball hat. He smiled up at me while hugging two brown paper bags.

"Hi there," he chirped. "Krueger's Grocery delivery."

"Great, thanks." I stepped out of the doorway, allowing the guy entrance.

He hesitated, looked just beyond me into the house. "Is it all right if I come in?"

How else was he going to bring the groceries inside? "Uh, yeah. Come on in."

He stepped onto the threshold of the door. "Thanks. I like to ask. Sometimes you just don't know." He trailed me down the hall into the kitchen.

I showed him where to put the groceries and followed him to the front door again.

"Sometimes, people tell me just to leave the bags on the front step. I do that too." He returned to the truck another time to retrieve two more bags. Then he carried them into the house and down the hall to the kitchen, still chatting away about his methods for quickest delivery. "Sometimes, I time myself. I've delivered eighteen bags of groceries into a house and gotten back into the truck in one minute and thirty-five seconds."

"Really?" I deadpanned. "That's impressive."

"I'm still trying to beat that record," he said, placing the last of the bags on the counter.

He turned to face me. "Anything else I can do for you, Miss Tullinger?"

Distracted by the sound of footsteps in the hall, I craned my head around.

Pearse stood in the doorway—barefoot, wearing a pair of jeans torn across one knee and a T-shirt with the neck cut out of it, revealing dark chest hair. "What's going on?"

A smile spread across the delivery guy's face. "Hey, Pearse. Just waking up?"

"No, I just got home from work." Pearse moved into the kitchen and within a foot of the guy. "Why are you in my house?"

I looked back and forth between the two of them. "Oh, you guys know each other?" I thought back to meeting Pearse in the coffee shop. This really was a small town for having a population of 90,000.

"Yeah," Pearse said. "I know him. Why is he here?"

The delivery guy shot out a fist and playfully punched his arm. "Hey, it's great to see you. And saw your band play at Odd Bods the other night. Pearse and I played music together for a while. Didn't we? When you first got to Asheville. Remember? With that other guy, Torin?" He shifted his gaze to me. "I'm Billy, by the way."

I nodded. "Avery."

"And Billy was just leaving," said Pearse.

"Hey, I'm just doing my job."

Billy's face was so hopeful, and Pearse's was so filled with animosity, I almost felt sorry for the grocery guy.

Pearse grasped Billy's arm above the elbow and forcefully moved him down the hall just as I rummaged three dollars from a side pocket in my purse.

"It was nice to meet you, Avery," Billy called over his shoulder. "See you next week."

"Not if I can help it," Pearse mumbled.

I trailed behind them, holding out the cash. "Wait," I called out just as Pearse pushed him out the front door. "Here." I rushed to the threshold and pressed the money into Billy's outstretched hand.

"Thanks." He smiled. "See you later."

Pearse shoved the front door, and I dodged out of the way to avoid being hit by the swinging panel.

I spun toward him, hands on my hips. "What is the matter with you?"

Pearse twisted away from me and started to walk down the hall. "Why did you have to let that guy in?"

"He was delivering the groceries. What else was I supposed to do?"

"Carry them in yourself? You look capable enough."

My mouth fell open. *What an arrogant ass.* "Hey, I don't know what your problem is, but you just live here. You don't own this place. I do."

"If you knew that guy, you wouldn't be friendly with him."

I continued to talk to his back. "Look, when my father's attorney told me there were tenants here, I had to think long and hard about allowing you guys to stay."

Pearse stopped walking and pivoted to face me.

"Then I thought maybe it was a good idea because it's such a big house and all, but you are not going to—"

"Why are you having groceries delivered?" His voice softened.

"That's none of your business. A lot of people have groceries delivered."

We stood in the corridor in front of the dim lighting of the kitchen. Pearse's dark eyes glowed. My adrenaline pumped; my insides trembled. When was the last time I'd told somebody off? My lack of contact with others had made confrontations unnecessary.

"Yeah, I mean, why don't you ever leave this house? You've been here a week, and I haven't seen you as much as walk to the mailbox."

And this was why I'd chosen to live alone all these years. *I should tell both of these guys to pack up and move on.*

I stepped back. "You met me before I ever came here. Last week. At the coffee shop. We talked."

He scrubbed his hand across the stubble on his jaw.

"You don't remember."

"Yeah, I do." He leaned forward, flashing white teeth. "I've been stalking you," he whispered. Then he gave a low laugh. "I'm just joking."

A shiver ran up my spine. Something about the way he looked at me. Intense eyes boring into mine and the stark, raw, expression of angst in the set of his jaw—not to mention the argument I'd overheard with Colin that morning. Was this guy even safe to have in the house?

For a fleeting moment, I wondered if he might put his hands on the wall on either side of my head, boxing me in. The thought sent panic to my chest, but it also triggered something low and deep in my core. My gun lay one floor above, stored in the safe by my bed. It wouldn't help me very much while I was standing down here.

But if Pearse touched me, I was ready to strike out. An elbow to the gut, a kick to the groin. I'd been able to throw a decent punch once upon a time.

"Don't do that," I said.

"Do what?"

"Look at me like that. I don't like that. And if you touch me, I *will* hit you."

Pearse took a step away, and the hall's odd lighting cast shadows over the planes of his face, which relaxed as he backed against the opposite wall. "Sorry."

"I don't know that this is working out."

Pearse held up a hand. "Can we start over here? I *am* sorry about the way I acted. It was shitty. You're right. I'm ... not feeling well."

My defenses subsided a little. He seemed to realize he'd overstepped a line. But after this, I would be wary of Pearse. I would be on the look-out for those tell-tale signs of drug use, and if I found out he was using, he was gone.

I took a deep breath. "Okay. Look, I'm just going back to what I was doing, and you can do the same. We'll forget about all this. For now."

He nodded, his head hanging forward.

I scooted sideways past him toward the kitchen. I expected him to saunter off into his part of the house, hoped he would. But as I put away the groceries, he came into the kitchen.

"Need some help?" He began to unpack the contents of one of the bags.

I held out my arm to stop him. "No. Please. You really don't have to."

He looked at me, his lips upturning slightly. "It's okay. I want to. Mea culpa."

At least he acknowledged that he was wrong.

We set out groceries in silence. Occasionally, he asked me where to put something.

I practiced my breathing. *Slow and deep.*

"Has anyone ever told you that you look like Nina Mayhew?" Pearse rested against the counter facing me.

"The actress?"

He nodded.

I laughed. "Uh, no."

"You do. I mean, you're a dead ringer."

"Wow. Um, thanks." I emptied the last bag and rushed around the kitchen, opening and shutting cupboards. Nina Mayhew. Right. I didn't come close to looking like her.

"My brother—well, Colin—I mean, he's crazy about that actress. You should ask him about the time he met her in New York when she was there on a movie shoot."

"That's cool." I could feel Pearse's eyes on me.

"He must have freaked *out* when he saw you."

My face burned. I desperately wanted to switch subjects. "So, you said you're in the medical profession. What do you do?"

"I work in the lab at the same center where Colin works—as a phlebotomist."

"So you draw blood."

"Yep. All day long."

I tensed—my typical reaction anytime I thought about having blood drawn. Also, not a subject I wanted to talk about. The light above our heads flickered once, and I remembered they'd been burned out, and Pearse had offered to fix them.

"Thanks for fixing the lights."

He looked up. "No problem. I think they still need some work."

"Let me know what I owe you."

He shrugged. "It was nothing. Really."

I creased the end of the paper grocery bag, folded it, placed it under the sink. "So. You're from New Orleans, didn't you say?"

Pearse pulled himself up to sit on the countertop. "Yep. The Big Easy."

I dragged a bunch of grapes out of a bag and reached past Pearse to drop them into the fruit basket. "What brought you here?"

He lifted his gaze to the ceiling lights and exhaled loudly. "A change of scene, I guess. A change of weather. A change of ... people." He slid off the counter and ambled to the refrigerator, grabbed a beer out of the side shelf. He unscrewed the top and then hoisted himself back onto the counter. "As it turns out, wasn't as much of a change of people as I thought."

"What do mean?" I rested my hand on the lip of the bag.

"There's assholes all over."

"What about your girlfriend? I heard Colin mention you had one. Lacey?"

"Yeah. Lacey isn't really my girlfriend. She followed me up here from New Orleans, and I'm sure she'd love it if I called her that but..." He wrinkled his nose, swilled from his beer. "Nah."

"Why's that?"

"She's just...." He looked down. "A nutcase, actually."

Pearse's body blocked the cabinet where the cans of tuna should have gone, so I stacked several on the wrong shelf. "You're *not* loving Asheville, then? Everyone else tells me how great a town it is."

He lifted a shoulder, wrenched his mouth. "There are some good things about it. I don't know. I guess I'm trouble no matter where I go. But I'll live . . . or not."

Earlier, he'd said he was sick, so now I wondered if he had a serious illness. But as I looked at him, I saw no sign of a physical malady. His arms looked muscular, as though he worked out. Everything about him seemed fit and solid.

And raw.

He looked at me but didn't say anything.

Neither did I.

The refrigerator hummed.

The icemaker dropped cubes.

Outside, a car whirred by.

A dog barked.

The doorbell rang.

He hopped down from the counter. "I'll answer it. It's probably for me."

I hung back in the kitchen, processing my thoughts. I didn't even know this guy.

Pearse's low voice echoed in the corridor, and I moved to the edge of the hallway to better eavesdrop on his conversation.

"I don't have any here," he said.

"Oh, come on. You've got to," said another male.

"I don't," Pearse insisted. "I told you. Right now, I'm trying to consume as little as possible."

"That's why you look like crap." A third voice sniped.

Shit. He is doing drugs.

"Let's talk about it. Show you how to handle all of this—best practices."

"No, you're not coming in here," Pearse said forcefully. "And I don't need to know best practices. I'm doing just fine on my own, thanks."

"There are methods, man. Ways of doing things. And this is *not* how it's done. People start to ask questions and get suspicious. The rest of the group will wonder if you're trying to quit the organization." There was a pause, and then, "Are you trying to quit the organization?"

"No. But I'm closing the door now. Get off the front step and get the hell out of here."

"You're making a big mistake. Don't alienate us. We can help you."

Pearse shut the door.

Quit what organization?

I hurried back into the kitchen, grabbed a tomato from the fruit basket, and attempted to look busy with a knife and cutting board. I didn't know what to believe. Maybe it wasn't drugs. But whatever it was, it probably wasn't good.

He's got to go.

I was sorry for whatever he was going through, but I couldn't risk having someone dangerous in my house.

I waited a few minutes, hoping that Pearse might return to the kitchen.

But he never did.

Chapter Thirteen
Monday, January 27

"**D**r. Darnell has a cancellation at eleven today," the receptionist on the phone said. "Can you make it in here by then?"

Could I? I wasn't sure. Could I even make it out of the house in less than an hour? And what about driving myself to an unfamiliar place?

"The paperwork is all online, so you can fill that out and bring it in, drop it at the front desk."

"Will I have to have my blood drawn?"

"Yes. Dr. Darnell would like you to sign in for the lab first. He's put in orders for several tests. Then he'll see you after."

As I printed and filled in all the paperwork, my heart beat out a a cadence. That part was easy. Now I had to think about transportation. My 2007 Honda hadn't moved from its spot in the driveway since I'd arrived last week. The effort of figuring out where I was going and how I would get there was daunting. What if I made a wrong turn or got lost?

I could almost hear Dr. Murphy's voice: *Then you turn around and backtrack and find the right road.*

She always made it sound so easy. But one wrong turn often precipitated another...

I got dressed and made my way downstairs.

Pearse was shuffling from the kitchen into the hallway, carrying a mug of coffee.

"Hey." His eyes trailed down to my purse. "Going somewhere?"

"To the doctor's, actually."

He nodded, sipped his coffee. "Good luck."

I wasn't sure how to take that. "Are you working today?"

"Not today."

I opened the back door and looked out. The old, rusted thermometer hanging on the iron gate registered a temperature below thirty. Maybe I'd make chili when I got home. Something to look forward to.

If I'd had more work to do, I could beg off this appointment—say something came up. Client needs work right away. Sorry, have to reschedule.

Work had slacked off a little since coming to Whickering Place a week ago. A casualty of the winter season, maybe?

I scurried out to the driveway. Taking a deep breath, I jerked open the car door and threw myself into the front seat. My fingers shook as I plugged the address into my GPS.

A twenty-minute drive. The trick was to avoid the highways.

I can do this.

I slowly backed out of the driveway, my fingers grasping the steering wheel, my pulse pounding in my palms. *Slow and deep.*

The first few turns weren't bad. Start out on Broadway, then a left turn onto West Walnut Street, then onto Biltmore Ave, then—

Ka-thump, ka-thump, ka-thump.

My heart chunked in time with the somersaulting rubber of my tire. I hit the brakes, rolled off to the side. *Please do not let this be happening now.*

The worst thing I could've imagined—a flat. When I'd left Morganton a couple of weeks ago, my tires looked a little low. I'd only driven my car a couple of blocks a day in the past nine years. One of my neighbors had told me my tires were rotting. Why hadn't I done something about it before?

For the same reason I didn't want to get out of my car now. Going out in public.

I threw open the door and stepped out. Cars flashed by, going both ways.

My chest hurt as I set foot on the pavement, propelled myself out, and whirled around to look at the wheels. The front tire on the driver's side looked like it had melted into the icy pavement.

"Cold enough for you?" A man walked down the sidewalk toward me. Grizzled beard. Weather-beaten face.

I backed up against the car and dug my fingernails into the paint.

"Need a hand with that?"

"Um..." I shot my gaze at the tire and then back to the man. What was I going to say? No? "I'm okay, thanks." *You idiot.*

"You got a tow service?"

"I'll call one."

He glanced down at the tire, shook his head. "Probably take 'em an hour to get here. I can do it in ten minutes or less."

"Oh, you really don't have to."

Ignoring my response, he moved toward the back of the car. "You got a spare in your trunk?"

"Uh, I think so, yeah."

Hoping to get this over with as quickly as possible, I reached into the floorboard and popped the trunk. The man hauled out a tire, a jack, a breaker bar. "The weather people are saying an ice storm's coming this week. Probably gonna be bad. Treacherous conditions."

My heart sped. *He's just being helpful. He's not going to abduct you. You should thank your lucky stars he's so willing to help.*

While he squatted down by the wheel, I leaned against the rear passenger door and focused on the building in front of me. It looked like a club. A font style that reminded me vaguely of something cabaret or spooky spelled out the name *Odd Bods.*

"Ever been to that place?" The guy glanced up, jerked a thumb over his shoulder.

I pointed. "There?"

"Yeah. Odd Bods."

"No. What is it?"

He smiled, ran a hand over his bearded face. "You must not be from here."

"I'm not."

"Crazy place. Attracts a whole different element. Lots of weirdos. People who think they're vampires." He positioned the breaker bar on a lug nut and wrenched it back and forth, finally unscrewing it with smudged fingers.

I stared up at the structure, remembering what Colin had said about his patient with the vampire fetish. Then I switched my gaze back to the man.

"But really, they're just a bunch of messed-up and dangerous humans—*if* you want to call them humans."

"Dangerous?"

He nodded, lifting the tire and placing it on the ground. "Oh, yeah. Those people are into human sacrifices and all kinds of craziness."

Human sacrifices? What kind of town had I moved into? "Why don't the police come in and bust the place?"

"They've tried. Never been able to make any charges stick." He shifted in his seat. "Those people—well, they're kind of a cult, you know? They're not just a bunch of drugees and low-lifes like you might think. They're well connected—lawyers and town council members and even police officers join up." He hoisted the spare wheel and secured it in place. "A friend of mine, they offered him money one time to give 'em his blood. He told 'em no way. They ain't takin' any of my bodily fluids."

The cold air worked its way through the openings of my jacket. "That's just sick," I half-whispered, mostly to myself.

"Oh, I know it. But a lot of homeless are choosing to go over to the vampires 'cause they're offering them a place to stay, food to eat, telling them they'll give them a new life." He raised his eyes to look at me as he tightened one of the nuts.

My nose started to run, and I brushed a gloved hand under it. "This seems like a wild town."

"Actually, I hear these weirdos are popping up in cities all around the U.S. It's not just Asheville."

I wrapped my arms around myself. This guy was freaking me out. Why was he telling me all this? I glanced at the other side of the street, thankful for once to see people milling around. There were two or three restaurants, a clothing store, a wine shop. It was broad daylight. *Remember, he's helping you.*

He finished twisting the nuts in place and then used the front of the car as a brace to help him to his feet. "I'm a tour guide for Blue Mountain City Bus Tours," he said, wiping his hands together and then against the front of his jeans. "And I used to see this homeless guy every day, sitting at the corner of the building at the first stop where people got on—with his cup and cardboard sign. Then one day, he walks up to me while I'm taking people's tickets, says, 'Remember me? I used to sit right there with a cardboard sign?' Guy was cleaned up, well-fed, pep in his step and all. Told me he had everything he ever wanted. Money, women, respect. But," he held up his finger, "but his eyes were dead. He'd sold his soul to something evil. Something wicked and depraved."

I shivered violently.

He collected the tire, jack, and bar and walked them around to the trunk. "They're advertising on singles websites and in weight loss clubs. I guess they want to make Asheville their mecca or something."

Climbing back into my car, I shut the door and started up the engine. I hoped the guy didn't want money. I didn't have any cash.

He closed the trunk and walked around to the window, which I rolled down about five inches.

"Can I pay you for your time?"

He shook his head. "Nope. That's my good Samaritan deed for the day."

I relaxed. "Thank you."

"No problem. Hope I didn't scare you with the story." His eyes crinkled at the corners, and he coughed out a raspy laugh. "Don't worry. You look like a smart woman. I'm sure you wouldn't be roped in by any of those crazies."

"I'm sure I wouldn't." I shifted into drive. "Thank you again."

I pulled onto the street, clutching my chest and gasping for air. My whole body trembled, and I fumbled my cell phone, trying to swipe up my directions again.

I missed a red light, ran right through it. Horns blared.

"Shit, shit, shit." It was all I could do not to scream. I wanted to scream—might have felt better if I had.

I made the last turn into the parking lot by the sign for Asheville Center for Internal Medicine. Colin and Pearse's place of business. Hematology Associates.

I pulled into a space and tipped myself out of the car. On legs that felt loose as oatmeal, I made my way into the lobby.

The blast of heated air moved through my lungs like a toxin, seizing the muscles and blocking me from taking a full breath. I scanned the waiting room. Children cried. A woman stood at the window, arguing with the receptionist about her insurance card. At the other end of the room, a man paced, his hands tucked behind his back, his eyes fixed straight ahead. An assortment of tightly seated patients bowed their heads over cell phones.

Which of you is dangerous? Murderer? Vampire?

The man's words had unsettled me, reminded me why I didn't like having my blood drawn. It was my blood. I wanted it to stay inside of me.

I couldn't do this. I yanked all of my paperwork out of my purse and thrust it into the hands of the receptionist. "I'm sorry. Something urgent has come up. I need to reschedule." Then I rushed back outside, climbed into my car, and sobbed.

Chapter Fourteen

A small setback. I'd try again. Maybe next week.

But I wouldn't tell Dr. Murphy about what happened. Or Colin.

I dumped cumin into the pot, followed by pepper and curry.

Voices echoed from the front parlor. I'd left the television on, and the volume was ridiculously loud.

As I moved down the hall to shut it off, a tap on my shoulder, as though someone had used two fingers to poke me in the back to get my attention, spun me around.

No one was behind me. The corridor was empty.

My skin iced, and I rubbed at my shoulder blade. Phantom sensations. Sort of like when I was asleep and thought someone held me down—hands closing over my throat, preventing me from breathing.

Today's outing had done a number on me. Pivoting slowly, I continued down the hall and turned into the front room, where the television blared. Had I raised the volume that much?

I grabbed the remote and pressed the power button. But it didn't shut off. Several more attempts proved fruitless, although I was finally able to reduce the volume.

"Hey."

I turned.

Colin stood in the doorway.

I met his eyes briefly before shifting my gaze back to the television and pressing harder on the remote. "Hey."

He jangled his keys. "You cooking something?"

Giving up, I threw the remote on the couch. "Yes. Chili. Want some?"

"Thanks, I might." He bounced his keys in his hand several more times before shoving them into his pocket.

Colin followed me as I returned to the kitchen. My chili had started to boil. Globs of red sauce popped out of the pot and dotted the counter like blood clots.

Shearing off a paper towel, I pressed it to the surface and wiped up the mess. "My aunt's recipe. She puts a little cinnamon in the mix. Some people don't like it, but I think it adds something."

I spooned the chili into a bowl and handed it to Colin.

"I also made some bread." I pushed the basket toward him. It was still warm.

"Wow. So, you're a cook."

I sat down at the table. "Cook or starve."

Colin joined me and immediately shoveled in a mouthful of chili. After a few seconds, he made a sound that I guessed meant he liked it. "My dinners normally consist of a sandwich from Joe's Deli on the corner, or occasionally I run out for a bite with one of the doctors I work with. This is"—he spooned in another mouthful—"absolutely amazing."

I couldn't help but smile. I'd done something that actually pleased someone. A first in a long while.

He set down his spoon and looked at me. His eyes were a lot like his brother's but lighter—a greenish-hazel color.

"Man. You really look like Nina Mayhew. The actress?"

My face heated. "Your brother told me that too."

"Is my brother home?"

I shook my head. "He went out earlier."

"Did he seem all right? Was he alone?"

"Yeah, he was alone."

Colin exhaled air through his nose.

I pulled off a piece of bread and popped it into my mouth. "So, Pearse seems kind of angry."

"He hasn't always been. Not until recently." Colin stood and carried his bowl to the sink.

"Just leave it in the sink," I said.

"No way. I can wash my own dishes." He rinsed out the bowl, grabbed a towel, dried it, and then set it on the counter.

He smiled. "Thanks for the chili."

"No problem."

I cleaned up the rest of the kitchen and then started toward the front room, where Colin usually camped out after dinner. But halfway down the hallway, I paused. Should I go in and sit with him or just go to bed? Did he even want company? Maybe he just wanted to be alone. *Somebody tell me what to do, how I should act.*

In the end, the decision had been made for me. The front room was empty.

The news played on the television. A reporter covered a house fire across town. Then they aired a breaking news report.

"This week's incident at the skatepark in which a local teenager was found dead is still under investigation. But now, the body of another teenager has been found—this time along Tunnel Road. An unidentified female—approximately fourteen to seventeen years of age, was found in the woods behind the Krueger Grocery Store. Cause of death is pending, but police suspect foul play."

Krueger Grocery Store. That was even closer than the last murder. I switched off the television. It was early—not yet seven o'clock—but I just wanted to curl up in my bed and sleep.

As I made my way up the stairs, I paused at a noise—a rustling sound—as though someone was wrapping a gift with tissue paper.

I inched up one step, then another, as the scratching and scraping intensified. When I reached the landing, I scanned the shadows.

Nothing appeared to be moving. But as I started again, the crinkling stopped.

Thump ... ssslither.

Where was it coming from? Down the hall that led to my room? Off to the right? From my father's studio?

Holding my breath, I rushed forward, bound for my bedroom. Just as I grasped the doorknob, something cold brushed against me. Sharp points dug into my skin.

I shrieked, shouldered the door, and fell inside. Slamming it, I threw my back against the panel. I hadn't imagined it. Something had grabbed me. I still felt the indention of the claw-like fingers burrowing into my wrist. A surge of adrenaline flooded me, fueling my heart.

"Avery?" From downstairs, Colin's muffled voice reached me. "Avery? Are you all right?"

No, I wasn't all right. But I couldn't tell him what happened—couldn't even name it myself. I cracked the door and called out to him. "I'm fine. Bumped into the wall. Going to bed now."

"Okay," he called back. "Good night."

Chapter Fifteen

The Colony, as it is known, began here at Whickering Place. Tuberculosis, and one ambitious doctor's quest to cure it, started it all. "The mountain air will be good for those who suffer from the illness," he claimed. "Build wide verandas and allow patients to sleep in the open."

Whickering Place was built under Dr. Shafton's specifications. And the patients came. A few were cured at first, but many others died, their expectorated bodily fluids drawing the likes of the succubus and incubus and other creatures of the night who thrived on the blood of the living. A few of us were strategically placed to bring the doctor to despair, and we claimed the life of his beloved in the second-floor master bedroom while she stared up at us with fixed eyes of horror.

The doctor, desperate to see his beloved again, engaged the use of a spirit board to bring her back—if only for a night.

More of us came instead.

At first, the touch of the succubus delighted Dr. Shafton, and he assumed his wife had returned. Soon, he knew the nightly visitations were not human. Even so, his mind had turned, and seared against all decency, he bid us come. One by one, more of us congregated—conjured by his offerings of blood. We learned to imitate those who died here—their voices, their shape, their likeness. He welcomed us, and we allowed him to cure patients for a time. Until he was driven out of town by those who didn't like his practices. Then we waited for another to take up residence.

In the interim, we multiplied. An empty house is an excellent station for traveling demons on their way to the next mission. In this case, many of us stayed.

We knew more victims were coming.

Now, we must have Avery's attention.

It's important that she knows we're here. For the nonbelievers, especially, it sometimes takes longer to piece together the clues, but when the realization finally hits them, the horror is staggering.

Since her equilibrium is already off, unbalanced by the recent changes in her life, influence over Avery's mind and body should be easy. Of course, we have other pawns at our service within the house itself. Distraction and chaos are always excellent tools of manipulation.

Often, in the first blush of supernatural experience, mortals like to think that light brush against their face, the voice they hear in the night, or the cold spot in the hall is a visitation from a beloved relative who has recently passed. That always makes us laugh. We love to play that game with them.

"Yes, today I'm your Auntie Anita, here to hold your hand while you face that scary shadow in the corner."

"Good evening. Tonight I'm your Grandpa Jacob, here to bring you a kindly warning."

Then they strain and struggle and come up with all sorts of ridiculous notions as to who is trying to speak to them and why. The most amusing is when they bring in their mediums and their so-called paranormal psychologists. Stupid, impotent people who ask us questions like, "Who are you? Why are you here? Do you need help? What's your name?"

Oh, those days are the best. We toy with them and trick them. We speak through their voice boxes and electronic voice projection apparatus. We say all sorts of drivel. Then we listen to them fawn over their pathetic data while they get off on their paltry results.

"She said her name is Melanie. She died here. She was murdered and may be stuck here. Do you need help crossing over?"

You stupid shits. We think you're all a bunch of assholes, and we want to kill every single one of you.

Unless we want to use you.

The Colony was founded on men's desire for supernatural abilities and the realization that power could be found from the "other side," as humans like to call it. But modern-day pop culture, sexual fetishes, and continued interest in the occult have fueled the continuation of our control and The Colony's growth and spread.

But before Avery can be of any use to us, she must know we exist. She must fear us. She must distrust herself and her feelings. She must reacquire longings of her own, those dead and buried for many years now, so that they may be twisted, exploited.

Ultimately, the design for all who come to this house is complete destruction. Make no mistake. Our motives are not to protect or comfort those who commune with us. We are not angels. We are not what they think we are. The insipid and simple-minded may deceive themselves that we are here to serve them.

But they are here to serve us.

Chapter Sixteen

When I finally went to bed that night, I couldn't sleep.

Voices. Muffled. Talking in the room above me. Then in the hall. With my heart thrumming in my throat, I threw back the covers, and the chill penetrated my thin pajamas. Flipping on the light in the bedroom, I opened the door wide and thrust my head into the corridor.

Nothing.

Exhaling, I moved back inside, shut the door, and put my ear against it. Then I listened.

Silence.

I'd read stories and watched TV shows in which people felt they'd been visited by their loved one after death. As much as I didn't want to believe it, I wondered if what I was experiencing could be explained in this way. Could it be my father trying to contact me? Although apparently, my father had experienced something in the house too, so that logic didn't hold up.

I threw on a sweatshirt and jeans and made my way down the dark hall toward the studio, flipping on lights as I went.

No matter what time of day I entered the studio, it was never comfortable. The lighting was dim, the air smelled foul—like old books that had been boxed up, set in an attic, and allowed to molder.

I flipped on the light, and the walls dripped unnatural yellow illumination. It hung from the valances and bathed the floors, draping the furniture and the walls, distorting furnishings, elongating angles, and stretching lines.

Moving from painting to painting, I stared up at them. Ace's creations were mesmerizing. The one with the red background, the one with the black, the one with the silver. Some brushstrokes broad, some thin. The patterns and colors were meaningless to me but had meant something to my father. I wished I knew his inspiration behind them.

His desk was on the other side of the room—nearly camouflaged by the shadows. I'd never even noticed it before but didn't know how I'd missed it. It was piled high with partially used or blank canvases and tubes—some with indentions, others that looked like hammered metal. A few jars stained with old paint held brushes—the ends turned up.

The chair was worn and looked like it had once been part of an old dining set—bits of stuffing tufted from a corner of the cushion. I sat down and pulled open a drawer on the right side of the desk. It was stuffed with old newspapers and magazines, which I quickly sifted through and set aside to be thrown out. I couldn't forever live in a house with all this clutter. The east wing carried hints of the future hoarding my father might have done if he'd lived.

Underneath a stack of magazines and newspapers lay an old laptop, the cord protruding from the back. From the early 2000s, perhaps—big and clunky. Plugging it in and firing it up, I waited for ages before an antiquated operating system popped up.

What was I looking for? I didn't really know. What did a painter keep on a laptop?

Outdated icons spaced over the desktop: an old dial-up modem, a financial management program, several photographs of paintings. I opened the word processing program and clicked on File in the menu bar. A list of files came up, all ordered in titles—entry1, entry2, entry3—spanning through entry35.

I clicked on the first one, dated 2/16/1999, mostly comprised of sentence fragments and phrases related to paintings, oils, and textures.

It seemed strange that my father would have noted his thoughts in an electronic document. Chances were, the laptop was a novelty to him.

The second entry was more of the same, so was the third. The fourth, dated 10/17/1999, started out like a journal entry.

Can't sleep. Noises above my head all night. Sounds like someone dragging boxes. Went up to check it out. Nothing there. Just a spare room off of the attic. Running low on money. May need to rent out space for events.

Same thing I heard every night. The noises, the dragging, the thumping.

I closed out of that one and went on to entry5, dated 12/22/99.

First event here this evening. Joint gala of local painters. Lots of wealthies in attendance. Sold several paintings. Financial ruin spared at least this month.

In 1999, I would have been a little girl living with my mother in Raleigh. For years Mom complained that Dad hadn't paid child support. Now it made sense why he hadn't. No money. It wasn't too much later that the checks began arriving regularly, much to Mom's surprise.

Entry6, dated 1/5/2000.

Y2K was a bust. We're all still here. Still alive. Electricity on. Noises upstairs louder than ever. Can't sleep at all. Thinking about calling someone in to check attic for rodents ... or ghosts.

Entry7, dated 1/8/2000.

Third night with no sleep at all. Have contacted a psychic medium. Would be a laugh if the place was haunted. In the meantime, I'm sleeping in the front parlor. During the day, though. Not at night when

I should be asleep. I've taken to painting at night instead. Work not as good, but it's the best—

A sudden fluttering sound drew my attention up and away from the computer.

Something flew by my ear. What was that?

Shooting up from the chair, I scanned the room. The flapping stopped. But as I moved toward the door, it began again—not quite birdlike but heavier, more irregular.

I looked up at the high ceilings topped by the skylight. And there it was. Leathery black wings beating as the creature bounced off the ceiling, dipped down, and clipped the hanging light, its furry body bobbing.

"A bat," I breathed.

Not that I was particularly afraid of bats, but I couldn't have one living in my father's studio. How did I get rid of it? My first instinct was to ask Colin or Pearse for help.

This is your responsibility now. The words coursed through my brain with paralyzing clarity. *This is your house.*

Again I wondered what I had taken on. I could barely care for myself, and now I owned a house with tenants, a potentially haunted attic, and a trapped bat.

A cold sweat seeped from my skin as I backed out of the room, switched off the lights, and closed the door. I hurried into my bedroom and quickly sent off a text to Maris, praying that the incoming message wouldn't wake her at 1:51 in the morning.

You asked me to contact you if I needed anything. I need something. Help. Bat in the studio. Any suggestions?

Downstairs, I crawled onto the couch in the front room. My father had slept here too. It was beginning to feel like the only usable room in the house for sleeping or working. The sofa was long enough for me to stretch out, and the only noises came from the street—a car horn, a dog bark.

But no voices. No slithering.

And Colin was in the next hallway. He would hear me if I screamed.

Chapter Seventeen
Tuesday, January 28

I was in a state of twilight sleep when a tap sounded at the door. Shooting up from the sofa, I pulled aside the curtains and peered out. Maris's blonde hair gleamed under the outside light as she stood on the doorstep beside a man.

Daylight was barely breaking the sky's thick, gray wall of clouds. I pressed the button on my cell phone. 6:53.

Wow. I hadn't expected that quick of a response to my text.

Draping a throw blanket from the back of the couch over my shoulders, I lumbered to the door.

"Good morning!" Maris chirped. She looked impossibly put together for this early in the morning. Her blonde hair hung over her shoulder in a braided rope. A red wool coat matched her boots. She beamed. "I thought I'd wait until it was a near-human time of the morning to come over." She motioned to the man standing next to her. "This is Kevin."

The man wore a black coat and gray hoodie underneath. The hood was pulled up, partially hiding his face. Kevin pointed his thumbs at his chest. "I'm your bat guy."

I ushered them inside. "Yeah, I hadn't expected you to come out—especially at this hour and in these temperatures. But thanks. I really didn't know what to do. I didn't want to wake up my tenants to help me catch a bat."

"Darling, it's really no trouble," said Maris. "Ace had some headaches with bats when he lived here too. That was years ago, but they've no doubt found some way back in."

"And where there's one, there's more," said Kevin.

Kevin and Maris headed into my father's studio while I dressed. Then I rejoined them.

Kevin swiped his hands together. "He's gone."

"Already?" It had taken the man less than ten minutes to remove a frantic bat. "You're amazing."

Kevin shrugged. "Only needed to open a window and let him out."

"We call Kevin the bat whisperer." Maris lowered her voice as though sharing some piece of secretive information.

"He'll easily find his way back in," he warned, "so I'd like to check your upstairs and your attic. Likely there's another one or two up there."

I nodded. "Of course."

"They hibernate this time of year. This guy was probably looking for a good spot."

"How do I keep them out of the house?"

"Well, if we see more, we can treat the place so they can't find their way back in. Then they'll go elsewhere for a dwelling spot."

"Aren't bats toxic? Don't they have rabies and stuff?"

Kevin waved his hand, wiping away my question. "A very small percentage have rabies—like one-tenth of one percent. You'd have a better chance of being run over by a rhino." He shook his head. "You don't want them *in* your house, but you do want these guys around in the spring and summer. They eat half their weight in mosquitoes."

I led Kevin and Maris up the stairs to the attic. As we climbed, the temperature dropped severely.

Maris shivered. "I guess these rooms don't get much of the heat from the downstairs."

We reached the first room—the one that was empty except for the Oriental rug.

"This would've been a perfect storage room. Do you know why my father never used it?" I asked Maris. "His studio is completely cluttered with junk, so you'd think he would've spread it out since he had so much space."

"His knees were bad. He didn't like climbing the stairs." She pointed to a door that I would've mistaken for a closet. "The attic is just through there."

Kevin opened it, and a dark space yawned beyond.

Maris waved him on. "We'll leave you to it."

I followed her back to the stairwell. She walked in front of me, placing her heeled feet carefully upon each step. "I wanted to talk to you about some offers I've been getting." She twisted her head around, forcing her words in my direction. "Ace always left me in charge of these things, so people in town are still calling me about setting up events."

"Events?"

"Right. As I told you, Ace used to host parties in the great room—weddings, galas. Those sorts of things."

"Oh, yeah." I still wasn't sure how I felt about that. The money was appealing, but it would mean strange people in and out of the house regularly.

"The other day, I received another call from Cadel Johanssen. He's desperate for a venue. Banquet, lots of food, dancing, fundraising. He's expecting over fifty people. Anyway, he was hoping Whickering Place might still be available."

"Oh." I tried to imagine the great room of Whickering Place teeming with guests and caterers and decorations. "I'll need to talk to my tenants about that."

Maris waved her hand. "Well, I'm sure Pearse won't care. He's out most of the time anyway, isn't he?"

As we reached the downstairs, both Pearse and Colin stood in the entryway, putting on their coats and preparing to leave for work.

"Good morning," Maris greeted them.

The men looked up at her and muttered replies.

"Well, hello," she said to Pearse. "How are you, stranger? It's been a few weeks."

He dipped his head. "Hey, Maris."

Smiling, Maris stood back and surveyed the two of them side by side. "They look like twins, don't they?"

The brothers looked at each other. Colin laughed a little and shook his head.

Maris lowered her chin. "My goodness. If you both had the same hair, it would be impossible to tell you apart."

"And that's where the similarity ends," Colin said.

Pearse aimed his body toward the door. He seemed anxious to leave.

"Both off to work, then?" Her stare lingered.

It was a little embarrassing.

"Well, we better let you guys go," I said, eager to break the spell.

After the two men had left, Maris turned to me, her eyes ablaze. "How do you choose between them?"

"I'm sorry—what?"

"Well..." She placed a fingertip to her lips. "Two hot men living under the same roof—your roof. And you," she pointed, "you're young and attractive. I'm sure you can easily snag one of them."

I huffed out air. "It's really not in my plans, Maris."

"The doctor would be the logical choice, of course. But the younger could prove to have talents ... in other areas."

My cheeks warmed.

"You just *know* Pearse Gallagher is good in the sack."

Mustering up a disapproving glare, I shot it in her direction.

She eyed me, a smug smile stretching her lips, making me wonder if somehow Maris *did* know.

"What?" She held out her hands, eyes widening with feigned innocence.

"I assure you. I have no plans to do ... anything with either of them." I shook my head, attempting to dislodge the image she'd planted in my head.

"Why not? You'd be a fool to pass up the opportunity."

"Pearse has a girlfriend. Colin probably does too." Dropping my gaze to the ground, I swallowed hard. "And I have my own stuff to deal with."

She cranked her head to the side. "You know, Avery, you can't stay holed up in here your whole life. Have you even once set foot outside of this house since you got here?"

"Yes. I have, in fact." Not very successfully, but she didn't need to know that.

Maris placed her hands on my shoulders. "Look, I think it's about time you took a deep breath and stepped outside of your shell, both literally and figuratively. I mean, Asheville is an amazing town. Loads to do here—great restaurants, music, art—all sorts of things going on at night. You managed to leave Morganton to come here."

"Yeah, and that was a major ordeal. It took tons of preparation, therapy, and more meds than I ever want to put in my system again."

"Well, surely the more you do it, the easier it will get."

Suddenly Maris sounded like Dr. Murphy. She had my best interests at heart, of course, but I'd tried what she was suggesting, and yes, it had worked for a while. But then it had stopped working. "It's not that simple."

"Yes, it is," she insisted, perching on the arm of the sofa. "Have I told you my story?"

"I don't know. I don't think so."

"I was in an abusive relationship for several years when I was in my twenties. In fact, he almost killed me." Her eyes flashed as she blinked several times. "But then I got involved with a group of people who showed me a different way of living. They helped me get away from him. They helped me get rid of him. They showed me that I was powerful in my own right and didn't need to live under that kind of abuse. They made me realize I couldn't let him win. I learned I could take charge and be a different person."

"That's great. I'm happy for you."

"It's not an outcome that's exclusive to me. The same could be true for you. It's open to anyone who wants to grab it." She pushed off the couch, walked to the front door, opened it, and then stood back, allowing me a view of the sidewalk outside. "See, Avery? There's a world out there. I know a lot of people. I could introduce you to a new way of life."

I stepped away, shaking my head. Even the suggestion that I walk outside was threatening.

Maris straightened, crossing her arms. "Have you thought any more about selling? Maybe a smaller place would be better for you."

"I'm still thinking about it." Then, smiling, I gave Maris the same answer I gave everyone who'd tried to advise me about my agoraphobia over the years. "Thank you. I appreciate your encouragement."

"Hello?" Kevin's voice echoed down the stairwell as he stood on the landing.

"Yes?" I called back, thankful for the interruption.

"Yeah, you wanna come see something?"

Maris and I hiked back upstairs, through the empty room, and into the attic, which was every bit the old, creepy space I expected. Boxes, cobweb-covered furniture, discarded paintings, and canvasses—long-ruined from exposure to the elements. The air was musty, damp, and smelled of something foul. As I craned my neck back and stared up into the pointed eaves overhead, I glimpsed what looked like small tobacco leaves hanging.

"What is that?"

Kevin looked at me with a half-smile. "Those are bats."

Maris and I both sucked air simultaneously.

"I'd say over two hundred of them."

"What?" A wave of dizziness crashed over me.

Kevin nodded. "Yeah. This is a full-blown bat cave you've got here."

I blinked, and the hanging forms came into focus—furry, cone-shaped, upside down, and lightly swaying from the rafters in their state of sleep. A chill passed through me.

"Obviously, I have to bring in reinforcements for this," Kevin said. "I've never seen quite this many in one spot."

I didn't know what to say. One bat—no problem. But hundreds of them living in my attic?

"Why would they all roost here?" Maris breathed, staring up at them in awe.

Kevin shook his head. "Don't know. But for some reason, they like the conditions. Right now, they're all in a state of torpor. Their heart rates slow to like, ten beats a minute or something. They don't have to eat or poop or anything. A couple of months when the weather warms, they'll be ready to end their nap."

"How did they get in?"

"Oh, bats can get in through an opening as small as three-eighths of an inch. You've probably got a gap somewhere."

"What can we do?"

Kevin stacked his flashlight and gloves in his box. "Exclusion. It's a complex process. I'll call some of my buddies. It may take a bit of time to remove them all—especially this time of year. You'll have to be a little patient. But once they've all gone, then we'll need to seal up any and all holes."

I walked Kevin and Maris to the front door.

"I'll be back tomorrow. I'll bring my best guys," Kevin told me.

"Do I have to leave the house or anything?"

He shook his head. "No. No, it's not like bombing for bugs. No chemicals are used. It's all very humane and natural."

As I closed the door behind them, I exhaled a shuddering breath. This was where I encountered the odd dual nature of my illness. Knowing my house was infested with bats made me want to run out the front door. But as I looked out the window into the street beyond, it was as if an impermeable glass shield kept me from setting foot outside.

Imprisoned.

Chapter Eighteen
Wednesday, January 29

My outing for the day: standing in the garden behind the house, shielding my eyes from the sun, and staring up at the roof as Kevin stood on a ladder and fit netting over the attic gable vents. Then he secured them by drilling screws into the corners.

"How do the bats get out?" I called up to him.

He held up a flexible funnel that was corrugated like an accordion. "Through this."

With wire cutters, he snipped a hole in the mesh he'd just installed and inserted the tubing. "It acts like a one-way door," he called down to me. "They go out, and then they can't come back in, so they'll find another place to roost. I'll do the same thing on the other vent."

"How do we make sure they all leave?"

Kevin scaled down the ladder. "I'll come back periodically and check to make sure no stragglers are left behind." He jumped off the bottom rung and walked toward me, removing his heavy work gloves. "As it warms up, their activity will increase, and they'll start going out at night."

As Kevin and his helpers finished, I opened the gate that led outside to the sidewalk so they could easily access their truck parked on the street. Once they'd gone, I turned to survey the condition of the garden.

The place was a tangled, overgrown mess of weeds and dead bushes and flowers, but it had probably been beautiful once. In the spring, no doubt much of it would be green and growing.

Shivering, I pulled my coat around me. My weather app told me it was twenty-two degrees—too cold to stay out here for long.

High, stone walls encased the garden, and paths circled around either side of it. I trotted off to the right. At the end of the short path sat a gazebo, overgrown weeds surrounding it, the ceiling caved in. I stopped and looked up at the house. I could see all the windows on the back of the mansion from here. And high atop the roof, stone gargoyles flanked each of the four corners. I hadn't noticed them before—winged, hunched creatures covering their mouths as they laughed.

In the middle of the expanse, a stagnant pond was covered by an icy film. I remembered the pond from when I was a kid. I'd asked my father if I could swim in it. He'd said, "No. The fish live there."

Stepping over the snarl of vines, I stopped at the edge and looked into it. No fish there now. Just greenish-gray ice with leaves and moss and twigs encased within the top layer.

As I turned away, I blinked, and an image materialized. Swinging back toward the water, I looked again.

No.

Impossible. Staring hard at the surface, I tried to decipher between the mottled mess of moss and dead branches. But it was still there. I drew closer, squinting. Yes. A face. Reddish hair flowing out from the head—held in the clutches of the water. The eyes—a stark blue—wide open and staring upward.

I jerked back, a sharp wail tearing from my throat. I turned and half-ran, half-stumbled into the house and down the darkened hallway, my sprint ending as I collided with Colin's chest.

He grabbed my arms. "What? What's the matter?"

I pointed frantically behind me, only able to whisper. "Come see this."

"What? Out there?"

"Yes ... yes..." I answered breathlessly.

He followed.

My heart hammered my ribcage and temples as we burst into the cold air and trekked past the dilapidated gazebo to the edge of the pond.

"Look." I pointed at the icy surface.

Colin leaned forward and squinted. "Is it a koi pond?"

Heaviness in my chest forced me to lean over and look again. A tuft of reddish algae or aquatic fauna trailed out from a fossilized, waterlogged branch—white with age and winter trauma. The sky's reflection against the glassy surface glinted like two orbs.

That was what I'd seen. Not a body.

I shrank back. "I thought..." The air left my lungs in a cloud of condensation. "Yeah, I think koi swam in there when I was a kid. Not anymore, though."

I could feel Colin's stare as he followed me inside the house. He probably wondered why I'd brought him outside to look at a frozen pond.

How could I have mistaken algae and logs for a body? Creeping confusion and fear made its way up and over my shoulders, grasping my neck with its sharp claws and wrenching the breath from me.

Back inside, I sank onto the sofa in the front room and glanced up at Colin.

He stood in the doorway, his eyes meeting mine under heavy lids. "Are you all right?"

"Yeah."

Colin stepped forward and placed his hand against the entryway. "Met a friend for drinks after work. I'm still buzzing a little from two scotches, I guess." He plopped down on the couch, propped up his feet on the coffee table, and stared at the television with furrowed brows.

Cold air rushed across the floor as the front door opened and closed again.

Pearse's familiar footsteps sounded seconds before he appeared in the doorway, his face etched with a grimace. "Thanks for the ride, bro."

Colin didn't look at him. "Sorry. I needed some time to myself."

Pearse pulled a long, maroon scarf from his shoulders and tossed it on a chair. "Really," he deadpanned, standing over Colin, his legs pressing against the arm of the sofa. "Are we going to talk about what happened, or you just going to assume whatever and shoot me dirty looks for the next six months?"

I held my breath. *What happened?*

Colin scoffed. "Why would we talk about anything? You barely say two words to me most of the time."

"I've had a lot going on."

"Apparently."

Pearse dropped his gaze. "Look, I know you don't understand—"

"You're right. I don't."

I stood up, feeling like I should leave.

"Don't go, Avery," said Colin, still eyeing Pearse. "We're just having a brotherly brawl."

"Nothing new there, *brother.*"

I glanced up at Pearse. His face and lips looked pale, and dark circles underlined his eyes. Awkwardly, I jerked my thumb toward the hallway. "Should I go?"

"No, stay," said Pearse. "I'll go." He picked up his scarf, rewrapped it around his neck, and moved toward the door. "I've got somewhere to be."

"There's an ice storm starting out there, you know," Colin called after him.

The door slammed shut.

"Will he be all right?" I asked.

"Yeah." Colin rose from the couch, went to the decanters on the rolling cart in the corner of the room, and poured something brown into a short glass. "Do you want anything?"

"Like what?"

"Scotch? Gin?"

"I don't really drink."

Colin took another glass from the bottom shelf of the cart. "Come on. Join me. I hate to drink alone."

Why not? It wasn't like I was going anywhere. "Okay. Maybe just one."

"Scotch all right? Or would you prefer gin?"

I shrugged. One was as good as the other to me. I didn't think I'd ever had either. "Whatever you think."

"Scotch." He poured some amber liquid into a glass and handed it over the back of the sofa.

I muted the television as Colin sat beside me and set his glass down on the table. The heat from his arm radiated through my sleeve. My insides constricted, reminding me again of how little physical contact I'd had with men. I'd become one of those strange anomalies—a twenty-first-century spinster living a celibate life that hovered between Miss Havisham's and Rapunzel's.

I sipped the scotch and coughed, nearly choked. The pungent burn of the drink radiated through my chest, settling into my stomach like turpentine.

Colin smiled. "No? You don't like it?"

"It's terrible," I sputtered. But seconds later, the warmth spread through my face and hands, and my muscles inched out of their state of nerves-induced rigor mortis.

"It takes some getting used to. It's an acquired taste." He shifted his body toward me, bracing his elbow on the top of the couch and tucking his hand into his temple. "What did you do today?"

"Caught up on some projects for clients."

"What else?"

I shrugged. "Just worked, mainly."

He lifted his head off his hand. "What do you do again?"

This was always a hard question to answer unless people really understood web and mobile applications. "Well, the short version is that I'm a website designer. The more detailed version is that I help clients with user interface, applications, linked data—that sort of stuff."

"Interesting."

"Some days it is."

"How did you get into doing that?"

I grasped my glass and took another sip. "When becoming a police officer was no longer a possibility for me, website design was a no-brainer. I had a natural affinity for it, and I got a degree through an online university. No need to venture out to go to class."

"Is venturing out a problem for you?"

Here we go. The big reveal. "After the stabbing, I couldn't really ... leave the house."

He sat back, dropped his hand.

"It's been an ongoing struggle for over nine years now."

"Wow."

I toyed with the ends of my hair.

His gaze raked over me, trying to find some spot on my body—my neck, my cheek, my forearms—where the answer to his curiosity was tattooed. "So, you have agoraphobia?"

"I..." Taking a deep breath, I exhaled the words. "I have agoraphobia." Heat rushed into my face. "I mean, I'm trying to get better, but it's been a very long process."

The images replayed through my mind—Vince, lying on the ground—his blond hair matted to a bloodied forehead, his arms sprawled awkwardly. Me—screaming for someone to help us as blood flowed down my arms and dripped from my fingers. Then I must have lapsed into shock. I had no recollection of what happened after. I'd awakened in the hospital. Later, someone—a doctor, I think—filled in some of the missing details of my injuries. I'd colored in the rest.

Colin's gaze was unrelenting, and I turned away, sipped my drink. The burn caught in my throat, and I set the drink on the table. "I mean, I *can* leave the house, but it's pretty traumatic for me. I have to know exactly where I'm going, how I'm getting there, and how quickly I can get inside."

"What happens when you go out? What are you afraid of?"

"Dying." I shook my head. "It's an irrational fear, of course, and I know that, but if I don't have to go anywhere, I just . . . don't. And it's why I've put off getting treated for the blood thing."

Colin stood in front of me and held out his hands. Instinctively, I put mine into his and allowed him to pull me to my feet. He placed his fingers on either side of my neck, palpitating the glands. His hands were warm. My senses raced in synch with my heart.

Why couldn't I have gotten a sixty-seven-year-old tenant instead of this guy?

My physical reaction to Colin's touch felt foreign, painful. He moved his fingers from my neck and reached for my wrist, extending my arm and pushing up the sleeve of the sweatshirt. I tensed at the familiar sight of the scars on my forearms—flesh-toned lines, the skin a little thinner, a little shinier. Colin brushed his fingers over them, and my skin tingled.

He moved past the scars and pointed at a purplish-yellow blemish. "How'd that happen?"

"I don't know."

"Do you bruise easily?"

"Yes," I whispered, pulling my arm away and sinking onto the couch.

Colin sat beside me, closer this time, and leaned toward me, his gaze locked with mine. Immediately, I looked away, shifted my weight, and reached out for my drink.

He sat back, cleared his throat. "I'm sorry. I don't know what the hell is wrong with me. I think I'm a little drunk."

"It's all right. I'm sorry too. I'm adjusting to a new place and..."

Colin held up his hand. "No need to explain anything at all. I'm out of sorts. And very much out of order."

I glanced at the clock on the cable box. It wasn't even six-thirty. Too early to pretend to go to bed. "I think I should probably finish up some work."

Colin passed a hand through his hair and pushed himself to stand. "Yeah, I have some things I need to do too."

He lingered in the doorway, and I felt his stare upon me as I picked up glasses and turned off the television.

"You really do look like her—especially in this light."

I looked up. "Who?"

"Nina Mayhew."

"Oh." My face burned as a smile slipped over my face.

"Sorry. I know I keep talking about it." He glanced down at the floor. "I met her once in New York. They were filming at this old, abandoned building—one that had been repeatedly vandalized—all of the windows smashed out of it. Anyway, she was standing in the front parking lot after they'd finished filming, drinking coffee out of a Styrofoam cup." He smiled, apparently reliving the memory. "And I went up to her. She was the most beautiful woman I'd ever seen."

A laugh bubbled into my throat. "Good night, Colin."

"Night." He waved as he drifted off into the hallway.

As I went to bed, a warmth expanded in my belly—a feeling I hadn't had since I was a teenager. And I was pretty sure it wasn't because of the scotch.

Chapter Nineteen

Nina Mayhew. I looked her up before I went to bed that night. We definitely shared the same dark hair—maybe a similar bone structure, but her eyes gleamed with a starry, sparkling glow. Or maybe that was just the flash of the camera. But when I evaluated myself in the mirror, I saw a duller, lesser version of her.

As I nestled down into the covers and drifted off to sleep, I replayed Colin's face moving toward mine and wondered how it would have felt to kiss him ... and then I marveled that I actually wanted to kiss him.

SOMETIME DURING THE night, I awoke to the sensation of my hair being lifted from my shoulders. It was that unmistakable grade-school feeling of the girl sitting behind me playing with or braiding my hair during class. Groggy, I reached up and grasped for the braid just as it thumped back to my chest. My eyes snapped open. Now wide awake, I looked down and ran my hand along the full plait.

Sucking air, I shoved myself into a sitting position, holding the twisted hair out in front of me. A perfectly symmetrical braid. There was no way I could have done that in my sleep.

Shifting my eyes from one corner to the other, I barely breathed and watched for movement in the shadows.

My entire body jolted at a sudden scraping sound—a clawing noise outside my room.

"Yes?" I rasped, my eyes riveted to the door. Moonlight streaked through the window, beaming over the metal knob. Was it my imagination, or was the knob turning? The mechanical machinations inside the door creaked and popped as the metallic globe rotated and the door drifted open.

My heart throbbed in my throat, and I strained my eyes, desperate to see what was beyond the door.

Was anyone there?

Outside, the ice storm had begun, and sleet pelted the roof with loud clacks. A chill filled the room. Maybe the wind had blown the door open.

Then I saw it—a dusky fog that wafted and drifted like black snow. The mist piled and piled until it was as tall as a man—thin, scarecrow-like. Arms, legs, a head, but no face, no eyes—a dense, dark shadow.

I released the breath I'd been holding in exchange for the shriek that escaped my throat. I gasped in air and let it rip out of my chest again in a full-throated yell. Throwing back the covers, I bounded from the bed and ran, skirting around the ceiling-high, shadowy vapor.

Something sharp raked across my neck, wrenching another scream from my throat. I careened through the hallway and down the stairs, jumping off the fourth step from the bottom. Pain shot through my heels as I ran to Colin's door and rapped the fleshy part of my hands against it.

Seconds later, he stood in the doorway rubbing his eyes. "Hey."

"Something was in my room. It grabbed me." I bobbed up and down, resisting the urge to cling to his T-shirt.

He stepped out in the hallway and looked right, then left. "What? Who's in your room?"

"I don't know." Acid collected at the back of my throat, and my neck stung. I pressed my hand to it. It was slick and warm. "Oh shit," I panted.

"You're bleeding." Colin gently grasped my elbow and led me into the light of his bedroom. He pulled back my hair and ran his fingers over my neck, his brows knitted together. "Okay. Wait here and hold this." He reached over, pulled a towel from his desk, and pressed it against the space where my shoulder met my neck. "I'm going to check your room."

"No, Colin. Don't." Panic strangled my words.

"Press hard on that towel," he called over his shoulder.

As I listened to the sound of his footsteps overhead, an icy sensation crept over me. It hadn't even occurred to me to reach for my gun. It was still in the bedroom. Locked in a safe. Useless to either of us.

I would've sucked as a cop.

Sinking onto the edge of Colin's bed, I held the towel to my neck and tried to breathe. Had the thing followed me? What if Colin didn't come back? What if whatever was up there got him too?

I scanned his room, noting its orderly nature. Medical books lined the bookshelf. The closet door was open, and the clothes hanging within appeared to be sorted by color.

I looked down at my hair, still partially braided on the right side, and poked my fingers through the plaits to loosen it.

Anger flooded me. I hated feeling so powerless. Like a victim.

Think. What had I seen? Had it been a person? It hadn't looked like a human. Black smoke. Bats? Maybe it had something to do with the bats.

A frickin' gigantic bat. No, it had been something else.

I approached the staircase and stared up. The sound of doors opening and closing echoed. Colin was obviously traveling room to room. With a deep breath, I climbed the stairs.

"Colin?"

He swung out of one of the doorways and moved toward me with long strides. "I don't see anything up here."

I breathed out.

He gently lifted the towel from my neck. "It's still bleeding. Keep holding pressure on it."

"I need to get my gun." I shot past him.

"Gun?" Astonishment elevated his voice. "You have a gun?"

Ripping across my room and tripping over my sheets on the floor, I quickly punched in my code and gripped my Glock. Then I returned to the hall, carrying it barrel-down and against my side.

Colin stood, his mouth ajar. His gaze flashed from the gun in my hand to my eyes. "Do you know what you're doing with that thing?"

"Of course I do. I've won shooting competitions." I still took pride in saying that. Even though the reality of the accolades had long since passed. I hadn't shot a gun in years.

Colin walked several paces behind as he followed me downstairs.

On the landing, he brushed past me. "I've got a first aid kit in here."

I paused at the doorway of his bedroom while he collected another towel from the closet, a first aid kit from his desk drawer. Then he sat on the bed and motioned me inside, eyeing my gun. "But leave that over there, if you don't mind."

I set the gun on top of his chest of drawers and joined him on the edge of the bed.

He removed the bloody towel and pressed a clean one against my neck. "That's a nasty ... it looks like..." He pulled back. "Like a bite mark."

"A bite mark?" I met his eyes. "How could it be a bite mark?"

"What did you see up there?"

Mentally, I returned to the room. "A shadow. A giant shadow." I shook my head. "I don't know."

"A shadow didn't bite you."

"Well, I obviously didn't bite myself," I sniped. "Something was in there."

"Whatever it was, it's gone now."

That was hardly a comfort. I *had* seen something.

Silent minutes ticked by.

Colin pulled the towel away and inspected the wound again. "Why do you have a gun?"

I shot him a slanted look. "Why do you think? I told you. My original plan was to become a cop."

"But you didn't become a cop."

"What does it matter if I became a cop or not? You'd have a gun too if you'd gone through what I did." I shrugged. "My uncle—my mom's brother was a cop. He gave me the gun when I moved into my own apartment a few years ago."

Colin settled the towel in his lap, and I glimpsed the palm-sized blood mark on the terrycloth.

"Does it make you feel safer?" He motioned with his head toward the chest of drawers. "Having that?"

"Yes. So does the bow I have in my closet. It's just not as easy to grab in the middle of the night when you're fumbling around in the dark for a weapon."

Colin nodded. "I get it. I can understand your motives for having weapons to defend yourself—after what you've been through."

I rolled my eyes and huffed out air. "Good. I'm glad I could satisfy your requirements."

He held up a hand. "Easy. I'm a doctor, remember? I'm used to asking a lot of questions."

I cranked my head to the side, allowing him access to the wound. "Is it still bleeding?"

"Don't worry. I won't let you bleed to death. No major arteries are involved. It may just take you a little longer to clot. Once the bleeding's stopped, I'll put a bandage over it." He turned his face to the ceiling. "Listen to that. The sleet is really coming down out there."

The ice pattered against the roof and pinged off the window panes.

I met his eyes, wondering what he was thinking.

He ran a hand over the top of my head and through my hair. Goosebumps streamed down my arm.

Finally, he removed the towel. "Seems to be slowing. I'll get a bandage." From the first aid kit, he fished out a bandage and tape. He unwrapped the sterile gauze pad. Pushing back my hair, he pressed it to my neck. Then he cut several pieces of surgical tape and carefully placed them over the gauze.

When he was finished, he sat back. "What do you think happened up there tonight? You were running. Maybe you brushed against something, scratched yourself?"

"You said it looks like a bite mark."

Colin stood. "I know, I just . . . I'm trying to find an explanation that's more—"

"Scientific?"

"Yeah."

"Well, I'm the biggest skeptic you'll ever meet, so I'd like to find one too."

Colin stared up at the ceiling and growled a long, close-mouthed sigh. "I don't really know what to think, and I'm too tired to figure it out."

I touched the gauze. It was warm and damp. Underneath it, the skin burned.

"I should let you get some sleep." Pushing off the bed, I hovered in the doorway, not sure what to do. I definitely wasn't going back to my bedroom. Scraping my gun from Colin's dresser, I moved down the hall to the living room and settled onto the couch. Pushing the gun under the sofa, I pulled down the blanket draped on the back of the sofa and settled it over me. Then I stared at the ceiling and listened to the sound of my own breathing and the ice as it drummed out a cadence against the walls of Whickering Place.

Chapter Twenty
Thursday, January 30

The gray morning light filtered through the window sheers. The sharp, staccato smack of sleet had lessened to an occasional tap.

I slung my feet over the side and pushed myself off the couch, my skin stinging with the shock of cold air that met my bare ankles. Drifting to the window, I pulled back the sheers. Outside, the world was encased in a clear coating that matched the color of the sky. A snap—loud enough for me to hear through the thick-paned glass—signaled a tree limb giving way. Seconds later, it crashed to the ground.

Returning to the couch, I swept my gun off of the floor underneath and carried it upstairs. As I approached my bedroom, everything that had happened last night replayed—the images of the shadowy figure, the burning pain.

Everything was as I'd left it—my sheets thrown onto the floor, discarded clothing over the arm of a chair. Once I stepped inside, a rush of cold raised the hair at the base of my neck.

I popped the gun back into the portable safe. Then I grabbed underwear out of my chest of drawers while glancing into the mirror, where I caught sight of the bandage on my neck. Leaning in, I grasped the edges of the gauze and pulled it away from my skin. Colin was right. The wound looked like a definitive bite mark, jagged, inflamed.

The top outline of the teeth was pronounced; the bottom profile seemed fainter, and the indentions hadn't broken the skin. The flesh was red, bloodstained. Shuddering, I stacked socks, shoes, and clothing on top of the gun safe and carried everything into a spare bedroom, where I showered and changed.

By the time I'd returned to the downstairs, Colin was in the front parlor. He looked as casual as I'd ever seen him, wearing a light blue sweater and jeans. He stood by the bay window, holding an oversized coffee table book and flipping through the pages.

He glanced at me over his shoulder. "Have you checked out this book on Whickering Place?"

"No."

"I guess I'd never noticed it before." He pointed down at the page. "Did you know all these famous people stayed here in the 1920s?"

"Yeah, I think Maris said something about that." I peered over his shoulder. Old black and white photos reflected the rooms as they had looked a century before. "It looks so different."

"Apparently, the original owner was a doctor." Colin read from the page. "*Dr. Shafton moved to Asheville in the hopes of finding a cure for tuberculosis. Tuberculosis-infected persons were sent here with the belief that sleeping in outdoor, enclosed porches and breathing the mountain air would improve their ailment.*"

"And did it?"

Colin shrugged. "Some of them, I guess.

He closed the book and motioned to the window. "We're not going anywhere today. Ice is an inch thick out there."

Not like I would've been going anywhere anyway.

"YOU WENT TO BOARDING school?"

Colin nodded. "Yep."

"Where?"

"In Florida."

"I guess I could see that—you at boarding school."

He cocked his head to the side. "What does that mean?"

"Nothing. Just that you're very ... polished."

We'd been sitting in the front room for over an hour, chatting about what life had been like when we were young. I hadn't talked this much since I was a kid.

"Is that a good or a bad thing?"

I suppressed a smile. "It's not terrible."

"What about you?"

"I did not go to boarding school," I said, putting emphasis on the *not*.

He laughed. "No, I just meant, where did you grow up?"

"In Charlotte. I've never really been out of North Carolina."

"Would you like to?"

"Someday." I shifted my gaze. "So, you and Pearse are half-brothers. How did that happen?"

Colin leaned forward, clasped his hands between his knees. "My mom and dad were married briefly. They divorced when I was three or four but were always on good footing, even if they didn't work out."

"Where are they now?"

"Mom's in Colorado. Dad's in Florida."

"Do you still see your dad a lot?"

"Not as much. But we talk every week."

"And Pearse? What's his relationship like with your dad?"

Colin lowered his eyes. "I don't think Pearse and Dad ever really saw eye to eye. His mom was a one-night stand, and Dad didn't even know about Pearse until he was around ten years old. There's some bad blood there. Pearse's mother comes from a pretty well-known and affluent family in Louisiana. I don't think they were too happy about Pearse coming along. I'm not even sure he has much contact with them now."

"When did you meet him—Pearse—for the first time?"

"Not until he was around thirteen, and I was getting ready to go off to college. But he visited my father around the same time of year as me. We were sort of close for a while."

"Then what happened?"

He shrugged. "In a lot of ways, Pearse has had it rough. I think his mom did the best she could, but she raised him as a single mother, and she may have had money, but she also had family issues. Pearse and I ... we're very different people."

No denying that. Pearse exuded something feral—in his eyes, in the set of his mouth. He was like those geysers in New Zealand I'd read about—steam rising from the surface, boiling beneath. Cracks in the landscape glowing red and orange, promising that one unappointed day in the future, he would blow.

Chapter Twenty-One

In the beginning, blood pacts were performed in the garden over a receiving vessel. A chalice, a bowl, a platter. The donating member ceremonially spilled their blood into a container to be partially consumed by the members of The Colony before pouring it onto the grounds of Whickering Place.

The second owner of Whickering Place lacked dedication to the cause and was swiftly eliminated. Unfortunately, this meant ownership of the house passed into the hands of non-Colony members. Without a Colony member in possession of the house, the access to power for members of the group was lost. The Colony does what is necessary to keep Whickering Place in the hands of loyal servants.

By the time Ace Tullinger moved in, we had expected more sacrifices from the members—that they might retain our favor. There could be no passive donations or animal sacrifices. We required real blood, all the time, directly ingested into the house's walls, its pores.

The wall was an ingenious creation, which arose through our whispered suggestions to Ace that he paint with human blood. And he exceeded our expectations. Donor after donor invited to Whickering Place complied with his request, anxious to have their blood on one of Ace Tullinger's paintings. Once they realized they could hold power in The Colony by submitting their blood—slicing their hand and placing it against the wall, thereby allowing us to feed on the life force—more people than ever volunteered.

Occasionally, Ace brought an extra vial or two from unwitting or even unwilling victims: the perfect additive to our collection. This idea was passed on to other Colony members in other states. The blood pact wall became part of The Colony code. Members saw it as their direct line to power. And it remains so to this day.

Chapter Twenty-Two

The day wore on, an ice-laden time freeze. Outside, nothing seemed to be moving—no cars, no animals, no humans. Inside, the house had quieted—no slithering, no thumping.

Only the sleet pattered against the windows.

"More ice? We won't get out of here for days," Colin said.

My heart lurched. The idea both excited and terrified me. Just the two of us here.

For a few hours, I could almost imagine Colin and I weren't landlord and tenant, but friends holed up in the middle of an ice storm.

Around three o'clock, Colin returned to his room to make some phone calls and send some emails, and I dragged myself upstairs to my father's studio, where I'd set up my desktop computer. I seriously needed to work and catch up on social media and advertising for the business.

After a couple of hours, I couldn't concentrate. Images plagued me. The frozen pond—the woman's face under the ice. The black shadow from last night—its breath against my neck as it bent over me and sank dark fangs into my skin.

I jabbed at my eyes. *Stop it. Get out of my head.*

When I pulled my hands away, I was confronted by my father's paintings. Red paint appeared to drip down the canvas's surface. I put my finger to it. It was dry. It only looked like blood. *Breathe, breathe.*

"Hey, Avery." Colin's voice echoed up the stairwell.

Exiting the room, I moved to the top of the landing and peered down at him.

He held up a bottle of wine. "What do you think? Too early?" He looked at his watch. "It's not quite five o'clock ... or does it really matter?"

I smiled. "Definitely doesn't matter."

He nodded, stripping the foil from the top of the bottle as he strolled off.

A surge of excitement coursed through me. Then I stopped myself.

This was not real. Dr. Murphy would say I was allowing myself to fantasize about the Gallagher brothers because they were the only men I'd encountered in years.

On my own, I had control. Bringing other people into the mix was dangerous.

But that didn't stop me from joining Colin downstairs, where he'd already poured a generous portion of wine into two glasses. He handed me one of them.

"I can't remember when I last drank wine," I said. "Maybe once or twice back in Morganton when my mom and uncle brought a bottle to my apartment for my birthday."

Colin clanged his glass against mine. "I'm introducing you to all sorts of things, aren't I?"

The wine tasted like blackberries and slipped down my throat, warming my insides. I experienced a sense of contentment—temporary and fleeting as it may have been.

We both sat on the couch simultaneously.

"Have you heard from your brother?"

Colin shook his head. "No."

"Are you worried at all? The news said the conditions out on the roads are really treacherous."

Colin sipped his wine. "I'm sure he's fine. He's probably with Lacey."

"Lacey. Have you met her? Do you like her?"

Colin looked at me over the rim of his glass. "Yeah, I've met her. She's a nurse. She works at the center. No, I don't like her. I don't even think Pearse likes her. He just keeps her on the string for convenience, although I think she wants it to be more. Pearse has that effect on women." Colin gave a short laugh. "What about you? Do you—are you seeing anyone?"

I raised an eyebrow. "Agoraphobia makes dating pretty difficult. The guy would have to be into breaking and entering. No, I haven't dated anyone since Vince."

"Vince. Your boyfriend who was killed?"

I nodded slowly.

"That's a long time."

"Yep."

"So not even an online relationship or anything like that?"

"Too risky."

He was quiet. The corners of his mouth folded.

The wine was starting to hit me. If I stood, I'd probably be dizzy.

The television came on, and the room exploded with sound. We both jumped.

"What the hell?" I pushed myself up from the couch and searched for the remote. "How did that happen?" I finally located it on the mantel, right beside the coins, which were arranged in a triangular configuration. I quickly pressed the volume on the remote, and the sound faded.

We sat in silence for a few moments, staring at the television. Then we both laughed.

"Weird."

The five o'clock news played, displaying Asheville's ice-covered streets. A reporter mentioned the number of power outages and highway accidents. People should remain inside.

No problem.

The story cut to a street bathed in flashing blue and red lights and a female reporter bundled in a puffy navy-blue coat. "... as what police are saying is the third local murder in a week has authorities concerned. The most recent happened last night, right here in the Montford Historic District, shocking neighbors and stumping police as the body of twenty-seven-year-old Dawn Smith, missing for three weeks prior, was found in Riverside Cemetery less than a mile from her home."

A thirty-something woman was on the screen, her head covered with a fur-ringed hood, condensation framing her face as she spoke. "It's really hard to believe. This is a quiet neighborhood." She looked over her shoulder. "We've lived here for three years, and no one's even run a stop sign."

The reporter held the microphone a little closer. "Did you know the victim?"

The woman shook her head. "No, not well. I'd seen her jogging sometimes in the morning, taking out her garbage, going to her car or whatever." She shrugged. "Seemed like a nice woman."

The news cut back to the reporter. "Police believe the recent murders may be connected and are calling them 'The Vampire Killings.' Although autopsy reports are pending, Smith's wounds seem consistent with last week's murders, when two victims were drained of what coroners say consisted of roughly sixty-five percent of the blood in their bodies." She turned a little and motioned to the gravestones behind her. "Neighborhood watches are in place, under the assumption that there may be a serial killer on the loose. Reporting from Riverside Cemetery in the Montford Historic District, this is Ashley Cossio from News 8 Asheville."

"Sixty-five percent of the blood in their bodies?" Colin's mouth hung open. "That's incredible. I mean, the killer would've had to practically pump the blood out of them."

"She was twenty-seven. My age. And it happened right here." My chest tightened. "In *this* neighborhood."

Colin grabbed the remote and pointed it at the television. "Let's not watch the news. It's depressing."

The screen flickered off.

But I couldn't shake the reporter's words. "How does that much blood loss even happen?"

"Well, it's not hard to die from blood loss if you hit an artery." Colin's voice was low. "But sixty-five percent blood loss is overkill."

We drank our wine and sat silently. I tried to think of something to say—anything to move my mind away from the news report.

Colin picked up the book about Whickering Place from the coffee table and thumbed through the pages.

"You're really into that book."

He nodded, his eyes fixed on the page. "It's interesting. The history of the house."

I didn't know why I hadn't looked through it. If I was going to live here, I probably should know some of the house's history.

Colin smoothed his hand over the page. "Dr. Shafton, the tuberculosis doctor who owned this place, he married one of his patients."

He tilted the book up so I could see a photograph of the young woman, her hair long and wavy, hanging over one shoulder. The other side was swept up and fixed with a jeweled barrette. The women on previous pages had hairstyles fashionable in the twenties, short and bobbed.

"She was beautiful."

He read from the caption under the photo. "She was a concert pianist. The doctor had the ballroom built for her."

The ballroom Maris wanted me to use for events and galas. "Hm."

"Unfortunately, she died from the very thing Dr. Shafton thought he'd cured her of. Five years after he married her."

"How sad."

Colin lowered the book. "I don't think I've ever seen the ballroom."

I finished my wine and stood. "I can show you if you want."

"Sure."

The ballroom was just off of the main entrance, but it was locked, so I had to find the right key to open it.

I hadn't paid much attention to the ballroom when Maris showed me. I'd been too overwhelmed. The high, ornate ceilings and black and white tile floor had completely escaped my notice.

"It looks like something out of *The Great Gatsby*," Colin noted. "Look at those columns."

White columns with gold antiquing punctuated all four corners of the ballroom. At the back, three archways led to the wall mural—the panel that produced the secret passage. Three crystal chandeliers shaped like upside-down mushrooms drooped from the ceiling.

"You can almost imagine what it would have looked like in here with people dancing." I breathed, envisioning men in their tuxedos and women in sleeveless gowns that clung to their bodies.

Chairs were stacked neatly along the walls, but numerous sheet-covered tables flanked the sides of the dance floor. A small stage was backed by a mural of mountains and trees.

"And the band would've been up there," Colin waved toward the stage.

I circled slowly, staring up. "Look at the detail on the ceiling and the walls." I stopped, suddenly aware of Colin standing very close to me, his body heat radiating into my back.

I twisted around.

He held out his hand.

Not really sure what he was doing, I took his hand, eyeing him suspiciously. "What?"

He drew me against him, pulling me hard into his chest and putting his arm around my waist.

Understanding, I stiffened. "I don't dance."

He lifted my left arm and slipped it over his shoulder. Then he held my right hand against his chest as we began to sway.

"Don't worry. I won't make you do the Charleston." He stared down at me. "You think this is what it would've been like?"

"Probably not," I managed. The muscles in my back trembled with tension. I didn't want to dance. I didn't know how to dance. Maybe once at a junior high prom, I'd jumped around with a bunch of my girlfriends, but this... Standing so close to him that I could smell the wine on his breath. It was too ... real.

"No? What do you think it would have been like in here? Back in the day."

"Lively. More people. More ... music."

"We can pretend."

"My imagination isn't that good."

"Oh, come on." He smiled and shot a glance to the back corner of the room. "Imagine F. Scott back there dancing with his crazy wife. And over there, I don't know." He laughed. "Maybe Ernest Hemingway or somebody like that."

"You do have a vivid imagination."

I wanted to relax. I wanted to "revel in the moment" as romance books said I was supposed to do. Instead, I clenched his hand with the force I would've used to pull back the string of my bow. I fought the urge to break away, run to an upstairs room, and close myself in with what I understood—solitude and safety.

"There are all these people out there being murdered, and we're in here dancing," I said, just to say something.

Colin leaned in, and I felt his lips against my forehead as he nuzzled my hair—felt the stubble of his chin as he rubbed it over and across, back and forth, his warm breath spreading down my cheeks and onto my neck. My body went rigid.

"Let's not worry about serial murderers tonight. Or dancing," he whispered in a low tone.

No. This wasn't really happening. Was it? My control had slipped. Some rarely used part of me responded—slowly and painfully.

He pulled back the collar of my sweatshirt and ran a finger over the bandaged bite mark. "Does it still hurt?"

"No," I breathed out, my senses firing as his body pressed against mine. I felt the muscular contours of his chest under my fingers, his hand moving in circles at my lower back. Then his lips moved to my collarbone, his tongue trailing along my skin and up my neck. He paused, his mouth centimeters away as our breath mingled in small pants. Finally, he pressed his lips to mine, and our lips opened together as his hand slid into my hair. Instinctively, I grasped and clutched at him, some primitive part of me taking over.

His thighs pushed at mine, urging me backward until I collided with the banquet table. Its feet screeched against the floor tiles as it shifted against the wall. Suddenly, I was on top of the rectangular platform, and Colin was crawling over me, settling himself on me—the weight of his body flattening my back against the hard surface. Colin moved his hands over my sweatshirt, finally creeping underneath the material. Grasping the edges, he pulled it up, running his tongue along my midsection.

"Wait. I—"

He looked up at me. "What?" His breathing was ragged, his eyes heavy. "Is it too soon?"

I shook my head. But maybe it was. I didn't know. How did things progress from here? "I—haven't actually ... done this. Before."

"What?"

Shit. I shouldn't have told him.

"Really?" His mouth hung open, his eyes shifting off to the right. Then he suddenly pushed up and climbed off the table. "I guess I sort of wondered. After you told me about your last boyfriend. At least I should've put two and two together." He dropped his gaze to the floor, raked a hand through his hair, swallowing hard. Then he held out his hand to me, pulling me to a sitting position.

I groaned, which sounded more like a protest. Strangely, I'd started to enjoy this.

Breathing hard, Colin lifted my hand, folding my fingers into his. "I'd have felt like a real asshole if I'd ... well, I mean, look. You're on a table." He laughed.

I slid off of it and stood in front of him. "Some people might think sex on a table is hot."

He smiled. "No. I'm drunk, and I think you may be a little as well ... it wouldn't be cool." He ran a hand over his face. "How is it you're still a virgin? What about your boyfriend?"

Embarrassment crept in, heating my cheeks. "Vince and I had just started seeing each other ... when he was killed."

Colin looked down at the floor again. Then he nodded resolutely. "This can wait."

"Okay." *I want to die right now.*

He glanced up at me. "I'd actually like to get to know you. There's no rush for the physical relationship."

My stomach tightened. "Here I thought tonight was going to be my lucky night. In the middle of an ice storm."

"There will be other nights. And other ice storms."

Chapter Twenty-Three

No. Colin is *not* part of our plan. He never was.

We will have to deal with him. Swiftly. We've had to neutralize others in the past who threatened our plans. And we have very special plans for Avery. Virgin blood is not an easily acquired commodity.

Let us relay a tale about an unfortunate girl named Beverly Moorhead.

Beverly Moorhead was not part of our plan.

Ace became acquainted with her one evening when he'd slipped out of our control. He met her at the bank, of all places. She was a teller. Oh, to look at her—she wasn't much. A twenty-five-year-old virgin who'd scarcely dated a man in her life. But Ace was desperate for female companionship. In much the same way that his daughter now yearns for male company. He'd been alone a long time. Never mind that Beverly was fifteen years younger. In his mind, Beverly was a comfort to him.

We instantly plotted her demise. It was nothing personal. She simply was not the right sort. She wasn't worthy of living.

Blood was the only reason we allowed her in the house. Again, that eternal quest for virgin blood. Why, you may ask? Oh, we could tell you it tastes better. But really, it's all about destruction and desecration. That's why we're here, after all. Our very existence is dependent upon negativity and depravity. To take a virgin's blood, especially if it results in death, is our highest form of ecstasy. What was meant for man's consumption, or in some rare cases martyrdom to God, is consumed by us. Oh, the victory is delicious.

But we warned Ace. He was not to touch her. She was to be the sacrifice for the night of The Colony's gathering. If he took her, there would be severe consequences.

But Beverly threw herself at Ace, and he finally succumbed. With our prized sacrifice lost, we had no choice but to eliminate her. Whenever she was in the house, we drove her mad—whispering in her ear, "Kill yourself, you little slut. Slit your wrists or we'll do it for you."

In the end, her blood was hardly worth our while.

Beverly was a meddling bitch.

Her death was necessary.

Chapter Twenty-Four
Friday, January 31

Ada showed up by herself, bucket of cleaning materials in hand. It had taken her five minutes just to unwrap herself from layers. Coat, sweaters, scarves, and gloves.

"I can't believe you're here," I said. "That street is a sheet of ice."

Ada sat in the kitchen and tugged off one of her Arctic-conditions snow boots. "Honey, as long as the creek don't rise and the rapture don't come, nothing else keeps me away from my jobs." She dropped the boot on the ground and jerked at the other. "These girls the company hires, they're all wimps. A little bit of ice ain't keeping me away." Once both of her boots were off, she massaged her big toe. "I may be on my own today, but I'll get the job done just as fast."

"Can I help you at all?"

She poked her foot into a tennis shoe. "No. I got a system." She raised her head. "You're liable to mess it all up."

I raised my hands. "Got it. I'll stay out of your way."

She stood and arched her back, releasing a pop. "You know, if you want to be helpful, you could see if that dryer of yours is working today. Or you might consider getting a new one. Every other time we come in here, that machine goes on the fritz."

Ada hobbled off, and I wandered into the utility room. The old white dryer was massive—probably a leftover from 1985. Time to buy a new one. I turned the dial, hit the on the button. The machine coughed and then quaked into action.

I found Ada in Pearse's room, pulling the sheets off the bed.

"It's working."

"Good."

She threw the brown sheets onto the floor and shook out fresh ones, spreading them across the mattress.

I scanned the room. Against the wall, a biohazard box sat next to a tower of tissue-box-sized containers printed with their contents: alcohol swabs, BD Winged Blood Collection Set Safety Lock Needle 23G 50/bx, Latex Free Tourniquet Blue 20/bg, Clear Plastic Surgical Tape.

"It's like a laboratory in here," I said.

"Hm," Ada grunted. "Remind me of Mawmaw's house."

"Your grandmother?"

"Mm-hm."

I tried to connect the dots between Pearse's bedroom and Ada's grandmother. I scuttered around to the other side of the bed, gripped the edge of the top sheet, and helped her place and tuck it. "Why's that?"

With her eyes, she motioned to a football jersey hanging on the closet door—a black V-neck with a gold fleur de lis on the front. "*New Awlens* Saints."

"Yeah, Pearse is from New Orleans."

"So am I."

Now I had a place for her strong accent, although it was slightly different from Pearse's. "Oh."

"Born and raised in the *Quatah*."

"How long have you lived up here?"

"Fifteen years. I moved up after Katrina took my house."

"I'm sorry."

Ada positioned a pillow under her chin and fit the cover over the edges. "It's fine. The good Lord had other plans."

I picked up the second case and then shook the pillow into it while I threw another gaze across the room. A red electric guitar, the paint partially chipped away from the body, sat in a stand in the corner—a boxy, white amplifier beside it, umbilically connected by a curly cord. One of my father's larger paintings hung above the bed like a headboard. It looked like one of his earlier works. Green and silver smears covered the canvas, treads of his knuckles separating the paint, as though he'd been finger painting rather than using a brush.

"So you said the room looks like your mawmaw's house?"

Ada tossed the pillows against the headboard. "It don't look like it. It feel like it."

I still didn't know what she was talking about, but I helped her pull the comforter from the floor and spread it over the bed.

She eyed me. "You know about the voodoo, right?"

"Heard about it."

Ada smoothed her hands over the brown comforter, pushing out the wrinkles. "Mawmaw loved her voodoo. Every time I went to her house, there was things just floatin' in the air. I could feel 'em." She straightened and swept her gaze across the ceiling. "Feels like that in here." She shook her head. "I never wanted any part of it."

"I don't think Pearse is into voodoo, though."

She looked back at me, raised her hands to her hips. "No. He got other issues. That boy in trouble."

"*In* trouble or just trouble?"

"Both." Ada stooped, swept up her bucket of cleaning supplies, and carried it into the bathroom.

I sat on the edge of Pearse's bed and stared up at the ceiling, trying to feel whatever it was Ada sensed. The tap whistled as she cleaned the sink.

"How well did you know my father, Ada?" I called to her.

"Well enough."

I nearly laughed. "Do you think he was into voodoo?" For lack of a better word.

Ada leaned out of the doorway. "Your father was into black magic. There's a difference."

"What kind of black magic?"

She turned off the tap and stood in the bathroom doorway. "You ever been up to that room beside the attic?"

I nodded.

She took a deep breath. "That room was always locked up when your father lived. I only went up 'dere one time. After he died. When the painters come here. And that was real recent. The wall was red, and they were painting over it. But the red wasn't from any paint."

"What was it?"

"Blood. It was red from the blood. I know the smell. The smell of blood is real distinctive." She compressed her lips. "And they can paint over the wall all they like, but the curse is still there underneath it all. Curses like that don't just go away. They a binding agreement with something evil." She shook out the cleaning rag and turned back to the sink. "I'm sorry to tell you, honey, but you've inherited a lot more than just a house. A lot of things living here. They ain't human, and they drawing more to them. Inviting more to come."

BY THAT AFTERNOON, the ice had begun to melt.

I climbed up to the attic room and stood in front of the freshly painted wall.

I'd been thinking about Ada's words, trying to make sense of them. It was hard to imagine an entire wall covered in blood. Maybe it just looked a lot like blood.

I stood with my nose centimeters away from it. The stringent scent of new paint was embedded behind the whitewash, but I couldn't smell any blood. Whatever blood smelled like.

And the idea that my father had been into black magic had been eating at my insides. Who really did that kind of crap, anyway? And why? Since coming here, all of my expectations, perceptions of reality, and notions about my father had been upset. It made me wonder if I could really trust myself to judge truth and circumstances through the lens of a life that had been put on pause for so many years.

Returning to the downstairs, I spotted Colin in the hallway. As much as I wanted to talk to someone about what Ada had said, Colin wasn't the person. If my dad had actually been into some kind of witchcraft, I didn't want anyone to know about it—especially Colin. It was embarrassing.

"Hey." Colin looked up at me. He wore his long wool coat and grasped the handle of a leather bag. "I probably won't be gone too long. I have a couple of clients this afternoon that I didn't want to reschedule unless it was absolutely necessary. As it is, I think the roads are thawing."

I motioned toward the front room. "You'll probably find me here—in the same spot—when you come home."

Colin's mouth raised a little on one side, but his eyes looked sad. "You know, I'd love to try and help you get outside a bit. If you're interested. Maybe I could take you out to dinner tonight."

A muscle in my face pulsed. I slanted my eyes away from his.

He set down his bag and moved toward me, rested his hands on both of my shoulders. "Avery, it can't be good for you to sit in this house all the time. I mean, you can't enjoy that."

"Of course, I don't enjoy it. But I also don't enjoy the panic attacks."

"But what if I was with you?"

He wants to be the hero that finally breaks me out of my agoraphobic prison. "You know, you're not the first person who's tried to get me out of the house." The words came out harsher than I'd intended.

He nodded a little and looked away, dropping his hands from my shoulders. "I understand." Pivoting, he moved toward the door. "I'll see you later."

My words had sounded so gruff, unlike me. But I was pretty sure I was getting my period soon, which could account for my foul mood. Or maybe all the wine I'd had last night. Maybe this was what a hangover felt like.

Was the safety of the house, a building, any form of a structure, merely a psychological safe haven? What if I tried to go out and something terrible resulted?

I could almost hear the voice of Dr. Murphy: "What do you think is going to happen?"

An armed robbery at the local convenience store. A car driving into the front of a restaurant. A terrorist bomb going off downtown. Vampires draining me of all my blood. A crazy woman with a knife stabbing me to death... Or just making a fool of myself in front of a crowd of strangers. That possibility was scarier than all the others.

Chapter Twenty-Five

After Colin left, I pulled out my father's old laptop. Curious to see if I could find evidence of the black magic Ada talked about, I curled up on the couch and located the entry where I'd left off.

Entry 10
1/15/2000
Something strange happened today. On the way into my studio, I heard a voice. It spoke to me. Clear as if someone stood beside me. It greeted me. Yes, I was scared at first, but then, as it continued to talk to me, I realized it didn't mean any harm. The voice, the presence, was interested in my paintings. Wanted to help me.

Do I imagine this? Or can it be real?

If real, it could be beneficial. Maybe these conversations will awaken something in me. No matter what, I no longer believe I'm alone here.

So my father had heard voices. I'd thought I'd heard voices too. Interesting, but not proof of black magic.

Entry 11
2/2/2000
Is it possible to have a relationship with a spirit? It is happening to me. I cannot talk to anyone about this. They would think I was crazy. But it's the most fantastic experience I've ever had.

The woman—she comes to me at night. Often there is an immediate physical component to our interactions, or sometimes we talk first. Always there is guidance about my paintings, the inspiration for what I should next paint. My muse tells me I must follow her instruction, and my art will be successful. As long as I am listening to her, work, life, love will thrive.

Today, I sold a painting for $150,000. From here on out, I will do what she says.

Reading these entries gave me a funny feeling in my gut. My father was focused on these conversations and interactions with an unseen muse or entity. It was creepy. I wondered about his state of mind. Maybe it explained why he'd suddenly cut off all contact with me.

Entry 12

3/5/2000

It's a miracle. Red. For the first time in my life, I can see the color and actually detect that it is red. My muse has allowed me to see colors previously absent from my vision. How? I don't know. But she wants me to paint with red—every shade of it. Last week I sold two paintings for $175,000 each. Both of them red washes with deep purple circles embedded.

I've also met someone. Her name is Beverly Moorhead.

Chapter Twenty-Six

I needed to talk to someone. I was beginning to think I was breaking with reality. I called Dr. Murphy. After several tries, I finally reached her.

"Avery, great to hear from you. How are you?"

My voice shook a little as I responded. "I'm doing okay."

"You're living in your father's house in Asheville now. Correct?"

"Yes."

"How's that going?"

"Okay. There's a lot of junk I need to get rid of here. I think my dad may have been a hoarder."

"There are some very reputable junk removal companies."

"Yeah, thanks." I felt like a moody teenager. I'd contacted her and now couldn't get out why I'd called.

"Are you still taking your medication? I notice you haven't refilled recently."

"I take it when I need it. I don't like the sluggish way it makes me feel."

"What about the meditation techniques?"

"That doesn't really help me. It never has."

"How are you coping with the change?"

I hesitated. "I think all right. I mean, the house is enormous. With a lot of weird night noises. And I have tenants."

"That's good. Are they nice?"

"Yes."

"Good. That's good for you. To be around new people."

"One of them," I blurted. "I mean, I think I might kind of like him."

"Really? A romantic interest?"

"Maybe."

"That's great, Avery. I'm so happy to hear it. Does he feel the same?"

I looked down. I was clenching the bedspread. "I think so. But I'm not sure I'm the right person for him."

"And what would constitute the right person?"

I suddenly felt like I was back in therapy. "Someone without all of my baggage, probably."

"You think other people don't have baggage?"

Yes, they did, of course. But there couldn't be too many with a life as weird as mine. "He's a doctor."

"That's not a bad thing."

"No, but..." I put my hand over my mouth as I spoke, muffling my speech, knowing she'd ding me for saying the next words. "I just can't imagine that he'd want to be with me—once he really gets to know me."

"Is that you feeling sorry for yourself? So, is that a healthy thought process, Avery? Convincing yourself that you're not good enough?"

I sighed. "The weird thing is, I'm also sort of ... I don't know, I guess I'm sort of attracted to his brother too."

Silence.

"Hello?"

"Yes, I'm still here." It sounded like she was typing something. "Hm. Interesting. What's he like?"

"Completely different. Kind of ... dangerous."

"Dangerous?"

"I don't think he's actually dangerous, but..."

"Could it be that you're attracted to him *because* he's dangerous. You've lived the last ten years of life trying to be as safe as possible. Maybe a little danger is appealing."

I bit my lip. "Yeah, maybe."

"Avery, I think this is just like before. You feel that everyone else is better than you—that everyone is judging you."

Now I felt like she was judging me.

"Relationships may be challenging for you in the beginning due to your background and some arrested development in the area of socialization."

Yes, we'd discussed this before. Emotionally, socially, I was more like a teenager than a twenty-seven-year-old. Romantically inexperienced. Socially stunted.

"What if I just came back to Morganton?" The back of my neck felt hot. I lifted my hair off my shoulders. "I could move back into an apartment."

"Have you been thinking about doing that?"

"Some."

The typing stopped. "Wouldn't that be moving backward rather than forward?"

"Would it?" Why did I feel like she was patronizing me?

Dr. Murphy's voice was level. "I told you there would be some bumps along the way. Have you been venturing out of the house?"

"A few times."

"And?"

"Not good."

"Then you need to do it more."

It was so easy for her to say that.

"Look, Avery, you know as well as I do, the only real treatment for agoraphobia is to confront your fears—something you really haven't been willing to do on any consistent basis." She sounded brusque, frustrated.

What happened to "call me anytime you need to talk"? Now that I was out of treatment, I was like that annoying friend that was too dependent and needy.

Dr. Murphy continued. "Like we talked about before, if you don't practice some steps toward recovery, your anxiety will increase."

A lump had formed in my throat. "Okay," I managed.

"Ask your new guy to take you out. Not out to paint the town, but down the street on a walk or to a café. It'll help to have someone with you."

Now I wished I hadn't called. I guess I'd expected her to tell me something I didn't already know.

I was on my own. No safety net. A realization that sparked a dull pain in my stomach and quickly radiated down my arms and legs. I slid my hand under my hair again. My neck was slick with sweat, and my breathing picked up.

My purse was in the front parlor. I quickly went down to find it, took out the anti-anxiety meds, and popped one. I would be vigilant with these over the next week or so. Maybe taking them as prescribed could actually help me.

Pearse came through the front door, followed by a woman around my age. She wore a short leather skirt and purple tights. The word that came to mind was *robust*. She eyed me. Her shortish auburn hair swung across her cheek as she looked from me to Pearse.

"Hey." Pearse stopped at the threshold of the front parlor.

"Hey."

He gestured to the woman. "This is Lacey."

The famous Lacey. Pearse's sort-of-but-not-really girlfriend.

"Lacey, this is my landlord, Avery."

She forced a tight smile and raised her hand.

"Hi," we both said in awkward unison.

Five seconds of silence followed. Somehow, she wasn't what I expected. She was taller, plumper.

Lacey shrugged out of her leather jacket, revealing a forearm covered in tattoos. There was one on her neck too. I'd imagined someone blonde and petite and perkier. This woman looked like she could kick Pearse's ass.

Pearse motioned toward the hall. "Well, we'll just be..."

Yeah, I knew where they would just be. Interesting, since he'd seemed put off by her before. But what was that adage my mother used to say? All cats are gray in the dark.

I picked up the laptop and trudged upstairs to my father's studio.

Maybe I'd call the junk removal people. Or I could read more of the journal entries. I opted for the latter and scrolled down past the last one I'd read, where my father had met a woman named Beverly.

Entry13

3/23/2000

She won't leave me alone. They won't leave me alone. There are several of them now. Anytime Beverly is here, they whisper in my ear, telling me what a whore she is, how I shouldn't be seeing her. But Beverly was a virgin when I met her. Now they're angry with me. They wanted something from her. Her soul? My soul? I don't know anymore. The only time Beverly and I have peace is when we go to her place or to a hotel, but even then, I hear them talking in my ear—like a buzzing fly or some sort of mosquito that stays close in the sweat of summer.

And I'm beginning to think I'm spending too much time outside of the house. They tell me I should be inside, working.

They tell me that I must start painting with my own blood. Or Beverly's blood. What a shocking piece of art. They'd sell for even more than what my paintings are currently bringing in.

A jolt like an electrical shock ripped through me. Here it was—the blood. Just like Ada had said. I'd just assumed my father had become a self-consumed artist over the past two decades, and that was why he was a stranger to me. Instead, there was this.

A sound from the vent by my right foot caught my attention.

Oh no.

When I'd lived in the efficiency in Morganton, I could sometimes hear the neighbors downstairs having loud sex. Obviously, Pearse's room was right underneath my father's studio.

I rose from the chair and squatted beside the vent. Mostly, I heard Lacey shrieking with high-pitched wails. But once she'd finished, I heard him.

My stomach flipped over. I bit my lip, clasping my hands together so hard my nails cut into the dry skin of my palms.

And then it was over, and there were only soft moans, heavy breathing, and muffled words.

My mouth dropped open. I scrambled away from the vent and returned to the desk. It was weird knowing the source of the sounds. In my efficiency, I never knew the people. Here, it was different. And it gave me a sick sort of thrill. Listening to them lent some inkling as to what it would be like to be with Pearse in that way.

Then I felt guilty and creeped out for even thinking that.

The room darkened as the sun went down. I turned on the lamp and read more of my father's journals, trying to dislodge the images, the sounds. Subsequent entries were only about his paintings, nothing about Beverly or the thing he called SHE or THEY.

Footsteps at the door. Shuffling.

I froze.

I hadn't heard the slithering or thumping in days. But the footsteps were distinct. Something was definitely there—on the other side of the door. My gaze trailed across the room to the panel, separating me from whatever was there. Underneath the door, a shadow moved.

Thump.

A knock—one, two, three of them. *I'm sick of this.* My father may have coexisted with the weirdness in this house, but I didn't plan to do so. Anger propelled me across the room, and I jerked the door open...

Pearse's dark eyes met mine.

Air seeped out of my throat. "Oh, hi." I looked away from him. Heat crept into my face. "You scared me."

"Hey. Did you need something?"

His feet were bare. I swept my eyes up his body. Jeans. A black T-shirt. I guessed this was what one threw on after sex.

"Huh?"

"I saw you standing in the doorway."

I finally met his gaze. "What? What doorway?"

He dropped his shoulders and seemed irritated with my answer. "The doorway to my room."

"When?"

"Just now."

"I wasn't standing in the doorway to your room."

This was more than unbearable. And confusing. I'd been listening at the vent, but not the door of his room.

"Well, someone was. Someone was standing in the doorway. I could see her shadow. Lacey saw her too."

Then we stared at each other. His mouth hung slack; brows compressed. He was obviously as perplexed as I was.

He shook his head a little. "What the hell just happened?"

"I don't know." Cold chills took flight up and down my back. First of all, that he thought I would stand in the doorway of his room while he had sex with Lacey, and then that they'd obviously seen someone that looked like me standing there...

"And it's cold in my room too. Did you shut off the heat?"

"No."

He motioned for me to follow him. My skin prickled as my brain churned, trying to figure out a logical explanation. As I followed Pearse downstairs, I understood what he meant. It felt colder in the hallway as we approached his room. I clasped my arms around myself as we passed by the cracked-open door of his bedroom, glimpsing a sliver of an unmade bed on the way to the thermostat.

"Maybe one of the heat pumps is broken."

But when we reached the hallway that contained the thermostat, a blast of heat warmed the narrow corridor. "Feels warm back here," I noted.

"Yeah. That's weird. In my room, it's like we're standing outside."

We stopped in front of the thermostat.

"It says sixty-eight degrees," I said.

He shrugged. "Maybe it's just my room. Maybe the vents are closed."

I wanted to tell him they were definitely open.

"Anyway," he said. "Thanks for checking."

I followed him back down the hall, and as we reached his door, he paused and spoke over his shoulder. "Actually, it feels a little warmer in here now."

"Yeah, great."

He turned. "That's where she was standing." He pointed at my feet. "Right where you are now."

Then he closed the door.

Chapter Twenty-Seven
Saturday, February 1

"**A**very Tullinger?"

"Yes?" Shielding my eyes from the late afternoon sun, I blinked at the man and woman standing on the steps leading into Whickering Place. I'd never seen them before. And I hated the idea of random people coming to the door.

The man held a leather wallet in his hand. He let it fall open, revealing a badge. "Detective Nick Stoney." He motioned to the strawberry blonde standing next to him. "This is Detective Hannah Mears."

Police. My heart thudded. "Yes."

He stepped forward. "Can we come in for a minute? We'd like to ask you a few questions."

"About what?" My response was more of a reflex than anything.

"You're the owner of Whickering Place?"

"Yes."

The female stepped forward. "You have a tenant residing here. Pearse Gallagher?"

I nodded.

"Can we come in?"

I stepped out of the way, allowing them entrance, my heart galloping.

Until the stabbing, I'd wanted nothing more than to be one of these two people. After the stabbing, the presence of police gave me anxiety, reminded me of the day of Vince's murder when I'd had to give my statement.

Some of those feelings rushed back to me as I gauged the seriousness of the detectives' expressions and the somber tone of their voices. The fear. The grief. The horror.

My hands were slick with sweat. I wiped them against my jeans and motioned for them to follow me into the front room.

"So you want to talk to Pearse?"

Detective Stoney cleared his throat. "Actually, we'd like to speak to you, Miss Tullinger."

The inside of my throat thickened. "Okay." I gestured to the sofa. "Please. Sit down."

Detective Stoney grasped the front of his pant legs and tugged them up before sitting. Detective Mears didn't take her eyes off of me as she lowered herself onto the sofa.

She spoke first. "How long have you been living here, Miss Tullinger?"

"Almost two weeks."

"Where were you living before?"

"In Morganton."

"This must be quite a change for you."

I sat on the loveseat across from them. "It was—it is."

"Did you visit your father a lot when he was living?"

"Almost never. A few times, when I was a little girl."

"You weren't close, then?"

"No."

What do you want? Why are you here? My chest tightened. This whole scene was sending me on a slow slide into panic mode.

Detective Mears scooted forward to the edge of the sofa, her marble-green eyes wide. "Miss Tullinger, were you at all familiar with the religion your father practiced?"

I wrinkled my nose. "Religion? I don't think my father practiced any religion. At least none I know of." *Black magic.* My mind looped back to Ada's words and the most recent entries that discussed his supernatural muse. But I still didn't think that constituted a religion, per se.

Stoney scooched to the front of the sofa. "Have you ever heard of a group called The Colony?"

"Nope."

Mears sniffed and shook her shoulder-length hair away from her angular face. Her sharp features were attractive—a thin nose and pointed chin. "You wouldn't know if your tenant, Mr. Gallagher, is part of the group? The Colony?"

"What?" The thudding in my chest accelerated. "I don't even know what the group is, detective."

She licked her lips. "The Colony is a very dangerous cult, Miss Tullinger. They consider themselves vampires, and we believe they are responsible for the spate of recent homicides happening all over the city."

Stoney lowered his chin and gazed up at me. "You've heard about those, I assume? The homicides?"

The news reports—bodies found in the Montford District, the cemetery. Drained of blood. I swallowed. "Yes."

He extended his arm and opened his palm. In the center sat something round and dark. A coin. Like the one I'd gotten from Whickering Place as a kid. Like the ones sitting on the mantel now and the bag I'd found upstairs. "These coins have been found beside each body."

He held it up, revealing the side with a likeness of the house minted into the bronze. To emphasize, he pointed at the writing. "It says Whickering Place."

I swallowed again, feeling like I was choking on the mucus in my throat.

He flipped it over. "And there's writing on the back too. In Latin. It says, *Tenebrae vincunt*. Darkness prevails. Have you ever seen these before?"

Air streamed from my throat. "Yeah, there are some on the mantel."

Mears elongated her neck, her eyes focused on the fireplace. "Up there?"

I nodded. "My father let me have one when I was a little girl. I thought they were souvenir coins or something."

She strode to the fireplace. I noticed then that she wore black orthopedic shoes with her knee-length skirt.

Stoney leaned forward. "Listen, Miss Tullinger, we don't believe you're involved in any of this. We know your ... situation."

Meaning my illness.

"We know you just arrived in town and have no record of affiliation with any of these people."

Mears lifted a coin from the mantel and held it between her thumb and forefinger. "May we take a few of these?"

I shrugged. "Sure."

"Do you know what they are?" Detective Hannah Mears's voice was smooth and cool—like ice cream.

"I don't. I don't know why my father had them. But I've seen them around the place."

Mears pivoted from the fireplace toward Stoney. She handed him the coin. "The autopsies show most of the victims were drained of their blood. Not from multiple wounds either. One wound to the neck or one to each wrist. And no other. No major organs touched."

"Why would you think my tenants are involved in anything like that?"

The muscle in Stoney's jaw pulsed. "Because Whickering Place has a longstanding affiliation with the cult. Rarely has there been an inhabitant of this house who has not been a member of The Colony." He glanced at Mears. "And we know for a fact that your father was a member of the organization."

"What?" Bile rose in my throat, burning. "Who are these people?"

Mears leaned forward, bracing her hands on her thighs. "Detective Stoney and I have been investigating The Colony for several years now. They call themselves twenty-first-century vampires. They have a whole underground setup of clubs and rituals and initiations. If you talk to any of the spokesmen, they are very polished and come off like media-savvy politicians. They claim to be like the Masons or a hiking club—just a group of folks with a shared interest."

"That's what they tell you," Stoney interjected, the corners of his mouth drawing down. "But the reality is very different. They have an elaborate system that allows them to cover their tracks amazingly well. Members of the group span every level of local, state, and federal government. They fly under the radar, and they keep to themselves. But make no mistake, they're a bona fide cult. Brainwashers, killers."

"And my father?" I choked out the words.

"Your father joined the organization in 2000. He was an active member, and he publicly attributed his professional success to The Colony."

Detective Mears cleared her throat. "The group is heavily immersed in the occult. They use Ouija Boards, blood pacts, and the conjuring of spirits as part of their practices. As well as sacrifices."

Black magic.

"Sacrifices? Like, humans?"

Mears nodded. "They generally believe thirteen a year—per regional colony—is the magic number. They've even sacrificed a few of their own to reach that number. We believe your father was one of the thirteen from last year."

"But he committed suicide."

Stoney blinked. "There is an uncanny history of suicides among The Colony members. At first glance, it might look like they're just an unhappy bunch of people. But there's more to it. And in the case of the more recent homicides ... well, those definitely were not suicides."

I drew back. This was too much. I couldn't believe my father would've been involved in this—let alone Pearse. "This sounds insane."

Stoney nodded. "It *is* insane. And criminal. And why we're investigating them so heavily."

"Why haven't you arrested them already?"

"There have been arrests from time to time. But like I said, they are remarkably well-protected. You've heard of the mafia? Well, The Colony is Dracula's mafia. They're smart. They have doctors and lawyers and medical professionals at their disposal and on their team. It's very difficult to catch them at their game."

"Am I in danger?"

"You may be," said Mears. "Especially since we believe Pearse Gallagher is heavily involved with them."

I rubbed my temples. "Why do you think he's involved?"

"He frequents Odd Bods, a vampire club. And it's been suggested he was involved in The Colony in New Orleans as well."

"Have you seen any strange behavior from your tenants?" asked Stoney.

I nearly laughed. I hardly knew what was strange and what wasn't anymore. "I don't know."

Mears reached into her pocket and pulled out a card. "We'd like you to call us if you see anything noteworthy. Anything at all. Even if you think it's nothing."

I took the card. "Okay."

Stoney stood, smoothed his pants. "And we'd actually prefer it if you said nothing to your tenants about our visit. It will be easier to ascertain information that way and ... it'll be safer for you."

"We'll be keeping an eye on the house," Mears added quickly. "And you'll notice increased police presence in the area anyway—due to the recent Montford murders."

My legs quivered as I stood to walk Stoney and Mears to the door.

Why had I ever come here? Why hadn't I stayed in Morganton where it was safe, where I'd never heard of anything as ridiculous as people pretending to be vampires.

As soon as I shut the door, the phone on the hall table rang. Slowly, I turned and stared into the foyer.

Ring. Ring. Ring. Ring.

Ignore it. It will have to stop eventually.

But it continued to vibrate and clang—the abrasive, tinny sound rattling my inner ear.

Thirty-five, thirty-six, thirty-seven...

Striding toward the phone, I stared at its trembling brass structure. What if I just took a sledgehammer and smashed the damn thing? Threw it in the pond outside?

Forty-eight, forty-nine...

The pond was frozen solid. If there were a sledgehammer in the house, I wouldn't know where to find it. Instead, I carried the phone out through the backdoor and into the garage where the garbage cans lived. Pressing the antique phone on top of the trash bags, I forced the lid down on top of it.

Chapter Twenty-Eight

"What are you afraid of?" Colin sank onto the couch and stretched his arms over the back. "It's just dinner."

"Maybe some other time."

Disappointment spread across his face like liquid. He lowered his eyes. "Okay. Well, if not tonight, then how about tomorrow night?"

I tensed. *Here we go.* "Like a date."

He shrugged. "I guess it would be sort of like a date—if you wanted it to be. We wouldn't have to go far. There's a café at the end of the street."

I willed myself not to panic. The end of the street was only a couple of blocks. No big deal.

Colin's mouth flattened into a line. "Or maybe I'm misreading all this—and being totally inappropriate since I'm your tenant."

"No, it's not that." Finally. My tongue worked again.

"I'm not your type."

"No. It's not that either." I laughed a little, covering my face with my hand.

"You're completely creeped out by me saying you look like Nina Mayhew."

I pulled my hand away. "No. I want to go. I just . . . I don't want to embarrass you."

"I can assure you that you will not embarrass me."

Tears pushed at the backs of my eyes, and I turned them to the ceiling. "Colin, the last time I went out to dinner anywhere with anyone—like, to a real restaurant—I was nineteen."

He nodded. "I know. I understand."

"No, I really don't think you do." I sank onto the edge of the opposite sofa. "I don't know how I'll handle leaving the house ... at night. Even if I'm only going a block."

"I'll be with you. I'm a doctor. Remember?"

I forced a smile. The poor guy was really trying, and I was being a Negative Nelly. Maybe this was my turning point. Maybe I'd be absolutely fine.

"If we get there and you're feeling really uncomfortable, we'll go. I'll bring you straight home."

I let out a long stream of air—the desire to go with him crowding out the will to resist. "I'll go."

BASED ON WHAT I'D ENCOUNTERED inside the house over the past few days, the idea of going out seemed much more doable, if not desirable. But I was caught between the two extremes: preferring the safety of the familiar and longing for freedom from its clutches. Home was no longer my sanctuary. There was no safety at Whickering Place.

"Are you okay?" Colin's voice was gentle, calm as he led me toward his car.

Stepping onto the sidewalk brought pain to my chest. For the past few hours, I'd rehearsed this trip over and over in my head. Three steps down to the sidewalk, approximately five steps to the curb where I'd climb into Colin's car. Less than three minutes to reach the café, which was two blocks away on the corner of Montford. We would eat dinner and then we would come home.

I'd taken an extra half of a lorazepam. Just in case.

"You'll love the food in this place," Colin assured me. "You said you liked Italian, right?"

What if I faint? What if I cause a scene? Or throw up?

"Yes," I managed.

"Didn't you say your mother's Italian?"

"Half, yes."

Colin opened the passenger door of his red Miata, and I sank into the seat.

He settled into the driver's seat, and I had to remind myself that he wasn't a stranger. Not entirely.

"You okay?"

I forced myself to nod.

He started the ignition.

We were on our way.

"Where does your mom live?"

"My mother?" How to even begin? "Mom moved back to Milan."

He quirked an eyebrow. "Really?"

"I haven't seen her in a few months now." I thought of the last postcard I'd gotten from her marked with a blue *Par Avion* sticker.

"Wow. Do you miss her?"

"Yes. But we text and talk on the phone a lot. She was ready for a change too. And when she found out about my father's suicide ... I think she thought it was time."

Colin was trying to make conversation. Keep me distracted.

I struggled to keep talking, my eyes darting from one side of the street to the other, searching for ... for what? Dangers. Threats. Anything suspicious.

But his conversation had worked. Suddenly we were at the café. He held my hand as we walked, and within twenty steps—yes, I counted them—we were inside, where a hostess led us to our seats.

This was almost normal.

A memory of Vince flashed through my mind. Our one-month anniversary. He'd just gotten paid from his job at the sub shop. He wanted to take me to Lassiter's. He'd told me to get anything I wanted. I'd ordered prime rib. And we'd talked about going to the parade the next day...

"You did it."

I glanced up. Colin was smiling.

Oh, you poor deluded man. It's not over yet. I opened the menu and stared at it. "It took a lot of preparation," I whispered. I didn't want anyone to hear me, even in the private room.

He opened his menu. "What did you do to prepare?"

"I made a list of the horrible things that could happen. I did that before I left."

"Really?"

"Yep."

"What was on that list?"

"Car crash. Hit and run. A building fire."

Colin smiled. "We would have to be two very unlucky people. We were only going two blocks."

We ordered. During the wait, an uncomfortable silence settled over us. I climbed into my head, wondering what he must be thinking, what the server must think, what I *should* be thinking. All thoughts that I shouldn't be having right then. I wanted to talk to him about what the detectives had said. But they'd specifically told me to keep it quiet.

"Do you think I should sell Whickering Place?" I blurted.

"Um, I don't know. Do you want to sell?"

"Not really. But then, some days, I feel like it might be the best plan."

"Okay." He nodded. "I'll step up my search for a house."

"No, you don't have to do that. I haven't made any decisions."

Our server came by with our wine.

I took several sips. "Colin, is Pearse is dangerous?"

He looked at me. "Dangerous? What—to himself or to someone else?"

"Someone else."

His brow creased. "I ... don't think so. Why? Did he do something? Say something to you?"

I closed my menu and set it aside. "No, I just—well, you said he might be involved in some stuff—and that you were concerned about him. And I overheard a conversation you two had about the possibility of Pearse doing drugs—and I just wondered if he was involved in anything illegal or dangerous."

Colin swilled from his wine. "I'll be honest with you, Avery. I don't have any proof that Pearse is doing drugs. I know he's got some issues and some interesting behaviors. But I don't think he would hurt anyone. I don't think."

"Okay."

"But if you're uncomfortable having him in the house, or he's done something to scare you, I mean—"

"No." I waved my hand. "He hasn't done anything."

Our food arrived. The server put our plates in front of us and then stepped back. "Can I get you anything else?"

Colin shook his head. "No, thank you."

After she left, Colin paused, his gaze fixed on his plate. "If he's done anything to make you not want him in the house, then he'll have to go."

"No, he hasn't done anything to me. I'm just feeding off of your words. That's all."

Colin exhaled. "He's my brother. I don't want to think badly of him, of course. But I really can't say for sure."

We ate. I forced mouthfuls of chicken parmigiana into my mouth, and it settled into my stomach like a rock. I wanted to eat as fast as possible. To leave as fast as possible.

"If you're up to it," Colin said, his voice slowly registering as though someone had turned an imaginary volume knob. "I was thinking maybe we could go see a play on the weekend."

The theater? A crowded theater where I'd have to worry about having an attack amid hundreds of people? I'd have to make sure I got an aisle seat in case I had a meltdown and had to run out.

"I don't know."

"Or we could just go out to eat again."

"Maybe." I didn't want to be too committal. My tone sounded hesitant.

"Or whatever you want to do." Colin's voice was low. "I'd just really like to spend more time with you alone. If possible."

I laughed. Or maybe I just laughed in my head. "Aren't we always alone?" He meant out of the house, of course.

He motioned to my plate. "Is it good?"

I'd stopped eating, so he probably wondered. The cold sweat crept over my back. "Yes, but I'm starting not to feel well."

His plate was still piled with food. He motioned to the waitress. "Could we get to-go boxes?"

Chapter Twenty-Nine

Colin was disappointed. I could tell by his lack of conversation. But I couldn't worry about that.

We drove home in silence, and I concentrated on slowing my breathing, counting the minutes until we'd pull into the driveway. It had only taken five minutes to get to the café. Only three more until we were home. Another thirty seconds to get back inside.

As soon as he pulled the car around the house and parked in the garage, I sprang out and ran toward the door. Two more seconds and I'd be inside. Close the door, and ... the sigh of relief wracked my whole body. I went straight into the front parlor and collapsed on the couch.

Colin came in and sat next to me. He put his hand on my leg.

I looked up at him. "That was really hard."

"It'll get easier."

I dropped my gaze to my hands. They lay in my lap like dead birds. "I don't know."

"I promise. It will."

"How can you promise that?" My eyes shot up to his. "I mean, really, Colin. How can you promise that? I've been living with this for ten years. How do you know it's magically going to get better?"

"Well, I know one thing that helps agoraphobia is to confront your fears. Getting out of the house even if you don't feel like it." He slid his hand against my cheek, caressing my face. "If you want me to, I'll keep taking you out until it's normal for you. We *can* have a normal relationship."

I pulled away, stood. I didn't like the swoony feeling sliding through me, worming its way in and out of my chest, my stomach. It took me off guard, made me feel unprotected. "No." I faced the fireplace, determined not to look at Colin. "No, Colin. I don't want to start thinking about relationships or what things could be like in the future. No dangling carrots. I can only deal with right now. This minute." A knot swelled in my chest and hardened.

I felt the heat of his body as he stood behind me, his chest against my back, his arms around my waist. "I understand." He whispered into my ear as he turned me around to face him.

I fought the pull of his arm. "No. This is such a bad idea."

"Why?"

My mind was a jumble. I couldn't come up with anything in the few seconds before he kissed me. Once his mouth was on mine, it seemed too easy to just go with the moment. Maybe there could be a future between us. Maybe things could be normal.

But then the long parade of what-ifs marched through my mind. As he deepened the kiss, I pushed at him. "I'm serious, Colin." I took several steps back, kept my eyes down. "This isn't going to work."

But I wish it could.

"Avery..." His voice died off. "I really think we have something here."

"You're only interested in me because you think I look like Nina Mayhew. But I'm not her." I hadn't meant to say that.

He bit his lip, scratched the back of his head. "That's bullshit. Why are you trying to sabotage this?"

Another few seconds and I'd break down. From there, things would devolve.

Colin moved toward me. I didn't protest. I let him kiss me. I let him lead me into his bedroom.

We kissed and made out. That was all.

But I realized how easy this could be. I liked Colin—his touch, his kiss, the way his bare chest felt against my midsection, and I kept waiting for him to remove more of my clothing—my bra or my pants. But he didn't. He was waiting for me to give the signal, and I held back. A future with him seemed as unrealistic as the idea that I would travel the world. I didn't want to hope for something that remained so completely out of reach.

Colin flopped over on his back. "I'm sorry, Avery. All of a sudden, I feel really sick."

I sat up. "Are you okay?"

He stared up at the ceiling, rolling his head back and forth against the pillow. "I'm not sure. I just feel like I could puke."

"I have that effect on people," I joked.

He forced a smile. "No, but..." Sitting up, he leaned over the side of the bed. Then he stood. "I think maybe I just need to walk around. Walk off whatever this is."

He was gone a few minutes, and during that time, I heard him murmuring to Pearse in the hall. I wondered if he was telling his brother that I was in here.

I really, really hoped he wasn't.

A few minutes later, Colin returned to the room and collapsed onto the bed.

"Feeling better?"

"A little. But my stomach is still ... must have been something I ate." He propped himself on his elbow and looked down at me, toying with a lock of my hair. "Hey, I meant to tell you. I have to go on a business trip in a couple of days."

"Yeah?"

"Yeah, and I'll be gone for three weeks."

Three weeks? "That's a significant amount of time."

"I know." He fell back on the pillows. "I'm being sent to a medical conference in Denver. It's only a four-day conference, but my mother lives there, so I figured if I'm going all the way out, I should visit her. Haven't seen her in a while." He ran his finger under my chin. "I'm sorry. Dr. Arnold just decided the other day that I was one of the doctors going."

"It's fine."

"I wish you could come with me."

I sat up and picked up my shirt off the end of the bed. "It doesn't matter. It's not like we're boyfriend and girlfriend or anything. I mean, you're my tenant, so..."

Colin raised up beside me. "You keep saying that. Is that what you really think? You really don't see anything else between us?"

I thrust my head through the neck of my sweater and pulled it down. "I don't know, Colin. I maintain what I said before. It seems pretty implausible. Don't you think?"

He shook his head and lay back on the bed, covering his eyes. "You know, it's like you're *trying* to push me away. You don't believe anything good could happen to you, and you're determined to prove that you're right about that."

I shrugged. All my defenses were up. "Sorry, but I don't need you to psychoanalyze me. I've had plenty of that."

"It's just crazy."

"Maybe that's because I am—crazy." My voice broke as I forced the word out of my throat and stood to leave.

"No, you're not." Colin pushed up on his elbows. "I really like you, you know."

I paused at the door and threw a glance at him out of the corner of my eye. "I like you too."

"So what's the problem?"

I shut the door. I didn't know what the problem was. Or maybe there was more than one.

Chapter Thirty

O ur timing is impeccable, as always.

Food poisoning should provide the perfect deterrent. No need to kill Colin just yet. No need to invite more scrutiny to Whickering Place and ruin our plans. But it's essential that there's no more contact with Avery of the sexual kind.

The detectives may pose a problem. Too much detail could spark Avery's moral outrage, coloring her opinions before we've had a chance to move the critical players into place.

The next order of the game is to push her, test her, rend her heart and mind into a place of fear and trembling. We have people for that, of course—humans to bend her, show her how to be what we want.

Convincing humans to kill themselves or kill others isn't as hard as one might think. It's a matter of inflicting the three d's: discouragement, defeat, despair. Then desperation sets in, and they are much more willing to hear our voices. And when they no longer care about anything, only want the pain to stop, they will do almost anything we tell them.

Pearse's will has been tougher to break. He remains aloof and removed from our influences. And although he is an instrumental pawn in this unfurling plot, he is also a work in progress. We still have much in store for him.

Now the games are about to begin. Starting with the name game. Most humans are shocked that we know their name. Once someone enters our sphere, lives in our space, we know their name as it's spoken.

Names have power. Names form the threshold of recognition, accolades, passion, prominence, and fear. When used most unexpectedly, a person's name can unleash a previously unknown level of terror.

When you hear your name muttered in the dark, it's not your ears playing tricks on you. It's us—toying with you, letting you know we're there. Watching you. When you wake in the middle of the night thinking someone is whispering in your ear, only know that if you had eyes to glimpse the supernatural, you would see us, standing at your bedside, leaning over, and thinking about all the ways we want to violate you ... all the ways we want to kill you.

Chapter Thirty-One
Tuesday, February 4

Ａll morning, Colin had been preparing to leave for his business trip. I'd heard his footsteps in the hall. I'd seen him on his phone confirming his flight. My heart rose into my throat. Soon, for all intents and purposes, I'd be alone in the house. How would I cope when the house was empty, and I was left with whatever was here?

It was close to noon when he rolled his suitcase to the door. I hovered in the entryway of the front room. The least I could do was tell him goodbye, have a safe trip. He strode toward me and held up a green box. "Here."

I took the box, flipped it over in my hand, and read the label. "Desmopressin acetate."

"I know you said it caused you headaches before, but I think you should give it another try. For the von Willebrand."

I smiled at him. "Thanks, Colin."

"Use it twice a day to start. Then we'll see about adding an oral component in a few weeks when I come back."

He put his hands on either side of my face and kissed me. "I'm worried about leaving you here alone."

"Your brother is still here."

He laughed a little. "That's the other thing I'm worried about."

I smiled. "Don't worry, Dad. I won't allow any wild parties while you're gone."

He kissed me again. His phone buzzed, and he pulled away, looked down at it. "My ride's here."

"Have a good trip." I stepped back, putting a few feet of distance between us.

Colin's expression dropped a little. "I'll call you tonight during my layover."

"Whatever. I know you'll be busy."

I HADN'T DONE AN INTERNET search on my dad's name in years. He had a website that featured his paintings, but he never did social media, and articles about his successful art showings were pretty repetitive. Sitting in front of my computer in his studio, it felt strange to type in the keywords *Ace Tullinger, The Colony.*

A list of hits popped up—write-ups about my father's artwork and one on an art colony, but I couldn't find anything about his involvement with a group called The Colony. My next search was *Ace Tullinger and the supernatural.*

This brought up several articles, one from the *Asheville Citizen-Times* dated October 2016. *Local Artist Claims Muse Comes from Inside the Walls of Whickering Place.*

I skimmed. Much of it was about my father as the well-known local painter whose work was widely featured in downtown galleries. Off to the side sat a photograph of Whickering Place and Ace standing in front of it, brandishing a paintbrush.

When asked what inspires Tullinger to paint work that has been termed as "dark but luminescent; frightening but enthralling," Tullinger is quick to cite his muse. "There's an entity living within the walls of my house. It tells me what to paint, and I do it."

An entity in the walls of his house? Sounds a little like Amityville. But Tullinger is quick to point out that he has coexisted with spirits for some time. "I think there may be multiple entities. But they've always been there. I have allowed them to stay, and in turn, they provide me with inspiration for my paintings. They allow me to see colors I wouldn't otherwise be able to see. It's miraculous, really. And maybe that's why I like to use red so much now. But traditionally, red has been symbolic of fire and blood. It's the color of passion. Of primeval desire."

Nothing new that I hadn't read in his journals. Only here, he'd shared his crazy with all of Asheville.

I fished Ace's laptop out of the drawer where I'd last left it and resumed reading his journals. I skipped over a few that were just notes on paintings and finally settled in to read one with substance.

Entry22 7/14/2000

I am now in a relationship with two women. But I can no longer ask Beverly to the house. The succubus wants me all to herself.

In the article, he'd termed whatever was leading him as "muse" and "entity." Now, he gave it a name: succubus.

I'd heard the term before. Leaning over to my computer, I quickly pulled up the browser and typed in the word. Over eighteen million hits came up. I clicked on one that gave a basic definition.

A demonic entity often mentioned in folklore; the female equal to the incubus. The succubus has been said to come to men in the night and have sex with them.

Ew.

As I looked down the list of hits, there were a surprising number of personal accounts—people who claimed to have been attacked by a succubus or an incubus. I read through a few paranormal encounters, many of them too skeevy and lurid to finish. Dad apparently wasn't alone in his experience, whether it was real or imaginary.

I kept reading, couldn't help myself. There weren't that many entries left, and as creepy as they were, they offered some insight into Dad's frame of mind.

Entry 23 7/20/2000

I must stop seeing Beverly. I'm afraid for her life. The succubus sticks close to me all the time now. She says that even if I leave the house, she can attach to me and go along. She can make me do things I wouldn't otherwise do—because she's inside me. I'm strangely and equally thrilled and terrified at the same time. What is it about this entity that leaves me so addicted to her touch, her voice, her commands? I find I cannot wait for her to come to me every night, yet her presence scares me more than I dare say.

My blood chilled. I snapped the laptop shut. I'd read enough. I looked around the room, my gaze bouncing from easel to easel, empty jars, dormant brushes. My skin prickled, the hairs rising on my arms like antennae. It was freezing in here—as cold as the outside.

I stood, rubbed my hands up and down my arms, waiting to see my breath cloud before my face. But the coldness passed. Within a minute or less, the temperature returned to what it had been before, as though a blast of heat had chased away the frigid air.

It was late when I closed the studio door and, carrying my father's laptop with me, made my way down the stairs. Halfway down, I heard the front door open, and Pearse's shambling footsteps echoed in the hallway. He was soaking wet—his dark, curly hair stuck to the sides of his face in wet clumps. He jerked his head up as though he knew I was standing there, staring.

"You're up late."

I smiled a little. "You too."

He lowered his gaze and shrugged out of his wet leather jacket, letting it drop to the floor. His black button-down shirt was plastered to his chest. "Yeah."

"It's pretty wet out there, huh?"

"Yeah. I walked a ways, so..."

"Were you out with Lacey?"

Why had I asked that? It was none of my business.

"Lacey? No." He motioned toward me, his eyes almost meeting mine. "What about you? Why are you up so late?"

"Just finished some work."

"Ah." He nodded. "Colin here?"

"No, he left for his trip."

"Oh, yeah. That's right. I forgot."

Pearse began unbuttoning his shirt, and a shock of electricity bolted through me as he peeled the sopping wet material from his shoulders. He wiped the back of his hand across his forehead. "Well, I'm going to go get out of these wet clothes." He leaned down and swiped his leather jacket from the floor.

I turned away, heat rising in my face. "Oh, of course. Yeah, you must be freezing." When I looked up again, he was gone.

Chapter Thirty-Two

L ater that night, I lay on the couch and tried to sleep.
I pondered the detectives' warnings, Dr. Murphy's words.
Maybe you're attracted to the danger. But was Pearse dangerous? I
didn't know him well, and although he seemed to positively drip sex,
he didn't strike me as dangerous. But I couldn't trust myself to know
for sure.

Unbidden, my mind replayed the scene of him standing in the
foyer, unbuttoning his shirt.

Bolting upright, I willed away the stray image, pulled my father's
laptop out from under the couch, opened it, and clicked on File.
Then I scrolled down to the last journal where I'd left off.

Entry 24 7/21/2000

*I have consulted a medium about my dilemma. She thinks we
should attempt to communicate with the succubus through a spirit
board—to tell her that I need her to move on, leave me alone. We will
try it tonight.*

Entry 25 7/22/2000

*Last night, we communicated with the succubus. The pointer
palette of the spirit board moved all on its own, just like people say it
does. And when the medium asked the entity questions, she answered.*

"Why are you tormenting Ace?"

The pointer spelled out, "He is mine."

Medium: "Are you here alone?"

Answer: "No. We are many."

The medium's final question was, "What do you want with him?"

The answer: "His life. His blood."

The medium thinks that for me to have any freedom, I must bring blood to the entities from outside sources. The succubus wants blood she can access, feed from, draw life from.

So this is what Ada had talked about—the dark practices, the blood, the black magic.

Setting aside the laptop, I located the manila envelope Maris had given me, which contained paperwork and a key to access the file closet. Then I marched to the billiard room.

As I turned the envelope up and tilted the contents onto the pool table, the papers slid out, and the key bounced on the green felt.

Crossing to the door in the far corner of the room, I slid the key into the lock, and the closet opened into a darkened space that smelled like molding paper—pungent, damp, and rotting. I swept my hand along the wall and located a switch. The light blinked on, fluorescent bulbs struggling to waken. The room was the size of a narrow walk-in closet lined with several mildewed boxes and three army-green filing cabinets that looked like they were from the 1950s. The brand name, Arrow, had the slanted tell-tale font of post-World War II brands.

I opened the first drawer and peered in. It was stuffed with files, mostly financial ledgers spanning back decades. The two drawers below it contained the same.

The second cabinet held one file labeled *Settlement*. Opening the folder, I rummaged through the legal papers, finding one dating back to 1995. The transaction had taken place on December first—between someone named Harrison Kane and Ace.

According to the documents, Harrison Kane had been the owner before my father. I wondered if he was still around or even alive. And could I contact him?

As I backed up to the wall, my foot scuffed against one of the partially decayed boxes. The flaps were open.

Kneeling down, I separated the flaps. The box was filled with books. I picked up the one on top. *The Practice of Witchcraft*.

I fanned through the damp pages, noting the scribblings on the edges. My father's handwriting? The rest of the books in the box were the same. Various manuals, some appeared handwritten. A few spiral notebooks that contained Latin and what looked like possible incantations. I dropped them back in the box.

Stuffed along the side of the books were several black velvet drawstring bags. I looped one of the strings around my pinky finger and lifted it out. Slowly, I drew the bag open.

It was filled with coins. The same kind from the mantel. The same ones that the detectives said were left beside the bodies of the recent victims.

The pop of wood against wood drew my head up. It sounded like someone was playing pool.

I dropped the file and peered into the dark game room. Only the light from the hallway spread a swath of orange across the floor and onto the billiard table. I zeroed in on the balls that had been so perfectly positioned within their triangle. Now they were broken—one of them still rolling across the length of the table to bounce off the far end.

"Hello?" I called out hopefully.

Nothing.

My shoulders sank.

"Hey."

Pearse's voice made me jump. He stood in the doorway.

"Did you just break the balls?" I asked.

He drew his head back. "Huh?"

I pointed. "The pool balls. Did you just shoot them, break them?"

"No. I don't generally play pool by myself.

He reached around and slid his hand against the wall, brushing the light switch. The overhead glowed. Then he sauntered in, his dark hair half hanging in his face, one side tucked behind his ear—a black thermal undershirt stretched across his chest. "Can't sleep?"

"Not really."

He looked down at the table, then back up at me. "Heard from Colin?"

"No." I ran my hand across the tabletop and then waved it parallel above the surface, feeling for—what? Invisible strings?

Pearse leaned against the table. "He's gone for three weeks, right?"

"Yep."

He palmed one of the balls and gave it a push. It shot down the table, bounced off the green ball, and rolled into the side hole.

"Nice shot."

He walked around, picked up a stick from the rack on the wall. "Three weeks is a long time."

I wondered where he was going with this. "As long as he pays rent, he's free to come and go as he pleases. Just like you."

Pearse bent over the table, positioning the stick against the white ball. With a quick jerk, he sent the white ball spinning into the red one. "So that's where you're at."

"What?"

He straightened, held the stick upright. "I'm just messing with you."

I shrank backward, stepping toward the file closet. Grabbing the file, I turned off the light and locked the door. Then I made a beeline for the exit.

"Wanna shoot a game with me?"

I caught onto the threshold and twisted around. "Oh, thanks, but no. It's late."

He rested the stick against the table and took several steps toward me. "Have I done or said something to upset you? I mean, other than that first time, which I know was an asshole move, but..."

I was already shaking my head. "No. Why?"

"Something Colin said."

Damn it. "What did he say?"

"Just that he thought I was scaring you."

"You're not scaring me," I said too quickly.

"Okay." He looked at me evenly and then flashed a brief smile. "It's just that right now, you're standing there, looking like you want to tuck tail and run."

I exhaled, hating that he could read me so well. "No. I'm fine."

"Okay."

After about thirty seconds, the silence was awkward. His stare was intense. *Say something. At least change the subject.*

"Do you remember the day we first met? At the café in town?" I blurted.

He nodded.

"It's kind of weird, isn't it? I mean, the coincidence. That you would end up being my tenant."

"Life's full of coincidences."

"Yeah, but, well, that was just—"

Somewhere upstairs, a door slammed shut.

A lightning bolt of alarm jolted my heart.

Pearse's eyes widened. "What was that?"

"Is someone else here?" I asked. But I already knew the answer.

"Not that I know of."

Another door slammed.

He looked up at the ceiling. "I'll go check it out."

"Don't bother," I waved my hand in the air. "You won't find anyone. That's like the third time that's happened."

Pearse stopped at the doorway, his gaze still directed toward the foyer. "There's a lot of weird shit about this place." His arm brushed mine.

"Why did you and Colin decide to live here? I mean, didn't the real estate agent tell you this place has a history? And not a good one?"

"No."

"So, how long after moving in did you start to experience everything?" I asked.

"Everything? Oh, you mean the thumping noises at night. The cold spots..."

"Yeah. All that."

"Not until you came."

"What? You didn't hear anything before?"

He shook his head. "Not really. We were here for three months without anything weird." He met my eyes. "Maybe it's you that's haunted."

I gave a half-hearted laugh. "Great. Let's add that to my other list of ailments."

He leaned against the door jamb. "What other ailments?"

"Never mind." I wondered if I could actually fit my foot into my mouth.

"You're sick?"

"No, no. Not really sick per se. It's just a blood disorder. I was born with it. No big deal." I wished he'd go out into the hallway and not stand so close. But then it occurred to me that I could move too.

"Tell me."

"Clotting disorder. Von Willebrand disease. But your brother hooked me up with this medicine now. So it's supposed to stop the heavy bleeding—although I still don't want to..." I broke off. Saying too much.

"Don't want to what?"

I squirmed, pressed my back hard against the opposite door jamb. "I still don't want to get my blood drawn. Colin says I should. It's been years since I had my blood tested. But I have this fear that I'm going to die if I do ... even though I know that's ridiculous."

"I can do it."

"Do what?"

"Help you with that." He pivoted out of the doorway, throwing a glance and smile over his shoulder. "Stay there."

I stared at the edge of the rug and its stringy tassels. What was he going to do?

Then I remembered the boxes of medical supplies I'd seen in his room. Realization crept over me. *No, no, no.*

I shot into the foyer, glancing over my shoulder toward the light shining from his bedroom. "Don't worry about it, Pearse," I called. Then I made my way quickly into the front room. I scanned the furniture, actually thinking about the possibility of hiding behind one of the couches. This wasn't normal. Didn't blood draws have to be done in a hospital? Or at least a lab?

I can't do it. I can't let him do it.

But a moment later, Pearse was back, carrying a see-through plastic bag. Inside, there were tubes, vials, needles in wrappers.

The old panic hit me with gale force.

"No, no." I crouched in front of the sofa as though that would somehow protect me from his advance. "You can't."

He held up the bag. "I'm a phlebotomist. Remember? This is what I do."

If the sofa hadn't anchored me, I would've crab crawled away from him. Instead, I pressed my spine against the base, shaking my head. "No. Really. You don't need to do this."

He knelt down in front of me and began taking items out of the bag. "Come on. Let me. It's fine. This way you don't have to go anywhere. And then it's done."

"But how will you store the blood, and-and-and don't you have to keep it cold or something?" I stammered, my lips trembling.

"Yes." He smiled. "You have a refrigerator, right?" Pearse stretched out the tubing and glanced up at me.

He must have seen the fear in my face. He dropped his hands and then grabbed mine. His fingers felt warm, and my hand had suddenly gone ice cold.

"Avery. Trust me." His voice was low, reassuring. "I do this all the time. Dozens of times a day. You will be fine." He emphasized each word, his eyes widening. "You said yourself—you're on medication now."

He already thought I was scared of him. And I did not want him to think I was scared of him. But the shaking began in my stomach and moved outward to my limbs. My face heated as I looked down at my sweater. It was obvious the muscles were quivering behind the chenille.

Pearse ran his hand down my arm. "Relax. Just relax. I promise I won't hurt you."

But what if I bleed and bleed and can't stop bleeding?

"I promise you won't bleed to death."

He'd read my mind, seemingly.

He turned my arm palm up and stretched it out in front of him. Slowly, he pushed the sleeve of my sweater up.

I shuddered, anchoring my eyes to the ceiling.

"Avery."

I lowered my head.

"I know what I'm doing."

"I know."

Pearse pulled a red rubber strap from the bag and wrapped it around the top of my arm. "This is probably the most uncomfortable part." He cinched it tight, and the rubber tugged at my skin.

I tried to control my breathing. *Slow and deep.* But the breaths were coming hard and fast and loud, and my heart actually felt like it was cramping.

Pearse held the tubing and vials and rustled a wrapped needle from the bag.

Tears pressed at the backs of my eyes.

He circled his fingers over the crook of my arm.

A cord somewhere inside me broke—like a thin rubber band had snapped. This whole experience suddenly seemed—dare I even think it—sensual.

Cradling my elbow, Pearse continued to circle the crook of my arm with his thumb. He held the packaged needle in the other hand and tore open the wrapping with his teeth. "Hold your arm perfectly straight."

I cranked my arm into place.

He ran an alcohol swab over my skin. "Don't look," he said. "Look at the fireplace. Not at what I'm doing."

I shifted my gaze to the cold fireplace. Distraction.

My mind shot back to what he was doing, waiting to feel the prick of the needle. I inhaled sharply and held my breath, allowing my eyes to flicker down as he positioned the point over my arm.

"Don't look. Just a little sting."

I closed my eyes.

It was quick. The sharp point broke through the skin and probed my vein—ushering in an uncomfortable spike in sensation. "Ow."

"Look at me."

I opened my eyes. Pearse was staring at me. He snapped the rubber band off of my arm. Then he glanced down and changed out the vial with a second empty one.

"Are you all right?" he whispered.

My stomach flipped. Except now, it had nothing to do with the fear of having my blood drawn.

I nodded slowly, unable to pull my gaze from his. He could've kissed me right then, and I would've been totally okay with it, even with the needle still in my arm.

Finally, he broke his stare and looked down as he withdrew the needle.

I glanced at my arm. A drop of blood welled into the crease, but just as I started to swipe it away, Pearse bent down and pressed his lips over it.

My mouth fell open. What was happening?

He sucked, drawing the skin up. *He is a vampire.*

Taking a sharp breath, I raised onto my knees.

But he didn't let go. Instead, he grabbed my arm with both hands and sucked harder.

A little moan escaped my throat—part revulsion and part something else.

I should stop him, push him away. But I didn't want to.

When he pulled back, a glance passed between us—one that said something powerful had just happened, but I wasn't even sure what to call it.

He pressed a piece of gauze to my arm and stretched tape over it. "Don't lift anything heavy for an hour." His voice was rough, raspy.

I slumped back against the base of the couch and watched as he placed the vials inside a metal box marked BIOHAZARD. Then he got to his feet.

"I'll drop these off at the clinic on my way into town in the morning. For now, I'll just put them in the fridge."

As he turned to leave, I felt like I should say something. What? Thank you?

Instead, I sat silently. Then I pressed on my bandage and relived Pearse's lips against my skin.

Chapter Thirty-Three
Wednesday, February 5

The next morning, from the window on the upstairs landing, I watched Pearse walk from the house to the garage. He was dressed in scrubs, his leather jacket over the top, and he carried the biohazard box he'd used to store my blood. I'd been replaying the scene in my mind until I wasn't sure what had actually happened and what my mind had manufactured. When I looked down, there was the bruise in the crook of my arm surrounding the tiny hole.

After, I moved into my father's studio and circled the mouse to wake up the computer. Then I spread out the paperwork from the manila folder, the information from the house closing in 1995, and typed in the name of the previous owner: Harrison Kane.

A few internet searches produced several Harrison Kanes in North Carolina. What were the chances that this same guy still lived in the Asheville area? But as I checked through the White Pages and scanned previous addresses and potential ages for the Harrison Kanes listed, I eventually discovered that the one who had lived at Whickering Place between 1986 and 1995 was deceased.

A Harrison Kane Jr. was listed under Harrison Kane Sr. as a family relation. From what I could tell, Junior lived in Asheville. A few more searches and I'd unearthed that he was thirty-seven and owned an antique shop in the River Arts District. He was an expert in rare and ancient coins and stamps.

The dilemma. The shop was a seven-minute, 2.8-mile drive. I hadn't driven the car since the debacle that led to my flat tire. Hadn't even gotten the tire replaced.

If I did—that would be two outings in one week. And if I actually got out of the car and went into the shop to talk to a stranger about this house and possibly the coins—well, that would be worth calling Dr. Murphy and celebrating.

KANE'S ODDITIES AND Antiques looked as old as Asheville itself, and the place probably hadn't been cleaned since it was built. Like all antique shops I'd ever entered, the place was cluttered with other people's long-forgotten junk. Old chairs' arms and legs all tangled together, heaped in one corner.

I drew a deep breath of relief that I appeared to be the only customer in the shop.

A man approached from the back of the store. "Hi. What can I do for you?"

He pushed wire glasses on top of his head.

My mouth felt dry. "I—I'm here to talk to Harrison Kane."

"That's me."

A wave of dizziness swept over me, an overload of adrenaline. "I'm hoping you can tell me a little something about your father and a house he owned from the eighties into the nineties."

"Whickering Place?"

The swiftness of his reply surprised me. "Yeah. Wow. I wasn't sure if you'd know what I was talking about."

He nodded, walking backward. "Come on back."

I followed him, weaving around the shelves that held chipped and yellowing teacups and passing through stacks of children's toys from the sixties, seventies, and eighties—dusty plastic rocking horses, colorful rubber rings, discarded board games. At the back of the store, glass counters housed old coins, knives, stamps.

Harrison lowered himself into a seat behind a desk with a blindingly bright, adjustable lamp and motioned to the yellow plastic chair on the opposite side.

He switched off the lamp. "What's your connection with Whickering Place?"

I sat. "It's mine. I own it. I live there."

He didn't blink.

"Did you ever live there?"

Slowly, he nodded. "Until I was ten."

I ballooned my eyes.

"My mother and I finally convinced my father to put it up for sale. Before it killed him."

"Before *the house* killed him?"

Harrison turned his eyes toward the ceiling. "Well, let's see. When I was about five, Dad was up in the attic patching some holes when the roof collapsed on him. Broke his arm, some of the insulation got into his eyes, damn near blinded him. A few years after that, he was struck by lightning while walking in the garden. Sunny day, a little overcast, and then boom!" Harrison raised his hands. "Knocked to the ground. Had to be rushed to the hospital. But it was ruled a freak accident."

"That's horrible."

"When I was around eight, things started getting really freaky. Dad was just lying in bed, and the way he told it, something literally picked him up and threw him across the room and against the wall."

My fingers gripped the edge of the table. The other two incidents had a chance of being explained by extraordinary bad luck. Being tossed across the room by an imaginary force was pretty hard to wave off. Sort of like being bitten by an invisible entity.

"He got a concussion from that."

"Did you ever experience anything?"

Harrison looked over my left shoulder, his eyes glazed. "Yeah, but you know, I was a kid. Everyone tells you it's just your imagination. Some memories are so fuzzy I'm not sure exactly what happened." He shook his head. "Anyway, the final straw was when my dad fell down the stairs. Ended up in a wheelchair. But he later told us that someone had pushed him. No one else was in the house. Mom and I found him like that when we got home. After that, we put the house on the market. Took two years for it to sell."

"And then my dad bought it."

He nodded, leaned forward. "What about you? Why'd you want to talk to me about the place?"

"Ever heard of a group called The Colony?"

Harrison flopped back in the chair. "All too often."

"Was your father involved with them?"

"No. But they wanted him to be."

"Who's they?"

"The leaders of The Colony. They recruited him hard. But my dad didn't want anything to do with them. Or their practices." He leaned forward, lowered his voice. "But since you're living there, you should probably know that it's very important to The Colony that the owner of Whickering Place be a part of them."

"Yeah, I keep hearing that. Why?"

"Because it allows the members access whenever they want it. They believe spirits live within that house. They believe those spirits can give them power. Have they approached you yet? About joining them?"

"No."

"How long have you been living there?"

"A few weeks."

He sat back. "They'll be around."

A chill passed through me. What about Pearse? He hadn't so much as mentioned The Colony. He would be a logical recruiter if, in fact, they intended to try to recruit me.

The bell on the shop door jingled. Harrison elongated his neck to look over my shoulder. "Oh, hey, Alex." Then he sat back again. "Just my coworker. He's cool."

"Know anything about these?" I grabbed one of the coins from my pocket and held it in my palm.

Out of his leather vest, Harrison pulled a magnifying glass. Old school. Then he settled in, squinting at the coins, turning them over. He dropped the coin on the mat, moved the light closer, picked up a set of tongs, and prodded it. "I don't really like to touch these things, to be honest with you."

Same thing Ada had said. "Why?"

"They're binding coins."

"What are they?"

Harrison darted his eyes off to the left. "Well, I'll tell you this. These were the final nail in my father's coffin."

"What happened to your father?"

"He killed himself. A year after we moved out of Whickering Place. These things kept turning up on our doorstep, our windowsills. A few times, we even found them inside the house."

I shook my head. "I don't understand. What are they for?"

Harrison nudged the coin with the tong again as though it were a dead roach. "These binding coins are probably around circa nineteen twenty-five. They originated inside Whickering Place. Dr. Shafton, the first owner, used to have a coin-making machine in his basement. He needed to make something small, portable, sendable."

"Why?"

"Okay, so the purpose was to procure the will of others. Dr. Shafton would send or bind, so to speak, a spirit to the coin. Then they would leave the coin on the person's doorstep or something like that. When the person found it, the spirit—demon or whatever—would have access to them. Once the person had the coin, the demon could make them sick, make them do something they wouldn't otherwise have done."

"Sort of like a voodoo doll."

Harrison waggled his head. "Kinda like that. Objects make for easy possession. Or even animals. Ever read the Bible?"

"No."

"Well, in The New Testament, Jesus cast out a legion of demons, and he sent them into a herd of pigs. With objects or animals, there's no human will or resistance involved. That was how Shafton engineered these coins—as a demon's free ride to wherever he needed it to go."

My body felt heavy. I might have overdone it a little on the pills to make it through the outing. "You know, the police have found these coins on the bodies of the Asheville murder victims—the people found drained of blood recently."

"If The Colony are still using the coins like they once were, then I'd wager the members have everything to do with the murders."

"Yeah, but right now, I have a ton of these things all around the house. It doesn't really look good for me—or for my tenants. Especially since the police don't have a scrap of evidence to convict any of the individual members of the organization."

Harrison met my eyes. "Here's what I'd do. I'd get rid of every coin I could find. Put 'em all in a bag. Throw 'em in the French Broad River. Let 'em sink to the bottom."

"Can't I just throw them in the garbage?"

He shook his head. "Nope. Cursed and possessed things come back. You gotta take them far, far away from your house."

I breathed out, a shiver wrenching my body from top to bottom. "Okay. I'll start looking for the rest of the coins and get rid of them." Now that I knew what they were, I didn't want to touch them either.

"My best advice to you is to get out of that house. Don't stay there if you don't have to. The longer you stay, the better the entities get to know you. They'll learn your weaknesses, your greatest fears, and then ... they'll go after you."

I was pretty sure they already had.

Chapter Thirty-Four
Thursday, February 6

"**O**ur last phone call was kind of abrupt, and I'm sorry about that."

Dr. Murphy called me. I was surprised when I saw her number. Quite honestly, I hadn't expected to ever hear from her again.

"I was really swamped that day, Avery, and couldn't give you my full attention."

"It's fine. I'm managing."

"I got your message about over-the-phone sessions."

Oh, that's right. I had left her a message about a week ago.

"Are you still interested in doing that?"

"I think so. Maybe."

"Great. Well, let me take a look at next week's schedule, and we can start up soon if you like."

"Okay."

"How are things?"

"I'm managing," I repeated. *Managing* seemed the best word to describe my status. Coping. Alive. Not dead. Yet.

"What does managing look like to you, Avery? Are you venturing out?"

"A little." At least that was true. "I'm actually quite proud of myself. I took the car out yesterday to an antique shop."

"That's wonderful. That's real progress. And your relationship? Didn't you say you were seeing someone?"

I winced. "Colin. Yeah, well, I don't really think that's going anywhere. He's out of town right now, and I think we're too different." *Plus, his brother sucked my blood last night, and I kinda liked it.* I could never tell Dr. Murphy about that.

"I see. Well, that's okay. Start slow with these sorts of things. One step at a time."

"Hm."

"And his brother? Still dangerous?"

"Yep."

"What about other friendships? Have you met other people? I remember we talked about the importance of relationships to your recovery—making sure you form attachments with people who can support you."

I ran through the list of the people I'd talked to in the last few weeks: Maris, two detectives, Pearse, Colin, Kevin the bat guy, Harrison... "Sort of."

"Well, work on that. And then let's talk next week. I'll be in touch with a time."

"Okay. Thanks."

I disconnected the call and sat back on the couch, chewing at my thumbnail.

Since coming home from Harrison's shop yesterday, I'd had one mission: find and locate any and every binding coin and get them out of the house. I'd collected what I could into a plastic Krueger's Grocery bag.

The one place I hadn't looked was the basement. According to Harrison, that's where the coin-making machine had once been. But the idea of going down there was almost as horrible as venturing out of the house.

More than anything, I wanted these weird voodoo coins gone.

I stood in front of the basement and took a deep breath. Finally, I grasped the knob and jerked the door open. The stairwell yawned, black space with descending steps. I flipped on the light, and the flickering yellow-green illumination nearly made the descent look more ominous and unwelcoming.

Gritting my teeth, I forced myself down the stairs. Then I ran my hand along the wall until I found another switch that lit the basement.

A cavernous area stretched before me filled with boxes, folding tables, and chairs, and empty vases lined a shelf on the wall. The concrete appeared damp, with a few small puddles near drains in the floor. Steel poles stretched from the floor to the pipe-laden ceiling.

I pulled my phone out of my pocket and swiped on the flashlight. Shining it from corner to corner, I scanned the space for anything that looked like a coin-making machine. But this seemed more like a storage area—and a desperate one at that. It would be difficult to find any coins down here unless I pulled out every box and scanned every shelf. Not appealing.

Just as I was about to turn and head back up the stairs, my phone torch beamed over a gleaming object that was all too familiar. I stopped. The antique phone.

No. Couldn't be. I'd thrown it in the garbage. The garbage had been picked up several days ago. Maybe it was a second phone. After all, there could've been more than one in the house. Slowly, I moved toward it. With every step, I grew more confident that this phone was identical to the other one.

Harrison's words returned to me: *Cursed and possessed objects come back.*

The sound of the brash, metallic bell flooded the basement—its harsh bray slicing through my chest.

My involuntary shriek accompanied the ring as I spun and bolted for the steps, tripping on the landing and catching myself with my outstretched hand. The jagged corner of the wood stair scraped my wrist, inserting several splinters under the skin. But I popped up and leaped several steps at a time until I'd reached the top and slammed the door behind me.

From the basement, the ringing continued.

I gathered up the bag of coins from the living room and carried them outside.

It was getting dark. I'd managed one trip outside the house this week, but I didn't think I could do a second. And definitely not on an errand to the French Broad River. Instead, I opened the front door, leaned over the railing, and tossed the bag under a boxwood hedge. Then I ran back inside.

The phone was still ringing.

"Forty-six, forty-seven, forty-eight..."

I counted the rings as I picked the splinters from my wrist.

Chapter Thirty-Five
Friday, February 7

I'd been alone in the house for two nights. Pearse had never come home after Wednesday morning when I'd seen him carrying the biohazard box with my blood. I also hadn't heard from Colin. Or Maris. Or Kevin the bat guy.

I was beginning to have that I'm-the-last-person-alive-on-earth feeling.

I should get in the car, take the coins and dump them in the French Broad, just like Harrison suggested. But leaving the house for the outing to the coin shop had taken a lot out of me. I wasn't sure when I could do that again.

Throughout the day, the phone in the basement rang intermittently, muffled by the floorboards. I jumped every time. Sometimes it rang twice; sometimes forty-two times, sometimes fifty-six times. It was maddening. The phone was going to the river as well. As soon as I worked up the nerve.

Ada usually arrived early on Fridays—by ten o'clock. But now it was close to noon, and I still hadn't seen her or her team.

Absently, I trailed down the lower hallway and passed Pearse's room. It hadn't occurred to me before, but if Pearse was involved in The Colony as the detectives suggested, there might have been coins in his room—or something else of interest. Something to indicate just how dangerous he really was. Maybe I'd just take a peek or do a little investigating of my own. I'd need to unlock the room so the cleaning crew could get in anyway.

The spare keys were in the chest in the master bedroom. I quickly moved inside, slid open the drawer, and grasped the ring with the keys. Pearse's room was marked #7.

Then I wandered back downstairs and stood at his door.

My hand shook as I pushed the key into the lock and turned it, my adrenaline pumping with the notion that I was doing something sneaky, wrong, but necessary.

The door creaked open, and I stepped into the blackened space. The blinds were drawn, heavy curtains pulled over the top of them, making the space as dark as if it were night. I marched over to the windows, pushed back the curtain, twisted the rod to open the blinds. A grayish light filtered in. I turned on the squat Asian lamp on the bedside table and pivoted in a full circle—taking in everything.

Except everything wasn't much.

The cover on the bed was thrown back, the sheets bunched up at the base like a wadded-up fast-food hamburger wrapper. The pillows lay on the floor, and I fought the temptation to pick them up and put them back on the bed. Ada and her crew would do that when they came in to clean. His nightstand contained scattered remnants of an emptied pocket, a condom, loose change—none of them the coins I was seeking. Three guitar picks—two blue, one red. I picked up one of the blue shards of plastic and inspected it. *Odd Bod*s was printed across the triangular space. The vampire bar.

A stack of books rested on the floor by his bed.

Pearse didn't strike me as the type who read.

The top book was on the history of New Orleans. The one below appeared to be a medical book on anatomy. I fanned through its pages. Some were marked with yellow and orange sticky notes. The material seemed dry and academic, but several of the marked pages addressed the arterial system. Obviously, a reference manual.

The bottom of the stack surprised me the most. A paperback copy of Thomas Wolfe's *Look Homeward Angel*. Asheville's own literary son's controversial novel. The pages were crisp, unmarked. Unread, I guessed.

I pulled back the lid on the biohazard box. It was empty, but there were several test tube racks inside.

The high chest of drawers was cluttered with a pile of clothes, a waxy yellow candle—its structure melted down into a ceramic bowl—and a small black box, latched by a button the size of a lentil and a loop of thread. I reached up and lifted the box, carefully holding it as I unlatched the loop. A black card fluttered to the ground, and I squatted down and scooped it up.

The inside was black velveteen molded around tools that resembled ornate scalpels. Long, wooden handles carved with Celtic symbols ended in a pointed tip that looked a little like a calligraphy pen. Another piece nestled into the box had a similar point, but it was a decorative thimble that fit over the tip of a finger. A small glass vial with a screw-on top completed the collection. Turning the card over in my hand, I read the silver writing.

Drink up, my love. Cheers! Love, Lacey

Lacey. The stalker. The sometimes lover.

I popped out one of the instruments and rolled it in my hand. The point was sharp as a razor blade. It would hurt to have that pushed into a vein. Shuddering, I returned the knife to the box and replaced it in its spot atop the chest of drawers.

A fast peek in the bathroom revealed tiles covered in discarded towels. No coins and nothing else in Pearse's room that would give me any insight into his life besides what I already knew. I didn't really know what I'd been looking for anyway. A journal entry stating he was planning to commit murder in the Montford cemetery?

I moved out of his room and pulled the door shut.

"Lose something in there?"

Gasping, I spun around.

Maris. A coy smile wrenched her lips.

My mouth fell open. "Uh, I ..."

She stared, waiting for my excuse.

I breathed out—couldn't think of any reason why I would be in his room. "I was just unlocking it for the cleaning crew. I thought I'd open the blinds for them."

Now she beamed, triumphant. "Find anything interesting?"

I shook my head. "No."

Maris turned and began to walk down the corridor. "I knocked several times, but no one answered. I still have a key that Ace gave me, so..." She held up a silver key dangling from a hoop.

Maris had a key? I hadn't known that. I tried not to feel affronted that she thought she could just walk into my space. Note to self: Change the locks.

She called over her shoulder casually, "Kevin's upstairs. Checking his bat traps or whatever."

"Oh. Okay."

While we were standing in the kitchen, Maris opened my refrigerator, pulled out a bottle of beer.

"Pearse won't mind if I borrow one of his."

I said nothing.

"So how's it going?" She knew exactly where to find the bottle opener. Drawer beside the fridge.

Dr. Murphy said I should cultivate some friendships. So far, Maris was the closest thing I had to a female friend—even if she didn't respect my privacy. "Um, it's okay, I guess. I'm managing."

Managing. Same word I used when talking to Dr. Murphy.

Maris pressed the bottle to her lower lip. "How're things with the guys?"

"Fine. Colin's on a business trip for three weeks."

She raised her eyebrows. "The older one's away. Time to make your move on Pearse."

Why was she so desperate for me to get it on with Pearse?

I frowned. "No thanks. Pearse has some ... issues." I used Colin's word.

"Like what?" She leaned forward.

"I don't really want to get into it." But that's what friends did. They got into it with each other, shared confidences, secrets.

"Does he have a disease? Or is it something worse? Has he spent time in prison?" She chuckled and swatted my arm. "I guess I should have asked him more questions before I let him move in."

"Yeah, did you do a background check or anything?"

"Oh, of course."

"So, did he have any prior criminal behavior? Felonies? Misdemeanors?"

"He's managed to avoid being caught for anything like that yet." She laughed again.

I didn't.

Then she cocked her head. "Sweetie, no. Of course not. Why would I let someone live here who'd committed crimes?" She tipped her head back and poured the beer down her throat. "Pearse is perfect. Trust me."

I eyed her. Blonde hair spilling over her shoulders, red sweater, black jeans, and knee-high boots. She always managed to make me feel like a frump, even if she never said it.

"Maris, I appreciate your interest in my love life. But really—I'm in no shape for a relationship right now."

She raised her eyebrows. "Doesn't have to be a relationship, honey. There are more simplistic elements of pleasure that have nothing to do with a relationship."

My mind flashed back to Pearse sucking blood from my arm, and a little chill of pleasure ran through me. I turned my eyes to the ceiling. "I prefer to keep my life simple and celibate. It's a lot less complicated."

Maris stopped. I could almost hear the scrape of the needle against the record as what I said sank in. "Celibate? I'm sure you've had your fair share of relationships. What else would you have been doing with yourself? Cooped up inside all these years?"

I swallowed, feeling the sting of her words. "Dating has been the least of my worries."

"Well, we all need a little physical attention from time to time." Maris rolled her eyes before resting her gaze on me. "Am I right?"

"I guess for some people. Opportunities for sex are not abundant for the agoraphobic."

"Well, you're *not* saying you're a virgin, are you?"

"I'm not saying anything."

Now her mouth stretched open, and she smacked her fingers against it, giggling. "What? You're not serious."

It was time to change the subject to something she *could* help me with. "Actually, I'm glad you're here because I could really use an ear right now."

She leaned against the counter. "I'm *all* ears, sweetie."

"Did my father ever talk to you about journals he kept?"

Her brow creased. "What kind of journals?"

"I found this old laptop of his where he kept his electronic journals."

Her face went flat. "No. I don't know anything about that?"

I looked at her, wondering if she'd even believe any of this. "Well, he wrote a lot of weird stuff in them about this woman he knew and the entity in the house—"

"Have you felt anything?"

I couldn't bring myself to say that I had. To give voice to it, to admit that I'd experienced something supernatural would somehow make it all real. "Not really."

Maris moved toward me, her arms outstretched. "Oh, sweetie." She pulled me into a hug. "I've been so worried about you being in this house. And with your history. I can see why it would be overwhelming to you." She stepped back, holding me at arm's length. "Just let me take care of everything."

"What do you mean?"

"Well, you want to sell the place, right?"

"I think so. Maybe. I still don't know."

Maris nodded, clasping my face between her hands. "It makes sense. Your father would have understood." She stepped back. "We'll get you out of this place in no time."

I took another step back from her. I didn't want to feel rushed or pressured into selling. Especially if I changed my mind.

"You only need to give the tenants thirty days' notice. People do it all the time. I would even consider keeping them on as tenants for another few months."

"No, I know. I need to think about it." I didn't like the idea of someone swooping in and taking over everything in one day. I hadn't gotten control of my life yet, and I wasn't ready to give someone else dominion over my inheritance—even if it made my life easier.

Maris swilled from the bottle, narrowed her eyes. "I understand. Take your time. Let me know when you're ready. I'll draw up the papers."

I drifted to one of the kitchen table chairs and sank onto it. "Maris, did you know that my father was involved in a cult?"

She carried her bottle to the table and sat down in the chair opposite mine. Then she fumbled in her purse. "Who told you he was in a cult?"

"Like I said, I've been reading his journals."

Her face grew stony. "Ace wasn't involved in a cult."

Her phone chimed, and she drew it out of her purse, swiped her finger across the screen. "Oh, it's Cadel calling about the venue for the twenty-third." She looked up at me, blinking. "What do you think, sweetie? Can I tell him it's a go? You don't have to do a thing except open up the great room and make it available."

I shrugged. Whatever. "I guess so. That's fine."

She beamed. "Wonderful. I'll send him a text and let him know."

I sat back in my chair, feeling like I'd lost a battle. I watched her fingers move across the screen, sending her reply. Had she really not known about Dad's involvement with The Colony? Or maybe they weren't as close as she thought.

My phone buzzed. I looked down at the screen. A text from Colin.

Miss you.

I ignored it.

Clunking sounded from down the hall, and both of us looked toward the kitchen door as Kevin appeared. "You've still got a lot of bats up there."

"Ugh," I groaned. "Have *any* of them left?"

Kevin pressed his fingertips into the tabletop and leaned toward us. "Oh, yeah. Some have gone, but as I said—it's not their active time. They're pretty lazy in these temperatures. Give 'em a few more weeks."

Maris stood up, plonking her beer bottle onto the table. "We've got to go, Kevin. I almost forgot. I have a client coming by the office in an hour."

Kevin followed her into the hallway. "I'm all done here anyway."

Maris rounded the table, bent down, and kissed me on the cheek. "I'll call you later, sweetie. Let me know if you need anything." Then she circled back again. "And don't forget about the twenty-third."

I watched them walk out the front door, past Ada and her crew as they approached. Immense relief flooded my chest. I didn't know why Ada was such a comfort to me, except that she was the most normal person who'd walked into this house since I'd gotten here.

Ada smiled at me as she entered. Then she reached into her pocket, pulled out a small gray satin bag, and placed it in my hand. "For you, honey. To keep you safe."

Chapter Thirty-Six

"What is it?" I asked, pulling the drawstrings on the bag and turning it up and into my hand. The chain spilled out first. Then a wooden cross.

"That was my mama's, and she gave it to me. Whenever our daddy took us to my mawmaw's for Sunday dinner, I wore it for protection against any spirits that might try and do something to me."

I turned the cross over in my hand. A red stone was inlaid in the center of the wood. The charm was simple, but the chain was heavy silver.

Ada pointed. "That 'dere cross is made of cypress wood, and it was blessed by the Reverend DuVrais from New Iberia. I started wearing it when I first come into this house. And now I'm giving it to you."

My heart surged with emotion. I raised my head and smiled. "Thank you, Ada. But I can't take this. It's yours. It's valuable. It has sentimental value."

She shook her head and closed her hands around mine. "No, no. It's yours now. I want you to have it. It's served its purpose for me. You need it more."

No point in trying to tell Ada that I didn't want to give any more credence to the supernatural than I had to. And I knew she wouldn't take no for an answer.

I slipped the chain over my head. "Thank you. That is really nice of you."

"Wear it all the time," she said. "Especially around those people."

192

"Those people?"

"The ones who come here looking to take your power." She shook her head, her eyes soulful and sad. "Don't give it to 'em." She raised her eyes to the ceiling and whispered, "And I don't really wanna say no more. Don't want 'em to hear me. Don't want to give 'em any more information than what they already have."

I assumed she thought the spirits were listening to our conversation.

TWO HOURS AFTER THE cleaners left, the ground outside was a mixture of crystallizing ice and snow cone mounds. I watched it all from the window in the front room.

The neighbor across the street ran outside in a T-shirt and jeans, the ice pellets bouncing off his arms as he extended the windshield wipers on his and his wife's car. The twin boys in the house next door rolled out of their front door, their small bodies stuffed into snowsuits far too big for them.

The automobile traffic usually so present on this end of the street had ground to a halt as the roof and hoods of the cars quickly took on a sheet of white.

Colin's red Miata turned into the driveway and wound around the house toward the garage. For a moment, my heart stuttered. Was he back already? But then I remembered he'd flown to Colorado. Pearse must have driven it—and that meant he was back.

I moved to a different perch, the landing on the stairwell affording me a glimpse of the back window, where I could watch Pearse saunter up the walkway, his face hardened against the sleet and snow, the white precipitation settling into his hair.

He shoved his cell phone into his back pocket and pulled his leather jacket closed. Then he disappeared under the awning of the house.

Seconds later, I heard the back door break open, his feet shuffling inside. The door creaked closed.

Leaning over the banister and trying to keep my hair from hanging down too far, I listened for the sound of his key scratching at the lock on his bedroom. Instead, he bypassed his room and stood, looking up at me from the entryway below.

"Hey, Avery."

"Hey." I straightened. "Thought Colin had come home unexpectedly."

His eyes shifted. "Oh, 'cause I was driving his car. My car is making some weird noises."

I nodded. "Okay."

He pointed behind him with his thumb. "Yeah, it's getting bad out there."

"Sounds like it."

A few seconds of silence passed. Things were awkward now between us. Or maybe it was only weird for me.

"Feel like joining me for a drink?"

"Um..." I smiled, replaying the scene from the other night when he drank blood from my arm. "What kind of drink did you have in mind?"

He raised a hand to his temple, looked at the ground, licked his lips, looked up at me again. "Uh, I've got some beer."

My little attempt at humor had obviously flopped.

He took a step back. "I mean, don't feel obligated or anything." His voice echoed in the foyer.

"No—it's..." I started down the stairs. "I was just kidding." It would be even more uncomfortable if I had to explain the joke.

His gaze followed me from beneath dark brows. "Okay."

"Yeah. That's fine. I'll have a drink with you."

As I stepped onto the landing, he was already moving toward the kitchen, and I followed him. He walked to the fridge, pulled out two beers, and placed them on the counter. Then he rolled open the drawer, grabbed the bottle opener, and popped the tops.

"Have you heard from Colin?" He handed me one of them.

Colin. I had all but forgotten about his text.

I curved my fingers around the bottle. "Uh, yeah. I think he texted earlier. I haven't had a chance to respond."

Pearse ran one hand over the top of the island while bringing the bottle to his lips with the other.

I watched him. A little injection of adrenaline coursed through me. "Anything on my blood samples yet?"

Pearse looked up at me and swallowed. "Haven't gotten the results back yet."

"What did you tell them? The people at the center. About the blood samples?"

"I didn't tell them anything."

"Isn't that illegal? I mean, just bringing in blood samples from the outside."

He smiled. "Yeah, probably."

I wavered and then managed to blurt out the next question. "Have you ever gotten in trouble for anything like that at work?"

"No."

"Have you ever been in any kind of trouble?"

He turned up his beer again and swallowed. "What do you mean?"

I looked down at the floor, where the tiles needed replacing. "Well, I didn't know you guys when I moved in. I guess I'm just wondering if there's anything I need to know."

There, I've said it.

"About me? Or Colin?"

"Both of you."

Pearse pushed himself away from the counter and walked toward the kitchen door. "Like what?"

"I don't know." *Have you ever murdered anyone?*

"Like, have I ever been in jail?" He looked at me over his shoulder and smiled.

"Have you?"

"No."

He carried his beer out of the room, and I picked up mine and followed him. In the foyer we stopped, turned toward each other but stared at the floor. Pearse still had his coat on, and I wondered if he would be leaving again.

He rested his back against the wall. "What else do you want to know?"

I felt my face heat and raised a shoulder in a half-shrug. "No. Nothing. It's fine."

When he next spoke, his voice was low. "Avery, I feel like there are some things you *should* know. For your own protection." His expression was serious, his eyebrows knitted together.

Here we go. This was what I'd been waiting for. Info for Stoney and Mears. My stomach tightened. "What?"

He ran a hand through his hair—a motion that was like Colin's. "I know some people who are—"

The doorbell rang. We looked at each other.

"Who the hell would be here? In this weather?"

I wondered the same thing. The road outside had been pin-drop silent. The pavement was iced over.

Pearse opened the front door. Maris and two men stared back at us.

Maris's lips were stained with black-cherry-colored lipstick. "Hi there," she chirped. "Sorry to drop in like this, but our car got stuck at the bottom of the road. We had to practically crawl on our hands and knees to get here." She moved inside and into the hallway, but the men lingered at the threshold.

"What're you doing out in this?" I stammered, annoyed.

"Trying to get Torin home." She motioned to one of the men. "He lives in the Pisgah neighborhood, but we finally realized it wasn't going to happen. The roads are completely impassable. So I thought maybe we could hang here until the thaw."

Until the thaw? That could be tomorrow. But cold air was blowing across the threshold, and the two men were standing outside.

Maris looked from me to Pearse. "May we come in?"

I nodded and motioned them inside.

Chapter Thirty-Seven

As soon as the men stepped across the threshold, I experienced a sense of disappointment. I really didn't feel like entertaining tonight.

The men wore similar black jeans, black shirts, and leather jackets. They looked to be around my age—possibly late twenties—and both had large, pale eyes.

Maris put an arm around the man closest to her and tilted her head to rest on his shoulder. "These are my new friends. I'm showing them around, and I thought you might want to meet them—make them feel welcome." She turned to the man standing to the left of her. "This is Torin." Then she twisted toward the other man. "And Ian."

Ian was slightly smaller than Torin. He stepped out of Maris's hold and shook Pearse's hand. "Hey, how's it going? You're Colin Gallagher's brother, right?"

Pearse nodded. "I am. How do you know my brother?"

"He was my doctor." He put his hand to his chest. "Chronic anemia. But it's a problem for a lot of us, right?"

Torin spoke next. "I met you recently at Odd Bods. My band plays there sometimes too. But you probably don't remember."

Pearse's face hardened.

"Maris says you're a phlebotomist," said Ian.

Now Pearse's face resembled a stone. His eyebrows lowered, his mouth set.

"That must come in handy," Torin said.

Ian laughed.

Pearse didn't.

"Where is Dr. Gallagher?" Ian asked. "Is he here?"

"No," said Pearse, his voice low. "He's out of town."

"Perfect," Maris exclaimed. "Shall we all move into the front parlor, then?"

What was going on? I tried to process. Clear as it was to me that Maris was a cougar who liked good-looking young men half her age, I couldn't figure out why she would show up in this weather with two of them in tow. An uneasy sensation nestled into my stomach. Something was happening that I didn't understand.

We filed slowly, silently into the front parlor.

They carried brown bags—the sort used to conceal bottles purchased from a liquor store.

"Can I get you anything?" I asked.

"Could we trouble you for some glasses with ice?" Maris held up her brown bag. "We've brought our own entertainment, but we might need some *accoutrements* for party purposes."

Maris's gaze was glued to Pearse, a little smile tugging at her lips.

"I'll go get the ice." I left the room to retrieve the glasses. When I returned, Maris was sitting next to Pearse on the couch, leaning forward, her elbow on her knee. They were whispering but stopped as soon as I came into the room.

I set the glasses full of ice on the table in front of them.

Maris sat up. "Thank you, Avery."

"You know, Ian and I were in New Orleans just last year," said Torin to Pearse.

"Were you?" Maris raised her perfectly sculpted eyebrows. "What were you doing there?"

Ian's mouth twitched into a smile. "Mardi Gras. Partying with some friends. Great place. Great food. Great time."

Pearse grabbed his beer off the coffee table. "Most of us stay far away from the city during Mardi Gras."

"Too wild?"

Pearse nodded.

Torin shrugged. "I have wild tastes."

"I can vouch for that," Ian said.

Maris motioned toward the more muscular of the two men. "Torin just got a job at the hospital."

"At Mission?" Pearse asked.

He nodded. "I work in Admissions."

"Seems like everyone in the whole damn town works in the medical field," said Ian, his chiseled cheekbones raising with a sardonic smile.

"Are you in the medical profession as well?" I asked Ian.

He looked up. "No. I'm between jobs right now. But Maris is helping me with that, aren't you?"

She smiled at him. "You know it, baby."

I cringed, watching her claw-like fingernails walk the path from his knee to his thigh.

Out of the paper bag, Ian pulled a bottle containing something yellowish with a label that read Absinthe Green and a fairy on the front. "Absinthe, anyone?"

"The green fairy is here." Maris laughed. "Pearse, you should feel right at home."

Pearse exhaled and rolled his shoulders.

Ian's steely eyes widened as he popped the cork off of the bottle. "Yep. I learned to drink this stuff in the Quarter."

Torin pointed at the glass. "Did you bring the sugar?"

"Yes." Ian picked up the glass, carried it over to the fireplace, and dumped the ice into the grate. "No ice needed for mine." Kneeling down beside the coffee table, he produced a bottle of water and a flat, silver spoon with tiny holes in it. Then he placed the spoon across the lip of the glass and looked up at Pearse. "Oh, do you want to do the honors?"

Pearse gave a quick shake of his head.

Ian shrugged. "Just wanted to offer you the chance. As you probably know, the ritual is just as important as the consumption. This is the traditional French preparation."

Ian tore open a plastic bag filled with sugar cubes and held up a small square. He placed it on the spoon and then poured drops of water over the cube, dissolving the sugar into the glass. "Then there's the Bohemian preparation, which involves fire. Also, the Ernest Hemingway version—'Death in the Afternoon.' One part champagne, one part absinthe." He took his time and explained each maneuver. "The sugar is used as a buffer against the bitter taste." Once done, he looked up—his eyes jumping from person to person. "Who else is up for trying some?"

A second or two of silence passed before Maris spoke up. "I'm game."

Ian's gaze rested on me. "What do you say, Avery? Feeling brave?"

"No, thanks."

"Oh, come on. I think we should all try some," said Torin. "How often do you have the chance to drink quality absinthe? And look at the weather outside. It's not like you're going anywhere today."

"Or any day, for that matter," I heard Maris mumble.

Around her, I was back in high school. She was the prettier, smarter, meaner, popular girl who wanted to point out all of my inadequacies and remake me into her own image.

I glanced at the window. The precipitation fell harder now, battering the pane with a mixture of ice pellets and snowflakes.

Ian dumped the ice out of the other glasses and began preparing the sugar cubes.

The air buzzed with a strange, heightened sense of excitement—as though something extraordinary was about to happen. Maybe it was the snowstorm, or the self-assuredness of Ian's absinthe preparation, or Pearse's dark eyes staring at me from across the room.

Ian handed me a glass first, and I hesitated.

"Sip it *slowly*, Avery," Pearse warned. "It's 75 ABV. It'll knock you on your ass."

"Pshh," Maris waved her hand at him. "Who are you? Stop directing her. Just let her drink it."

I tipped the glass up and allowed a little to flow over my tongue. It wasn't bad. A little sweet, slightly bitter. "Tastes like licorice."

"That's the anise and fennel." Ian smiled and handed Pearse a glass.

"Despite his reticence," Maris said, "I happen to know that Pearse is a big fan of absinthe. Aren't you, Pearse?"

"I've been known to drink some. From time to time." Pearse put the glass to his lips.

The clock on the mantel struck eight. Minutes later, it seemed, it struck nine.

My vision swam a little.

"Avery," Maris sat beside me on the couch, her hand on my shoulder. "We have some things to talk about."

"We do?"

"Yes." She glanced at Torin. "We may have a bit of a bidding war for you. I've told you that I'm interested in buying Whickering Place. Well, so is Torin."

I swiveled my head toward Torin. He smiled back at me with Day-Glo white teeth. "I'm prepared to offer more than the asking price," he said. "Twenty percent more."

My reactions slowed. "There is no asking price. I'm not sure if I'm selling yet."

Maris swept her arm across my shoulder and squeezed me close. A puff of floral perfume wafted up from the neckline of her sweater.

"Avery, I thought we talked about this earlier. You said you wanted to sell."

"I said I was thinking about it."

"But you told me you weren't happy here."

My cheeks burned. I really didn't want Pearse and the others to hear what I'd confided in Maris. But now Pearse's stare bored into me.

"The noises, the stress," she continued. "It's a lot of house for you to live in all by yourself."

"Colin and Pearse live here too."

Maris glanced at Pearse. "Yes. But they won't always live here. Will they? And Torin and I are very willing to take it off your hands now. A guaranteed sale. Guaranteed money."

"Why is it so important to you that I sell you this house?"

I swept a look toward Pearse just as his eyes slid away.

Maris fluttered her long lashes. "As I've said many times. Your father was very important to me, Avery. I have a lot of beautiful memories here." She swallowed, turned her head away, and swiped under her eyes with extended forefingers. Then she pivoted back around. "I guess there's no harm in you knowing that I cared for your father. We had a special relationship. This house holds sentimental value for me."

Her words faded out as time flowed, passed, shifted, and glided together like pieces in a kaleidoscope. The conversation waned in and out. I struggled to follow it. Someone played records on the old turntable in the corner—jazz or ragtime music.

I looked down at my glass. It was empty. I wasn't sure when I'd finished it.

Ian refilled the glass. I pushed it away. I hadn't intended to finish the first. Anyway, it was late. I wanted to go to bed.

Maris stood and approached Ian. Her movements were slow, seductive as she pressed her body against his, her hand sweeping up and into his hair as they started to sway. I watched them, my eyelids growing heavy.

"Avery."

I looked up and met Torin's gaze.

He sat down beside me. "That's an unusual name."

"But Torin is run-of-the-mill. Common as John."

He smiled. "I guess we both tend toward the exotic."

The music changed to a slow, waltz-like tune, and I skimmed my eyes across the room to Pearse. He was looking right at me.

I stood, and the room tilted slightly. Torin caught me under the arm and pulled me close to him. "Are you all right?"

I jerked my arm away. "Yes, I'm fine. Just a little dizzy." Pearse was right. That was a strong drink. I should have avoided it. I sank onto the couch again, and Torin sat very close to me, our legs touching. His breath puffed against my neck—short, hot pants, the smells of licorice surrounding us like incense.

He moved his fingers into my hair, lifted a handful from my shoulder, and inspected it like material he found interesting. "I love your hair."

My mind swirled with disconnected, fragmented thoughts. Why were they here?

I pushed to stand up again and weaved over to the fireplace, where I ran my hand across the mantel. The coins used to be here.

The coins.

I'd left them outside. I'd never taken them to the river.

The needle scratched against the record—the music had stopped.

I glanced toward the sofa where Pearse leaned down to speak to Maris, their voices amplified as though they whispered into microphones.

"Have you talked to her about it?" Maris asked.

"I might've had a chance if you all hadn't shown up so early."

She waved him away. "Well, plans have changed." Then she called out to me, "Avery, how do you like the absinthe?"

"It's not my thing."

"Come sit." She patted the seat cushion next to her.

Slowly making my way back to the couch, I slumped down next to her. She put her hand on my leg. "We all care deeply for you, Avery. I know how much you've had to endure these past ten years. How much you've missed. And I know how hard you're trying to change, get better." She glanced around the room. "We've all been through difficult things, haven't we, Ian?"

I flinched in response to a light touch on my arm and cranked my head around, meeting Ian's steely eyes as he perched on the armrest of the couch. A small smile pulled his lips away from his teeth, revealing pointed canines. Too pointed. People didn't have teeth like that.

Vampire. The word reverberated through my mind with distant alarm.

Maris grabbed my chin, turned my face so that I had to look at her. Her voice softened. "Remember when I told you I was once in an abusive relationship and how I had gotten involved with a group of people who changed everything for me?"

I leaned back, trying to dislodge my cheeks from her fingers. She let go, and I shifted away. I wasn't really sure if I remembered or not. But I didn't want her to touch me again.

Maris nodded as though answering for me. "Well, I've been living this new life for about fifteen years now." She motioned toward Ian. "And Ian here just joined our organization this week. How's it been for you, Ian? Have we made you feel welcome?"

Ian beamed, again showing his canines. I wanted to push on them to see if they were real.

"It's been the best week of my life. New friends, a new purpose." He spread his hands palm down in front of him and circled them. "Everything is coming together. This experience has completely empowered me. Made me a whole person. I was only living half a life before. I was depressed. Angry. I'd lost my job. I'd been evicted from my home." He sipped his absinthe. "Then I met Maris and the others. Ever since, it's like I'm home. It's the most amazing feeling."

Why did I feel like I was watching an infomercial with testimonials of people trying to sell me a new product?

"Mm-hm," Maris chimed in. "I feel the same. Life with The Colony is so superior to my old one. I have an outstanding group of people surrounding me. We share mutual respect and adoration for one another. We are intellectually, psychologically, morally, and spiritually on the same page."

My heart pounded. The Colony. Maris was in the cult too?

I spoke slowly as if each word weighed five pounds. "That's wonderful, Maris. I'm so happy for you."

"None of us are alone anymore. Someone is always looking out for us."

"Oh, yeah, someone always has your back," Ian added.

"I have found..." Maris stopped, her eyes turning to the ceiling. "Immense personal growth and connection through this group." Grabbing my hands, she shifted toward me until her knees touched mine. "There is so much room for female leadership here, Avery. There are no glass ceilings. You can be anything, anyone you want. You can recreate yourself, learn new skills, climb the ladder, so to speak. Advancement is encouraged. I'm running my own team now, and I lead more than fifty other people. The possibilities are endless." She squeezed my hands.

"My father was a member," I managed. Now it made sense why she refused the idea that he was in a cult. People in cults never thought they were in one.

Maris nodded, her eyes sparkling. "Yes, he was. A wonderful, highly valuable member, and because he owned this house, he became a regional leader. And that's why I thought of you." She punctuated each of her words by tapping her finger on my knee.

I sat up a little straighter. "Me? Why?"

"Your legacy. Your father was in a powerful position simply by owning Whickering Place. This was the source point of all of our meetings and events. He hosted the best parties you could ever imagine, and many, many powerful and elite people came through those doors." She pointed toward the foyer.

"Until he committed suicide."

Her eyes clouded. "That was a complicated situation."

"I hear a lot of people in The Colony commit suicide."

Maris's eyes did not move from mine. "Where did you hear that?"

Where had I heard it? Stoney? Harrison Kane? "I don't—"

"I'd like you to consider coming to our meeting in two weeks—the one I was telling you about—on the twenty-third. Here. At Whickering Place. Meet some people. Get to know us. See if there isn't something we can offer you."

Right then, I wanted out of the conversation. "I'll think about it."

Ian stood, sauntered over to the turntable, and put on another record. "You'll see the world with us, Avery."

See the world? I could barely leave the house.

"Maybe she doesn't want to see the world," Maris said. "Maybe she only needs to be queen of her domain. Right here."

A slow song, a sixties tune I recognized, flooded the room. Something about laying across a brass bed.

Maris sat back. "Ace used to love this song." She rose from the couch and joined Pearse, who stood by the window, his back to us.

I caught parts of her whispered words. " ...only needs a little time. That's how all of us found this life. A little time is all any human has anyway. So worry less about how much time you spend with someone. It's all relative. The important thing is the house. Appeasing the house."

Exhaustion wormed its way through my brain like a fog. When I looked back at them again, Pearse and Maris were kissing. Then he pushed her away. I closed my eyes.

What is going on?

The clock on the mantel struck and chimed, but I couldn't count the strikes, lost track after only a few. How long had we been here? Time was passing ... or standing still.

I felt heat against my back and craned my head slowly. Torin sat beside me, his hand touched mine. Blood smeared his face.

"What?" Sucking air, I shied away from him.

He wiped at his chin with the back of his hand? "Do you want some? There's plenty in the other room."

My mouth fell open. "No. No."

"Sure?"

"Yes."

A silent scream crouched in my throat. My gaze trailed over to Maris and Pearse. They were gone. So was Ian.

Shock and repulsion assailed me, along with fear, which drew me to my feet. Vampires. Just like Stoney and Mears had said. These were the vampires. And Maris was one of them. So was Pearse. I had to get away.

Torin laughed. "Wow. Girlfriend, you are skittish." He stood in front of me and gripped my shoulders.

Maris suddenly reappeared on the threshold of the room. Her voice held the commanding tone of a parent. "Torin, come here. She is *not* for you."

Like a scolded dog, Torin dropped his hands.

Behind Maris, Pearse reappeared. He lurched forward, his fingers closing around my wrist, and then he tugged me into the hall. "Stay away from her," he called to them over his shoulder.

I stumbled behind him and into his room.

He closed the door and faced me. "I don't want you anywhere near them."

A knock on the door was followed by Maris's voice. "Pearse?"

"Yeah? What do you want?"

"Remember what I told you."

He turned back to me, his voice a whisper. "Stay in here until they're gone."

"But—"

"Do *not* come out of this room tonight."

My mouth hung open as I watched Pearse slip out the door. Then I promptly fell like a tree onto the bed.

On my back, I stared at the ceiling, straining to hear anything other than my heart pounding in my ears.

Exhaustion finally overtook me, and I slid into a dreamless sleep.

Chapter Thirty-Eight

H umans never cease to amaze us with their diabolical and often creative ways to be just as evil, crafty, and manipulative as are we.

"Where there's a will there's a way" has never been more accurate than when a person is obsessed with possessing something or someone—a concept we share with the human species.

Whickering Place binding coins have been a sought-after prize for members of The Colony. The vampire in possession of a binding coin can command and carry spirits with them. They can bend an unsuspecting human's will to theirs or get rid of said human altogether. Traditionally, however, the coins have remained at Whickering Place until needed.

Today, that changes.

Avery did not dispose of the coins as she had intended. An oversight? Perhaps. Or perhaps we were at work, our fingers in her brain, distracting her and ensuring our will was done.

As Maris departs Whickering Place in the wee hours of the morning, we grasp her head and tilt it, allowing her line of vision to graze the ground under the bushes. A velveteen sack resting under a hedge. A lucky find.

Some of us travel with her to her next location, the downtown vampire lair, Odd Bods.

Now, inside, Maris approaches the bar, where a woman with long, flaxen hair looks up at her. "Hey, Maris."

"Cassie, is Cadel in yet?"

The girl shakes her head, runs a rag over the top of the bar. "I haven't seen him."

Maris leans in. "He's supposed to be arriving in town today. Call me the second he comes in." She orders a hemo-martini and sits at a table. For now, the room is empty, but soon, the place will be teeming with other vampires.

We tremble with anticipation and salivate. Here, amongst so many who are willing to do our bidding, the possibilities are endless.

We climb on top of Maris's head—the perfect lookout.

She pulls out her cell phone and types a group text.

We have a mole amongst us. Far too many police are asking questions. Watch what you say and to whom.

Moments later, an auburn-haired woman ascends the stairs at the other end of the room, crosses, and sits at the table next to Maris. "Just got your text. What the hell is going on?"

Maris sighs, slams her hands down on the table. "I got a text from Ebony. We've got a bleeder, Lacey. Someone is playing us, feeding information to select members of the police. Feds are getting involved."

"Do you know who it is?"

Maris frowns. "Don't know who it is yet. But I'll find out. I have lots of connections with the local police."

"Shit. What are we going to do?" Lacey points up at the bar toward the flaxen-haired girl. "Cassie told me that some detectives were in here last week—one afternoon before the bar opened. Said they asked her a bunch of questions."

Maris raises and lowers her hands. "Calm down. First of all, we have our own people in place, working to make sure no one has anything concrete on us. Right now, they only have suspicions. The most important thing is to find out who is leaking the information. And ..." She looks up, scanning the room. "We have to be careful how much we say. It will be much easier once we reestablish our headquarters at Whickering Place."

Lacey nods. "What about that girl—the one who owns it. Avery? Any luck there?"

Maris twists her mouth. "Not yet. I've assigned Pearse to keep working on her. But he's not to touch her."

Lacey's forehead compresses. "But I thought that was the plan. Didn't you tell me you wanted Pearse to tap that, or whatever, and then we get her to join up, so we can get the house?"

Maris shoots Lacey a smile of restrained contempt. "Your boyfriend has not *tapped* her as you so delicately put it. No one has. Ever. She's still a virgin."

"What?"

Maris nods, raises her eyebrows. "Will wonders never cease. Pearse has gotten sloppy. Or lazy. Lucky for us in this case. When's the last time we've had a virgin to sacrifice?"

Lacey looks off, considering. "I don't know. Not since New Orleans. Like, I was a teenager the last time I saw a virgin sacrifice."

"First choice is to convince Avery to sell the house to us. She seems to be teetering at the moment. But if we can't force her hand on that, then we convince her to join us. That way, we get Whickering Place, and we get virgin blood as part of her initiation and her blood pact, which will be beneficial to all of us no matter what."

Lacey eyes Maris. "Didn't you say you had a thing with her father? Weren't you in love with him or something?"

"In The Colony, Lacey, we can't afford to love *like that*. That's a naïve and impermanent type of relationship. We have to keep our attachments loose. Eventually, we have to let them all go. So don't get too attached to Pearse." Maris flips her hair over her shoulder, raises her chin. "But yes. I cared deeply for Ace."

"But you let him sacrifice himself?"

"He made the ultimate sacrifice for The Colony. But he made a huge mistake in leaving the house to Avery. As his attorney, I begged him not to do it." Maris straightens, her face hardening as we squeeze her head, blocking out any feelings that could distract from her purpose. "But he had another attorney draw up his last will and testament, not me."

"Ouch." Lacey sips her drink.

We slowly push down on Maris's chest, pressing out the air.

She stands, downs her martini. Then she reaches over, grabs Lacey's drink, and downs it too.

Lacey frowns. "But if Avery won't join, then what?"

"Then we kill two birds with one stone. Literally. A full sacrifice of a virgin will open up all sorts of new portals within Whickering Place, and the succubus and incubus will disseminate powers and gifts amongst the members. The succubare love nothing more than virgin blood. We will be immensely rewarded for that kind of sacrifice."

"But how are you going to get the house if she's dead?"

She leans in, whispering. "Avery's twenty-seven years old. She doesn't have a will. She will die intestate. Then we'll acquire the house. Stop asking all of these questions. Just trust me. And do your part."

Maris looks up.

Cassie, the bartender, stands by the table. "Can I get you guys something else to drink?"

"Isn't tonight a two-for-one on the hemo-martinis?" Maris asks.

Cassie nods.

"Then we'll both have a couple more." She reaches into her purse and pulls out a coin, pushing it across the table to Lacey. "Here. A little gift to get you started."

Lacey's eyes light up. "You got more coins."

"And there are more where they came from. Little Miss Careless left them in a place that made them easy to take."

"So, should I..."

Maris nods. "You know what to do."

We all gather around Lacey. The real fun is about to begin.

Chapter Thirty-Nine
Saturday, February 8

Daylight. I pry my eyelids open. Where was I? Lying on Pearse's bed. I rocked my head to the side. Pearse wasn't in the room.

My tongue was glued to the roof of my mouth. I pushed myself slowly into a sitting position. My head felt like someone had pounded it with a hammer. I reached up and touched my forehead to make sure there was no blood or some kind of head wound. When my hand came back dry, I scooted to the edge of the bed and stood. Using furniture as a crutch to move across the room, I finally reached the door and cracked it open.

The corridor was quiet. No sign of anyone.

In the front parlor, glasses cluttered the coffee table. Sugar cubes were scattered across the glass top. An empty bottle of absinthe lay on its side.

I stopped by the mirror on the wall and slowly raised my head. The simultaneous glimpse of blackened pits under my eyes, along with Pearse's seemingly lifeless body jolted my heart. I spun around.

He lay on the couch, his arm hanging over the side, his face partially buried into a throw pillow. I darted toward him, glimpsing the swath of blood across his shirt. There was so much of it. Like he'd been shot.

Nausea ripped through me. "Pearse?" I grasped his arm and tugged.

He jerked awake and his eyes popped. With a quick inhalation of air, he pushed to sitting and lifted a hand to his forehead.

"What happened?" I motioned to his blood-stained shirt. "Are you hurt?"

"No, I'm okay."

"Is that your blood?"

Pearse looked down at his shirt. "Yeah. I think so." He pulled the neck away from his chest and looked into the opening. "It's fine."

"Why are you bleeding?"

Pearse shook his head and remained silent.

"Are they still here?" I whispered.

"No. They've gone."

I glanced out the bay window. The snow was falling. "So, you're *all* in The Colony."

He sat forward, his clasped hands hanging between his knees. "Yeah."

"How long have you been involved?"

"A few years."

"And Maris? You've known her all along?"

He nodded. "Yeah, I've known her a while."

"Why? Why are you a part of them?" I sank onto the edge of the couch.

Pearse looked down. "I don't want to be a part of them. They're all bastards." He shrugged. "It's hard to explain. I left New Orleans to get away from The Colony, but Lacey followed me here, and then it just started up again. The members came out of nowhere, and then I was right back in it. They're everywhere. I can't get away from them."

I pointed to his shirt. "And this vampire thing. I mean, why do you—*what* do you do? Bite each other?" My breathing sounded ragged.

He met my eyes briefly, and then his gaze slid back to the floor. "Not really. Biting isn't normally part of it."

"Ian has fangs."

"Those are just caps. You can buy 'em for a few thousand dollars at the dentist. But you can't really break the skin with them. They're just for show. That guy's just a little too into his own hype." He sounded almost embarrassed.

"How do you do it, then?"

"Sometimes we use a sort of lancet—like the kind diabetics use to draw blood from their finger. Or small razor blades."

"Or needles—like when you took my blood?"

He nodded once.

I jerked my head to the side and huffed out air. "This is kinda sick, Pearse. How long have you been doing this?"

"A while." He pushed to his feet. "It started out with me just dabbling in soft-core vampirism at clubs in New Orleans. Just here and there. Just for fun. We drank from each other or willing donors. Never like this."

The acid bubbled in my stomach, trying to make its way to my esophagus. It felt like something was about to explode inside me any second—bile, anger, a blood-curdling scream.

Pearse looked down at me. "Are you okay?"

I swallowed hard, nodded.

He shuffled over to the mirror, and after catching a glimpse of himself, he turned away, circled back toward me. "I'm so sorry that you had to find out about everything the way you did. Last night feels like a bad dream. I don't know how I let that happen."

"Maris tried to get me to join."

"Yeah. That's been the plan all along."

"The plan all along?" My insides iced. "I'm part of a plan?"

Pearse sank onto the couch again. "You know how you mentioned our meeting in the café that day, that you thought it was such a coincidence and all? Well, the naked truth is that Maris planned for your arrival here at the house for months."

A piece of the puzzle shifted into place. "She was my father's lawyer, so she would've known I was coming."

"No, but it was more than that. Maris needs you to be okay with us—members of The Colony—coming and going at Whickering Place."

I froze, my head pounding.

"Maris arranged it so that I could live here," he said. "And then Colin's lease was up, and he wanted a place to crash temporarily, so he asked if he could rent a room too. That sort of threw a wrench in the works. Maris hoped you'd want to sell. They were all ready to buy if it went on the market." He passed a hand over his mouth. "Avery, The Colony started tracking you as soon as you came to town."

I stared at him, my heart double-timing. "I can't believe this."

"That day I saw you at the coffee shop? They knew that's where you went every morning. I was to try and meet you ahead of time."

"They were watching me? Why?"

His face reddened. "I guess they thought..."

I knew what they thought. Maris's words to me last night—and even before that—about Pearse. She'd thought if I slept with him, then I'd be more willing to join them. How could I have misread Maris so completely?

"When you didn't want to sell right away, the backup plan was to get you to join up."

Panic swelled in my chest. "Why are you telling me all of this?"

"I don't know. I'm probably putting you and myself at risk, but I want out, Avery. They just won't let me go."

"Why? Why not tell them you don't want anything to do with them?"

"Because it just doesn't work that way. I tried to leave before and—" He held out his hands. "They found me."

"Why can't you just call the police? Tell them what's going on?"

"When I say The Colony has members everywhere, I mean everywhere—the police included. Maris has a lot of friends in the police department. We can't trust anyone."

I let his words sink in. I was in danger. The police may or may not be involved. What about Stoney and Mears? Were they part of this too?

He shook his head. "I'm so sorry, Avery. Things have gotten way out of control." His phone dinged, and he pulled it out of his back pocket. "It's from Maris. Something's happened." He ran his thumb across the screen. "Apparently, there's a mole. Someone's leaked information."

"What kind of information?"

He shrugged. "Don't know. Maris is telling everyone to be on their guard."

Fear gripped my chest and squeezed. Now I knew about them. They knew about me. "What about Colin? Have you told him?"

Pearse's Adam's apple bobbed. "He doesn't know."

I took a deep breath. "He'll flip out."

"I'd rather him not find out."

"What should I do?"

Pearse stood and padded toward the hallway, but then he stopped and placed his hands against the wall, bracing his weight, his head hanging. "For now, I think you should act like you don't know anything about this. You can say you were drunk. Don't remember what happened last night. Don't let on what I've told you. We need to come up with some kind of plan to get you out of here." He looked up at me. "I want to make sure you're safe."

Safe. What a joke. I'd been deluding myself with that word for almost ten years. "I'm not leaving this house just so they can take it over, Pearse. There's no way."

"Avery." He dropped his hands to his sides. "I'm trying to save your life here."

As the hard reality of Pearse's words hit me, a knot formed in my throat.

He trudged into the hallway. "I'm gonna take a shower."

As soon as I heard the door to his room shut, I rushed to the bay window and looked out. A police cruiser sat parked across the street. They were watching the house. Just like Stoney and Mears said. How would I know if I could trust them? Maybe they were just waiting to gain access like the others.

My mind whirled. I didn't know what to do or who to believe. Maybe I should tell Pearse to pack up and get out now, but then I'd be here in the house alone—with a colony of vampires that wanted in. And no one in my corner.

I scanned the room—the carnage left behind from last night—the walls, covered in my father's paintings. My eyes stopped at a framed picture.

My knees felt weak as I moved toward it.

Probably 8x8, the black wood framed a coin—the etched likeness of Whickering Place facing out. A binding coin. *The coins!*

I raced toward the front door. I'd forgotten all about the sack under the hedgerow for the last three days. As I blasted into the frigid air, hugging myself and hopping barefoot down the stone stairs, I already knew. I grabbed the banister and swung around it, the frozen iron stinging my palm.

The bag of coins was gone.

Breathing out a cloud of condensation, I instinctively peered up and down the street. Anyone could've taken them. Neighborhood kids. A passerby. Maris.

My heart sank as I threw my head back.

The gargoyles were looking down at me. Laughing.

I lumbered back into the house, closing and locking the door behind me.

Riiiinnng!

I spun around. The phone from the basement sat on its original perch in the hall. Was this all just an elaborate prank? Was someone moving it around to freak me out? Maybe this was part of The Colony's "plan."

Clenching my fists, I moved toward the phone. Each ring vibrated through me like an electrical current.

Then it stopped.

I stared it down, waiting for the ringer's knell. When it didn't blare again, I picked up the receiver and placed it to my ear.

"Hello?" A male's voice.

"Hello?" I answered. A reflex.

But then another voice spoke—a whispery growl. "Ace..."

A shiver began at the top of my head and drove freezing sparks throughout my body.

"Yes?" The man answered.

"It's time for you to do it," the voice rasped.

What was I hearing? My father's voice?

"No," he responded. "No, I can't. I can't do it."

"You will do it," said the voice. "You will kill her. You will drink her blood. You will feed the wall."

"No, no. Please." Distant sobbing.

My fingers squeezed the receiver so hard it made a cracking sound. I held my breath. How was it possible that I heard my dead father's voice on a phone that wasn't hooked up to anything?

Static flared on the line, obscuring the voices. I pressed the phone harder against my ear.

The growl intensified, no longer uttering words but only horrible sounds—chewing, smacking noises. Finally, the voice screamed a final command. "Kill her."

Chapter Forty

I desperately wanted to talk to someone about the phantom conversation. But Pearse was the only one in the house, and the last thing he needed was me harping on about a haunted phone.

But I had to get rid of it. I should just take it to the river like Harrison suggested I do with the coins. Except now, after what Pearse told me, I was too terrified to leave the house.

And as much as I wanted the phone gone, a part of me was intrigued by what I'd heard. A conversation that lingered from long ago? An echo from the past? Kill who? And why?

Two texts from Colin waited for my response. How was I? He hadn't heard from me.

I texted him back that everything was fine. Anything to avoid a conversation with him about everything going on here. But I wished he hadn't left or that I was with him right now in Colorado where it was...

Safe?

Where was safe, anyway? Did safety even exist? Wasn't the world just one big dangerous jungle? It didn't seem to matter whether I stayed in the house or hurtled out the door into oncoming traffic. Nowhere was really, truly safe.

I hovered on the bottom floor, near Pearse's closed bedroom door, listening and watching. He was having a phone conversation, but his voice was too low to hear even when I stood right in front of the door. Who was he talking to? What were they talking about? Plotting? Did it involve me?

Shit. I was becoming paranoid. My breathing quickened—a warning sign of an anxiety attack.

I took a lorazepam and stationed myself in the front room by the bay window. The police car never moved. Whether friend or foe, they were making their presence known and obvious. Was that for my benefit or The Colony's?

I worked. Then I dozed. Around two in the afternoon, the clang of a pan, the sigh of the refrigerator door told me Pearse was moving around in the kitchen.

A few minutes later, he arrived in the doorway.

"I'm going out. I won't be back until really late."

"But the roads—"

"Avery, I have to go. I don't have a choice." He barely looked at me as he spoke, his brows pushed low.

"Okay." I bit my lip. It wasn't really about the roads. It was about me being left in this house alone. Not knowing what to believe. In some ways, the vampire I knew was better than the other devils—either in the house or out of it.

"I guess I don't have to tell you not to let anyone in," he said.

"No." *But what about what's already in here with me?*

"Lock all the doors."

I listened to the clump of his boots against the tile as he walked down the hall. Staring up at the ceiling, I shut my eyes and counted his steps to the back door. A few seconds passed. He must have taken a detour into his room. A few more seconds. More footsteps. Clacking of the handle on the backdoor.

I pushed off the couch and rushed up the stairs and to the landing, where I could watch him tramp the path to the garage.

He carried a biohazard box.

Chapter Forty-One

One of the best parts of attaching to a human is free travel. We may have spent the past thirty years at Whickering Place, but now we have free passage to the city, to clubs, where we can spread out and attach to others. But some of us continue to cling to Maris, trekking through the woods, staring out at the dark sky.

Some of the vampires complain about the cold temperatures. Others are too rapt with twisted anticipation to care. We stop in front of a cabin and wait.

All of the vampires look ridiculous. Dressed like Gregorian monks in hooded capes and masquerade masks. Many look more like birds than humans, with their long, beaked disguises protruding from their robes.

A male vampire wearing an ornate mask and a garment obviously meant for a much larger person stands beside Maris. "What are we waiting for? It's frickin' freezing out here."

Maris looks at him through the holes in her mask. "Pearse. We're waiting for Pearse."

"Oh."

And that seems to satisfy the complainer for a while as the night blackens and the air turns colder. Finally, headlights flare at the end of the road, the grinding hum of tires on gravel brings everyone to their feet, and they peer into the glare, shielding their eyes with their hands and bell-shaped sleeves.

"Here he comes," someone calls out.

The vampires circle the car like wolves surrounding their prey.

A woman in a costume cape climbs out of the car and quickly dons her mask—a cat face, complete with synthetic black whiskers. She opens the back door and yanks at another human's arm. The man emerges blindfolded and stumbles out of the backseat. He does not fight as the caped woman leads him into the cabin. We all follow, leaving the cold for the warmth, lit by a fireplace and candles on nearly every surface.

Several of us grasp the hands, the heads of the other vampires, inserting a talon into their ear—injecting bloodlust into their brains. Spittle drips from the mouth of one of them. His desire to taste the warm, metallic flavor of blood overwhelms him.

We stand high on Maris's shoulder, surveying the scene, waiting for what will come as she steps forward and puts her hand on the man's arm. He's breathing hard, sweating, even though he's just come from freezing temperatures.

Maris pushes his leather jacket from his shoulders. "You know the drill, Pearse."

He nods, says nothing.

The woman who dragged him from the car returns to the back seat and now enters the cabin carrying a white and blue metal box marked BIOHAZARD.

The members sigh, moan, lick their lips, and gather around as she sets the box in front of them and opens the lid.

"Remember," says Maris. "Only the new members—Ian, Torin, Ebony, and the twins—will drink from the vials. The rest of you have full access to fresh blood from our donor."

Clearly, the man assumes he is the donor. He rolls up his sleeve and appears surprised when the blindfold is pulled away from his head. He looks straight into Maris's eyes behind the holes of her mask.

She laughs at him. "Surprise, Pearse. It's not you tonight."

He's obviously confused. He looks from side to side. But the group is already focused on another figure.

Two vampires lead a female through the cabin door, her screams and sobs audible before she's even entered. She is directed to the group's center, two vampires clamping either of her arms and one pushing her from the back. Dressed in a similar robe to the rest of them, the girl twists and turns her body in an attempt to pull away. A folding chair is placed in the center of the circle, and her two masked captors force her to sit.

"Please, please stop. Please don't hurt me."

A typical, sniveling human.

Maris holds out her hand, presenting the girl to the group. "Here she is. Here is our donor." Then Maris pats Pearse's arm. "Go on. Do your magic."

He looks at the girl, his face practically melting. "What? No. No, I can't."

The girl jerks again, screaming, kicking out with her feet, but she's held fast to the chair by one of the robed figures on either side of her. "Please! I don't want to. No!"

"Hurry up, Pearse," Maris calls above the girl's cries. "We're all hungry."

He stares at her, his lip curling in horror as he shakes his head. "I didn't bring my kit."

"We have everything you need right here." Maris points to an array of needles, vials, and tubing laid out on the table behind her. Then she addresses the group. "Creatures of the night, I thank you all for your willingness to come to the woods on this especially cold evening. Normally, of course, we would have our festivities at our favorite club. But rest assured, our usual banquets will resume next month, once we've taken care of our mole. But that doesn't mean we can't feast tonight." She turns to Pearse and smiles. "Whenever you're ready."

Pearse glances at the equipment and then back to the girl. "She doesn't want to. Let me be the donor. I thought that's why you brought me out here."

Maris smiles tightly, shaking her head. She approaches Pearse, standing just inches away from him. Her voice is low. Her voice is our voice. "You are not in the rotation tonight. We have chosen our donor, and it is her."

"But..." He thrusts his hand toward the girl. "Look at her, Maris. She's freaking out. She doesn't want to do this." He steps away, bows his head. "No. You either let me be the donor, or I'm not doing this."

Maris glides toward him again, and her eyes change—a metamorphosis from human to beast—dark venom filling the blue irises behind the mask eyeholes.

We all speak in unison. "You are not giving the orders here. We gave you the opportunity to be a leader, and so far, you have rejected us. So," she stretches out a graceful hand toward the girl, "these are the consequences. You do what we tell you to do."

Pearse snaps his eyes up to meet ours. "Maris, please." His face lines with pain. "She looks like she's sixteen years old. I mean, shit! I don't think I can do it. She doesn't want this."

Maris moves toward Pearse until her robe touches his shirt. We look up at him through the holes in her mask and growl, "We are vampires, Pearse. It doesn't matter what she wants. It's about what we want."

Maris reaches into the pocket of her robe and pulls out a dagger with an ornate handle. She turns, approaches the girl, and places the dagger to the girl's forearm. Then she rakes it across the skin. A thin line of red appears.

The girl shrieks and batters herself against the back of the chair as the circle of vampires closes in.

Maris carries the knife upended and places it to Pearse's face, pressing the point into his cheekbone, smearing the blood. "If you won't do it, then I will. And I'll do it with this. And it's going to hurt a lot more. You know it will."

Pearse's eyes harden, and he swallows. Then he shifts away from us and toward the table where he goes to work sorting through the wrapped needles and vials.

It is then we notice the most interesting detail. Pearse is the only one not wearing a mask or a robe.

If the girl lives, she will have seen only one face tonight.

Chapter Forty-Two

I t was afternoon, and Pearse wasn't home.

I crawled onto the couch at six that evening. Exhausted. Sick. My head spinning with all that had happened and all I now knew.

Thanks to Dr. Murphy, I had both lorazepam and Xanax on hand. I usually took lorazepam, but Xanax would work quicker. I took two and slept.

My phone went off at 1:32, waking me out of REM sleep. The screen read *Pearse*.

I immediately answered.

But it wasn't Pearse's voice on the line. "Hi, Avery. You don't know me, but my name's Cassie. I'm a friend of Pearse's." She spoke quickly, the words tumbling out. "He asked me to give you a call."

I sat up. "What's going on?"

"He's in bad shape. We're in an Uber right now. I'm riding back to the house with him, but I'll need your help once I get there. We're just a few minutes away."

I fumbled around for my shoes, trying to wake up and get my bearings. "Okay, I'll meet you outside."

Waiting by the front window, I watched until car lights beamed over the lawn and the car's tires crackled over the gravel driveway. With my heart pounding in my throat, I stepped outside, the cold air cutting through my sweatshirt.

As I approached the side of the car, a girl with hair as long as mine but ruler-straight and pale as moonlight got out.

"Hi," she breathed, yanking open the back door. "I'm Cassie."

As soon as I looked inside, I saw why she needed help. Pearse was slumped in the backseat. Cassie pulled at his arm, and he flopped toward us.

"Grab his other arm," Cassie instructed.

"What's happened to him?" I grasped his left wrist and tugged.

Pearse's head lolled back. We weren't getting any help from him.

"Do you ladies need assistance?" The driver grunted in a deep voice, already climbing out of the car.

I stepped out of the way and allowed him to extract Pearse from the backseat. Once he got him standing, Cassie and I tossed one of Pearse's arms over each of our shoulders.

"Got 'im?" the driver asked.

We both panted that we did, but suddenly, I knew what was meant by the term "dead weight." Half-carrying, half-dragging Pearse, my knees threatening to buckle under the strain, I pulled my side of the human yoke, nearly losing my balance as we crested the steps of the entryway and somehow managed to maneuver him inside and into his bedroom.

We backed him up to the end of the bed.

"Here, turn him." Cassie pivoted, ducking out from under his arm so that he sank onto the mattress.

His other arm slid off my shoulders, and he fell back.

Breathing hard, my heart pumping, I stared down at him. "Will he—is he all right?"

Cassie stood back, her shoulders rising and falling, her hands on her hips. "I think so. But you'll need to keep an eye on him. And we should probably get him on his side, in case he starts getting sick, so he doesn't choke on his own vomit."

We rolled him onto his right side, trying to fold his legs up onto the bed best we could.

Sweat pooled between my breasts, and I wiped the back of my hand across my forehead. "What happened to him?"

Cassie motioned me out of the room, although we left the door open. "Can I get some water?"

We went into the kitchen, where I grabbed two glasses from the cabinet, pushed them against the lever on the fridge. The water hissed as it filled one glass and then the other. I handed one to Cassie. We both collapsed onto kitchen chairs and guzzled water.

Cassie finished off her glass and rolled it between her hands. "I'd say that's what bench pressing one-sixty feels like, wouldn't you?"

"Is he drunk?"

"Yep." She placed the glass on the table. "I've never seen him like this. When he showed up at the bar, he was already a mess."

I noticed a tattoo on the fleshy part of her hand, offset from her thumb, which looked like some kind of Celtic symbol. "Cool tattoo."

She ran the fingers of her opposite hand over it. "Thanks. It's a triskelion. The symbol of strength. I've got another one on my arm. They used to be something else. But I had a tattoo artist turn it into this instead."

"How do you know Pearse?"

Cassie stared straight ahead as she talked. "I'm the bartender at Odd Bods. You know it?"

Oh no. Was she one of them too? "I've heard of it."

"It's a vampire club." She announced it so nonchalantly—as though telling me it was a Greek restaurant or a home supply store.

My gaze dropped to the lettering on her T-shirt. Odd Bods was printed on the front, a bat logo set behind it.

"Pearse comes in a lot. We talk all the time."

I wondered if she had a speech impediment. Her words seemed garbled—like she had a mouthful of taffy. She seemed to realize the same thing and leaned forward, bringing her hand to cover her mouth and spitting something into it.

"Forgot to take these out." A glistening retainer-type contraption with canine fangs attached to the wiring rested in her outstretched hand.

"Do you *all* have those?"

"A lot of us do. I wear 'em to work. That's all." She shrugged. "Anyway," she sat back. "I consider Pearse a friend. I don't want to see him get hurt."

I nodded, wondering if that meant they were more than.

As though she'd heard my thoughts, Cassie turned and met my eyes. "Just friends."

"Okay."

Cassie shifted her gaze back to the wall. "Pearse says he trusts you."

I nodded again, trying to hide my discomfort.

"He's a good guy. Nothing like the others." She paused, looked at me. "How much has he told you?"

"About what?"

"About his lifestyle. The people he's involved with."

"Some."

Cassie met my gaze and held it. I could tell she was trying to read me.

"I'm not part of them," she said. "The Colony."

I exhaled. "Okay."

She rocked her head left and right. Her neck cracked. "I mean, I consider myself a vampire, but I'm not one of them. I used to be part of a group like them, though. A long time ago. That's how I got the original tattoos." She rubbed her fingers over the tattoo on her hand. "These used to be brands."

"Wow. That's um, extreme."

"Some of us who practice vampirism are just normal people. We're not out to hurt anyone or even to explore the dark side of this life. But some get off on it. It took me several years to get out of one of those groups." She glanced up at me and then shook her head as though clearing the memories. "Anyway, because I work at Odd Bods, I hear a lot. And then Pearse tells me stuff too."

I nodded.

"They ..." she placed her black-lacquered fingertips to her forehead. "The Colony. They're horrible people. And they treat Pearse like shit."

I latched on to her statement. "What do they do to him?"

"I know he hasn't told me everything—I think some of it's just too embarrassing—but he's basically their slave."

"Really?" I leaned forward. "What does that mean?"

"My understanding is that The Colony was grooming Pearse to be in leadership—like, they wanted him to head up a region. But he wanted out. He tried to run. So now, they use him for whatever's needed—blood donor, blood procurer—since he's a phlebotomist, he's got skills they can use. And he has regular access to blood."

I rubbed my forehead. "I guess I don't understand why he can't just quit?"

Cassie pressed her lips together. "Because he can't get away from them. Once you're part of The Colony, you don't just decide to leave. They have you. Right now, they have Pearse where they want him." She turned the glass, inching it in a circle on the tabletop. "They have something on him, something that they're using to keep him in line."

"What do they have on him?"

She shook her head. "He didn't want to tell me. Didn't want to involve me. And really, he's right. I mean, it's better if I don't know. But I wanted to let *you* know what I heard, so you can do what you need to do."

"What do you think I should do?"

"Get the hell out of Dodge as soon as you can. It's the only thing you can do."

"But I can't leave the house for them to just move in and take over."

Cassie shrugged. "I would. A house isn't worth your life."

I huffed out air, shook my head. Unbelievable.

Cassie banged the bottom of the glass against the table. "Well, I'd better call another ride and get going." She stood. "I would've brought him in my car, but if someone saw me..."

"You're welcome to stay. We have several spare bedrooms."

"Thanks." She turned her face to the ceiling. "But I think I'll go. It's better if I steer clear of this place—it's got too many ties to The Colony."

She walked to the door, swiping at her phone screen.

"Thanks for bringing him back safely." I felt like a wife or a mom—thanking the good Samaritan for rescuing a loved one.

She gave me a half-smile. "I wasn't going to leave him there. The parasites at that bar would've drained him dry in his condition." She jerked her head toward his room. "Keep an eye on him."

"I will."

I went into the kitchen, filled a glass of water, and took it into Pearse's room. Placing the glass on his nightstand, I sat on the edge of the bed and debated how much work it would take to remove his jacket.

He lay right where we left him. He looked dead. Only the lightest rise and fall of his shoulder indicated he breathed. I grasped the edge of his jacket and slid it off one shoulder. There was no way I could get it off of him from this angle without his or someone else's help. Underneath the jacket, he wore a black shirt, and as I tugged at the coat, the neck of his shirt slid to the side, revealing the flesh under his collar bone.

The edge of a gauze bandage peeked out. I stretched the neck of his shirt down. The bandage was the size of a playing card, the center of it spotted bright red, and all around it, one- to two-inch gashes had scabbed over.

Cassie said they used him as a donor. His shirt had been covered in blood yesterday after Maris and her cronies left. Obviously, this vampirism thing went both ways. Pearse appeared to be just as much of a food source as he was a feeder.

He coughed and I jumped. I watched for signs that he might throw up. But then he drifted off again. I pushed the strands of hair away from his face. Staring at him then, something in me stirred. Pearse was like a wounded wild animal—one I was keeping in a spare bedroom of my house. I knew I shouldn't really have it here—one day soon, it would heal and possibly turn on me—but I couldn't just put it outside and leave it for some other animal to attack.

He needed my help.

And I liked that feeling.

Chapter Forty-Three

The girl is left in the cabin in the woods. A binding coin on either eye. Whether she is dead or alive when we go is unclear, but a dead body is of little use to us. Therefore, we travel by our live human hosts, now on foot, to an awaiting car by the highway.

Maris climbs in along with Ian and Torin, and we head back toward the city. Masks and robes are removed and stuffed into plastic bags.

Maris lifts the bag of coins and jingles them. "Mission accomplished."

From the front seat, Ian cranes his head around. "Can he be trusted? Gallagher?"

"Pearse Gallagher has a lot of history with The Colony. Not all of it good." Maris cocks her head to the side. "Why do you think he was the only one of us exposed? No, of course he can't be trusted. He has far too much of a conscience. So, until he falls in line, he will be treated accordingly."

"What about the girl? His housemate? Avery?" Torin asks. "Does Pearse know about the plan?"

"Only that we're trying to get her to join, and we need his help. But if we wait too long, the full outline may get back to him. So, I'm planning on moving him out of the house as soon as I can find him some other lodging." She leans her shoulder into Torin's. "Maybe he can come live with us. We can turn our little arrangement into a ménage à quatre."

Torin makes a sound of disgust. "Ugh. No, thanks. That guy's an ass."

Maris shrugs. "You don't get to make those kinds of decisions, Torin. Maybe when you reach my level, things will be different. But in the here and now, you don't get choices. Neither does Pearse. He has to do what we tell him. Especially after tonight." She glances between Ian and Torin. "I'll probably need your help again for moving him out of Whickering Place. There's a lot of police presence around the house. We need to make sure if there are any arrests, it's Pearse and not one of us."

Ian's eyes sparkle. He smiles, revealing his pointed teeth. "So how many does that make? Five, six?"

"If the girl dies, that makes eight. Five more to go to achieve our thirteen sacrifices before October."

We sink our talons into her brain, reminding her of the most prized sacrifice—the one we're waiting for.

"But," she brightens. "A virgin sacrifice will count for at least three lives."

"So, when are we doing that?" Ian asks.

Maris shakes her head. "Not immediately. After tonight, we'll need to lay low for a few weeks. We don't want to be careless. The night of the gathering—on the new moon—it has to happen then. But we need to move fast on getting Pearse out of the house. If my suspicions are correct, Pearse is eyeing Avery a little too much. He may have begun to form feelings for her. And we need to make sure he doesn't screw up our sacrifice. Literally."

Chapter Forty-Four
Sunday, February 9

I awoke to the sound of water running.

Lifting my head sent lightning-sharp pain down the back of my neck. I was sitting on the floor beside Pearse's bed. Based on the location of the shooting pain, I'd obviously been sleeping with my head flopped onto my chest. My gun sat in my lap. I'd gotten it out of the safe last night before coming in here to sleep.

My neck popped as I turned toward the sound of the water. The bathroom door was shut. Pearse was obviously in the shower.

As I stood, all my muscles cringed with pain and stiffness. The digital clock on the bedside table read 11:23. I'd probably been in that position for at least nine hours.

The shower shut off.

Rocking my head side to side to loosen the tendons, I quickly exited the room.

When Pearse finally found me, I was in the kitchen on my second cup of coffee.

"Good thing it's a Sunday," I remarked. "You would've slept through your alarm."

Pearse sank down in the chair beside me, stretching his legs out in front of him and blowing out a long stream of air. His wet hair dampened the collar of his sweatshirt. "How did I get back here last night?"

"You sort of Ubered. With help." I offered a half-smile. "Your friend Cassie made sure you got home safely.

He rubbed his hand across his jaw. "Cassie. That was good of her."

"She was worried about you. Told me to keep an eye on you and make sure you didn't choke on your own vomit."

He ran his hand through the top of his wet hair, turning his eyes toward the ceiling.

I waited.

When he didn't say anything, I leaned forward, sliding my hand across the table toward him. "Pearse, tell me what happened."

He dropped his gaze. "I can't."

"Why?"

"I don't want to involve you."

"I'm already involved. I'm living here with you in this crazy, haunted house ... with-with a phone that rings even though it's not plugged into anything, and my dead father's voice on the other line..."

Pearse cranked his head back. "What?"

I nodded. "Yeah, so whatever is going on here has been happening for a long time. And I'm part of that legacy, apparently. So if your problems have anything to do with The Colony, they're indirectly related to Whickering Place, and I'm involved anyway."

He shook his head. "You don't want to be involved in this. Believe me."

"I want to help you."

"You can't."

I drew back, tapped my fingernails against my coffee mug. "Cassie told me something went down last night. Is that what this is about?"

He raised his eyebrows. "Cassie told you that?"

"Yes."

"She shouldn't have told you that." He glanced off to the side. "Cassie's not part of The Colony, and she's been through enough. I don't want to involve her either."

"What happened?"

He flattened his hands against the tabletop. "Don't ask me, Avery."

"How can you get away from them?"

"I can't."

"You could file a restraining order."

He exhaled a bitter laugh. "If only it were that simple. They have shit on me, okay?"

"What kind of shit?"

"The kind that could land me in jail." He steepled his hands and covered his mouth and nose. "Until last night, I'd never had to ... I can't even imagine what you'll think of me if I tell you."

I swallowed. Dread clawed its way up my throat.

"They drove me out to the woods." He dropped his hands, looked down at them, shaking his head slowly. "Then they brought out this girl."

Shit. He's right. I don't want to know. "Did you know her?"

"No. I didn't even know what was happening at first." He rubbed a hand over his face. "I shouldn't be telling you this."

"What happened to her? Is she still alive?"

"I tried to stop before she..." He squeezed his eyes shut, bowed his head. "I don't know. She finally passed out. I had to leave her there."

"Did you call the police?"

"No, Avery. I told you. I can't call the police. Don't you think they'd know who made the call?" He shot up from the chair. It tipped onto its back legs and then fell forward again, clattering against the tile as he bolted from the room.

Seconds later, I heard the hall bathroom door slam.

Muffled sounds of retching.

The trickling of water through the pipes.

I waited. Numb. But also horrified.

He returned to the room, wiping at his nose and mouth as he slung himself back into the chair. "I didn't want any of this," he whispered, pressing his fingers to his eyes. "So, they've got me. I try to leave or tell anyone or anything—they have plenty of witnesses who can testify that I was there. I was the only one without a disguise. And they have plenty of my blood that can be traced back to the scene, I'm sure. They know I want out. So now they're making my life a living hell. Lacey's got me for a sex slave, and the rest of them ... well, I'm the resident blood donor around there."

Sex slave? I hadn't expected that detail.

"What are you going to do?"

"I don't know. If it gets too bad, I'll just ... turn myself in, I guess."

I shouldn't care about this. I should tell him to turn himself in. But I didn't want him to go to jail. Not really.

After a few moments, he looked up at me. "I'm sure you've noticed that the police have been sitting outside the house for days now. Maris and the other members of The Colony know it. Something's gotta give soon."

"I won't tell them anything. But what if you went to them voluntarily, told them what happened?"

"It's impossible to know which of the police are involved."

I wondered again about Stoney and Mears. "Someone's got to be able to help us—help ... you."

Pearse shook his head. "If that girl turns up dead—"

"Wait. What?" *Turns up dead.* White-hot panic flooded through me. "Are you telling me you killed someone?"

"No. I mean, I didn't intend to hurt anyone. I didn't—I wouldn't..." He threw his hands up. "Look, The Colony has ways of doing things. And sometimes people end up dead. I tried to make sure she wouldn't die." He raked his fingers through his hair. "But if they finger me as the suspect, they might ask you to testify."

I couldn't understand what he was talking about. But despite the horror building in my stomach, my heart twisted. Something about Pearse—maybe his vulnerability, his humility—reminded me of Vince. Then I pictured Vince's lifeless body. And pity welled up in me. "Maybe it won't come to that."

"Maybe. But I've been living in this house with you for the past few weeks, and you pretty much know what's going on."

"I won't say anything."

"You may not have a choice. And why wouldn't you? You don't owe me anything. I've put you in danger just by being here." Pearse pushed his chair back and stood. "Anyway, I just got the word this morning. Maris wants me out of here."

"Out of where?"

"Whickering Place. They'll be moving me to a different location soon."

"Where? Where will they move you?"

"I have no idea. But unless I suddenly decide to take them up on their offer of leadership in The Colony, I have no power whatsoever."

"What if you agreed to become a leader like they want you to? Or you pretended to?"

"I'm tired of pretending."

"Better yet, what if you owned Whickering Place? This is their hub of power, right? I mean, supposedly? What if you took the power out of their hands?"

He leveled his gaze. "Avery, obviously that's not possible. I can't afford to buy this place." He swiveled in the chair toward me. "But I want to make sure you're safe. Do you have someone you can stay with? Someone in another city or state or country, for that matter?"

I shook my head. "No, Pearse. My mother's in Italy, and I'm not going there. My uncle's all the way on the other side of the country in

Arizona, and he's not well, so I'm not taking this to him." I looked up at him. "You know about my agoraphobia. I can't just walk out of the house and go live somewhere else. It doesn't work that way for me." I sat back. "Anyway, don't worry about me. I can take care of myself."

His frown lines softened. "Yeah, I saw your gun."

"And I'm a damn good shot."

The corners of his mouth twisted up. "I'll bet you are."

"I've got a compound bow upstairs too."

He chuckled. "I would never have pegged you for a warrior. Vampire hunter."

I felt my face flush, and I fought the smallest of smiles. "So don't mess with me."

"I wouldn't dream of it."

MY HANDS SHOOK AS I unscrewed the lid of my Xanax and popped one. Then I popped another for good measure. Then I lay down on the couch and let warring thoughts take over my brain.

In one night, everything had changed.

A small part of me wanted to call Detective Stoney and Detective Mears and tell them everything Pearse had said to me. Was I naïve to believe him when he said that he'd been trapped into this whole thing, led down a path of deception?

He still drank blood. On the other hand, people ate insects and monkey brains and bull's testicles, so maybe drinking blood wasn't so different. As long as no one died in the process. *But a girl may have died last night.*

As the extra pill kicked in, I started to drift—the stress artificially draining away from my body. My mind floated with images of doors and walls. A red wall. Paint? Or blood?

"Avery."

Someone was calling my name? But I was almost asleep. Maybe I was dreaming.

"Avery."

My eyes popped open. Not a dream.

I didn't move. Couldn't move. Oh, shit. It was happening again. The dreams I'd been having for years. Something was on top of me, breathing in my face, holding me down. Dr. Murphy had called it an old hag attack—a sort of sleep paralysis where my brain woke up before my body.

But the smell was horrific. I'd never smelled that stench or felt the brush of something against my cheek, like hair.

The voice growled, like the ones I'd heard in this house before, like the voice on the telephone. "Death is coming for you."

I tried to scream but couldn't open my mouth.

"You are the sacrifice we've been waiting for." Then the voice grew angrier, growling, "We're going to kill you. We're going to stab you. You'll bleed to death."

I managed to move my arm, beating at the thing that held me down. But my hand passed right through it, and I smacked myself in the chest. In that millisecond, I grasped the cross that Ada had given me and thrust it forward. If the thing had been solid, I would have touched its forehead with the necklace.

With a piercing shriek that vibrated my eardrums, the thing lifted off of me.

I bent at the waist as though propelled upward by springs. Gasping, sputtering, I still held the cross with one hand and wiped at my chest and my neck and my face with the other, trying to rub away the feeling of the thing sucking my air. Then I scrambled to the nearest lamp and twisted the switch, flooding the room with light.

Nothing was there.

This can't start up again. Not now. Maybe it was a side effect of taking the second pill. I should have stuck to the one.

It took some time for my breathing to return to normal, to convince myself I'd dreamed it. Admitting this was real made the idea of staying here unbearable.

So much for sleep. I curled up on the couch, grabbed the remote, flipped on the television, and scrolled through a long list of home improvement, food shows, and true crime dramas. I settled on the women's movie channel and turned it up in an attempt to drown out the lingering voices in my head.

Nina Mayhew was on the screen, and a sudden pain niggled at my insides. Colin's girl. It was one of her older films, back when her hair was as dark as mine. Now she was usually photographed with shorter, caramel-colored hair. But in this film, I actually noted the resemblance between us.

She played a federal agent who'd fallen in love with a Russian defector. I'd seen the movie before. It had been popular a decade ago. I'd forgotten a lot of it but remembered the scene where she told the Russian—played by some hot American actor whose name I couldn't remember—that she would give up her job, her life. They could move out to the country—anything to keep him from going back to Russia.

Following that film, another Nina Mayhew movie came on. Apparently, the network was having a Nina Mayhew marathon.

As the sun peeked over the mountains and the shadows in the room turned to a gray wash, an idea budded in my brain.

And each of the movies encouraged it to bloom.

By morning, I was ready to present it to Pearse.

Chapter Forty-Five
Monday, February 10

He might never agree to it, and maybe I'd forever regret it. It was crazy—totally insane, actually. But it could solve several problems. And create several new ones.

My hand shook as I raised it to knock on Pearse's door. Seconds later, I heard the pad of his feet as he made his way over to open it.

When I actually saw him standing there in boxer shorts and a T-shirt, I faltered. "Hi."

"Hey." He held the door partially open.

"Did I wake you?"

"No. I was awake."

For a minute, the words left me and I couldn't think of how to start. My cheeks burned.

He pulled the door open all the way, and I moved inside and stood awkwardly in front of him.

Pearse's shoulders rose and fell. "I'm thinking the best thing to do is to call Colin and tell him everything. He can arrange something to get you both out of here. At least out of town until things calm down. Then I'll take my chances. Turn myself in."

"No." I swallowed. "I have a better idea."

"What?"

"We could get married."

"What?" His face compressed with a have-you-lost-your-mind expression.

If my cheeks had burned before, they were scorching now. "In name only, of course. I know it sounds crazy. But here's the thing, if we were to get married, you'd be part owner of Whickering Place. I can add your name to the deed—well, I mean, I could add your name anyway, but it has more of an effect if we're in this together. If you're part owner, aren't you suddenly one of the most powerful members of The Colony? And you get Lacey off your back—"

"That wouldn't get her off my back. She'd just come after you."

"And," I continued, "As an added bonus, if we're married, then no matter what, I can't be made to testify against you. If it comes to that. And I'm sure it won't." Now I was just babbling.

Pearse's face seemed frozen.

What had I done? This was a ridiculous idea. It made so much sense in the wee hours of the morning, but now it seemed outrageous.

Pearse gave a weird sort of chuckle.

I tensed. "This is a crazy idea, isn't it?"

"Yes, it is."

I broke off, watching his expression change. "I just thought," I dropped my face into my hands. "Never mind. I don't know what I thought." I stepped back. "Maybe I can just give you this house. You mentioned that would be something that could help you, and I don't really want it anyway, and—"

"No, no, no." He put his hand on my shoulder. "Thanks, Avery. It's a very ... generous offer, but that really won't solve anything in the end. The Colony isn't all that crazy about marriage and—"

"Ah! Another reason to do it. To piss them off."

"None of it matters if I'm in jail. Or dead. Anyway, your testimony wouldn't be as important as the members who were there that night."

"But if you're the owner of this house," I held out my hands, "then everything changes."

"I can't let you do that."

"Why not?"

"Because if something were to happen to you, I'd never forgive myself."

"Then at least we tried," I said resolutely.

"I just... No. Why would you want to do something like that for me?"

I sank down on the edge of his bed and stared up at him. "Pearse, for ten years I've lived my life locked inside—completely self-absorbed—literally, I've had no one else to think about but myself. All I've focused on is keeping myself safe."

His expression softened.

"For probably the first time in my life, I've got the chance to think about someone else. This situation is as unsafe as it can possibly be, but..." I looked up at him. "I want to do this. To help someone else. To help you." But I didn't want him to think I was holding him to some obligation or stalking him like Lacey. "It would be an arrangement. Like a business agreement. No strings. No need for it to be more than in name only. Then, with you in control of Whickering Place, that will buy us some time, won't it?"

His eyebrows lifted. "What about Colin?"

I shrugged.

"It'll kill him. I won't have to worry about The Colony. *He'll* kill me."

"Colin and I would never have worked anyway. He's far too sane for me." I attempted a laugh.

Pearse passed his hand over his mouth and chin, his eyes boring into mine.

"What do you think?" I stood slowly. The trembling started deep in my lower abdomen as the reality of what I was offering sank in. "I know it's a stab in the dark, but..."

I broke off as Pearse stepped toward me.

"Are you sure about this?"

I couldn't form the words, but I nodded, swallowed.

He paused for a second before putting his arms around me. I could feel his fear. And his gratitude.

"This is crazy," he whispered against my hair. "And I'm not sure there's a hope in hell of it working. I'm not sure they'll believe I've had a change of heart. But if it can buy us some time, then maybe I can figure a way out of all this."

The sheer gravity and intimacy of the moment—the intensity of what we were doing and the danger of it all potentially backfiring on us—ripped a shiver from deep in my body. "I'm scared too," I whispered. "But let's do it."

Wow. I'm engaged.

Chapter Forty-Six

It was going to take too long to get a marriage license through the online process.

We needed to accomplish this as fast as possible, so I took a Xanax, clenched my fists, and rode with Pearse to the Register of Deeds office for a marriage license.

Not that my anxiety was gone entirely, but having something else to focus on—like the fact that I was about to get married to a vampire for reasons that I barely understood myself—distracted me from the fear of the strangers and the unfamiliar space.

I never thought I'd marry. I certainly never thought I'd get married like this or for these reasons. A few weeks ago, if someone had told me I'd be entering into a marriage that would put me in grave danger, I would've reentered Morganton Psychiatric. A month ago, I could barely leave my apartment.

But this was my decision. No one else had suggested it. I had no idea what I was doing. But during the last ten years, while I'd done everything in my power to stay safe, stay alive, my life had completely lost all meaning. Now, as scary as it was, there was some purpose for the danger. But no matter what, I'd have to live with my decision.

I asked the clerk for a copy of the deed to Whickering Place. My father had filed a quitclaim deed before he'd committed suicide.

"What do I need to do to get his name on this too?" I jerked my thumb at Pearse.

The clerk looked at me over her wire-rimmed glasses. "You'll need to go to an attorney for that. Then it'll be filed here."

I glanced at Pearse. "We'll find an out-of-town attorney."

"As long as it's not Maris, I don't think it matters who we get," he said.

After we'd filled out all the paperwork and paid the $60, the gray-haired lady behind the desk handed us the license. "That's good for sixty days anywhere in the state of North Carolina," she told us, her thick North Carolina accent drawing out each word.

"Now what?" Pearse's hand shook as he took the marriage license from the clerk.

The woman's eyes darted back and forth between the two of us. She shrugged. "I guess you get married."

I leaned into the counter, keeping my voice low. "How do we find a justice of the peace?"

She pointed out the window. "Well, you can just run down the road a pace to the Courthouse. The magistrate is on the second floor and usually does marriages at eight-thirty in the morning and three in the afternoon."

"Today?" Pearse asked.

"Yeah. See if he can fit you in for his three o'clock. It'll cost you twenty dollars. Cash only. Then you can run over to Mellow Mushroom and have a pizza." She snickered. "I'm just kiddin' you."

In the span of an hour and a half, counting the time we had to wait, we were married.

It hardly seemed real. It felt more like one of those games I'd played as a kid—pretending, standing up in front of friends with a piece of lace thrown over my head like a veil, wearing a white nightgown. Except I was wearing jeans and a wool sweater.

Even stranger was that everything went right back to normal as soon as it was over. Pearse drove us home. I went into the kitchen to clean up some dishes. He followed me, poured a cup of coffee, sat down at the table.

"Now we just have to find an attorney who can add your name to the house deed." I leaned against the counter and scrolled through the listings on my phone. I paused on one of the names. "Here's someone. He's in Hendersonville. Michel Babineau."

Pearse nodded. "I like his name. Sounds like he could be from *Looziana.*"

"Anyway, he does real estate law. I'll give him a call."

When I looked up at Pearse, he was smiling.

"Weird, huh?" he said.

"What?"

"I feel like we should be toasting with champagne or something."

"Yeah. Maybe we should've picked up a bottle on the way home."

Pearse was quiet.

My phone rang. I glanced down at the screen. "It's Colin."

The smile slid from his face. "Having any regrets yet?"

I shook my head. "Nope."

Then I let the lie hang between us.

The call went to voicemail.

My head spun—the weight of what we'd done suddenly hitting me with the force of an anvil. I was married. To Pearse. Someone who could be going to prison. I was going to give him my house? Had I completely lost my mind?

I turned toward the sink, laid the cell phone aside. I reached for a plate, washed and then dried it.

Pearse's phone dinged.

He stared down at it. "Colin. I should get it. He never calls me."

As he answered, Pearse's voice hardly sounded like his own.

The phrase echoed in my mind: *Have I made a huge mistake?*

I had a sneaking suspicion the same sentiment was running through Pearse's head too.

After Colin's call, we stood and stared at each other.

Now what?

"He asked me where you were."

"What did you say?"

"That you were around here somewhere."

I shifted from one foot to the other. "What are we going to tell him? About this?"

Pearse pinched the bridge of his nose between his thumb and forefinger. "Maybe we don't tell him anything right now."

I shook my head. "It's still gonna hurt him whenever he finds out."

"Well, it's a little late for an attack of conscience." His phone lit up again. He slid his thumb over the screen. "Maris is texting."

My heart jolted.

"I'm being summoned."

"Don't go."

Pearse looked up at me.

We'd only been married a few hours, and I was already telling him what to do. "I mean, do you have to go?"

He nodded. "I do."

"How long will you be there?"

"I have no idea. Depends on how things go."

I exhaled shakily. "Okay."

He took a step toward me. "Will you be all right?"

"Yes."

"Just lock the door behind me. Don't let anyone in."

"I won't." My voice broke a little, and I cleared my throat. I stood by the door while Pearse pulled his leather jacket over each arm and fished Colin's car keys out of his pocket.

I opened the door and held it for him. "Still having car problems?"

He crossed the foyer and paused in front of me. "I just don't want people following me. They know my car."

I nodded.

Pearse's gaze moved from my eyes to my mouth back to my eyes, and there was something tender about it. For a second, I almost thought he might lean in to kiss me. Instead, he placed a hand to my cheek. "Thank you. For what you did. I know it's a sacrifice."

"It's not." But of course, it was.

As soon as Pearse left, I shut the door and threw the locks.

My gaze landed on the phone on the foyer table. For some reason, I expected it to ring. I approached it, stood right in front of it, my hand poised over the receiver—ready to lift it as soon as it yodeled its shrill sound.

But the phone was silent.

The house felt eerily calm.

Chapter Forty-Seven

After Pearse left, I called Michel Babineau and retained his services to add Pearse's name to the deed. All I had to do was send over the necessary documents. Babineau would draw up the paperwork, and then Pearse would be part owner of Whickering Place. I put everything together in an envelope, wrote out a check, and walked the twenty-three steps to the mailbox to make sure it went out the same day.

That night, I sat in the front parlor watching movies. No Nina Mayhew marathons on the women's movie channel, so I pulled up an old one on Netflix. A newer one—a thriller set in New York City. Not nearly as good, but watchable.

My phone pinged, and I grabbed for it. Could be Pearse.

But it was a text from Colin.

All good there? Helping my mom move today.

He'd sent a picture of himself carrying two boxes and glancing over his shoulder. His mom had probably taken the photo.

Looking at the picture was like glimpsing someone from my past. Even though he'd only been gone a week, a lot had happened since he'd left.

I texted back, *Glad she has you there to help her.*

How's the Desmopressin working out? Any headaches?

I groaned. The last few days, I'd completely forgotten to take it. It was difficult for me to remember, stay on schedule. It was the same with my anti-anxiety pills—or any medication, really.

No headaches.

The clang of the doorbell launched me from my seat. I reached under the couch and slid out the gun safe, typed in the combination.

The doorbell rang two more times. Then knocking.

My heart pounding in my throat, I traipsed back to the foyer, holding the gun at my side. "Who is it?"

"It's Detective Stoney and Detective Mears."

I relaxed my shoulders. But then I remembered Pearse's words. I had no idea whether or not they were members of The Colony. I tucked the gun into the back of my jeans and peered out the peephole. Stoney's pale face looked back at me.

Huffing out a sigh, I opened the door.

He and Mears moved inside. "Sorry to bother you so late. Is Pearse here?"

I stood silently, my arms crossed, determined not to give them any ammunition to use against Pearse. "No."

Mears looked unfazed by my attempt at dismissing them. "We wouldn't have come this late if it wasn't important."

Stoney motioned to the front parlor. "Can we sit?"

I rubbed my forehead. "Can't we just stand? I'm really tired and about to go to bed."

He looked at Mears.

She nodded.

"All right. Have you seen Pearse Gallagher in the past twenty-four to thirty hours?"

My expression didn't change. "Yes."

"Do you know how often he was in and out of the house during that time?"

"I don't know. I'm not keeping tabs on him."

"Do you know where he is now?"

"No."

"What about two nights ago?"

"What's this about?"

Undaunted by my sullen demeanor, Mears lifted her eyebrows. "Do you? Know where he was?"

I shrugged.

"Something's changed," said Mears. "What's happened?"

The words exploded from my mouth. "Pearse and I got married today."

"What?"

"We got married."

They glanced at each other.

Mears's voice was cold. "Was that something you were planning?"

"Not really. It just kind of happened."

Stoney seemed nervous. He swiped his hand across his mouth. "Okay. Well, that is certainly an interesting development."

I sucked in my lower lip.

Mears took a step toward me. "A young woman was found in a cabin in Black Mountain early yesterday morning, barely alive, a Whickering Place coin on each eye. Eighteen years old. Drained of blood. Like the others."

I sucked harder. *Pearse couldn't have done it.*

Mears's voice was steady. "The victim stated that the man who drained her blood—she heard the others call him Pearse. He was the only one she could identify—the only one not wearing a mask. But she said he used needles, tubing, even a tourniquet. Just like someone would use in a lab to draw blood."

Oh, God. Please no.

I released my lip and tried to appear unfazed.

Stoney was quick to add on to Mears's compilation. "The girl described Pearse—'the one they called Pearse'—that's what she said—about six feet, black hair, dark eyes, wore a leather jacket." He lifted his shoulders and let them fall again. "Sound familiar?"

I exhaled what felt like all the air in my body.

Mears pinched her temples. "Miss Tullinger—or should we now call you Mrs. Gallagher?"

I flinched. Good lord, I nearly blushed. What was wrong with me? This was serious.

"Pearse *is* a phlebotomist. Isn't he?"

I hesitated. "Are you going to arrest him?"

"At this stage, we'd just like to talk to him."

My heartbeat was erratic. "Well, like I said. He's not here."

Stoney coughed, pulled a handkerchief from his pocket, and wiped under his nose. "When he comes back, will you have him contact us?"

Mears's eyes bored into me. "It'll be better for everyone if he comes to us voluntarily."

After they left, I sank to the floor, put my head in my hands, and let my hair fall over my face like a shroud as reality washed over me. He'd drained her blood. The girl had nearly died. Pearse had done that?

It was starting. Much sooner than I'd thought.

I don't even know this guy.

Despite what he says, he could be a maniacal killer.

For all I knew, he could be planning to kill me.

Chapter Forty-Eight
Tuesday, February 11

P earse didn't come home that night.
Or the next day.

And I didn't hear from him.

I reminded myself that this had been my idea. He owed me nothing—not even a phone call. This was an arrangement. Nothing more. I'd said those words to him.

Maybe it was better if he didn't come back.

But as day again darkened into evening, I worried. Really worried. Had the police found him? Arrested him? Had something else happened? I'd been walking around, gun in hand or in the back of my jeans, unwilling to put it down except when I went to bed. It was under the pillow when I slept—which hadn't been much anyway.

A wave of nausea cascaded over me as I rolled off the couch and straightened. I hadn't eaten anything since last night and didn't really feel like eating now but knew I should. My blood sugar was probably low. There was leftover lasagna in the fridge.

I trudged toward the kitchen.

But the smell. It was horrible. I covered my mouth and nose. Was the stench coming from the kitchen? No. A draft of wind wafted down the corridor, carrying the stink of rotting meat.

Then I stopped walking. Couldn't take another step. It was like in my nightmares except I was standing, and my legs locked as though my knees were held in place by a restrictive brace.

It looked like a mist. It advanced slowly from the end of the hallway, taking shape as it moved. Little by little, I could see that it was a woman—taller than me and encased in shadow. Her long, black hair seemed to move independently from the rest of her, like Medusa's serpents. Her movements were less of a walk than a glide. As she stepped out of the shadows and approached me, she actually seemed to be comprised of shadows ... with two glowing eyes.

Unable to move my head to look up at her, I stared into the swirling black emptiness that would have been her neck. She stood inches away, and a blast of hot breath cascaded over my head. The stench that had filled the hallway moments before flooded into my nostrils.

My gun was in the back of my jeans. If I could only reach it. But I couldn't even flinch. Paralyzed from the hairline down.

Succubare. The word came to me as though it had been spoken aloud.

This woman was my father's captor. And now she was to be mine.

But then the succubus left the way she came, gliding backward down the hall, her red eyes fading into the shadows.

My fingers twitched, but I still couldn't move my arms, my legs.

A minute passed, then two. The smell dissipated until only the faintest metallic odor lingered. A warmth drenched my body, starting at the top of my head and dribbling down my face, neck, shoulders, torso. One cell at a time, I could move again.

Jerking my arm in a reflexive action, the muscles wrenched as I grasped the handle of my gun, pulled it from my waistband, racked the slide, and fired. The explosion was deafening as a burning shell bounced off of my cheekbone, followed by the sound of glass breaking. Smoke filled my nostrils. The entire sequence of events took ten seconds.

I trembled violently. Even my teeth chattered as I backed into the front room, my thoughts whirring, adrenal gland pumping. What had just happened? What had I seen? Even more disturbing, what had I done? The response had been wildly reactive, uncontrolled. I'd never shot a gun inside a house before. A massive violation of Gun Safety 101.

Staggering to the fireplace, I dropped the Glock on the mantel. Then I collapsed on the couch and stared at my shaking hands.

But I couldn't stay here. That thing—what if it came back? Scrambling to my feet again, I sprinted toward the front door, threw it open, stumbled out ... and smacked face-first against a glass wall. I could go no further. Glancing over my shoulder and through the open door of Whickering Place, the realization of my imprisonment became clear.

A couple strolled by on the sidewalk and glanced up at me. I realized how this must look as I stood, balancing on the top of the steps, trying to jump off, but unable to do so, my arms outstretched as though I might take flight.

"Is everything all right?" The man asked.

I forced myself to bob my head up and down. "Yeah. Yes."

They walked on.

Pivoting, I faced the house and looked in through the front door, down the foyer and the long hall—the hallway in which I'd seen the succubus. *I could run through, straight back to the garden.*

With a deep breath, I plunged into the house, grabbed my coat off the hook, and ran headlong to the back as laughter echoed all around me. The soles of my shoes crunched over glass—the bullet had broken one of the window panes on the door leading to the garden. Then I burst through and darkness embraced me. I tripped over a tangle of bushes, some disintegrated bricks. Planting my feet, I stood and stared up at the dark house.

Cackling boomed and rolled through the air. *The gargoyles*, I thought as I caught a glimpse of one of the darkened stone figures, its wings extended as though it would take flight. But its hand cupped its mouth as it called out to a partner on the opposite corner of the house.

"Shut up!" I covered my ears.

The laughter faded away as the wind whipped through the garden, blowing my hair back from my face.

I was as much a prisoner in the garden as I'd been inside the house. The only light came from the streetlamps shining over the top of the high walls. A few feet away from me was the frozen pond—no doubt still clutching its drowned algae-haired log that looked like a body.

But I couldn't go back inside. Not with her in there.

After a few minutes, my eyes adjusted, and I picked my way along the overgrown trail to the ruins of a bench. As I lowered myself to the cold, cracked stone, a chill zigzagged through me.

"Pearse will be home soon," I spoke the words aloud ... to reassure myself.

But I knew that might not happen. He hadn't come home last night. There had been many nights when he hadn't come home.

My fingers and butt numbed with cold, and I rocked back and forth. What time was it? The icy grasp of the air around me tightened.

My rushing adrenaline cooled, and a crushing despondency came over me like a cloak of despair, the pain of it nearly physical. My whole body trembled, and I clasped my arms across my chest.

Even now, the inability to move, the red eyes, the undeniable stench of rancid breath circulated through my senses, reminding me what I'd experienced. This thing—disembodied spirit or succubus or whatever it was—had breathed on me, and I'd practically heard the words. It had known my father. Now it was coming for me.

A light glowed from a window in the east wing, and I jumped. Watched, waited.

A few windows over, another light flared. And then another. One by one, the windows blazed as though someone moved from room to room.

I held my breath, waiting to see the succubus moving across the upstairs.

Instead, a minute later, the back door flew open, and yellow light spilled out into the garden. Pearse stood in the doorway.

"Avery," he called out forcefully.

I stood slowly, stiffly. How long had I been sitting here? How much time had passed?

Pearse stood with his hands on his hips. As I hobbled faster and drew closer, I felt the vibe of anger radiating off of him.

"Where were you? I was searching the house for you. There was glass all over the floor and the window was broken, and I thought—"

"I'm fine." I brushed past him and careened over the threshold, where the rush of warmth brought uncontrollable shivering. Air as thick as molasses enveloped me, and from somewhere inside the house, something growled.

But Pearse didn't seem to hear anything. We stood on the broken glass, his boots pulverizing the shards as he grabbed my shoulders. "I thought..." He lowered his voice. "Why were you out there?"

"I broke the window. I shot the gun, and the bullet went through the window," I babbled.

"What? Why did you need your gun?"

Gasping, I peered around him at the shadows beyond. "I'm sorry. But you didn't come back, so..."

"Were you trying to freeze to death out there? It's twenty degrees outside." He dropped his hands from my shoulders, his face softening.

My skin crawled. Despite the broken window, the air in the house was oppressive. "I—I thought I saw someone in here, and—"

"Who?"

"It wasn't ... a solid person."

His shoulders slumped. "Oh." He cranked his head around and looked into the shadows behind us. "Shit, we've got to get out of this place," he breathed, shrugging out of his coat.

"I know."

He threw the coat over the banister. "I need to talk to you."

"I need to talk to you too."

His eyes were rock hard. "What is it?"

"The police came here last night."

His face blanched. "What did they say?"

"They were looking for you."

He drew his hand to his forehead. "Shit."

"That girl lived. She knows your name, and she gave it to them."

Pearse grew silent. His eyes darted back and forth. "I know."

I swallowed hard, dreading my next question. "Did you *actually* drain her blood?"

His face tensed. "They made me, Avery. I didn't have a choice. I told you. They're killers."

"And you aren't?" I flattened my mouth. "Or you just don't think of yourself that way?"

He dropped his gaze. "Obviously, the girl didn't die."

"She could have."

"Yes. She could have," he said, subdued.

A giant shudder wracked me from the inside.

He ran his hand through his hair. "I didn't want to. God knows I didn't want to, but if I hadn't done it, they were going to use a knife."

"Wow. You know it's bad when the logic of draining a person's blood with a needle is somehow better than using a knife. The end result is the same."

"Not always."

"What? You've killed people with a needle before?"

"No, of course not."

"Have you helped them kill before?"

"No." His eyes flashed.

Nausea from earlier returned. Acid roiled in my stomach. "Where have you been for the last day and a half?"

He inhaled slowly, his shoulders rising. "When they found out the girl lived, Maris sent me into the woods—to one of their hiding places—until they could figure out how they're going to handle this. I guess they got cold feet about letting me take the rap for attempted homicide. Probably worried about what I'd say. Who else I'd take down with me."

"Was Maris with you?"

"Maris wasn't there."

"Who was with you?"

He hesitated.

"Was Lacey there?"

He nodded.

I flinched.

"And I told her we're married, that I'm part owner of Whickering Place now."

I felt a prickle at the back of my neck—a tiny thrill that he would tell her the news so fast. "How did she take it?"

"Not well. She was pissed—like, crazy pissed. Which is probably a pretty good indication of how the rest of them will take it."

My chest tightened. "Now what happens?"

He placed his keys on the table beside the phantom phone. "I don't know."

"Have we made it worse by doing this?"

"I don't know."

"What should we do?"

"We wait."

"And hope the police don't come back here for you? Or worse, that members of The Colony won't come for us?"

"Would you rather I go?"

"No," I said a little too loudly.

He took a couple of steps toward me. "Why would you want me to stay?"

A knock on the back door startled both of us. We stared at each other.

"Police?" Pearse breathed.

Why would the police come to the back door? Unless someone in the neighborhood had called them after hearing gunshots. "Go." I waved him off into the shadows and tromped through the broken glass.

"Hello?" Cassie's pale gold hair gleamed through the remaining panes. "What happened to your door?"

I motioned her inside. "Why did you come to the back door?"

"The back gate was open. I didn't want to come through the front in case someone saw me. Is Pearse here?"

"Yep, I'm here." He swept out of the shadows and stood under the flickering hall light.

The three of us moved into the kitchen and sat at the table.

Cassie seemed out of breath as she spoke. "Congratulations, by the way."

I glanced up at her, then Pearse.

He lifted his shoulders and dropped them again. "I texted her. She knows." He shifted his eyes to Cassie. "Has the news reached everyone yet?"

She nodded. "Yep."

"And?"

I held my breath.

"They are handling it as you might imagine."

"Badly," I said.

Cassie arched an eyebrow. "That would be one way to describe the reaction."

Pearse leaned forward. "What are they saying?"

"Oh, all sorts of stuff. Maris was running around the bar, pulling Colony members aside and having private conferences with them. Those two new members—Ian and Torin?—they were sitting up at the bar. It was really noisy in there, so they probably didn't realize I could hear them. But they were talking about an upcoming sacrifice. Of a virgin—the highest possible sacrifice they can make to the succubare. Apparently, they've been waiting for a long time. It's a really big deal to offer virgin blood to the 'vampire gods,' or whatever." She made air quotes with her fingers. "Anyway, I got the impression that they thought Avery was it and that Maris has been considering her for the offering." She looked at me. "Until Maris came up to the bar and told them that Pearse had 'effed up everything.'" She used air quotes again.

"So they were planning on killing me?" Liquid anger and shock pulsed through me. Could things get any worse? I held up my hands. "Well, stupid me confided in Maris about my sexual status before I knew she was a psychopath." I gave a short, sharp laugh. "Aren't I the lucky one?"

Pearse stared at me. "What? Are you really a virgin?"

"For real?" Cassie squinted. "I thought they were talking bullshit."

My cheeks burned. I pushed my chair back and mumbled, "I figured your brother would've told you."

Pearse's mouth fell open. "No. Holy shit. I can't believe it."

My mind rewound to the moment I'd told Maris. "Look, it's not something I regularly tell people. It's not anyone's business."

"Well, now it's everyone's business," said Cassie.

"But you and Colin didn't—"

"No," I said quickly. "We didn't."

Pearse stood. "So that's why Maris told me to keep my hands off of you." He made a strange sort of laughing sound. "Great. Just great." Terse lines formed across his forehead.

Suddenly I knew this information held a deeper meaning for us both.

"I think you two should get out of here," Cassie said. "Like, I'd be really surprised if Maris hasn't sent people over here. You *know* there will be some kind of retribution."

I pushed up from the table. "But Pearse is part owner of Whickering Place now. Doesn't that give him some special status with the organization?"

Cassie's lips tightened. "Not until they decide to recognize him in that role. Plus, he's gone against a Colony order. That's not going to endear him to anyone."

A new layer of panic settled over me. "So, this was a big mistake."

Pearse pivoted away from me, wandered into the hall, and circled back again.

"Let me drive you guys somewhere," Cassie said. The wooden chair legs screeched against the tile floor as she stood. "You really shouldn't stay here. You're sitting ducks here."

Pearse stepped toward me, grabbed my chin, and forced me to look up at him. "Avery, whatever happens, I'm not going to let them hurt you."

Tears stung the backs of my eyes. "Pearse, you can't protect me. You can't even protect yourself." I gulped air and stared up at the ceiling. Everything was happening too fast. I didn't want to make any more plans. I wanted to run. I looked down the darkened hall. "The vampires can take the damn house. I don't even care. Let's just go."

Cassie pulled her phone out of her back pocket. "Hey, I know a guy who works at the Grant Estate Mountain Resort. It's like forty-five minutes away, just past Hendersonville, in Flat Rock, I think. Anyway, he owes me a few favors. I'm sure he can get you guys a room. You could check-in under different names. Hide out there for a few days until Maris has a chance to calm down."

Pearse cleared his throat. His eyes grazed mine. "I know it's not ideal, but..."

"None of this is ideal, Pearse."

"I'm just trying to check their every move."

I choked out a bitter laugh. "And I'm the pawn."

We stood in silence, both of us staring at the ground. I listened to the sound of Pearse's breathing and mine mingling.

"You should leave your phones here," Cassie said, holding her cell phone up to her ear. "So they can't track you. And while you guys are there, why don't you just take care of this for real? I mean, shit. You *are* married." She rolled her eyes, turned, and walked into the hall.

Pearse's eyes were dark and wide, his voice low. "I know you wanted this to be a business arrangement, with no strings attached..." He grimaced. "And this is gonna sound sleazy, but Cassie's right. What if we just take the option off the table?"

A funny fluttering crept over my shoulders and into my neck.

He held up his hands. "Totally up to you, of course. But I mean, Maris will assume we've already done it anyway. So we could cover our bases. So to speak."

The irony of all this wasn't lost on me. But my mind felt blank. Paralyzed by fear. I was right on the edge—standing on the cliffside looking down at the ocean while the cavalry rode directly toward me.

I looked up at Pearse. "Just ... not here, okay? Let's go somewhere else. If Cassie can get us a room, then let's go."

Pearse went to get his coat.

Chapter Forty-Nine

I t was after midnight when we arrived.

The Grant Estate Mountain Resort was a five-star establishment that hovered on the edge of a lake, its stone structure lit with green and midnight-blue illumination from embedded spotlights. Any other time I might have been awed by its location and the sheer size of the resort, which stretched out as far as I could see. Now, my anxiety was in overdrive. I fumbled in my purse for my pills and popped two.

I tried to keep my thoughts at bay. Everything we did from here on out had to be a practical consideration. I'd jumped into this mess feet first. Now I had to swim. Or drown.

I waited in the car while Pearse and Cassie went inside to talk to her friend. In my head, I replayed therapy sessions with Dr. Murphy. The deep breathing exercises she had taught me. The mantras I could repeat to myself to calm down.

Within five minutes, Cassie and Pearse were back. Cassie climbed into the driver's seat. "Good luck." She looked at me and blinked. "Have fun."

Pearse opened my door. "We've got a room for three nights. That should buy us some time." He held out his hand. My fingers slipped across his palm, and he hoisted me to my feet.

I walked on legs that barely held my weight and felt like I was having an out-of-body experience—watching some other couple enter the hotel.

A high ceiling greeted us in reception, along with gas-log hearths on either end. During regular hours the lobby was probably bustling with people. But now, it was a ghost town, quiet and dim.

As we moved down the hallway, we passed a salon, a spa, and several gift shops, all closed up, their darkened display windows crowded with North Carolina sweatshirts and kitschy tumblers.

The halls were equally deserted, not a soul around. Blissfully silent. No voices. No shadows. No flickering lights.

We rode the elevator, both of our heads down. The rumble of the machinery was accompanied only by the sleeve of Pearse's leather jacket scraping against the wall, and the swish of denim as my purse brushed against my leg.

On the third floor, we walked like automatons to the door of our room. Pearse fumbled the key card, dropping it before successfully inserting it into the slot. As I waited, my entire body began to tremble.

Once opened, I hurried out of the hallway and into the room. The door shut behind us, blocking out the rest of the world.

A king-sized bed occupied one end of the room—its white comforter edged with a teal-blue throw and matching pillows. Chocolate-brown drapery covered the windows, and a sash in the same blue held back the curtains on either side. The room was luxurious, new, and nothing like Whickering Place.

We both stood, scanning our surroundings, reciting trite phrases about how nice the room was and what relief we felt to be out of *that house.*

And then all the words evaporated. There was nothing more to say. The elephant in the room was bigger and more nerve-wracking than I'd thought it would be.

We locked gazes.

"We don't have to do anything tonight, Avery." Pearse shrugged out of his jacket and hung it over the back of a chair. "I'm exhausted. I'm sure you are too."

I shook my head. I'd already made my decision. "No. I don't want to wake up tomorrow and have to think about it. Let's just do it."

He made a little exhalation, and for a moment, I wondered if he was going to protest.

"Okay," he said finally.

My heart racing, I started to undress, and in between shedding each article of clothing, I pulled back the comforter on the bed and then the sheets.

"Do you want the lights on or off?" he asked.

"Whatever. Doesn't matter. Yeah, off, maybe."

He switched off the lamp by the bed, but a small one on the chest of drawers across the room still cast a dim glow.

When I glanced over at him again, Pearse had removed his shirt and sat on the other side of the bed, his back to me. I stared at the muscles of his shoulders as he took off his watch and placed it on the bedside table.

Am I really going to do this? This is crazy. The safety zone was in my rearview mirror.

But I needed to get out of my head. It was a little late for logic.

When I was down to bra and panties, I climbed under the covers.

When Pearse turned around, he was naked.

I bit my lip. I'd never actually been in the same room with a completely naked man before. But he *was* gorgeous. He was lean and muscular and other than the bruises around the crooks of his arms and the scabbed-over incisions under his collarbone, he looked like one of those guys in a hot fireman's calendar.

So this could've been a lot worse.

My heart was pumping so hard I could see the tiny rise of the sheet that covered my chest. I stared up at the ceiling,

Pearse lowered himself to his elbow. "I know this isn't how you thought it would happen," he said in a low voice.

"I never thought it would happen at all," I said to the ceiling.

He rolled toward me, and his fingers grazed my hip.

I flinched.

His face was encased in shadows as he leaned toward me. "Just try to relax, Avery. I know this is weird and ... really awkward, but it doesn't have to be so bad." A flash of a smile. "You might even enjoy it."

"We'll see." Right then, I couldn't get a solid breath.

"You know what's really bizarre about this?"

"What?"

"We're married."

"I know."

"And it kind of feels like we're two teenagers who just checked into a hotel for the night."

"I wish that were the case."

Pearse drew back a little, and the planes of his face loosened. "I also feel kinda like I'm stealing my brother's inheritance or something."

"Please don't say that. Don't talk about Colin right now."

He brushed my hair back from my forehead—a gesture that seemed intimate and even merciful. "Are you sure you want to do this?"

"Yes. And please don't ask me a bunch of questions while we're doing it, like, are you okay, and all that. Let's just not talk."

"Whatever you want."

Leaning in, he kissed me then, and despite everything—the fear of what I was doing and where I was, the horror of what I knew about Pearse and the people he was involved with—my body responded on its own.

I reached up, ran my hands over his shoulders and into his hair, arched my back, and pressed against him. I'd never felt anything like this before—the anticipation—the sheer physical sensation of racing adrenaline brought on by one person's skin touching another.

He reached down and ran his fingers between my legs, and I shuddered. Then he shifted the crotch of the panties aside, and I sucked a sharp intake of air as his fingers made contact with me. He pulled back—his dark eyes searching mine, apologetic.

Then he kissed me again. As the kiss deepened, he slid off my panties and touched me until I couldn't keep my hips from moving.

"Hang on. I need to get a condom."

He rolled away, and I waited while he tore open the wrapper and put on the condom. All at once, I was not only a willing participant but an eager one. I wanted this to happen. I wanted Pearse.

My ribcage felt like it would explode as he settled himself on top of me, bracing his arms on either side of my head and scooting one of my legs away from the other with his knee. I held my breath, and then he was inside of me. I cried out from the burst of pain and the astonishment that we were actually having sex. But seconds later, ripples of pleasure eclipsed any sting.

"Sorry," he whispered against my ear.

"It's fine. *This* is good."

As Pearse moved back and forth over me, the thought trailed through my brain that Maris had lost her sacrifice.

And I was safe.

Chapter Fifty
Wednesday, February 12

I awoke to the patter of water hitting the tile in the shower. I sat up, remembering where I was and what had happened the night before.

The corners of my lips turned up as I looked down at the bed where we'd slept. The smear of blood across rumpled sheets. Everything was different now. I felt different.

Pearse came out of the bathroom wearing a towel. His hair was wet and dripping and clung to the side of his face and neck. "Hey."

"Hey."

"You all right?"

I nodded. "Yep."

He sat down beside me on the bed. "Are you really all right?"

I bit my lip and nodded harder. I might have been glowing.

He ran his thumb along my cheek. "I don't know how you're feeling about all this—and I know it's a lot to take in, but..." He slid his hand further back into my hair. "Everything else aside, what happened between us last night was ... really good."

An unstoppable smile stretched my cheeks. "It was."

"I'm glad you thought so too."

He leaned forward and kissed me on the forehead. Several drops of water dripped onto my face.

"I'm starving," I said.

He stood. "I was going to go down and get us some coffee, but maybe we should order room service."

"That sounds good." I scooted to the edge of the bed, still holding the sheets up to my collarbone.

"Yeah. And I should call Cassie and find out what's going on. And I need to call work."

"Yeah, what about work?"

"God knows what Lacey's told them," he breathed. "I may already be fired."

"What will you tell them?"

He dropped the towel from his waist and lifted his clothes from the chair by the bed. "I'll go with ... family emergency."

"It's sort of true."

I didn't know what I was going to do yet about my clients and finishing the websites I'd started for them. I didn't even have my laptop. Or my phone.

I watched Pearse as he dressed. In one night, my feelings for him had exploded into something so much deeper than they had been twelve hours before. "I wish we could just stay in this room. Like, forever."

Pearse looked at me over his shoulder. "Why's that?"

I shrugged. I didn't want to say too much. After all, I was renegotiating our original contract. Married in name only. No strings. "I like it in here. It's a nice room."

AFTER BREAKFAST, I stood in the shower, letting the warm water run over my body and replaying last night—the way Pearse's hands had felt when he'd touched me.

When wet, my hair practically cocooned me, covering the whole top half of my body like a water nymph or a mermaid.

Right then, I made the decision. There was a salon downstairs. It was time. I was going to venture out of the room and downstairs. On my own.

I took my medication out of my purse and stared at it. I'd been taking it faithfully for weeks now, but today, I wasn't even sure that I needed it. I felt great. No thump, slither noises were going on above my head. And if I tried really hard, I could almost believe Pearse and I were just a normal couple. For the first time, I realized that's what I wanted. But I also had to admit that the pills had been working.

I popped my usual dosage and left Pearse to make his phone calls. Then I poked my head out and looked both ways up and down the corridor. A man was leaving his room, and I waited, watching his back until I couldn't see him anymore. Then I shot out, hustled down the hallway, and propelled myself onto the elevator.

And forced myself to breathe.

Three floors down, and I was in the lobby.

People were everywhere. Walking, sitting, eating.

A moment of panic almost sent me back to the room.

But no. Today, I was a different person. Things were going to be different from now on.

I spotted the salon right next to one of the gift shops. Inside, a woman sat with tin foils in her hair. She was drinking out of a mug and staring down at her phone.

I forced my legs to move forward.

I'd read that in some cultures, the cutting of the hair symbolized rebirth or reparation.

The girl who cut my hair was young and had a strong accent—maybe from New Jersey or New York. "Why do you want to cut it?"

"It's time for a change."

She spun me toward the mirror. "I wish I could grow my hair this long," she said. "My hair's so fine it just breaks off after I get it past my shoulders."

"I didn't grow mine this long intentionally."

She draped the cape around me. "Would you like to donate it? You know, to Locks of Love or something?"

"Yes, I would, actually."

She nodded, sweeping my hair into a low ponytail. "If you're cutting ten inches, it would make sense."

I only winced slightly as I heard the scissors saw through the rope of my hair—practically twenty years of growth.

"There you go!" she said, holding up the ponytail for me to see.

"Wow."

Slow and deep.

Tears sprang to my eyes when she rotated me toward the mirror again, and I saw the ends of my dark hair settled around my shoulders.

New person, not hiding behind my hair, I reminded myself.

I actually felt lighter as I left the salon. I hadn't realized how heavy hair could be.

A gift store next door to the salon sold champagne, so I bought a bottle. It seemed like the right time for a celebration.

BACK IN THE ROOM, I shut the door behind me and put my forehead against it.

"What happened to your hair?" Pearse exclaimed.

I turned around slowly, my eyes filling with tears. "I went to the salon downstairs and had them cut it. I thought it was time for a change."

"Wow."

I tried to gauge his response as I approached him. "Do you like it?"

"Yeah. You look different." He smiled.

"I feel different."

He put his hands on my shoulders. "Is that because of the new haircut or what happened last night?"

A small smile pulled at the corners of my mouth. "Did you talk to Cassie?"

"Yeah. Everyone's looking for us. Police. Maris. Cassie said Maris asked her where we were."

"What did she tell her?"

"That we were on our honeymoon." He laughed.

"Good answer."

He nodded, squeezed my shoulders, and we reverse-walked toward the bed until the backs of my knees hit the base of it.

Pearse framed my face between his hands and kissed me, his tongue pressing against mine with urgency. Tipping me back onto the bed, he crawled on top of me and put his forehead against mine. "I wondered if last night might just be a one-off. Like, mission accomplished—now go away, you bastard, and leave me alone."

I grabbed the base of his shirt and pulled it up, running my hands across his chest. "I hope not."

He rocked back and pulled his shirt off. I sat up and did the same, frantically tugging at the button of his jeans as he ripped at mine. Then he lowered himself onto me. And this time, there was no hesitation.

Chapter Fifty-One
Thursday, February 13

We didn't leave the room at all the next day. We ordered room service, made love, and drank champagne.

I never, never wanted to leave.

"We have to go back, Avery," Pearse said, a line forming between his eyebrows. "We have to face this."

I slammed down my glass and raked my eyes over Pearse's bare upper torso. I'd turned into one of those pathetic, lovestruck women from the cheesy romance films. It was disgusting how my brain had turned into a mass of raging hormones—like I'd suddenly been let out of a cage.

"I don't ever want to go back there."

"I know," he said softly. "But we really have to."

"Why?" I made a fake crying sound.

Pearse refilled my glass of champagne and tousled the top of my hair. "I need to meet with Maris. See if we can come to some kind of agreement."

"They can have the house, Pearse. I don't care anymore."

He folded my fingers into his. "No. As long as we have the house, we have a bargaining chip. Now more than ever, we need to hold onto that."

"But for how long? I can't live my life peering through windows and wondering if a member of a killer vampire cult is lurking outside. I mean, how much longer are you going to keep trying to appease them?"

He squeezed my fingers. "There are some things that need to be resolved first. I *was* part of a crime—it may not have been my idea or my intention, but they've got me. I was the only person there that night without a mask. If this goes to trial, that girl will know me."

I sank back on the pillow. "We need to get you a good lawyer."

His brow wreathed. "Yeah, because there's more."

"What do you mean?"

He shook his head. "Some shit that went down in New Orleans. The Colony knows about it. They'll offer it up if this goes to trial. They'll have no problem sacrificing me—literally and figuratively."

"What else happened?" All of the air had gone out of my chest. "Please don't tell me this is when I find out you actually killed someone." I was joking, but not really.

"I was caught stealing blood from the lab I worked at in New Orleans."

"Why would you steal blood?"

"You know why," he breathed.

"Is the blood really that important?"

He dipped his head. "It happened after I tried to quit the organization the first time. Lacey worked at the same clinic then too. She saw me. She's the one that reported me."

My mind reeled. "What happened to my blood? You said you took the vials to the clinic."

His face flamed, and he shifted his eyes down.

"Did you? Drop it off at the clinic?"

Slowly, he shook his head. "I didn't."

"What did you do with it?"

"I drank it."

"What?" I shot up into a sitting position. "Are you joking? Tell me you're joking."

He lifted his eyes to meet mine. "I'm not joking."

I turned away, clutched my stomach. "You are sick."

"What? You know I do it."

"Yeah, but..." I covered my face. I didn't really want to believe it. It was so perverse, so disgusting. "I kinda feel violated."

He laughed a little. "*That* makes you feel violated? What we've been doing here in the room for the past three days doesn't make you feel violated?"

"No. That was with my consent. You drank my blood without me knowing—without asking me. Doesn't that seem wrong to you?" A flush of anger wove its way through me.

He exhaled. "Okay. I see what you mean. So, yeah, I guess it was a violation. I'm sorry."

"Did you give it to anyone else?"

"No. It was only two vials." He slung his legs off his side of the bed. "But that is one of my roles in The Colony—to help keep the blood bank stocked. That's part of the deal."

"Well, my blood is not part of the deal."

"I get it."

I eyed the scabs on his shoulder, the bruises in the crook of his arm.

"So, why do you have so many cuts and bruises all over you?"

He clapped a hand over what looked like a fresh laceration.

"How does it work? Do you draw your own blood, or does someone else do it?"

"Sometimes I do it, sometimes they do," he said.

"Cassie says they use you as donor a lot."

He nodded.

"So who drinks your blood?"

"Whoever needs it."

"Why would anyone *need* it?" I inhaled slowly. "I mean, it's not like you're really a vampire. It's not a physical need."

"I guess, after a while, it starts to feel like it is."

I didn't like that answer. Was this a fetish or an addiction? "Do you actually take blood from the neck—like vampires in movies?"

"Sometimes. Again, it depends on who it is." He ran his hand over the scabs on his arm. "I'm one of the few who will take blood from the neck. There are a lot of arteries there, so you have to be careful."

"Do you use the needles and vials and stuff?"

He laughed. "No, not in the neck area. Most of the time, I use a lancet, and some of us have special knives."

The box with the ornately carved scalpels. I wrinkled my nose. "What does it taste like? The blood? It can't taste good."

"It depends on the blood." A smile skimmed over his face. "Yours was wonderful."

"Gah." I threw my hand over my mouth and gagged. "It's disgusting." I shoved him in the chest. "I'm just so pissed off with you. Don't ever do that again."

"I won't." Pearse stood and went into the bathroom. Less than a minute later, he was back, holding something between his thumb and forefinger.

"What are you doing?"

He sat on the edge of the bed. "You wanted to know what it tastes like." He ran the edge of a razor blade along his forearm, creating a tiny puncture. Blood immediately welled onto his skin like a glistening drop of red rain. He held it up to me.

I shrank back. "No, no thanks."

"It's only a tiny bit. It won't hurt you. I mean, we've already shared other bodily fluids, so..."

Closing my eyes, I bent down and placed my lips over his skin, drawing the blood into my mouth. It was salty, slightly metallic. But I couldn't say I enjoyed the taste of it.

I pulled away, looked up at him. He ran his thumb over my lips and then kissed me, pressing his tongue against mine.

Pushing at his chest, I disengaged my mouth from his. "How often do you do this?"

"Once a week. Sometimes more."

I raised a hand to my forehead. "This is a lot, Pearse. I'm having trouble with this, I'll be honest. I don't get it."

"I understand."

"I mean, I know I've got problems—the agoraphobia and all that—that's not normal either, but this is just..."

He took my hand and began kissing my fingers.

"And I don't know what to do, Pearse."

"What do you mean?" He murmured against my palm.

"I'm scared," I breathed.

He released my hand and sat back. "You know, I'm scared too. I'm scared because..." He swept his hand up my neck and rested it at the base of my jaw. "You have wrecked me."

"What?"

He shook his head, and his shoulders raised as he took in a long breath. His eyes were like full moons, dilated and impossibly deep. My heart raced.

"I'm in love with you, Avery," he whispered.

I exhaled shakily, fighting the pressure at the backs of my eyes.

"I know—I know this isn't how it was supposed to be. You're supposed to be with Colin, but—"

"I love you too, Pearse."

He looked up at me. "You do?"

"Yes."

He grabbed the back of my head and pulled me forward until my mouth pressed against his collar bone.

"But I'm so afraid that if we leave this room, something horrible is going to happen," I said.

Pearse gently rolled me over and lowered his body on top of me, kissing my forehead, my eyes, my face. "I'm not going to let anything happen to you."

I nudged him back. "How can you promise that? You can't promise that. Especially not if you're in jail. This is serious. We need help."

"I know." He sat up, circled my wrists with his hands, and lugged me into a sitting position. "Maybe we'll just jump on the next plane out of town and go. Start over. Sound good?"

It sounded amazing. Only right then, it sounded impossible.

Chapter Fifty-Two

Nearly lifeless bodies are easy vessels to infiltrate. In the moments when they hover between life and death, their will is not their own.

Two nights ago, we divided our forces. Some of us traveled with Maris, and some of us entered the eighteen-year-old runaway, Greer Bennett.

Greer has been living on the streets of Asheville for over a year, ever since her mother's boyfriend started raping her. Life is safer in the shelters or under the bridge than in her own bedroom.

When a man named Torin approached her outside Odd Bods one night, offering her food, a place to stay, and a job if she wanted one, she took him up on the offer. Three days and nights followed of expensive meals, motel-room sex, and early morning cash left on the bedside table, with which she was instructed to buy new clothes and whatever she needed. Greer knew this was how prostitutes lived. But after fourteen months of exposure to extreme hot and cold, starvation, and fending off dirty, crazy men with beards full of lice and breath that smelled like a sewage drain, this life didn't seem so bad. Torin was young, good-looking, and he worked at the hospital. What more could she ask for?

The third night, however, Torin returned to the motel room wearing a long cape and fake teeth. He'd told her he was a vampire—not the undead kind, of course, but the sort that chose this lifestyle. He told her about all of the benefits—a network of friends always looking out for you. Money, never a problem. Food and housing? Always provided. But she would need to be initiated.

She would need to show her loyalty to them before they would accept her.

It had seemed easy enough. But Greer hadn't realized that there'd be such a high price to pay for membership. Torin had told her some of her blood would be required. She just hadn't realized how much. She hadn't expected to touch the brink of death.

Now, in the hospital, in protective police custody after giving a of the man who'd drained her blood—as well as a full account of the man who had put her up in a motel room for three nights—Greer talks to nurses who insist on taking more of her blood every few hours. She tells them about the sheets in the motel—how nice they were and how she'd come to love the man who'd called himself Torin. And how, even now, after everything, if he turned up at her bedside, she would still want to be his.

One of us has a firm hold of her head, pressing it between our palms, squeezing the memories of her night of terror from her mind so that all she can think about is her love for Torin.

Another one of us presses a finger to her eyes, stirring and addling her brain until she is riddled with fear and anxiety. We clamp onto her neck and suction all peace, all joy, all hope of a future. We breathe despair into her mouth.

When the male and female detectives return to gather more details, Greer suddenly has a new story.

"I lied."

The male detective cocks his head. "What do you mean you lied?"

"I was angry at Torin because I thought he was going to leave me. So I made up the story about what they did to me. It was all consensual. I asked them to take my blood. Things just got a little out of control."

The detective's face clouds over. His mouth tightens, twitches. "Greer, no one *asks* to have that done to them. They left you for dead. There were coins on both of your eyes."

We all laugh at him.

"It was a joke."

"This is bullshit, Greer," Mears says. "And I'm not buying it."

"Don't care," says Greer. "It's what happened."

Stoney's face reddens. "Why are you doing this?"

Mears steps forward, her jaw clenching. "We know what happened to you, Greer. And even if you did ask someone to do it, they still committed a criminal act. They should be held responsible. Pearse Gallagher should pay for what he did to you."

The girl shakes her head, and her voice takes on a shrill, panicked tone. "No, no. I wanted to die, don't you understand?"

"Why did you want to die? Why that way?"

"I didn't care how it happened. I just didn't want to live without Torin. I knew he was going to leave me."

The male looks desperate. He repeatedly wipes at his mouth and nose with a handkerchief. "Look, Miss Bennett, we understand that you're scared. But these are bad people. You've got to know that. And we need your testimony to put them away."

She swings her head back and forth. "I won't. I can't."

The detectives leave the room.

"One of them must have gotten to her. Changed her mind," says Stoney.

"Doesn't matter," says Mears. "We're still going after them."

"It'll be hard without her cooperation."

We kick the door shut behind them and cackle.

Chapter Fifty-Three
Friday, February 14

It seemed like a million years had passed since I'd last been at Whickering Place.

Ada had called and left a message that morning about the broken window—the one I'd shot out three days before. She wanted to make sure I knew.

Was that all? I half-expected to find the front door crowbarred, the house ransacked.

I called her back to tell her I knew. It was okay to clean up the glass.

By the time we got back to the house that morning, Ada and the cleaners had already been there—the telltale smells of the pine cleanser lingered in the air. The glass in the hallway had been cleared, a square patch of cardboard taped over the hole.

Nothing was out of place. The phantom phone sat on the table. The glass of water I'd been drinking the night we left was still sitting on the counter in the kitchen.

But the gun on the mantel was gone.

"No!" I shrieked.

"What? What is it?" Pearse asked.

"My gun," I panted as I lifted pillows, seat cushions. "It's gone."

"Where did you leave it?"

"Here. On the mantel." I scurried to the couch, dropped to my knees, and ran my hands over the rubbery bottom of the empty gun safe. I upended my purse and sifted through remnants of my three-day honeymoon. Receipts. Pillow mints. A protein bar.

Doing what probably looked like modified push-ups on the floor, I scrutinized every space under every chair, table, and carpet. I dug through couch cushions, shook out throw blankets, felt up my laundry bag, peered over ledges of high chests of drawers. I checked my bedroom, Pearse's. Even Colin's. It was nowhere.

The gun had simply vanished.

"Shit!" I screamed. I smacked my back against the wall by the staircase and slid down until I sat on the bottom step. "I am so stupid!" I covered my face with my hands, the tears stinging my eyes. "I left it sitting out. With a broken window in the house. With housecleaners coming in. Anyone could've taken it."

Pearse stood at the bottom of the stairs, grasping the banister. "Are you sure it's gone?"

"Yes," I wailed into my hands. "I've checked everywhere."

Ada hadn't mentioned it. I would call her back. If she hadn't seen it, that would be a good indication of how long it had been missing.

Our phones were where we'd left them—in a drawer in the kitchen.

I scrolled through the list of missed texts—one from my mother, three from Colin. Ugh. I'd missed a call from Dr. Murphy. And a voicemail message from Michel Babineau informed me that the new deed had been successfully filed with the Register of Deeds. One problem solved.

Then I phoned Ada.

"Missed you this morning, honey," she said.

"Ada, did you see a gun on the fireplace mantel?"

"A gun? Lord have mercy, honey, if I'd seen a gun, I probably would've sent my team outta the house."

Now I felt even worse. I'd practically accused Ada and her crew of stealing my gun.

"Although," she said, "I don't blame you for having one in that house."

I grabbed for the ends of my hair and then remembered that it wasn't hanging around my waist anymore. I couldn't twist it around my fists. "Yeah, well, I was an idiot and didn't put it back in the safe, and now it's gone."

Ada clucked. "Oh, honey. Call the police. File a report."

But I couldn't. The gun wasn't registered to me. It had been my uncle's, and that would just open up another box of problems.

"What about that broken window? Could someone have reached through and unlocked the back door?"

"No, the window was too high up. But thank you for cleaning up the glass."

"House was freezing cold this morning. I patched it best I could, but you'll need to get that fixed."

"Yep, thanks."

I disconnected the call. Dread, fear, anxiety—all of them clawed at my throat, poured acid into my stomach. Ada hadn't taken my gun—of course she hadn't. But plenty of other people could have.

I crushed my face with my hand. Maris had a key. I'd never gotten the locks changed. Any of them could have come in here over the last three days and taken it. It was just sitting out there—on display.

Pearse found me in the kitchen. He slid his hands around my waist and pulled me against his chest.

"Maybe I should call the police about the gun," I said.

I felt him tense.

"But I know I can't call them."

"Maybe it'll turn up."

"Yeah, in Torin's hands when he comes here to kill us both."

Pearse pulled me closer. "Guns really aren't The Colony's style."

I wished that gave me comfort.

"Babe, I have to go out for a little while," he whispered against my ear.

I spun around. "No. Where are you going?"

"I don't want you to worry."

"I am worried. Tell me where you're going."

He leaned forward and pressed his lips to mine. I clutched the fabric of his shirt in both of my fists, prepared to hold him there. When he pulled back, he wrapped his hands around my wrists. "I'll be back, Avery. I don't know when exactly, but I'll be back."

"Please, please don't." I hated the desperation in my voice.

"I got a message from them. They want to talk."

"Talk about what?"

He slid his hands up my arms to my shoulders. "Probably about you. And Whickering Place. And maybe they want to find out what kind of access to the house we'll give them. We may need to let them in for a while, let them have their events here ... at least until we can make a plan, figure out what we're going to do."

I exhaled through my nose. "At least tell me where you're going."

He closed his eyes, pressed his forehead against mine. "I don't know."

The tears rolled. I couldn't stop them.

"I'll be okay," he breathed.

"*I* won't be okay if anything happens to you."

He reached up and brushed hair from my face. "Yeah, you will."

Chapter Fifty-Four

A s Pearse was about to leave, the doorbell gonged.
I peered through the keyhole.

Detective Mears and two uniformed police officers.

Shit. What choice did I have? I opened the door.

"Hey, Avery." Detective Mears's pale aqua eyes stared at me from the other side. "Pearse here?"

"He's—" My voice failed, and I had to force sound from my throat. "He's here."

Pearse's sleeve brushed against my arm. "What's going on?"

Detective Mears's thin mouth flattened, and she unfolded a piece of paper. "Pearse Gallagher? We have a warrant for your arrest."

Had the floor dropped? I placed a hand to the wall beside me, anchoring my stance.

Detective Mears and the officers pushed into the house. Pearse held up his hands.

One of the uniformed officers produced cuffs and moved behind him, grabbing one arm and wrenching it behind his back.

The muscles in Pearse's face tightened.

Mears stopped a few feet in front of him. "Pearse Gallagher, we're arresting you on suspicion of attempted murder. You have the right to remain silent. Anything you say can and will be used against you in a court of law."

Everything slowed, blurred—frame by frame, second by second.

The officers led Pearse toward the door, Mears behind them.

I trailed and babbled questions. Where are you taking him? What can I do?

As they led him outside, Pearse twisted around. "It's okay. Don't worry, Avery. I'll be all right. I'll be home soon."

Words that bounced off of me.

Unmoving, I stared at his back as they led him through the door and out to the waiting patrol car, where they folded him into the police cruiser, pushing down his head as he climbed inside. Then they drove away.

PEARSE HAD BEEN GONE for three hours.

My mind flip-flopped between what had happened to my gun and what was happening to Pearse.

I called Michel Babineau and asked for a referral for a criminal attorney. Pearse was going to need one. Babineau had a lawyer friend who practiced criminal law, and he gave me his number. After a half-hour phone conversation and a credit card number, Sean Forceps—what a name—promised me he would take a trip to the Buncombe County Detention Center that afternoon.

I spent the rest of the evening sending emails out to clients, apologizing for missing deadlines, extending deadlines. Then I tried to work. Unsuccessfully. My mind was too full. My thoughts wouldn't rest.

I'd plunged into this new life—without a thought, without any real consideration for the consequences. It was unlike me. And maybe that's what had made it so thrilling. But now, reality set in. I didn't know who to trust. If something happened to Pearse, I would be on my own in this mess, scrambling to figure out who to call, where to turn, how to go on.

Without my gun.

I took a Xanax and waited for it to kick in.

Dr. Murphy had always been my rock and my confidante in times of crisis, but my life had never been on the line before. I didn't even know how to begin telling her what had happened—how things had changed so drastically in a few short weeks. She'd probably think I'd lost it. She'd want to increase my medication. She'd want to talk about how I was feeling and why and dissect every little nuance.

I wasn't in the mood for that.

After three days of adrenaline and Pearse and an environment that was blissfully different from this one, I was alone again. A decade of sitting inside on self-imposed house arrest had pretty much thinned out my support system. Now, I couldn't even find solace in talking to Dr. Murphy.

I stopped in front of the hall mirror, examining myself, trying to see if I really did look different.

Not really.

My hair was shorter. But I still looked like that haunted girl that couldn't leave the house for fear of disaster striking. Except now, I'd walked directly into disaster. I'd married it.

And then, I saw her.

Me.

Standing behind me in the mirror. Looking right at me. The me with long hair to my waist, no makeup, the sweatshirt from Orlando. The image walked out of the shadows, slowly materializing in the glass as a solid form.

A shriek tore from my throat as I spun around, but the air beside me was comprised of shadows and nothing more.

When I turned back to the mirror, the image was gone.

But a voice from somewhere in the house echoed through the hallway and called out, "Avery." Neither male nor female. A counterfeit sample of a human voice.

I clasped the cross hanging from my neck. "Leave me alone."

Laughter, low and sinister, rolled across the ceiling and vibrated down the walls.

Throwing my hands over my ears and bolting into the front room, I grabbed the remote and turned on the television. Then I pressed the volume button and allowed the sound to escalate and drown out all noises, voices.

Breathing hard, I sank onto the couch, glanced around the room, and watched the shadows grow long and dark as the day wore on. There was nowhere to run to escape them.

HOURS PASSED FILLED with mindless television, wall-staring, floor-pacing.

It was after seven, and I still hadn't heard from Pearse. Or his attorney.

The sound of metal prodding the keyhole and the creak of the front door shifted my heart into overdrive and brought me to my feet.

Springing up, I rushed into the foyer. "Pearse?"

Long wool coat. Short hair. A wrapped container of roses in his hand. Colin.

My heart dipped. He wasn't supposed to be home for another week.

A rush of disappointment and fear flooded me, and as emotion took over, my face crumpled into itself. Through tear-blurred eyes, I watched Colin drop his bags, lay the roses on top of them, and catapult toward me.

"What's wrong? What's happened?"

"What are you doing home?" My voice shrilled.

"Pearse called me yesterday. He said he thought you'd need me here. I got an earlier flight."

I couldn't speak. My mouth hung open. Sobs wracked my insides.

"What? What is it?"

I was beyond all pretense now. So far beyond it. "Pearse is in jail."

COLIN WAS CONFUSED. I could see it in his face as we sat together in the kitchen. While he drank strong, black coffee, I sipped the off-brand chamomile tea the grocery had delivered last week.

"I can't say I'm surprised, Avery," he said. "I mean, with the way he's been acting recently, it was kind of inevitable." He reached across the table, put his hand over mine. "I'm more concerned about you. Pearse was really worried about you when he called me."

"I'm fine," I whisper.

But my mind churned. Pearse had called Colin before he was arrested. He would only have asked Colin to come home in the case of an emergency. He must have thought something was going to happen to him—that there would be retribution—and that I'd need his brother around to pick up the pieces.

Now what? Colin probably wondered why I was less than enthusiastic about his surprise homecoming. And why I'd burst into tears about Pearse's arrest.

I could feel his eyes on me.

"Did *you* do that to your hair?"

Instinctively I raised my hand, smoothed a lock behind my ear. "Yeah. I mean, no. I got it cut."

"Why?"

I wasn't sure what to tell him. I knew how much he'd liked my ridiculously long hair. "It was annoying me. It was starting to feel like a shroud."

"Hm."

Obviously, he hated it.

He swilled his coffee.

With my eyes, I circumnavigated the kitchen. The roses Colin had brought me were now in a vase of water on the counter. Just the sight of them made my stomach buck.

"The flowers are nice."

"Well, it *is* Valentine's Day."

I exhaled. This was too awful.

"That was nice of you. Thanks." *He should know. I should tell him.*

"I didn't realize how bad things were here. Or what had been happening in this house," Colin said in a low voice. Then he swept his hand away from mine and sat back. "Avery, would you please tell me what the hell is going on? Do you know why Pearse was arrested? What are the charges? Was it drugs?"

"No. Attempted murder."

"What?" he hissed.

"Have you heard of a cult called The Colony?"

He shook his head.

I gave Colin a brief run-down on The Colony's practices, their beliefs, and then I told him the police had linked them to the local murders. And to Pearse.

"Pearse is a member of The Colony."

"Do you know that for sure?"

"Yes. He told me."

Colin rubbed a hand over his lower jaw. "I knew he was involved in something like this. I just didn't know how bad it was."

"He wants out."

"Out?"

"Pearse. He wants out of The Colony. He's not like them. He doesn't want to hurt anyone."

Colin's eyes hardened. "That night, when you asked me if he was dangerous, I should've told Pearse to leave then." He shook his head.

"And I should never have gone on this trip and left you alone with him."

He'd obviously launched into full-protection mode. And oh, how I dreaded telling him the truth. "I can take care of myself, Colin."

"Have you read about these murders? What the killer is doing to these people? Draining their blood to the point of death. Cutting their throats. Slashing wrists. I mean, they're serial killers." He compressed his mouth. "I just can't believe Pearse is one of them."

"He's not," I said quickly. "He's not a killer. He doesn't want to be involved with any of them."

"Well, he is involved."

"That's why he left New Orleans. To get away from them. But they won't let him go."

Colin's eyes narrowed, his mouth hanging like a broken gate. "Avery, Pearse isn't a teenager. He's certainly old enough to make his own choices and suffer the consequences."

We lapsed into silence. I focused on the sound of freezing rain outside—strangely soothing. I began to count the clatters. One, two, three...

He should know. "Colin."

He looked up at me. Passed a hand through his hair. The gesture reminded me of Pearse. When I first noticed Pearse doing it, it had reminded me of Colin.

"Something has happened. Something big."

"Something bigger than what I just learned about Pearse tonight?" Colin's eyes settled on me like a lead weight.

I nodded. "Yeah. This has to do with Pearse too." I cleared my throat. "And me."

"You and Pearse?"

My voice shrank away. "Yes."

"Did he ... did he touch you?"

"You could say that." I took a deep breath. "We ... um..." I dropped my gaze, shifted in the chair.

"Oh, shit."

I looked up at him.

"Please do *not* tell me you slept with him."

Closing my eyes, I blurted the words, "We're kind of married."

"What?" He laughed a little, but within seconds, his expression morphed from mild amusement to wide-eyed disbelief and then horror. His tongue darted over his lips.

"It was a snap decision, really. I just wanted to help him."

I jabbered the story quickly, gunning my words, ripping off the Band-Aid, trying to explain something I barely understood. But as I drew my gaze up to his, I saw the realization dawning.

"That was how it started. And then things snowballed."

His face became unreadable. Then he rested against the counter, grasping the edge, his eyes downcast.

"I don't understand," he said quietly. "Why didn't you just call the police?"

"Some of the police are involved. We don't know who to trust."

"We." He looked at the floor.

I clenched my fingers, twisted them. "I'm sorry, Colin," I whispered.

"When were you going to tell me?"

Now, obviously. "I—we didn't really have a plan."

"This sounds insane. You know that, don't you?"

I nodded.

"Avery, why would you do this? After what we had? Help me understand because I really, really don't. I mean, the way you've explained it, it sounds like you married him because you were looking for a charity case or something. What's happened to you? And—and, I mean..." He stopped, slung his hand over the back of his neck.

"I don't know what to say, Colin."

"There's nothing to say."

Pushing the chair back, I stood. "Everything just happened really fast, and on the drive to Flat Rock, I realized how out of control everything was."

He jerked his head up and met my eyes. "On the drive to Flat Rock? So, you can leave the house now?"

"Well, we had to leave for a few days and stay in a hotel, so..." I trailed off. I was making it worse.

"I mean ... shit." His mouth hung open a little, and he exorcised a breath. "I guess sex cures agoraphobia. Who knew?"

I winced. "I'm so sorry."

"Were you always attracted to him? Pearse?"

"Yes."

"Even when we were together?"

I shut my eyes tight and nodded.

When I opened them again, he was staring at me. His lip curled. "I should've known."

Somehow I needed to make it better, needed to restore his respect for me. I didn't want him to think I'd just had sex with Pearse or that I was a stalker like Lacey. "But now, I mean," I held out my hands helplessly, "now, I love him."

"You love him." Stark, raw pain raked his features. "Does he love you?"

"He says he does."

A muscle in his jaw twitched. "Well, why wouldn't he?"

The tension hung between us in prolonged silence.

"I know what you must think."

Colin shook his head, backing out of the room. "I don't think you do, Avery. You can't possibly know what is going through my mind right now. But I'll tell you this." He pointed his finger at me. "I think you've made the biggest damn mistake of your life."

Chapter Fifty-Five
Saturday, February 15

I'd fallen asleep in the early hours of the morning while lying in Pearse's bed—now my bed as well, I reminded myself.

But the sounds overhead had awakened me. For a few seconds, I lay there and listened. They hardly even bothered me now.

I swiped my cell phone off the nightstand to check for messages. A voicemail from Forceps, Pearse's attorney, glared at me from the screen. I'd missed his call.

"Damn!"

I sat up and quickly played the message.

"Hi Avery, this is Sean Forceps, Pearse's attorney. This doesn't happen very often, but the charges against your husband have been dropped. DA's not going to prosecute. I'll return the remainder of your retainer to you within the next few days. But if you need my services again, just give me a call."

I wanted to feel relief. Instead, I wondered why. What was the catch? Because there had to be one. I didn't trust that this was just a case of good luck. This could be like one of those movies where the mafia boss tells the guy he's free to go, only to shoot him in the back as he walks away.

And why hadn't Pearse called me?

I wanted to call Forceps, ask him if he had any more information as to why they weren't prosecuting Pearse. But in the end, it didn't matter. He would be released. He would come home.

Flopping back onto the mattress, I choked out a throaty sob. My cry reverberated off the ceiling. A cloud of dread settled over me, pressing down on my chest. What was The Colony planning now? Should I prepare myself for the worst?

The bedroom door floated open with only a small cry from the hinges.

I shot up from the waist, my eyes wrenched open, and I stared into the darkness so intently my ocular nerve ached.

Someone stood in the doorway.

"Pearse?"

No response. No movement. Although the silhouette looked like Pearse.

But then a prickly sensation swept up my spine. A few weeks ago, Pearse had told me about the figure in the doorway that looked like me. The girl who'd stood beside me in the mirror last night.

The entities. They could mimic us.

The phone in the hall rang. Its insistent clang—shrill, tinny—screaming at me to answer it. I fumbled with the lamp on the nightstand. The room flooded with light, and when I looked up again, the figure in the doorway was gone.

Flinging back the sheets, I thrust my feet out, leaped from the bed, and padded down the hall toward the phone. I didn't hesitate but snatched up the receiver, my hands shaking as I held it close to my face.

The voice was clear and sharp. "She's still here." It was followed by the loudest static I've ever heard, forcing me to yank the earpiece away.

I picked up the entire phone and hurled it, screaming at the top of my lungs. As I watched the base and cord slam against the wall, knocking a chunk from the molding, the phone clattered to the ground. Even from several feet away, I could still hear the static—and the voice—repeating the phrase over and over, "She's still here."

Chapter Fifty-Six
Saturday, February 15

Who was still here? Me? The succubus?

My head ached as I sat on the edge of the bed, staring at the wall of boxes that held Pearse's medical supplies. I could hear Colin in the next room. He'd been packing all day. Early this morning I'd awakened him with my scream. He'd come out of his room, checked to make sure I was okay. I'd told him I was. I'd had a bad dream. Then I told him they'd dropped the charges. Pearse would be coming home. At least, I thought he would.

"I'm going to find somewhere else to stay," he'd said before going back into his room.

It was for the best, of course. I couldn't expect Colin to live with us—watch us, hear us—all right under his nose.

I just wished Pearse would come home so I could stop worrying, get rid of this ache in my chest. How long did it take to be released from jail? Hadn't they given him his phone back yet? Where was he?

And once he was home, how long would we have to stay at Whickering Place? How long before we could sell this place and all of its demons and ghosts and bloody ringing telephones? I'd left the phone on the floor, the cord twisted around the handle of the receiver, attempting to strangle it.

I could pack up too. But no, I had to stay, had to pretend I was in control.

Maybe I should call Dr. Murphy. Except I didn't want to talk to her. I'd have to tell her everything. When I played the words in my head, I cringed—they sounded like the bleating of a sad, lonely woman who'd married a man out of desperation. Like those women who married men on death row. A Ted Bundy groupie.

At three o'clock, I dragged myself from the bed, threw on a dirty sweatshirt and jeans, and swept my hair into a ponytail. Then I opened the blinds. Outside, the bushes were tipped with ice, and a light dusting of snow flittered down from a gray sky. I was cold. And hungry. And too shit-scared to leave the room for food. I might've run into Colin. I just couldn't face him.

The doorbell rang.

I waited, hoped Colin would get it.

He didn't.

I cracked open the door.

"Are you going to get that?" he called from his room.

I trudged down the hall, braced my hands against the front door, and stood on tip-toes to peer out the peephole.

Maris.

No. This couldn't be happening.

"I know you're there, Avery."

I closed my eyes. "I'm busy right now, Maris."

"So am I, but I need to talk to you."

What could she possibly need to talk to me about? I knew everything, and she must've been aware of that. "What do you want?"

"I want to talk."

I stepped back from the door and stared at it, trying to decide what to do. "About what?"

"About Pearse."

"Where is he?" The question was instinctive. Maris had information.

"He'll be home soon."

With a deep breath, I tugged open the door.

Maris stood, her head cocked to the side, void of her usual smug smile. Void even of her typical red lipstick and heavy makeup. She looked deceptively young and vulnerable.

She held up a white shopping bag with black handles, the store name written in a swirly and unreadable font. "I brought you a gift."

A gift? The last thing I wanted was a gift from her. But I swung the door back and stepped out of the way. She was coming in anyway. I couldn't stop her.

"Well, Avery." She spoke my name like a school teacher calling down a pupil.

Thankful I'd taken my full dosage of meds, I clenched the edge of the door and tried to match her tone. "Maris."

This was the first time we'd met since the night she brought Torin and Ian here. Since the absinthe. The aura between us felt different now. I looked at her and saw a murderer. Someone who'd planned to kill me. A woman who'd orchestrated the death of others and so far had gotten away with it.

"Aren't you full of surprises?" Maris's hair draped over her shoulders. She tucked one curtain of pale gold behind her ear. "I never pegged Pearse for the marrying type. But then again, he's certainly not the most predictable of characters."

I lifted my chin, crossed my arms. *Speak to her as little as possible.*

She nodded, pursed her lips. "Anyway, he'll be home sometime today."

"Where is he now?" I couldn't trust her, but her words sent a shockwave of relief through my veins. At least they hadn't killed him.

She held up the carrier bag and marched past me and down the hall. "Right now, you should be showing a little gratitude, I think."

She marched into Pearse's bedroom, and I followed her.

She threw the bag onto the bed and pivoted, hands on hips, her eyes darting side to side. "I figured you would've done a little redecorating by now. It's very dark in here."

Colin's door banged shut. Luggage wheels whirred across the tile floor as he carted out his stuff.

Maris raised her eyebrows. "Sounds like Dr. Gallagher is back." She dumped a rectangular box out of the bag. "I'll bet he was the first to congratulate you on your nuptials." She raised the lid, revealing candy-apple-red satin.

I clenched my teeth as she lifted the dress out of the box and let the folds drop to the floor. "You see, Avery, I actually think you should be kissing my feet right now. The Colony is the difference between a prison sentence and exoneration. We could've let Pearse languish in jail, could've brought twelve witnesses to testify against him and say they saw him bleed that girl to the point of death." She laid the dress across the bed. "But lucky for him, the girl had a change of heart. She didn't want to testify. Made it easy for us."

"He never wanted any part of that. You made him do it."

"Perhaps. But he had choices."

"Choiceless choices."

Maris turned toward me, her eye contact direct, probing. "You must be under the delusion that your husband is a victim. Do you really think he's some squeaky-clean guy who was at the wrong place at the wrong time?" The corners of her mouth twitched. "Oh, Avery, we have plenty we could use against him. This isn't the first of Pearse's sins."

I swallowed. "I know about the stolen blood from the lab in New Orleans."

She snorted. "Oh, is that what he told you?"

I held my breath and braced myself.

"So, I guess he didn't tell you about the girl in St. Roch cemetery? He didn't even bother with the needle for her. Took some covering up. Luckily, she was just another runaway. No one really tried too hard to find her."

My chin and lips trembled.

Maris reached out and grabbed my shoulder, her fingernails digging into my flesh as her brows knitted. "Oh, sweetie. I know this must be hard to hear. I mean, he popped your cherry, and now you think you're in love with him. It's hard to imagine him as a cold-blooded killer, isn't it?"

I leveled my gaze on Maris and tried not to visibly shudder as my mind reeled.

She swiveled back to the dress and ran her fingers across the satin. "I wish I could've had someone like Pearse to break me in. My first time was a fast and furious romp in my boyfriend's garage. We couldn't go inside because his father was an alcoholic, always home, and owned at least forty-five different types of hunting knives." She wrenched her lips back in a bitter smile. "The whole thing took about thirty-five seconds. I'm sure Pearse took his time with you. He's like that."

Saliva pooled in my mouth. I wanted to spit. Or throw up.

Maris sat on the edge of the bed, pulling the fabric of the dress over her legs. "But the thing is, Avery, I really hope it *was* good with Pearse. I hope it was worth it. Because he's going to have to pay for it. He was disobedient, and that's one thing we don't tolerate in The Colony."

I swallowed hard. "What do you mean?"

She sat back, braced her hands behind her, exhaled. "We've agreed to recognize you both as owners of Whickering Place, and Pearse will be elevated to regional leader. But not before he's been reprimanded for his sins."

"He did it to save me," I said, hearing how weak the words sounded against Maris's calm, logical argument.

She nodded. "Yes, but actions have consequences. He'll take his punishment, and then he'll come home."

"What does that mean?"

She stood and approached me. "You'll understand what I mean once he returns." Eyeing me, she ran her fingernail under my chin. "You know what? I think you're the weak link. Pearse will fall in line—he knows better than to stir the shit pot. But you," she shook her head. "I just don't know about you. We can't trust you." The corners of her mouth inched into a smile.

I took a step back.

"Anyway," she spun around. "This dress is yours. For the new moon gathering on the twenty-third. As the owner of Whickering Place, you'll need to dress the part, you and Pearse. And knowing your issues about leaving the house, I took it upon myself to pick something out for you. I'd like you to try it on, so if it doesn't fit, I can exchange it before then."

I stared at the yards of fabric that made up the skirt. If I didn't trip over it and break my neck, it would be a miracle. But maybe that was what Maris was hoping.

The top was a fitted red bodice with a black lace overlay that formed an ornate off-the-shoulder style with long sleeves. I'd never seen anything like it. I'd certainly never think to wear anything like it. "Red isn't my color."

Maris's eyes darkened as they moved up and down my body. "What? Would you rather wear your usual frumpy attire? Jeans and a sweatshirt? Red is symbolic of power. Of fire. And I think we both know there's a tiny bit of fire in you somewhere—dim as it may be." She lifted the dress and gave it a little shake. "Try it on."

She tossed it toward me and I caught it, grasping the lacey bodice.

"Be sure you wear this too." Maris dangled a mask from a band of elastic. It was the face of an animal with a black, slightly elongated nose. Then she dropped it in the carrier bag.

"I'll try on the dress later."

"Now," she said.

Gritting my teeth and hating that I'd given in so easily, I carried the dress into the bathroom, the long skirts dragging at my side.

"Still so modest," I heard her say as I closed the door behind me.

I took several deep breaths, my heart pounding with adrenaline. I stripped off my jeans and sweatshirt. Then I unzipped the back and stepped into the center of it, pulled it up around me, and slid my wrists into the delicate lace of the arms. Reaching around, I worked the zipper up over my tailbone to the small of my back—that was as far as I could reach. I smoothed the satin skirt over my hips. The dress clung to all the right places.

As I stared into the mirror in the bathroom, I didn't want to like the dress. But the red actually suited me. If circumstances had been different...

The knock on the door made me jump. I needed to be on my guard at all times with her in the house. I didn't have my gun. I was at her mercy.

Maris pushed the door open. "Do you need me to help with the zipper?"

"It's all right. I get the gist of it without zipping it up. It fits."

She moved around to the back of me. Her cold fingers brushed the skin of my spine as the zipper whirred.

Grasping my shoulder, she turned me around to face her. My fingers twitched, and I nearly drew up my arm to smack her hand away.

She raked her gaze down the front of the dress. "Your father would have approved."

I dug my fingernails into the palms of my hands, willing her to go. Maris seemed to know exactly how to use my father to throw me off balance.

She turned, swinging the bedroom door wide as she went.

In the foyer, two suitcases and a duffle bag sat by the door.

Maris's eyes trailed over the luggage. "Looks like Dr. Gallagher isn't sticking around to watch the plot unfold." Then her gaze fell on me. "You should probably ask him not to rush off. Pearse might need a doctor."

"What? Why?" My stomach tightened.

She produced a cell phone and began moving her fingers across the screen.

Wait. That's my phone. I'd left it in the bedroom while I'd tried on the dress.

"What are you doing? That's mine."

"I know. I'm putting an address into your GPS." She handed it back to me. "Follow it. That's where you'll find Pearse."

Chapter Fifty-Seven

I intercepted Colin as he lifted his suitcases and prepared to carry them outside.

"I need help."

"What?" he groaned.

Another moment in time, I might've been more concerned about his broken heart, might've given him some space. But not now. Even so, the words didn't come easily.

"What?" he asked again.

"It's Pearse. I have to drive out somewhere to pick him up. And I think he's going to need a doctor."

"Why?"

"I don't know. But it was suggested to me that he might."

Colin dropped the suitcases and straightened. "He's your problem now. Not mine."

I didn't move. I stared at him. What else could I do? My heartbeat was erratic, and I could feel it everywhere—my throat, my temples, behind my eyes.

Then Colin turned his face to the ceiling and exhaled a growl. "I'm so tired of cleaning up his shit."

AS WE NEARED BLACK Mountain, the GPS said to take the exit. Colin turned off the highway and wound through night construction and an obstacle course of cones and bright lights and traffic merges before ending up on a dark, winding backroad. I stared out the window as we passed signs for a maintenance facility. Soon after, the streetlights disappeared, plunging the landscape into darkness.

Colin had been silent the whole way. I blinked frantically, forcing my lashes to beat back the tears, listening to the thumping of the tires over rough roads.

"Pearse is out here?" he asked.

"I guess."

"What is he doing out here in the middle of nowhere at night?"

"This is the address I was given."

"By whom?"

I didn't want to say. That would only complicate things. Colin would want to act, call the police.

"Turn right," the cheerful GPS voice directed.

Colin took a hard right down a gravel road, which ended in a clearing. He flicked on the high beams, illuminating the outline of winter trees and a backdrop of inky woods.

In the middle of the setting, a lone figure sat on a tree stump. He lifted his head slowly and stared into the headlights.

Pearse. He was alive. Although he seemed dazed. He didn't rise from the stump or move at all.

Scrambling out of the car, I marched with a single purpose—my jeans rustling in the weeds, my breath erupting in uneven, smoky puffs around my face. The beam of the headlights forged a path, and I followed it, several strides ahead of Colin.

When I was within a few feet of him, Pearse raised up slowly, using his hand to balance and then push off from the tree stump. As he straightened, his leather jacket fell open, revealing a blood-drenched shirt.

I grabbed the front of his leather jacket and attempted to hold him up as he teetered.

My mind grappled to understand what I was seeing. "What's happened to you? What've they done to you?"

Colin rushed forward and bumped me out of the way. "I've got him."

"Don't touch me," Pearse called out, his voice breaking with pain.

"Sorry, bro," Colin said, straining as he threw Pearse's arm over his shoulder. "Gotta touch you to get you in the car."

Pearse hissed a sharp intake of air through his teeth as Colin helped him into the backseat.

I fell into the backseat beside him while Colin climbed into the front and hit the overhead car light. "Pull up his shirt."

My stomach rolled as I separated the buttons on his blood-drenched flannel, then pulled up his T-shirt. Underneath was a dark, wet mass of blood.

I remembered the first night I'd seen this. The night of the absinthe when Pearse's shirt had been stained. But that had been a small wound—nothing compared to this. As far as I could tell, he was slathered in blood, front and back.

"We need to get you to the hospital," Colin stated.

"No," Pearse groaned. "No hospital. Just get me home."

I shuddered. "Colin, please help—he's really hurt."

Colin twisted around in the seat. "We need to get him to the hospital, Avery. That's it."

"No. You can't take me to the hospital."

Colin raised his voice. "Look, you've lost a lot of blood. Worst case scenario, you might need a transfusion. Best? You'll need stitches. Those wounds could get infected."

Pearse raised his head. "You're a doctor, Colin. Can't you help me? I'm telling you. I can't go to the hospital."

Anxiety filled my lungs until I couldn't get a full breath. "Can you help him, Colin?"

Colin turned back toward the steering wheel. "I don't know. I'll have to look at him when we get back to the house and see what I can do." He shifted the car into drive.

In the dark, I couldn't see the individual cuts, but there didn't seem to be an inch of him that wasn't smeared in dark red gore. When my hand brushed Pearse's side, he jerked away, and my fingers slid across the sticky wounds.

Colin glanced up into the rearview mirror. "What happened to you?"

"Let's just get home," Pearse groaned.

Colin weaved down the path, backtracking to the entrance of the maintenance facility.

As we returned to the city lights of Asheville and flashes of passing streetlamps highlighted the interior of the car, I gaped at my hands. They looked as though I'd immersed my palms and wrists in vats of blood. Past images reeled through my mind.

Blood dripping from my fingers. Vince lying on the ground.

By the time we arrived home, I wasn't sure Pearse hadn't passed out. But we managed to get him inside. In the bright light of Whickering Place's foyer, Pearse's appearance was shocking. His flannel shirt was soaked, along with the top of his jeans. Even his boots were spotted with gore. I grasped his hand, and my fingers slid against the blood.

"Let's get him to the bedroom." Colin propelled him forward, down the hall, and through the door. Pearse wavered at the foot of his bed until he finally sank down on the edge, wincing.

"I'll be all right. Just help me get the jacket off."

How had he gotten it back on in the first place? The pain must have been excruciating. Crawling behind him, I grasped the collar of his leather jacket, pulling it away from his shoulders. The back of his flannel was black with blood.

Colin started to lift the material of Pearse's shirt, but some of the blood had dried, and the fabric stuck to the wounds.

"We'll need to get the shirt wet before we can get it off of him." Colin bent over and began removing Pearse's boots. "Let's get him in the shower."

Colin and I both took off our socks and shoes. Then we helped Pearse to his feet and walked him into the bathroom. After stripping off his jeans, we stood beside him under the showerhead as it rained lukewarm water over our hands, arms, torsos.

I'd never really understood the idea of someone's skin turning green, but Pearse's pallor fit that description. As soon as the spray hit his back, he exhaled a string of curses and braced his hands against the tile. Within seconds, deep maroon water swirled around our feet.

When Pearse's shirt was thoroughly saturated, Colin began to pull the cloth away from his skin. It took several minutes, but little by little, the fabric came away, revealing long, deep slash marks that ran from his shoulders down to his lower back. Smaller slits striped his chest and shoulders.

"Holy shit," breathed Colin. "Who did this to you?"

"It's better if you don't ask me a lot of questions," Pearse croaked.

"The hell with that. This is barbaric, Pearse." Colin turned off the water and handed me a towel. "That's for you," he instructed. "We need to keep all cloth away from these gashes at the moment."

We squished into the bedroom on wet feet, helped Pearse back to the edge of the bed, and allowed his arms to slide off our shoulders.

Colin left the room and returned a few moments later with a glass of water and an assortment of medical supplies. He handed me the glass. "Get him to sip a little water. If he can't keep it down, I'll probably need to run an IV."

I held the water and Pearse took it. His hands had started to tremor, and liquid sloshed over the sides as he lifted it to his lips.

"You really should be having this done in the hospital. I'm an internist, not a plastic surgeon. These are gonna scar." Colin shot a syringe into the space beside one of the deepest gashes on Pearse's back, which looked at least six inches long.

Pearse sucked air through his teeth.

"You should press charges against them," Colin said.

"I can't."

"Why?"

"They have too much on me."

"Like what?"

Pearse didn't answer.

Colin blew out a long stream of air and turned back to the gaping skin, pushing the two sides together with his fingertips. "What did they use to do this? A hunting knife?"

"Mostly scalpels. Vampires carry their own."

"What the hell kind of people have you gotten yourself involved with?" Colin started the needle through the first gash.

"Bad ones."

Colin met my gaze. "So now you've involved Avery with this too."

I sat on the bed beside Pearse and threaded my fingers through his hand.

Pearse looked at me. "You told him?"

"I told him."

Shaking his head, Colin exhaled. "Damn you, Pearse."

"I knew what I was getting myself into," I said quietly.

A muscle in Colin's jaw pulsed. "Avery, there's more gauze in my bag by the front door. Would you mind grabbing it for me?"

I stared at the box of gauze against the wall, not two feet away. But I'd humor Colin if he wanted to talk to Pearse privately.

I stepped into the hall but hovered near the door, in the spot where I'd hidden when I'd first eavesdropped on them. That seemed like a lifetime ago.

Colin spoke in a low voice. "You know what really pisses me off? You knew how I felt about her, and yet you deliberately used her for your own twisted reasons."

"I'm not using her, Colin. And she's right, you know? It was her idea."

"And you just took her up on it. Like she was offering you a steak dinner."

"It made sense in the moment. But then ... I fell for her. You know? I love her."

I couldn't help it. My heart soared.

Colin gave a sarcastic laugh. "I loved her too."

"I know you did. I know you still do. And that's why I have to ask you a big favor."

"No. Whatever it is ... just no."

"If something happens to me, I need you to take Avery and get her out of here."

Several seconds of silence passed.

I mashed my hand against my mouth to keep from protesting.

"This is bullshit, Pearse."

"Colin, I'm not kidding. All right? If something happens to me, she's going to need protection. From them. I know I'm an asshole and you want to kill me, but this is for her. For Avery. Promise me you'll get her out of here."

My jaw clenched. A stinging lump rose deep in my throat. This was too much. Between the arrest, finding out from Maris that Pearse had lied to me about what happened in New Orleans, and then processing what The Colony had done to him as supposed "punishment," I was emotionally tapped out.

I forced one leg to move and then the other as I plodded to the front door and rummaged through Colin's bright blue duffel bag for the gauze. Then I hurried back.

Colin was drawing up a hypodermic needle full of clear liquid. He held the syringe in the air and allowed a small spray to fountain through the needle. "I'm going to give you a shot of amoxicillin for any infection." He looked at me. "He really should go get checked out, Avery. He could have internal bleeding. For that matter, he might need iron infusions after this much blood loss."

I sat on the bed beside Pearse. "Your brother's a doctor. You should listen." My gaze fell on a long gash that ran down his shoulder. He looked like he'd been whipped. No, he looked like he'd been stabbed. Shredded. "And they consider this punishment?"

Pearse winced as Colin started to stitch up another gaping laceration. "Bleeding is a form of punishment, yes. Each member of the team gets their turn. They can take as much blood as they want."

"Like a reenactment of Julius Caesar?" Colin asked. "Everyone gets a stab."

"Even if it kills you?" I asked, trying to shake off a wave of nausea.

"Yeah, sort of," Pearse said. "It's basically a feeding frenzy."

"It's heinous." Colin finished the stitches and cleaned the excess blood away with gauze.

"You could've died," I said.

Pearse looked up at me with a smile that didn't quite reach his eyes. "No. I had too much to live for."

Ugh. I just wanted to kill him myself. "Your charm isn't working for me right now."

Colin wadded up the bloody gauze and plastic wrappers. Then he gathered up his things and stood. "The painkillers will kick in soon," he said, moving toward the door. "They may cause drowsiness too."

Pearse slumped. "Good. 'Cause right now, I just want to sleep." He tried to recline and cringed. "Except I may need to do it standing up."

Chapter Fifty-Eight
Sunday, February 16

"You lied to me."

We were sitting on the bed, Pearse propped up with a multitude of feather pillows behind him. But each shift and movement of his shoulders brought a wince, a hiss.

He held up his cell phone and scanned his text messages. "About what?"

"About what happened in New Orleans."

"Huh?"

"Maris came here."

He dropped his phone into his lap and raised his eyes to meet mine. "When?"

"Yesterday." I stared at him. "She told me you killed someone in New Orleans. You told me you'd stolen blood from a lab. You lied."

Who was this man? Could I believe anything he said? I began to wonder if I was in the midst of an elaborate game—one in which I'd already forfeited the most valuable playing piece—Whickering Place—to a con artist.

He shook his head. "Maris is just trying to scare us. Just like the bleeding. It's all about sending a message. Reminding us that she's in control."

"I thought you were in control." I jutted out my chin.

"They're allowing me to be regional leader, but I mean," he broke off. "In the end, I have to do what The Colony tells me."

My heart dipped. To me, it sounded like this plan had plunged Pearse deeper into their servitude, not freed us the way we'd hoped. "So what you're telling me is, this was all for nothing."

"No, it's not for nothing. We're in a much better position than most."

"And that's why you're sitting here with a back full of stitches and a mouth full of lies about what really happened in New Orleans."

His eyes flickered, darted down. "I didn't lie. I *was* caught stealing the blood."

"Great. So you're a thief and a murderer."

He dropped his head. "I didn't murder anyone. It wasn't like that."

"Was it like what you did to the girl in Black Mountain? Maris said you didn't even use a needle on the girl in New Orleans."

"I didn't have any. And I didn't kill her. It was the first time I was a part of one of their rituals. I didn't know what they were doing. That girl was a voluntary blood donor. She wanted to be initiated into The Colony." His facial muscles tightened. "I was one of several vampires who ... cut her that night."

"And she died."

"Several days later, she did die, yeah. In the hospital."

I closed my eyes and imagined myself walking to my car, climbing in, and driving. Driving until I ran out of gas at the walkway of a gingerbread house in the middle of Sherwood Forest with a bunch of kindly dwarves ushering me inside where it was warm and safe and—

"Avery."

My eyes snapped open. Nope. I was still here.

"I would never intentionally hurt someone. Ever. I even called the police that night after it happened."

"And?"

He looked down at his hands. "That's when I found out how involved the cops were with The Colony. And then, when the others found out ... well, let's just say my loyalties were tested that night and found wanting." He threw his hand in the air. "You know the rest of the story."

I covered my face with my hands. *Someone tell me who to believe, what to do.* "How long do we have to keep this up, Pearse? How long before we can leave?"

"We need to be careful for the next few weeks—maybe even the next few months. We can't do anything to make them suspicious. It's too risky." He pulled my hands away from my face, forcing me to look at him. "Part of why I agreed to take the punishment was to secure this, Avery. We're going to need to buy some time. Make some plans."

We were always making plans. "How do we do that?"

He reached for the cup of water on the nightstand and drank from it. "Next weekend, we're hosting the gathering here."

Even though I didn't want to. "I really don't want any of those people—those *things*—in my house. In our house."

"Yeah, I know, but we have to. It's a really significant event—on the night of the new moon. They'll expect me to be on board." His eyes grazed mine. "They'll expect you to be on board too."

"What will I have to do?"

"Pretend. Dress in the clothes they tell you to wear, play the part of the hostess. They'll be announcing us as regional leaders that night. We need to look like we're important."

"Maris bought me a dress."

"Wear it."

Anxiety felt like concrete in my chest. "I don't know if I can do it."

"You can. We'll do this together. And when it's over," he glanced off to the side, "then we'll make Maris an offer. We'll sell Whickering

Place to her. She wants to be regional leader more than anything. She's made you an offer once before. There's no reason she won't take us up on it."

I'd have to become the best actress in the world to look like I was "on board" at the gathering. It would take at least that stupid mask Maris had given me to keep from betraying how much I wanted to send an arrow straight through her.

"After that," Pearse continued. "We'll go. We'll just pack up a few of our things and leave everything else behind. We'll start fresh wherever we decide to settle. We could go to Florida, the Keys, even." He put his fingers over mine, pulled my hand toward his.

If only we could fast-forward to the day after next weekend... I wouldn't have a moment of peace until then.

Two knocks sounded on the door. A few seconds later, Colin stuck his head inside. "Checking on his wounds."

"Come on in." I crawled off the bed and stood at the end, looking on.

Colin's eyes flickered toward me but didn't quite meet mine. He stopped a few steps away and held out two pill containers. "Have Pearse take these for the next few days. Antibiotics."

"Thank you," I said, my throat thick.

"And I'll leave you more desmopressin on the table before I leave. I still have some samples in my bag."

My heart ached. Even in the midst of what I knew must be disappointment and anger, Colin still cared enough to offer help. At least I could *try* to remember to use the desmopressin.

Colin asked Pearse to sit up so he could look at his stitches. "I'll come back in a few days to check you again." He focused on inspecting his work, running his finger along the length of several of the longer ones. "Do these still hurt?"

"No, they feel great," Pearse sniped. "Of course, they do. It hurts like hell."

"I'll give you some pain medication too."

Pearse sat back against the pillows, and his forehead wreathed with the pain of the small movement.

Colin took his blood pressure and timed his pulse. "Blood pressure's a little low, but not outrageously so." Then he stood back from his brother, observing him. "Your coloring still isn't good."

Pearse shrugged. "I'll live. Or not."

"Do you know where you're going to stay?" I asked Colin.

He glanced over his shoulder at me, but I immediately looked away. The guilt and sadness weighed a ton, made it hard for me to breathe.

"Yeah. I'm going to stay with a buddy of mine from the clinic." He stood. "I'll be back later in the week for the rest of my stuff." Then he moved past me but paused at the doorway, motioning his head toward Pearse. "Call me if he needs anything," he muttered. Then, allowing his gaze to fall, he added, "Or if you need anything."

Chapter Fifty-Nine
Friday, February 20

"You still wearing your cross?" Ada asked as she stepped over the threshold carrying her mops and buckets.

I grasped the wooden cross between my thumb and forefinger and held it out for her.

She patted my hand. "Good girl."

Ada lifted her face, almost like she was sniffing the air. "Wait a minute, baby. Something's different here."

I hadn't cried for at least two days and now seemed like a good time to let it all rip. The sobs overwhelmed me, starting at my shoulders, which jerked up and down with each hiccup of air. Then they traveled down to my stomach and buckled my knees.

The other women trailed in behind Ada and cast glances at me as they passed. One of the ladies headed toward the bedrooms upstairs, and the other one headed for the kitchen.

Ada raised her shoulders with a sharp intake of breath and then squatted down beside me. "Oh, honey. The air feels heavy in here."

"A lot has happened since I last saw you," I sniffed.

"Baby, I can tell. You wanna tell me about it?"

I shook my head, unable to speak.

"You find your gun?"

"No," I squeaked.

"What else?"

"I got married," I heaved.

"What? Girl, what're you saying?"

"It was sudden. It just kinda happened."

Ada set down her bucket of cleaning supplies. "Who did you marry?"

"Pearse." I pointed toward the door of his room. "The guy who lives in there."

Her eyes ballooned, and she sucked in her cheeks. "The vampire?"

Something about the way she said it seemed funny. I choke-laughed and nodded.

Ada drew her hands up to her hips. "Lord have mercy, honey. Why'd you do that?"

"It's a long story. But then he was arrested, and I'm not even sure if I can believe him, and-and the house is haunted, and now there's going to be a big party of vampires here on Sunday night." I broke off, feeling like I might hyperventilate.

She turned her face up to the ceiling again. "And they's just swirling up there like a merry-go-round of angry energy, just waiting to attack." She narrowed her eyes. "I can feel 'em."

"Who?"

"Those demons. You know it too, don't you?"

I looked up at the ceiling. Yes, I knew something was up there, but I didn't *feel* it the way Ada did.

She dragged her eyes down my shirt and stopped at my midsection.

I smoothed the fabric, looked down to see if I'd spilled something on myself.

"And you pregnant."

I wrinkled my nose and squinted. "What? No, I'm not." Although it occurred to me that I could no longer say the possibility was absurd.

She nodded. "Yep. It's early, but..." She placed her hand to my stomach. "You definitely pregnant. I'm a little bit psychic, you know.

Got that from my mawmaw. And I've been right about early pregnancies eight out of eight times."

I exhaled shakily. How could she know something like that? Of course, it was possible. We had not been at all careful since the first time. But it hadn't even been two weeks yet.

"But honey, you can't bring up a child in this house. You can't even go through a pregnancy here. It's not safe."

I wiped under my nose with the back of my hand. "I know."

Ada grabbed my wrist and pulled me to my feet. "I'm gonna pray." She planted her hands on her hips. "And then I'm gonna get to cleaning."

What good praying was going to do, I really didn't know. But I was almost amused by Ada's determined stride as she clenched her fist around the handle of her bucket and moved toward the staircase.

The front door opened and Colin walked in. "Hey. Hope you don't mind. I left some scotch and a few other bottles here. Thought I'd come by and pick them up."

"No, no. It's fine." Using the backs and fronts of my hands, I wiped the tears from my eyes and face and forced a puffy-eyed glance in his direction. I hadn't seen him in a few days, and today he actually flashed a smile. But he was focused on Ada.

"Morning, Ada. Everything all right with you?"

"Yes, Dr. Gallagher." She nodded at him. "You moving out?"

He stopped, placed his hand on the staircase banister. "Yes, um ... Trying to buy my own house. But how are you? I haven't seen you in a couple of weeks since I've been away. What're you up to?"

Ada took three steps, paused, and then turned to look at him. "I'm about to do something I never do. I'm gonna clean upstairs." She extended a finger and pointed toward the ceiling.

I huffed out a cloudy laugh. "Ada, you always clean upstairs."

"Not the way I'm cleaning today. Before I leave here today, I'm planning on telling those demons they got to go." She lifted her head and climbed up the rest of the stairs.

Colin turned toward me. "I *love* her."

"Me too." I looked at the floor, knowing my face was a patchwork of blotches. "How's the living situation?"

"Temporary, but fine." Colin's eyes didn't quite meet mine. "You okay?"

"Yep."

"Pearse?"

"He's back at work today."

He raised his eyebrows. "Oh. Well, I guess I'll see him there, then. I'm surprised he's already back."

"I'm just thankful they let him come back." I allowed my eyes to graze his. "Thank you if you had anything to do with that."

He looked down at his keys as he bounced them in his hand. "Everyone needs a break now and again."

"You've given him quite a few," I practically whispered.

"And ... well, you know, he has a wife to support now."

I swallowed, nodded. Every conversation with Colin these days seemed an exercise in my shame. "Thank you."

He pointed to the front room. "Well, I'll just grab those bottles now. And then I'll be out of here."

I strode to the bottom of the stairwell and looked up, wondering if I should go and find Ada. But as I took the first step, a blast of air, cold and stinging, slapped me in the face so hard it felt like a hand had struck me. I put my fingers to my cheek, where I could almost envision a handprint appearing.

No. I would wait downstairs.

Chapter Sixty

For nearly a hundred years we've lived here undisturbed. Some of us came later, but many have been here since the beginning.

It is an extraordinary thing to be ordered out of a longstanding place of habitation.

Painful.

Infuriating.

Although many of the weaker ones flee at the first murmurings of the Lord's prayer, there are others who hold on. We will not go so easily.

There are hiding places within the house. There are other lifeforms to occupy.

For many of us, hiding is not an option. We will exact revenge swiftly and violently.

In fact, the die has already been cast.

Or in this case ... the coin.

Our next victims have been chosen.

Chapter Sixty-One

After Ada and the cleaners left, I sat down in the front room with my father's laptop. I hadn't read any entries in a while, and there were still a few left.

The screen had begun to show signs of its age. Occasionally, pink and yellow lines scrolled down, or the entire surface blinked bright green or purple. I didn't know how much longer I'd be able to keep the thing running.

Entry32 12/22/2000

The attacks continue. The medium thinks SHE needs more blood. I'll never be free unless I bring offerings from outside sources. Perhaps that's why the succubus wanted me to paint with blood. She wants blood on a surface so that she can access, feed on it, draw life from it.

The medium suggests I create a wall somewhere in the heart of the house, where I can offer up blood to the succubus on a regular basis.

Entry33 12/26/2000

I have chosen a space for the blood offerings. Since most of the succubus's visitations to me have happened in the east wing of the house, I will use a room just off of the attic. I have offered up my own sacrifice of blood.

Beverly was kind enough to do the same.

It's been two days now. The succubus has left me alone.

The room off of the attic. The wall with the chip of white paint missing. The room that Ada said was cursed and she never went into.

Nausea struck me with gale force. My father's blood was on that wall. My father's girlfriend's blood was on that wall.

ENTRY 34 1/13/2001

The succubus is back. Two nights ago, she interrupted my sleep. Although I tried to fight her off, it was no use. She took what she wanted, and I had no control over my own body.

I'd thought the sacrifices would keep her at bay for longer. After all, I've been adding blood to the wall every week. Mostly animal blood from rabbits or mice or anything I can catch.

This morning I called the medium again. "What do you think SHE wants?" The medium thinks the animal blood isn't working. The succubus only wants human blood. And much more of it than she's getting.

I will need to become more creative.

The medium may know people willing to sacrifice for just such a purpose—a group particularly interested in the exchange and power of blood. They have ties to this house. People who lived here before me also had dealings with the entities in this house.

But I'm afraid of what the succubus might do if I bring in more strangers. Will she do to them what she did to Beverly?

But then again, I'm afraid of what will happen if I don't find more blood donors.

What had the succubus done to Beverly? What had my father done with Beverly? He never said. Never mentioned her again. And there was only one more entry...

Entry35 2/23/2001

The whole house smells of blood.

The wall is practically full now—nearly completely red. And would you believe it? I can actually see its dark richness filling my paintings with its vermilion hue. Members of The Colony have brought me sacrifices. Many of them have graciously given of their own blood to help me satisfy the succubus's insatiable thirst. I have joined them. In fact, I do not know what I ever did without them.

The attacks have stopped. For weeks now, she's left me alone.

Maybe I'll be able to live in peace within this house after all. With The Colony's help.

And that was it. The last entry.

"The whole place smells of blood." My father's words. Once, Ada had said those words to me—that the house had smelled of blood. Smelled of death. And here was the proof I'd sought all along. My father had been a member of The Colony. Proof that he had participated in their rituals.

I grabbed my cell phone, swiped up the internet, and typed in "Beverly Moorhead."

A multitude of hits came up. Beverly Moorhead in Vegas, in England, in Central Maryland. Many of them were alive and well. One woman with that name was eighty-five years old.

But another one had been missing since December of 2000.

Beverly F. Moorhead, 25. Last seen in Asheville, North Carolina.

I clicked on an image of her.

She looked like ... me.

Me with long, red hair. Haunted eyes.

She'd been a bank teller.

She'd been someone's daughter.

And now she was dead.

Chapter Sixty-Two
Saturday, February 22

"**I** think my father killed a woman," I said to Pearse as we lay in bed.

It was close to midnight, the night before the gathering. Neither of us could sleep. We'd made love, and then we'd gotten quiet, staring at the shadows on the ceiling.

"I think he killed her and hid her body somewhere in this house."

"Why do you think that?"

"What I read in his journals. He doesn't come out and say the actual words, but I mean, I guess it shouldn't be a complete surprise. My father was part of The Colony. The Colony is made up of murderers. If x, then y."

"I guess it's not the craziest logic."

"You don't seem too fazed by it."

He sat up, turned on the lamp by the bed. "Who was she?"

"A bank teller. She's been missing since 2000. She looked like me, only she had red hair. She was twenty-five. She was pretty much a loner. Just like all the others that The Colony goes after."

Pearse traced the veins in my hand with his finger. "You're not really a loner anymore, are you?"

"Don't change the subject. I want to talk about this."

"Okay."

"Because I think she's representative of all their victims."

"Why do you think she's still here?"

"The voice on the phone told me she's still here. Her body was never found."

He sat on the edge of the bed, his back to me. With my eyes, I followed the Frankenstein scars zigzagging across his back. Most of them were healing, but one near his shoulder oozed blood. All of them still looked red and angry.

"So, what does that do to your head? The idea that your father may have murdered someone?"

I ran my forefinger along his spine—the only strip of skin that didn't have a slash mark. "Sort of the same thing it does to my head to think that my husband may have."

Pearse craned his head around, his eyes meeting mine before sliding downward. Then he turned back around and faced the wall. "What do you want to do about it?"

I exhaled air through my nose. "With the position we're in right now, I'm not sure there's anything I can do about it. Until this is all over. If it ever is."

Pearse pulled on his jeans. "The house has been quiet."

"Yeah, no slithering. No thumping."

"No voices." He stood and walked to the corner of the room, lifted his red guitar from the clutches of its perch.

"Wonder why." I sat up against the pillow, grabbed Pearse's discarded blue T-shirt braided in among the sheets, and pulled it over my head.

He sauntered to a chair and lowered himself into it. Then he rested his guitar across his thighs and strummed a few chords.

"I've never heard you play."

He smiled a little. "I haven't played in weeks."

I leaned forward, rested my hands between my knees. "Play something."

"I'm not that good. I'm a hack. I just play for fun."

"Doesn't matter."

"Do you like Coldplay?" he asked.

"Sure."

He strummed through chords that I immediately recognized. Coldplay had been a band from my childhood. I'd had all of their CDs and wore out my mom's portable stereo playing them.

I grabbed a handful of T-shirt fabric over my heart and rocked from side to side. "Oh, this is one of my favorites. This song's heartbreaking."

"It's better on the piano, but I know the chords, so..."

I wasn't a musician, and I certainly didn't know what constituted good guitar playing, but even on an electric guitar that wasn't plugged into an amplifier, the tinny sounds of the strings evoked my memory of the full rendering of the song—piano, vocals, drums.

He stopped strumming and set the guitar back in its holder. Then he stood. "Avery, I need to talk to you about something important."

I tensed. "What?"

He took a piece of paper out of his pocket and unfolded it. "If anything happens to me—"

"It won't," I interjected.

"But if it does," he insisted, "I've asked Colin to get you out of here. To take you somewhere safe."

I shot up off the bed and moved across the room, my back to him. "Stop it, Pearse. I don't want to hear about that."

"Look, we need to be realistic and have a Plan B—in case Plan A doesn't work out."

I wasn't even sure what Plan A was. Pretend, wait, hope?

Pearse stood behind me, paper crackling between his fingers. "Here." He slipped his hand over my shoulder, holding out the scrap.

"What is it?" I took it from him.

"An address in New Orleans. Where you should go if something happens to me. You'll be safe there."

Safe. The word had a foreign echo, like a name from my past. I debated whether to tell him what Ada had prophesied. But I hadn't even missed my period yet. It wasn't due for another couple of days. And I didn't want to allow myself to think about it. Not with what we had to endure tomorrow. I wanted to get through the gathering first. Protecting a new life on top of protecting our own was too much.

"And you should read this." Pearse went to his chest of drawers and pulled out what looked like a parchment scroll with a red seal. He extended it to me. "I know it looks ridiculous, but it's meant to seem old and official. It's The Colony's literature. It's best you go into this thing tomorrow night informed."

"So what happens at these things—these gatherings? What should I expect?"

Pearse sank down on the end of the bed and looked up at me. "It's a celebration of the new moon. They can take place any time of year, but they're usually held before the spring, whenever a certain number of new members join."

"Am I going to be considered part of that number?"

"You could be. They might ask you if you want to be initiated."

"But I don't want to be initiated. Anyway, Maris has made it clear she doesn't trust me."

"Be on your guard at all times. Especially around Maris." He grabbed my hands. "You never found your gun."

"No."

"Have you thought about getting a new one?"

"Yeah, but I have to apply for a permit, and then there's the fact I was in a mental institution for a while." I shook my head. "I got the Glock through my uncle—he was an ex-cop. All very much under the table. Know anyone who can get me one on the black market?"

Pearse laughed. "No. Like I said, The Colony doesn't operate with guns."

"Just needles and knives and scalpels."

"Pretty much."

He pulled me against him, wrapped his arms around me. "Just stick close to me tomorrow night. Don't get separated from me. That's the important thing."

Chapter Sixty-Three
Sunday, February 23

A strange aura hovered over the house. There was a buzz of anticipation in the air, an unnatural electric current.

Downstairs, the guests were filing in. I could hear the rumbling of conversation, laughter, glasses clinking.

In the full-length mirror, my red dress looked like something out of nineteenth-century Venice. I held the carnival mask up to my face, covering all but my mouth and chin.

Two months ago, this woman who stared back at me from the glass would have been unrecognizable. A few weeks ago, I would've wanted to crawl into a hole—wouldn't have been able to handle the juggling act I'd have to endure tonight.

I shook a lorazepam from the container. If Ada's words were true, I probably shouldn't be taking it. But I wasn't going to call Dr. Murphy just to ask if it was safe to take while pregnant, and there was no way I could face this night without at least one. I dumped another one into my hand, popped them both in my mouth, and swallowed.

If we weren't about to embark on a night of nightmarish proportions, I might have appreciated how good Pearse looked.

In the last two days, his face had regained some color, and he appeared healthier. He wore an all-black tuxedo, and as he swung a black cape over his shoulders, I understood why so many were attracted to the campy vampire costumes. Barring elements of the ridiculous, there was a sex appeal to it.

I presented the dress, twirling for him to see the whole effect.

"You look amazing." He smiled.

"I look like I belong in a bordello."

He moved toward me, swept his hands around my waist, and pulled me against him. "Maybe a little, but it's working for you."

I pushed him away. "Let's just get through this night. That's all I can think about."

He picked up the scrolls on my nightstand. "Did you read any of this?"

"A little. Until I couldn't stomach it anymore. When I got to the part that talked about sacrifices ... I just couldn't."

The wording made it sound like the sacrifices were symbolic, spiritual—not actual human beings. But I knew enough to comprehend what the number thirteen meant. *Thirteen sacrifices a year must take place to appease the succubare*—like they were discussing a sales goal for the fiscal year.

Pearse tossed the scroll back onto the nightstand. "Yeah, I never read any of that shit. Maybe I should've. Then I wouldn't have gotten involved in the first place."

I grabbed one of the scrolls, unrolled it, and read aloud. "Clarifying the Blood."

Pearse made a scoffing sound.

"*A member of The Colony may clarify their own blood by consuming that of a virgin. Partial purification may take place if the vampire consumes the blood of an adolescent, regardless of sexual status. The ultimate goal, of course, is immortality, which is only attainable through the initiation of sacrifices and mass consumption of blood in all forms.*" I looked up at him. "So The Colony promises immortality—just like real vampires."

"Yeah," he deadpanned. "They say that."

"Their doctrine almost makes sense—if it wasn't so heinous and criminal." But this was how cults worked. They wore you down, convinced you they possessed sacred knowledge, made you feel as if you belonged to something special.

Fear crept in—of what we were to do that night, the roles we were to play, and the dangerous tightrope we walked.

I set the scroll aside.

Pearse sat on the bed beside me and put a hand on my thigh. Once more, I considered telling him what Ada had said. But what if it wasn't true? On the other hand, what if it was?

I hardly noticed the knock at the door, but when Pearse cracked it open, I looked up.

"It's Cassie." He stepped aside, and she breezed in.

"Hey, I just wanted to let you know that I'm here," she said.

Exhaling, I greeted her, pulled her into a hug. "Pearse told me Lacey asked you to bartend. I'm so glad. I feel a million times better just knowing you're here."

She stepped back, boxing her hands and framing my skirt. "Great dress."

"Thanks."

"And I guess you don't look too bad either, Pearse." She smiled.

"Same goes for you." He motioned to her red silk blouse and black tie under a tuxedo jacket.

"You guys ready to go down? Guests are arriving."

Pearse threaded his fingers through mine, and we followed Cassie to the top of the stairs. I looked down at the swirling colors and animated voices below.

There were too many of them.

Monsters.

Criminals.

And I was unarmed against them.

Some may have been just as desperate to escape their captivity as Pearse was—as I now was.

I couldn't remember the last time I'd been to a full-fledged party. High school? And I'd never been to a masquerade, but in some ways, all parties were masquerades. Everyone playing a role, acting the part.

At least at this gathering, no one pretended not to be pretending. All wore masks, capes. Many of them adjusted fake teeth in their mouth, pulling them out and pressing them back into place again.

And I was one of them. Or at least they thought I was. I slid the animal mask over my face.

Red silk ribbons hung from every allowable surface and waved like streamers at a Valentine's Day school dance. Wax candles in candelabras were interspersed with LED lights. Women in ball gowns, men in capes. The room swirled in reds, blacks, and purples—fantastic and terrifying.

As I descended the staircase, I sensed the vampires' eyes on me, and I was laid bare, exposed. As though Ada's pronouncement about my condition was visible to all—as if somehow, they could look into my body and see the life growing there.

Reaching the landing, I looked down at my dress and shook out the yards of material with my left hand. Pearse took my right hand in his, and we moved together through the foyer. A man wearing a suit with tails glided by, holding a tray with champagne glasses full of what looked like absinthe. A woman dressed in the same attire carried glasses filled with thick red liquid.

I checked my cell phone. 9:20.

"There you are."

I turned toward the voice. Maris. Ultra-red lipstick and a dark ring of eyeliner around both eyes made her look clownish. *Your age is showing*, I wanted to say to her. But in actuality, my goal was to say as little to her as possible and to stay as far away as I could.

She pointed at Pearse. "I need to put him to work."

I tensed. "Doing what?"

"Greeting the new members as they arrive." She smiled. Under the illumination of a black light bulb, her teeth were Day-Glo. "Making them feel welcome. Showing them where to leave their phones."

"Leave their phones?" I parroted.

"No phones allowed in the ballroom. Everyone is to check their phones with Leaf in the billiard room. No exceptions." She backed away, pointing down the hall. "So please go see Leaf first, then assume your role as host, Pearse."

"Where?" Pearse growled.

"Just by the front door."

His brows lowered. "Avery comes with me."

Maris held up a hand. "Avery must stay inside."

I looked at Pearse. *You said we shouldn't be separated.*

"At least one of you has to be in here to play host," Maris said.

Host. What a joke. I'd be lucky if I could muster up the courage to *pretend* to welcome anyone. Right then, I wanted to run out the back door and never look back.

Pearse squeezed my hand, met my eyes. "You'll be okay?"

I nodded for his benefit alone.

He leaned in and kissed me. "I won't be long."

I watched until his cape disappeared into the black flashing lights and crowds of vampires—all of them pressing in, forming their social circles.

I glanced at Maris out of the corner of my eye.

She was watching Pearse too. "His affection seems sincere."

"It is."

She arched an eyebrow. "I halfway thought the bleeding might have lessened that somewhat. It tends to have that effect."

"Obviously, it didn't," I choked out.

"Well, then," she breathed. "You must be doing something right."

FOR A FEW MINUTES, I thought I might get away without checking my phone. But an annoying female vampire wearing a creepy, smiling jester mask was circulating, patting people down and asking to see their phone check tickets.

When I saw her walking in my direction, I spun around and marched straight to the billiard room, where a vampire named Leaf sat in a medieval-style armchair with a high wooden back that blocked the entrance. Behind him, numbered cell phones lined the pool table and another fold-out platform beside it. Reminiscent of a coat check, Leaf handed out red claim tickets.

I took mine and returned to the ballroom.

The walls and floor were bathed in purple. The chandeliers had been dimmed, nearly extinguished, and black lights replaced illumination. A fog machine pumped out smoky tendrils of gray mist that curled around the revelers' feet. On the opposite end of the room, a small group of musicians played a stringed quartet.

"Not long now," Maris said.

The extra lorazepam started to kick in. A comfortable haze swept over my vision, blurring the edges of the sights and sounds around me.

A man wearing a gray velvet cape moved to the front of the room and raised his hand to signal an end to the music. A short but striking figure, his long, straight hair provided the perfect contrast to his pale eyes, red lips, and translucent skin. But it was his posture that commanded attention—shoulders thrown back, arms outstretched.

Maris's eyes lit up. "Ah. Our fearless leader."

The music left off with a final stroke of a violin bow, and the talking died the second he raised his hand. "Good evening, my lovelies. Happy New Moon."

A muttering of greetings rippled across the ballroom, followed by applause.

The man's gaze flashed over the room. An electric current shot down my spine as I realized he was motioning toward me. "I would first like to take this opportunity to thank Avery for the use of this grand facility—Whickering Place. For many of us, it's like coming home, as Whickering Place holds a revered place in our hearts. For so many reasons."

I found it hard to breathe until he finally allowed his eyes to trail away from mine and back to his rapt audience. "Many of you younger members may not know that Whickering Place and The Colony have a long history together, and now, I'm pleased to say, because of Avery and her new husband—many of you may know him as Pearse Gallagher."

A low rumble of laughter vibrated all round, and the weight of a hundred eyes settled upon me—some of them masked, others bare. Sweat formed behind the plastic of my mask, and the air flowing back and forth through the nose holes was hot, claustrophobic.

"These two lovebirds sneaked off last month and married without The Colony even knowing about it." He smiled, revealing gold fangs. "It's not our way, of course, as marriage is rarely allowed amongst the members, but sometimes, love and lust are hard to restrain, difficult to govern. Am I right? As Lord Byron once said, 'Love will find a way through paths where wolves fear to prey.'"

More laughter.

I forced my lips to twitch into a reluctant smile. I had to at least project complicity.

Leaning toward Maris, I whispered in her ear. "Who is he?"

She cranked her head toward me, her eyes widening, brows lifting. "That's Cadel. He's the executive director of The Colony—head over the entire organization."

I fixed my stare upon him as a shiver spread through me. So this was the man who decided who lived and who died. He hardly looked as ominous, threatening, or tall as I'd imagined.

He raised his hand, and his darkly painted, sharpened nails gleamed under the candlelight. "But now, dear friends of the night, this alliance will be a sweet asset to our family. For on this new moon, we announce that as owners of Whickering Place, Avery and Pearse will be elevated in the ranks of The Colony as regional leaders. And they have heartily agreed to allow us to use Whickering Place as our new headquarters and home."

More applause followed.

My stomach tightened at the images that *headquarters* and *home* brought to mind. I scanned the room for Pearse. Where was he? Was he still welcoming people?

A familiar shift in my breathing alerted me that I was transitioning into panic mode. Once the ceremonial part of the evening began, I wasn't sure how I would survive it. Would I be able to drink blood if they asked me to do it? Even the idea made me want to throw up.

The lights in the room dimmed again, and a series of songs played over the sound system, beginning with a Gregorian chant and morphing into organ music. Some of the vampires danced. Others congregated around the bar, where Cassie handed out drinks faster than she could pour them.

Over the next half hour, the noise level elevated, and the room filled with talking, cackling, howling.

I sank into a chair at an empty table covered in black lace. A skull holding a purple candle sat in the center. A masked waiter came by and asked if I would like a glass of absinthe, and I shook my head.

"Not an absinthe drinker, then?"

I turned. Cadel stood to my left, looking down at me.

My heart hammered into action. "Not tonight."

"May I?" He gestured to the empty chair beside me.

I tensed, forcing my shoulders to raise and lower. "I'm just waiting for Pearse."

Cadel sat and then looked out over the crowd as if scanning for him as well. "I'm sure he'll be here in a moment." He put his hand over mine. "You have beautiful veins. Prominent."

Fighting the urge to pull away, I pressed my fingertips into the tabletop and stared down at his numerous rings. A square sapphire crusted in diamonds. One with a large, round ruby. His own blue veins blazed a trail from his knuckles.

"I knew your father," he said.

I swallowed hard. "Well, then you probably had more contact with him than I did."

He drew his hand away from mine slowly, nodding. "I know you didn't have much relationship with him. So you couldn't have known what an outstanding member of The Colony he was."

Cadel struck me as someone straight out of a nineties' vampire movie, playing up the part of the sexy bloodsucker. His sharpened gold canines stuck out slightly from the other four in between.

"Ace joined the board in 2001, and he was always active and inspirational. He allowed full and unadulterated access to Whickering Place for all of our events and ceremonies, and he helped to form many of our foundational laws and bylaws."

Including the ones that said it was okay to torture and kill people?

I knew what he was doing—grooming me, wanting me to say that I would allow The Colony unadulterated access to Whickering Place.

Cadel waved a waiter to the table and lifted two glasses of absinthe, sliding one toward me. I shook my head. "No, thank you."

"I highly recommend it." He sipped from his. "All of our members drink absinthe."

So now he thought I was a member. "I haven't chosen to join yet."

He stared at me, amused, as though deciding whether to call my bluff. "Some of our practices may seem strange to you."

"Some? How about all?" But then I remembered I was supposed to be playing along with this whole charade.

"It's a little jarring the first time someone such as yourself sees a ceremonial act. A sacrifice is an extraordinary experience. Sacred."

"Killing, you mean?"

Cadel raised an artificially arched eyebrow. He probably plucked them regularly. "Semantics. It's just a word, really." He smiled again. "Do you think the wolf feels guilty after hunting down his prey? Do you think he considers it killing? No, it's simply what he does. He can't change that about himself. His instinct tells him to do it. If he were to deny that voice, then he would starve."

"But you're not going to starve without killing, without drinking someone's blood. It's not a physical need."

He raised a finger. "Ah, but you're missing the point of all this, Avery. We answer to a higher calling."

"A higher calling."

He held up his hands. "I'm sure you've encountered the spirits who live in this house. The incubus. The succubus. I suppose you could call them our pack leaders. And, like the wolf, we aren't led by the rules and regulations of this world. We have supernatural, otherworldly principalities that guide us. They are far more powerful and important than any mere mortal and his sad little philosophies on life."

I suppressed a shudder. Looking into Cadel's cold, ice-blue eyes was like looking into demonic orbs.

He patted my hand again, his talon-like fingernails raking against my skin. "You'll understand more as you grow in knowledge. It will all make sense as you learn our ways. Despite our misguided country's declaration of independence, I can assure you, Avery, that not all men and women are created equal. Some are far more worthy of living than others."

"And what stick of measurement do you use? For those who die and those who live?"

He nodded. "Again, we wait until we hear from the spirits. They tell us."

"So my father wasn't worthy of living?"

The smile slid from his face like melting butter. "Your father was a martyr. He chose to sacrifice himself."

"Why? Why would he do that?"

He narrowed his eyes. "Because he knew his reign had passed. The succubare told him that he was worth more dead than alive. As you see, he did the right thing." He extended his hand toward me. "Now the mantle passes to you. You are his legacy. You can go as far as you want in this organization, Avery. You could surpass your father."

Not if I have anything to do with it.

A gong sounded.

Cadel rapped his rings on the tabletop. "We'd best go. The festivities are about to begin."

I braced my hands on the table, pushing partially out of the seat, scanning the room again for Pearse. There was no sign of him.

Where are you?

Chapter Sixty-Four

The partyers shifted in one direction toward the center of the ballroom like a bevy of bats all crawling over each other to jockey for the best position.

Cassie moved away from the bar and stood at the edge of my table. She placed a glass of wine beside my hand. "You don't have to drink it. I just needed an excuse to come over."

"Where's Pearse? Have you seen him?"

She scanned the room. "No. But I wanted to tell you what's about to happen."

My mouth parched. All of my senses were on overdrive. "What's about to happen?"

Cassie glanced up at the crowd, which glided in synch toward the stage. "They're planning to have a sacrifice."

"What?" I hissed. "No." I shot to my feet. "No, this is supposed to be an initiation ceremony."

Cassie shook her head slowly. "I had a feeling there was something more to it than that. It's New Moon. And they're still short three sacrifices for the year."

My heart thumped wildly, and I skimmed the room for Pearse, my eyes darting from the door at the back of the room to the crowds pressing into the stage.

Then I saw him. He was wading through the hordes of vampires, his mask pushed atop his head, his eyes flicking up every few seconds to touch mine as he made his way toward me.

On legs that felt too wobbly to hold me up, I forced my foot forward. Then I fell into a stride, lingering at the edge of the crowd without entering into the wave of creatures whose eyes and noses were obscured by macabre, grotesque painted masks—their teeth sharp and carnivorous. I placed a hand to my own disguise, felt its rounded nose and the edge of the eye holes.

A starburst of a memory blasted through my mind. A flashing knife tip, blood smearing its surface. Dark red dripping from my fingers. Vince on the ground. A girl screaming, her arms held behind her by two men.

"You bitch!" she screamed. "I'll kill you. I'll stab you in the eyes, in the mouth, in the heart!" The death was meant for me. Not Vince.

Pearse grabbed my shoulders. "You okay?"

Coming out of the memory, I looked up at him. Dizziness swept over me—the lorazepam doing its work in double-dose fashion. "Yeah."

I reached down and grasped his hand. "Where have you been?"

He pressed his lips against my ear. "Had to make a phone call. Something's going on."

Cassie leaned toward him, whispered in his ear, presumably repeating what she'd said to me. He looked at her and nodded.

My heart seized. "What's happening?" Even though I knew. "Pearse, Cassie says there's going to be a sacrifice." I searched his face, desperate to act. "What can we do?"

Pearse looked over my head toward the crowds. His face said there was nothing we could do. "Just stay right here with me. Don't leave my side." He squeezed my hand harder.

Stoney. I wanted to call Stoney. Regardless of our conflicted relationship, I trusted him, didn't think he was one of them. But I didn't have my phone.

Maris stood upon the stage at the front of the room. She pulled the microphone toward her and called everyone to attention.

A woman in a short version of a ballgown with a billowing skirt of black ruched taffeta shoved in front of us. She whisked her mask off of her face, the elastic band ruffling her auburn hair. Lacey.

She looked at me, her gaze sweeping up and down my body, the downturn of her mouth betraying her bitterness and contempt. It was the same expression I'd seen in the face of Vince's ex-girlfriend as the men pulled her away from me. Lacey may not have been holding a knife in her hand, but her eyes were murderous.

A lump rose in my throat. I looked away and instead anchored my gaze to the stage where Maris talked about the significance of full moons versus new moons.

Dense, gray clouds billowed into the room. Someone had ratcheted up the fog machine. The vampires' ideal world consisted of smoke and mirrors and moons and blood. The Colony lived in an alternative reality where no one followed rules or expectations. And that's what made them so dangerous.

Chapter Sixty-Five

We have never been human. We don't feel human emotions. Compassion, empathy, and regret are not known to us. We do understand jealousy and avarice, at least from a useful point of view as we fervently pursue the devastation of humans—body and soul. Even without emotion, ruination brings a type of joy—to see torture and death meted out.

So, on this night, as we ride atop Greer, using her eyes to stare out upon a crowd that is entranced by bloodlust, unaware of their own logic, and practically salivating to see something terrible and beautiful carried out, we thrill at the darkness of the souls all around us. That so many have been corrupted by the pull of our temptation is worthy of celebration. What better way to top off the obliteration than to offer the ultimate deception?

Perhaps the humans will have their own small victory on this night, but we will wreak as much havoc as possible to ensure we win many deaths. Destruction is the name of the game, and souls are the prize.

Greer is not shaking. She is not scared. She knows what she must do, and she has been given the physical strength to do it.

Maris puts her arm across Greer's shoulders and draws the girl close to her. "Tonight is an extraordinary night." She smiles. Then her eyes turn upon Avery, who stands at the side of the room. "This may not have been the sacrifice we originally intended, but we feel certain that it will be acceptable and beneficial to the greater good of The Colony and the powers that shall be bestowed upon us all as a result."

Greer pulls a knife from her robes and holds it aloft.

Cadel appears from the shadows and smoke, his hooded cloak pulled low over his face. He places a ringed hand on Greer's shoulder and nods to Maris. She moves off the stage and goes to stand behind Pearse and Avery.

Now Cadel speaks. "My friends and family, we still lack three sacrifices to reach our goal before the solstice. When Greer told us she had decided to make the ultimate sacrifice tonight and assure her martyred place, we were all in agreement that she made the right choice."

There is a sigh of rapt anticipation from the audience as they look up at us in awe and reverence.

"But before the celebration begins, we must ask you all to allow us a one-time deviation from the norm." He smiles out at them, flashing his fangs. "Next to a virgin, the highest form of sacrifice is the self, where a member decides to take his or her own life. But instead, tonight, we ask that you join us in a different sort of sacrificial ritual, which may prove even more important to The Colony as an organization."

Cadel moves away from Greer and stands at the edge of the stage. His face hardens, his mouth turns down. "There are traitors in our midst."

The crowd's sighs turn to gasps as they pivot, looking around to see who the traitor may be.

"We must continue to seek out these threats. So we encourage you all to be vigilant and mistrustful of one another. Someone who may seem like your closest confidante may actually attempt to bring us all down."

Murmurs rip across the crowd.

Cadel places a hand on Greer's shoulder, and she kneels on the red pillow provided for her. Masked vampires carry two more red velvet pillows out onto the stage and place them beside Greer's.

"But the most traitorous ones of all stand among you. Therefore, instead of one sacrifice on this night, we will have three." He points his finger into the crowd, directly at Cassie. "We discovered a mole in our midst this year," he continues. "A hanger-on who seemed like a friend but turned out to be a traitor. Now, it is time for the true members of The Colony to take back Whickering Place. And that means traitors and moles must be ferreted out."

A shriek rises from the crowd as Cassie is seized, both of her arms held by two obliging vampires who walk her toward the stage.

"No!" she calls out, her legs folding under her.

Then we sit back and watch the fight, coliseum-style, as Pearse too begins to struggle through the crowds in an attempt to thwart what is about to take place, but he is blocked from reaching her.

What will happen? We wonder who will die first. The excitement is almost too great as we anticipate the smell of blood lingering in the air.

Once Cassie is hauled in front of Cadel, he wrenches the mask from her face and addresses the audience. "I'm sorry to deprive you of your bartender. But I'm sure we'll find someone else willing to stand in." He stretches Cassie's arm toward the crowd, pulls a scalpel from his waistcoat, and uses it to cut away the fabric of the sleeve. "Once, Cassie was a member of the Nocturne Brotherhood, one of the most powerful sects of vampire culture." He twists her hand, showing the tattoo. "This was once the mark of loyalty, but Cassie chose to abandon her kind, chose to obliterate her ties with one of the most preeminent orders. Instead, she's chosen the life of an imposter. An informant. Pretending to be a part of us, while communing with outsiders—authorities who would bring us down in the name of so-called justice."

A hooded vampire steps forward, knife outstretched, and grabbing her wrist, he drags the blade vertically down her arm.

Cassie does not scream, but her face twists with pain as a thin stream of red wells and spills over the skin of her arm.

Maris speaks in Latin, channeling our language of choice, communicating with those of us swirling in the air above the crowd.

Screams ripple throughout the room.

The crowd advances, closing in on Greer and Cassie, snarling and hissing.

We are nearly done here.

But then more of us arrive, hidden in the walls and the ceilings where we've lain dormant for over a week since that cleaning bitch sent us into hiding. Now there is a fight among us. Some of us rush forward while others are blocked from full access to the sacrifices—the coveted, spilling blood. All at once, we shriek in unison. We scrabble forward, clawing against an unseen force that weakens our powers.

Others rush into the masses below, clinging to them, possessing them.

It is chaos. It is war.

We see Greer and the victims below us.

Then we hold on to the walls and scatter across the ceiling.

Chapter Sixty-Six

My hand flew to the cross around my neck. I'd never prayed before. Wasn't even sure how or what I was doing, but I began to murmur words under my breath, pleading, asking Ada's God to help us. I bit my lip, tamping back a scream.

Pearse had successfully fought his way forward in the crowd in an attempt to reach Cassie. I stood, paralyzed, unable to move or dive into the circle of vampires to help my friend.

I was at the mercy of a roomful of killers.

Pearse nearly disappeared into the masses as he struggled against them, their hands at his back.

Suddenly, hands were on me too, clasping my arms, dragging me forward. I snapped into action, an old fight resurfacing in me. I bit at their fingers, tore at their wrists with my nails. They pushed me into the swirling crowd that enveloped and consumed me like a black hole. I felt like a leaf, picked up by the wind and tossed effortlessly. Black lights strobed all around, and the dense fog filled my nostrils.

I couldn't breathe as I was lifted and my feet came off the floor. I lashed out, kicking at anyone I could reach. My foot contacted what felt like someone's head, and I jabbed and jabbed until the person either went down or moved. Then someone let go of my leg, giving me enough momentum to propel myself forward, throwing my would-be captors off balance.

We tumbled to the ground, a twisted mess of legs and arms and far too much fabric for me to get up on my own.

Again, masked figures pulled me to my feet and jerked me forward.

Screams surrounded me.

Then I realized that the screams were my own. Over the din—the cries and cackles of the vampires—Cadel's voice cut like a sword.

"And behold our third and final sacrifice of the night. She is a legacy sacrifice, giving herself to the succubare as her father did before her."

Me. I'm to be the third sacrifice.

One of the vampires grabbed my hair, wrenching my head back until something in my neck popped, and an electrifying pain shot down and into my shoulder blade.

I struck out. Fists. Feet. Nails and teeth. Anything I had, I used. I would go down fighting. I screamed Pearse's name. I had no idea where he was in the mass of people or if he was in any position to help me.

Again, arms hoisted me into the air. It was as though I rode a black wave of tar that held me in its inky clutches and passed me along toward a shore where death awaited me. Flashes of color and lights disoriented me, and grotesque faces barked maniacal laughter into my face.

Upside down, Cadel's face came into view, his arms outstretched, motioning my transporting tormentors toward the final landing strip—a red pillow that would no doubt match the skirts of my dress, the color of my blood.

I landed half on the pillow and half off, my knees striking the hardwood of the stage. I cranked my head to the left. Cassie was there—head down, arms outstretched. She panted. Blood flowed from slits in her wrists. Cloaked vampires sat on either side of her, holding chalices under her hands.

I cried out, struggled to stand, but was pushed again to my knees. My thighs cramped. Forcibly, my head was turned to the right, where the young woman Cadel had called Greer raised her head to look at me. Her mouth drew up, revealing teeth reddened with blood. A slash bisected her neck from one side to the other—a death blow delivered by the knife held in her own hand and expertly guided by Cadel's red-stained fingers.

A scream ripped from my throat as I watched her eyes deaden, and she fell back from her kneeling position, her body tipped like a marooned boat, legs pulled up underneath her.

I thrashed against the arms that held me in place. An unseen hand slapped the side of my head, stunning me. My mask clattered to the ground, the hollow eyes looking right into mine. Then I realized what animal the disguise represented. A lamb. The rounded, black nose. Why hadn't I recognized it before?

Maris had chosen that for me. A lamb to the slaughter.

I raised my head and stared out at the crowd through blurred vision. Pearse came into focus, standing at the front of the mob.

His back was to me. "Stop!" He called out, extending his hands in front of him as though he would hold back the crowd's advance.

The room quieted, and the screams and growls turned to hisses.

Pearse spun toward Cadel, his cape fanning out around him, his eyes touching mine before settling on The Colony's executive director. "I am the regional leader. I have some say in this."

My entire body began to tremble. I would pass out soon. Hopefully, before they made the first cut.

I couldn't see Cadel's face, but I could hear the evil as it dripped from his tongue. "Maybe when this is all over, everything can go back to normal, Pearse. But you've caused enough trouble. If we'd been allowed to sacrifice Avery to begin with—as a virgin—then her death would've counted for three people. Instead, we are forced into this position. Because of your disobedience—and Avery's—we find ourselves here."

A shuffling noise prompted me to glance over at Greer's body. A masked vampire knelt beside her, holding a shallow bowl with a cut-out on the side, collecting the blood that spilled from her neck.

"You should never have underestimated us, Pearse," Cadel growled. "You certainly overestimated your own worth."

Pearse's face reddened, his shoulders rising in fast jerks. His voice broke when he spoke. "Please, take me instead. Not her. I was the disobedient one. Avery had nothing to do with it."

"No, Pearse," I cried out. "No."

He nodded, threw his mask to the ground, ripped his cape from his shoulders, and held out his hands. In a voice of complete resolve, he breathed, "Take me."

Cadel was quiet, and the room swayed and swam in my wavering vision. Pearse blurred and came back into focus, and bile rose into my throat and spewed from my mouth, coating the wood of the stage in front of me.

A hand shoved me in the back of the head. "Get up." Another set of hands lifted me roughly to my feet. But my knees refused to hold, and I sank to the floor again. Someone was dragging me, their arms locked underneath mine.

I looked over my shoulder. Pearse trudged onto the stage.

"No!" I cried out, the pressure in my chest building. "Pearse!"

But he wouldn't look at me. He stripped off his tuxedo jacket and then began unbuttoning his shirt. Several vampires rushed forward, ripping the fabric and pulling it from his shoulders. They shoved him into position, pushing down on his shoulders, forcing him to kneel where I'd been moments before. Only then did his eyes meet mine. And they were filled with regret, sorrow, and fear.

I couldn't speak. Sobs erupted from my throat, crowded out all other sounds, used up my breath.

Pearse's eyes locked with mine as he opened his mouth and started to speak.

A loud crash reverberated through the room.

Something had exploded. The glass from the high windows rained onto the floor. Amid the strobe lights, there were flashes—blinding—like fireworks and cracks and pops that were just as loud.

The vampires shrieked. The ones who had been holding my arms let me go, and I dropped to the floor, falling hard against my shoulder.

The room began to fill with a thick forcefield of pungent-smelling substance that crowded the air, and within seconds my lungs began to burn.

Over the din and the confusion, I heard Pearse's voice breaking through as he shouted, "Get out of here, Avery. Run!"

The vampires ran, some falling, trampling one another as they went. Genuine panic overtook the room. Desperately, I squinted through the flashing strobe lights and smoke in the hopes of seeing Pearse, but I could only make out darting forms, fleeing bodies, screeching monsters.

My eyes teared as I turned and sprinted in the opposite direction of the others—toward the back of the ballroom.

The secret panel. If I could make it to the back wall, then I could enter the passage to the master bedroom. And just maybe I could climb down the fire escape and flee into the night. Get help. If it wasn't too late.

Staggering, I propelled myself along, using chairs, tables, curtains. Staying as low as I could and still run, I focused all my energy on the door that led directly to the upstairs.

The vampires pushed through the double ballroom doors, screaming and coughing as I entered the shadows and hit the wall with my fists. The wall opened.

Panting, my eyes watering from something that burned like ghost pepper, I scrambled up the circular steps until I'd reached the landing and the door that led into the master bedroom.

The room was blackened save for the light coming through the windows. I scanned the street below for flashing and sirens. But everything was dark.

"Help will be here soon," I breathed as a prayer, my fingers touching the panes. "Someone has to come."

Downstairs the crash of breaking glass was followed by more screams. What was happening? Then I saw them. A line of vampires streaked into the yard below. They were quickly apprehended by men pointing weapons, shouting for them to put their hands up. As fast as the vampires exited, they were herded like cattle and out of sight.

A SWAT team. Like something out of a movie. My shaky sigh fogged the glass of the window. Maybe we'd be okay. Maybe we'd make it.

Wiping the tears from my eyes, I rushed to the door leading to the hallway and slowly opened it. Screams from downstairs swelled. Obviously, vampires were still trying to get out but were too afraid to throw themselves on the mercy of a tactical team. As I stepped into the hallway of the east wing, I scanned the shadows.

Cadel. Creeping up the stairwell. My heart bucked and I backed away. I pivoted on tiptoes and sprinted back into the room. My sweaty hand clutched the doorknob, slid over the metal. I closed the door as silently as possible.

Click.

I turned.

Her form was silhouetted against the light streaming through the window. A blast of red and blue streamed across the panes—police cars arriving—their lights offering a mist of illumination and allowing me to see Maris's outline ... and the gun she pointed directly at me.

"Looking for this?"

I breathed out slowly.

"You've probably been missing this, huh?"

Of course. Maris had taken my gun.

"Pretty careless to leave it sitting out on your mantel—especially for someone who was planning to be a cop." She pushed back a lock of her hair. "But I guess I have to cut you a break. You were on your way out the door to have sex with Pearse. That would make any woman a little air-headed."

I glanced over my shoulder. I'd never make it to the door. She'd shoot me in the back for sure.

Maris clucked. "Not registered to you, though—your gun. To your uncle." A white flash of her teeth. "That's convenient. For all of us, I'd say."

She moved toward me, and I stepped back, edging myself into the darkest of shadows, against the wall.

"Not very smart on your uncle's part, though. Especially since he's an ex-cop." Her voice was low, sharp. "Living in Phoenix, Arizona."

My mouth clicked open. "We need to get out, Maris. SWAT Team's here."

She took another step forward. "I'm sure I know at least one of them. See, here's the thing. We know people all over, in every walk of life. In every state. Our connections are vast. And there are ways around everything." Her figure drifted across the line of the window, but the gun was still pointed at me. "We gave you every chance to have a genuine change of heart. But ... you forced our hand. You and Pearse. His stubbornness is what destroyed him."

"I understand. I know you must be really ... upset with us." My voice squeaked.

"You know, you really were such a disappointment, Avery. To me, to your father. Why do you think he never contacted you?"

Time. I needed to buy some. Until the SWAT team made it up here. Eventually, they'd have to clear the building. They'd find us. "I know you cared for my father a lot, Maris. I know he meant something to you. And you to him. He said so in his journals." Lie, but somewhere in that stony heart of hers, she'd carried a matchstick of a torch for Ace.

She sighed. "I didn't want your father to be the sacrifice." She lifted a shoulder and let it fall again. "But in the end, Ace just wasn't strong enough. Even eighteen years after personally sacrificing his little girlfriend, the succubus stalked him day and night. She never, never left him alone. He wanted it to end. So he volunteered to be the one."

So, my father *had* killed Beverly. Just as I thought. "What did he do with her body, afterward?"

"He sent her to a watery grave."

"Here? At Whickering Place?"

"Well, he couldn't very well cart her to Myrtle Beach, could he?"

So now I knew. That afternoon when I'd thought I'd seen a woman in the koi pond—I had. Beverly. Or at least her likeness—one of the entities mimicking her.

"Surprisingly, after your father was gone, I missed him. I don't usually allow myself to have feelings for a man—or anyone for that matter."

More lights streamed through the window, and a bright white spotlight gleamed over Maris's blonde hair and the twist of her mouth ... which meant she could see me clearly, giving her a better shot. The light glinted off of the gunmetal.

"I actually shed a tear for him. I watched him do it, you know. I was with him while Cadel instructed him, guided Ace's hand to his own throat and helped him cut."

"These sacrifices aren't voluntary," I said, a reflex. "And they don't win you some kind of points with the great succubus and incubus of Whickering Place. There is no such thing."

"The succubus is real." Maris racked the slide on the gun.

My heart lurched.

"I'm surprised to see you so composed, Avery. Do you think what happened down in the ballroom was some sort of sci-fi special effect? You don't think that was real? The deaths? Those really happened. Greer's dead. Cassie's dead." She paused. "Pearse is dead. In your place. That wasn't the plan. The plan was to elevate him as regional leader—a position I could share with him. Once you were gone. But regardless," she snickered. "The succubare is pleased."

My throat tightened, and I fought to maintain control of the emotions sliding up from my core. Pearse was dead. They'd killed him. Just like they'd killed my father. And Cassie. And countless others whose names I didn't even know.

"Ace never wanted kids," Maris sneered. "Your mother told him she couldn't have kids. She trapped him. Then you came along—and he certainly didn't want you, especially after he found out what a weak, pathetic, mental basket case you were."

I nodded. "Well, I think that might have been the pot calling the kettle black. Didn't you just tell me that Ace wasn't strong enough to live?"

"He was still ten times stronger than you. You're nothing like your father."

"Good," I said, trying to keep my voice from shaking. "I'll never be a bloodsucker like him." My legs trembled violently, and my knees dipped.

"No, you just married one." She contorted her lips into that smug smile of hers. "Pearse could've been even greater than your father—he had much more potential to lead." She exhaled air through her nose. "You know, Avery, I had sex with both your father and your husband. I definitely preferred Pearse's abilities in the bedroom to Ace's. Much more masterful. More artful in some ways. But I guess that's the one thing we share in common," she continued. "We'll always have those memories."

Yes, I wanted to kill her. The rage boiled inside of me like nothing I'd ever felt before. But that's what she wanted. It would give her a reason to pull the trigger. I bit down harder on my lip. *Help is on the way. Just hold on a little longer.*

"But we don't have time for this now," she said. "As much as I'd love to continue the chat, we need to make our way upstairs."

"Upstairs? Why?"

"Don't you hear that, Avery? The glorious sound of slithering just above our heads? She's coming. You'll soon see her in her truest form. Her natural state. You'll be amazed by her beauty."

I hadn't noticed it before, but now I heard it—the thump, slither I'd become so accustomed to hearing every day.

"She's as old as time. She could have chosen anywhere to manifest, but she chose this house to be her temple." Maris's shadow moved back and forth, fracturing the light each time she crossed the window. "We were all honored. You should've been honored too. You could've been one of us, Avery. You could've shared in the gifts and the power that is to come."

She held the gun steady as she wiped under her eyes with the back of her left hand. "We'll go up to the room above us—in the traditional place—at the sacrificial wall. Where decades of blood offerings have kept the heart of this house beating. And there, your blood will become part of a legacy."

The wall—the one Ada said smelled of blood.

"Forget it, Maris. I'm not going up there."

"You don't have a choice."

"Yeah, I do. I choose to die right here. Shoot me."

In the end, it would be preferable. Death by bullet would be quick. I probably wouldn't even feel it. The von Willebrand would ensure I'd bleed out quickly.

"Move," she growled in a voice that sounded nothing like her own but like an animal speaking through inhuman vocal cords. "Upstairs. Now."

"No." My legs threatened to fold, and the silk of my dress trembled audibly, rustling in time with my shaking thighs. Pearse would've wanted me to fight. I'd at least go down in battle. I wouldn't allow him to have sacrificed himself for nothing.

The bright lights from the outside shut off, enveloping us in darkness again.

A loud bang shook the walls of the room and rattled my eardrums as the gun went off.

The bullet sliced through the top of my left shoulder, and I dropped to the ground. Seconds later, the white-hot pain exploded through my shoulder, and I instinctively crab crawled into the open closet. Grabbing the knob with my right hand, I pulled the door closed. My heart and adrenaline pumped in tandem.

Shit. That hurt. That hurt really bad. And why had I crawled to the closet? Now I was trapped inside—a rat in a barrel—waiting for her to pull open the door, take her next shot. Warmth spread over my shoulder, and I put my hand to it, felt the rivulet of blood gushing just as my back scraped against my bow. Grasping the grip in my right hand, I tugged it around to the front of me. With my left arm pulsing in pain, I fumbled for the arrows in their quiver.

Through the slats of the closet door, light flared. Maris must have turned on a lamp. "Best to come on out now, Avery. No point in prolonging the inevitable."

With my shoulder throbbing, I tried to extract an arrow from the quiver without making any sound, but the fabric of my dress swished, and my fingers froze, clutching the tip. The pain of every movement nearly took my breath. Thank God I had a compound bow. At least the cams would compensate mechanically and wouldn't require me to use as much strength once I was at full draw.

Maris paced back and forth, her shadow splintering the lamplight.

The closet was empty of most of my clothes since I'd moved many of them to Pearse's bedroom, and the space was just large enough for me to stand and raise the bow. My left arm was weakened, preventing me from pressing against the grip as much as I needed to. My hands shook so hard that as I fitted the arrow into the containment rest, the shaft rattled against it. I felt for the nock groove and attached it onto the bowstring.

Maris moved toward the closet. "I'm sorry it came to this. But as I'm sure you've figured out, sometimes a few must be sacrificed for the good of the many. It is one principle that we share with the rest of the world."

Through the slats of the closet door, the bodice of her black dress glowed like alligator scales.

One shot would be all I'd get. And I hadn't shot my bow in a long time. I also didn't know where I was aiming—I would have to go for whatever I could hit. Obviously, there was no time to line up my target. Blood ran down my aching arm, and it trembled violently as I drew the string back, anchoring it against the tip of my nose and the corner of my mouth.

Light flooded in as the closet door opened, and I had only a second to glimpse the side of Maris's face as I released the string. Another gunshot exploded, propelling a bullet somewhere over my head just as the arrow pierced through her black ballgown. A shower of blood spurted as she shrieked and fell back, clutching her chest. The gun clattered to the ground.

Crawling on my hands and knees, I scrambled forward and grabbed the gun with blood-slick hands. I didn't even look back at

Maris as I tore open the bedroom door and clambered into the hall toward the staircase.

I reached the top of the stairs and looked down. Below was pandemonium. Vampires staggered out the front door clutching at their faces. In the foyer, two were having an altercation with knives, stabbing at each other like they were in a street fight.

My eyes burned, blurring my vision with tears. Whatever chemical agent the SWAT team had used was disseminating throughout the house and finally reaching the upstairs.

I needed to get out. But I didn't think I'd manage the descent down the stairs. Already, my balance was starting to tip, and the blood flowed down my arm, filling in the lacey openings of the dress. At this rate, I'd die of blood loss.

I stepped backward, and my shoulder blades contacted the door to the attic. I could get out to the roof from there and maybe climb—or fall—down the fire escape. At least I could call out for help from up there. I didn't know how much longer my adrenaline would keep me upright.

I yanked the door open and tripped up the stairs. The air was freezing. Tears streamed down my cheeks like I'd just cut up a jalapeno pepper and rubbed my eyes. Up here, it was better. The chemicals obviously hadn't reached the attic yet.

Grabbing onto the top of the banister, I attempted to pull myself up, but my hands were slick with blood and I couldn't get traction. I collapsed onto the stairs, clutching the gun and crawling over the top step, my legs catching in the yards of material swirling around my legs.

I grasped the door frame of the anteroom and dragged myself to standing. Then I swung into the room and stopped.

Torin stood inches away from me. He held a 9mm that looked a lot like mine.

What the hell, Pearse? I thought vampires weren't into guns.

Torin's icy gray eyes stared at me. I raised my Glock.

"Ah-ah." He shook his head. "This now becomes a battle of wills, Avery. And from where I'm standing, your will looks like it's bleeding out pretty fast."

I glanced toward the window, the one that led to the fire escape. Steps away. It was open. Cold air pouring in.

Torin's eyes traveled from my face to the window and back again. "Trying to buy a little time before the pepper spray takes over." His eyes were red-rimmed too and glowed with tears. "Those poor bastards down there got the worst of it, though. At least we had enough sense to get upstairs."

Yeah, lucky me. If I'd just run outside with the rest of them I'd be in police custody right now. Not bleeding to death while facing off with another gun-toting psychopath.

"Your blood won't be wasted, Avery," Torin continued. "You're standing in the perfect room for your final moments." He patted the wall behind him. "We didn't even need to collect your blood and transport it up here."

The sound of shuffling feet drew my attention off to the right, and my heart dropped as Maris appeared, the arrow still protruding from her chest, the bodice of her black gown shining with a deeper, blacker stain of blood. She held on to the door jamb, smearing it with vermilion. "As you can see, Avery, your aim wasn't very good. My heart's slightly lower and to the left." She coughed. "But it sure hurts like hell anyway."

I didn't look at her, kept my eyes on Torin. I should just shoot him. And her. But to be fair, pulling the trigger was slightly harder than I'd thought it would be. I'd never actually shot anyone with a gun.

"Let's do this thing," said Maris to Torin, but her breathing was heavy, and she hunched over, still clinging to the wall.

"Put down the gun, Avery," said Torin. "You're not going to shoot me."

"I shot her," I motioned with my eyes toward Maris. "Why wouldn't I shoot you? It's easier to pull the trigger than a bowstring." At least that sounded true.

"What's the point?" Torin racked the slide.

Damn. This was bad. I'd started to shiver with the cold, the shock. My hands trembled; my muscles cramped and weakened.

"Why would you even want to live?" His gray eyes widened. "Your father's dead. Pearse is dead. You're probably going to jail after tonight. And from the looks of that flesh wound and the amount of blood all over you, I'd say you'll be passing out soon. Then we'll kill you anyway."

Nausea threatened to overwhelm me. My last memory of Pearse was of him being pushed to his knees. "I guess I value life a little more highly than you do, Torin. I think it's worth putting up a fight."

"So, what's it gonna be? Are you gonna pull the trigger, or am I?" Torin's finger moved dangerously close to the trigger, tapping it, teasing it. It was him or me.

Ada's words replayed through my mind. I might be pregnant. Even if I chose not to fight for my own life, I needed to fight for the baby. If there was one.

But then something caught my attention, drew my gaze up high on the white-washed wall behind Torin and Maris. A hole appeared. And a red trickle ran down the length of the wall. Seconds later, another hole opened in the middle, and another rivulet flowed. And then another. And another.

Maris gasped and staggered back. Torin didn't take his eyes from mine, and I tried not to pay attention to what was happening behind him. Blood. It gushed down the surface, turning the white wall into a red waterfall. The serum streamed onto the floor, soaking the carpet and pooling around Torin's shoes.

An instant later, the door to the attic blew open, and a scream ripped from my throat as the room filled with black creatures, all sailing through the air, their wings flapping frantically. They smacked into us, bouncing off and into the faces and hair of Maris and Torin before they flew out the open window. As though a storm blew in black clouds of screaming demons, the hordes of bats battered against us before exiting.

Two explosions sounded—Torin's gun.

And mine.

I'd pulled the trigger.

Torin fell against the bleeding wall and slumped over, his gray eyes wide, his expression registering surprise as he slid down, the blood from his chest wound running over his crotch, his thigh, and then mingling with the flow covering the floor.

Maris dropped to her knees, lunging for Torin's gun.

Instinctively, I racked the slide and fired again, hitting her in the arm she would have used to grab the handle. Clasping her shoulder, she fell back with a scream that barely sounded human.

She growled, wrenched her dress back, and drew one foot up and then the other. When she turned toward me, her eyes were onyx—flashing like an animal's.

It would have been easy to pull the trigger again. Finish her off. "I should just kill you. For what you did to my father. And to Pearse." I stepped across Torin's legs and worked the gun out of his fingers.

"Do it!" She held out her arms, allowing a full-on glimpse of the arrow. Looking at her then, I saw that my aim with the bow had been better than I'd thought. The front of her gown was slick, wet with blood. And now she was giving me a perfect target for a kill shot.

"I specifically didn't kill you," I panted. "I want you to live to see prison."

Outside I heard voices. Shouting.

I backed away from her. And following the exit route of the bats, I lifted my leg and braced the hand holding Torin's gun against the window frame. Dizziness chipped away at my balance, and I nearly fell backward before I could lift the other leg over. My skirts caught on the ledge, and I turned to pull the material loose. The edges of my vision blurred, narrowed as I looked through the window at Maris once more.

Inside, she stood, her gaze transfixed upon something within the attic. I rotated toward the object of her stare.

The thing nearly filled the entirety of the anteroom. Its black, leathery skin rippled as it moved toward Maris, and as it turned, its tail—like something that should be attached to a prehistoric creature—slid behind it. It stood upright on two scaled legs, reaching out with blackened arms tipped with talons. A long, snake-like neck ended in the face of a woman, her red eyes glowing, her head topped with what looked like ram's horns.

The foulest odor I'd ever encountered poured forth from the attic window in the form of a yellow mist as the thing hissed, lolling a lizard tongue from side to side as she slinked toward Maris.

Terror gripped my insides as I backed toward the edge of the rooftop. Navigating the fire escape might be impossible, but better to die trying.

Maris spread her arms. "Succubare," she breathed. "I have waited my whole life to see you. I have done all you've asked." She extended her blood-stained hands. "Yes. I've waited so long for this moment."

As the black body of the succubus eclipsed my view through the window, and Maris's scream—inhuman, like an animal in the throes of death—filled my ears, shouts behind me filtered through.

Male voices bellowed for me to put down the guns. I glanced over my shoulder. Three men dressed in full armor, their rifles trained on me, crept forward. Another one crested the wall at the fire escape ladder, climbed onto the roof and moved toward me.

I squatted slightly, set the guns on the ground.

"Hands in the air."

My left arm shook with pain, forcing a cry from my throat as I lifted my hands, my back to the approaching men. I gasped for air and sank to my knees, my vision narrowing into a gunsight-sized scope. The metal of handcuffs scraped against my wrists. Then the world went dark.

It was over.

Chapter Sixty-Seven
Sunday, April 4

"There were so many of them ... different from a normal hostage-barricade situation ... Blood all over the place ... Six dead inside. Two females. Four males. We didn't find anyone else."

Those were the words I remembered from that night as I lay on a stretcher, looking up at a stark, cold, star-filled sky. Probably a member of the SWAT team reporting their findings.

And Colin. He was there, leaning over the stretcher with assurances that he would ride with me to the hospital, telling me I would be okay.

Lucky for me, Maris had shitty aim. She had hit me in the uppermost part of my left shoulder, grazing the top, blowing off a huge chunk of flesh, and causing a lot of bleeding, but it wasn't a life-threatening injury. Wven though I hadn't used the desmopressin consistently, there had probably been enough of it in my system to promote better clotting. At least that was Colin's theory.

At any rate, I had survived.

And Colin had stayed with me.

Six weeks later, he was still with me. Or I was with him. But not in a romantic way. Just camping out in his new house.

"Are you sure you want to do this?" he asked, grabbing the handle of my suitcase and pulling it off the bed in his spare bedroom.

"Yes. I need to do this."

We'd just moved in three weeks ago following a stint in an extended stay hotel for a while after I got out of the hospital. I'd never set foot in Whickering Place again. Not even for my clothes.

I'd bought all new shirts, pants, a laptop, cell phone. All new everything. I didn't want anything from that place.

Colin had told me I could live with him as long as I wanted. Forever, if it came to that, but there were things I had to do before making any decisions.

A few months before, Pearse had given me an address in New Orleans and told me to go there if anything happened to him. I didn't know what I'd find once I got there, but I needed to go. Without him, the ache inside me—deep down in my core—was profound. The address was a connection to him.

Colin carried the suitcase to the hallway and set it by the door. Then he went back for his own. He'd agreed to drive me to New Orleans and stay until he was sure I was all right. Then, hopefully, he'd said, I'd want to come back to North Carolina. If not, he'd understand.

I was grateful for his help. Colin had been a rock throughout the past six weeks.

Ada's premonition of my pregnancy had been correct.

Confirmed in the hospital, the doctors had done everything they could to ensure I didn't miscarry after losing so much blood. Miraculously, I hadn't. And if all went well, I could expect the baby to be born before Thanksgiving.

"I told you," Ada said while visiting me. "I'm never wrong when it comes to predicting pregnancies. I can see the glow in a woman's eye even before she suspects she's having a baby. There's a new color to the skin—a flush, a whisper of things to come." She'd patted my hand then and urged me to eat my bland spaghetti swimming in orangey water on a plastic hospital plate. "And this baby's gonna be a fighter too. Just think, it's survived vampires and demons..."

I'd told her all about the last night at Whickering Place and my near-death at the hands of Maris and Torin and bats and a monster...

She'd nodded. "I knew when I prayed that day, some of those demons were leaving. But they'd have to go somewhere. I guess they just found their way into the hanging rodents in the attic. Lord only knows where they are now."

The police pretty much moved into Whickering Place after the night of the gathering. Not to mention the reporters, the paranormal groups. The whole house was a crime scene, the property wrapped up like a CSI present in yellow caution tape.

And if there were Colony members on the police force, they were laying low. The FBI was involved now, and those who hadn't been at Whickering Place that night, or the ones who'd escaped the ambush, were either on the run or scrambling for higher ground.

Torin's death was ruled self-defense. His body was found in the room off of the attic, along with Cassie's and Greer's in the ballroom. Three male bodies had been found in the foyer and the billiard room. Their throats had been cut—seemingly by their own or each other's hands. But none of them was identified as Pearse. Pearse's body had not been found.

And that gave me hope.

He could still be alive.

I knew Pearse's unknown status pained Colin. Once again, the burden of Pearse's disastrous decisions was Colin's to bear. But when I said that to him, he'd looked at me, his eyes full of compassion. "You are not a burden. I will do anything I can to help you ... and the baby," he'd muttered. "Pearse asked me to take care of you if anything happened to him. That's what I plan to do."

With Pearse missing in action, it gave me some peace that my child would still have Colin. That *I* would still have Colin. At least for a while.

I grabbed my purse, preparing to head outside to Colin's car—still a major undertaking for me on most days. Reporters had only recently stopped camping out on the lawn once they'd realized neither Colin nor I would talk to them. The paranormal psychologists? Well, that was another story. Every day I got an email or a phone call on my business line from them. So far, I hadn't allowed any paranormalist to investigate the house. I didn't think anyone should enter if they didn't absolutely have to be there.

As I opened the front door and stepped out, Detective Stoney was walking up the driveway.

"Got a second?"

"Well, we were just getting ready to leave, but ..." I looked behind me.

Colin stood in the foyer and set his bag down next to mine. "What's going on?"

Stoney crested the top step. "Could I delay you for a minute or two? I have some news you might want to hear."

"WE DRAINED THE KOI pond in the garden," Stoney said. His eyes had deep pits underneath them. No doubt this investigation and what they'd discovered inside that house had kept him up at night. "We found remains. Of a woman. Probably been there close to twenty years."

"Who was it?" Colin asked.

"DNA results confirmed today it was someone named Beverly Moorhead. Been missing since 2001."

I inhaled sharply. I wasn't surprised. I'd known all along that Beverly was dead. And the fact that they'd never found her body had given me even more reason to believe she was somewhere within Whickering Place or on the property. She'd been in the koi pond all along. Just like I'd envisioned. Just as Maris had suggested with her "watery grave" comment.

"How did she die?" I asked, even though I already knew.

"It's hard to tell because the remains were so decomposed. Based on the journals you shared with us, and what we know about The Colony's practices, I'd say it's the same as the others."

"My father killed her."

Stoney nodded. "So it would seem."

"What about the others that died? Cassie? Greer? The ones murdered at the cemetery and the skate park?"

"Cassie Graves had been working as an informant for about six months. She tipped us off about the gathering and what was going to happen." Stoney blew out a quick breath. "But we lost contact with her early that night, and it delayed our response time." He pulled out a handkerchief and passed it under his nose. "But to answer your question, all of the homicides are still under investigation. We're trying to sort out who were the actual knife-wielders versus the accomplices. It's complicated."

Pearse probably would be considered one of those accomplices. Maybe even one of the "knife wielders."

"One thing we do know," Stoney told me. "The Colony? Unfortunately, they're still out there. We may have tagged a few, but as you know, the network runs far and wide. And I hate to tell you this, but some Whickering Place binding coins have already turned up again. At the hospital."

The news was a blow. A real blow. The police were having to exert a lot of manpower around the hospital to ensure that all staff and visitors were carefully screened and monitored.

I'd hoped this would've all been over. That the terrible last night I'd spent at Whickering Place wouldn't have been in vain.

"We can get you into witness protection if you want," Stoney said.

But I declined. If there was even the smallest chance of finding Pearse or having him find me, I was willing to risk being discovered by the others.

"Any word about Pearse?"

Stoney shifted in his seat. "Well, with everything that's been on the news about The Colony, and Pearse's picture circulating through the media, we actually did get a strange tip-off this morning. A woman in Macon, Georgia, called us to say she was pretty sure she'd seen a man fitting Pearse's description."

"Where?"

"At a gas station." Stoney jerked his right shoulder. "Don't get too excited. There are a lot of dark-haired, dark-eyed men that could fit his description."

My heart sped. It was something. Anything at all was a thread of a lifeline. I'd had dreams he was dead. I'd had dreams that he was being held hostage. And then there were the ones where he walked through the front door of Colin's house. But I knew that one was the most far-fetched of all of them.

"He may have changed his appearance by now," Stoney said. "And of course, we don't know what his state of mind might be."

"What will happen now?" Colin asked.

"We'll look for him. But as you can imagine, we've got our hands pretty full at the moment. The district attorney's dealing with a huge group of vampires to prosecute. We're still trying to get them to give up names of the higher-ups. You'd be amazed at how hard it is to get them to talk. And we're still looking for Maris Manners and Cadel Johanssen."

I wanted to tell him they wouldn't find Maris. Ever.

Stoney and Colin chatted as they moved toward the front door, their conversation lost on me as I processed what the detective had said. Conquering The Colony seemed nearly impossible. But I clung to the hope that Pearse was still alive.

"What will you do with the house?" Stoney asked.

"Sell it. It's already underway. My realtor called today, said she has someone interested in buying."

He nodded. "Good luck." He turned once more as he reached the front door. "That place completely freaked out the investigators. One of the guys said a phone in the hallway kept ringing. Every time they'd pick it up, there were all these strange voices ... speaking in Latin. He finally carried it outside so they didn't have to hear it ringing constantly. Another investigator said he thought he saw blood running down the paintings. He thought the other guys were playing a prank on him."

I felt the corners of my mouth twist. Evil was still alive in that house. And I planned to give full disclosure to the new owner and suggest they have the place exorcised.

For me, remembering the traumatic events that had happened in Whickering Place reminded me of what I'd survived. And why I'd never go back.

"I know they're all eager to be done with that place," Stoney said.

"Me too."

After Stoney left, Colin and I finished packing up the car and headed out.

Colin drove for a while in silence.

Once we'd gotten onto the highway, he finally spoke. "Avery, I'm not saying this to be harsh, but what if Pearse never comes back? Or what if you find out he's dead?"

I didn't answer right away. It took me a few seconds to swallow and beat back the tightening dread in my chest. My hormones were crazy, and without the lorazepam or Xanax, I had to work a lot harder to control my emotions.

"Then he doesn't come back. Or I have to deal with the fact that he's dead." I looked over at Colin. "And I take everything one day at a time. I have other lives to think about now."

He nodded. "Would you ever consider ... look, I know you're in love with my brother, but would you ever let me help you raise the baby?"

I knew what he was asking. Somewhere down the line, it might not be the most ridiculous idea. But right then, I couldn't go there. "I can only do one day at a time."

He glanced over at me. The springtime sun glinted off of his hazel-green eyes. They reminded me a little of my own—the pain behind them. But there was strength there too.

"I know you consider yourself an army of one. Annie Oakley. Vampire slayer."

I laughed.

He shifted his head and ratcheted his gaze to the road. "But I guess what I'm saying is, the next time you decide to take on a houseful of vampires with a crossbow, I'd just like to be there to hand you the arrows."

I nodded. "Okay. You could be useful, I suppose."

He shrugged. "I mean, my exorcism skills are for shit, and I'm not even sure if I'd be much help in staking anyone, but I'm not bad at CPR."

"Anything else?"

"Well, I can tie a decent tourniquet."

I laughed. And then I realized I'd laughed twice in the last minute—the first time I'd laughed in six weeks. "And what if Pearse *does* come back?"

Colin's eye twitched slightly. "Then it'll be the happiest day of your life."

After that, he was quiet again until we passed the sign welcoming us to South Carolina. "I'm sure you wish you'd made a different decision four months ago, that you'd never come to Whickering Place. You could've stayed in Morganton. You could've stayed safe."

A smile tugged at my lips. "What? And miss all this?"

Colin shrugged. "You know what I mean."

I did. "I know it's hard to understand, but four months ago, I lived in a gated community that I never left. I felt nothing, I did nothing, and inside, I was dying. Now?" I looked out at the road stretching toward an unknown future. I'd just crossed over into another state. That was something I'd never done before. And there would be another state line and another after that. "Now, I'm finally living."

Friday, May 1
Asheville Psychiatric Care Center

T he woman sits staring out the window, her brain twisting with nervous energy. The voices have been bad today. Really bad.

Soon, she'll be meeting her new therapist. She doesn't know why she's getting a new therapist or what happened to her old one, but her anxiety levels are high, and the staff nurses are forced to increase her medication.

She focuses on the scene outside her window. Lots of trees. Mountains in the background... She turns over a coin in her hand. One of her friends here gave it to her, said it's supposed to bring her good luck. It has some weird writing on it and a picture of a house. Whatever. She needs all the good luck she can get.

"Hello, Laura."

She spins around, drops her legs from the window seat.

A woman with light brown hair that flips up at the ends stands in the doorway. As she glides into the room, Laura sees she's carrying a file. It's a heavy one. Full of a decade of notes on medications, treatments that haven't worked, transcriptions of long conversations with previous therapists.

"Hi."

"I'm Dr. Julianne Murphy." She holds out her hand.

Laura takes it. "You're my new therapist."

"Yes." She sits down in the only cushioned chair in the room. Blue vinyl. Matches the curtains. Dr. Murphy licks her lips. "So how are you feeling? The nurses said you were having a bad day."

The girl fights tears. "I'd expected my husband to visit today. But he didn't come."

Dr. Murphy opens the thick file, jots down something on a fresh sheet of lined paper. "Other friends? Do they visit you?" She doesn't look up as she asks.

"No," Laura answers simply. "Not really."

Dr. Murphy lays the file in her lap, the pen across the lined paper. She meets Laura's gaze. "It's important to have friendships. A group of people who can surround you, support you, help care for you."

When were they going to start talking about her long history of medical failures? That's what all the other therapists wanted to discuss.

"How are you sleeping?" Dr. Murphy asks.

"I'm feeling tired. I didn't sleep well last night. Do you know what happened to my other therapist?"

"No." Dr. Murphy shifts in her seat, crosses her legs. "But I'm glad I get to work with you. You're my first patient here in Asheville. I just moved last week from Morganton."

"Why did you move?"

"I bought a house here. From an old patient of mine. Just moved in."

Laura nods. "That's nice."

"Yes, it is. It's a home in the Montford Historic District. Have you ever heard of Whickering Place?"

Laura shakes her head. Suddenly, the voices are all talking at once.

She reaches for her good luck coin.

She hopes Dr. Murphy might be the one who finally helps quiet the voices.

AVERY'S JOURNEY CONTINUES IN THE THIRD BOOK
OF
THE LEGACY OF DARKNESS SERIES.
COMING IN 2020.

ACKNOWLEDGMENTS

Saying "thank you" hardly seems enough praise for these folks who helped make this book possible.

To Asheville, North Carolina: you are one of my favorite towns in the U.S. Thank you for providing the inspiration for this story, even though, to my knowledge, no vampire cults actually exist there.

To my beta readers—Bob Campbell, Kelly Alderson, Misha Chernov, Tammie Arnold, and Deborah Harris, your comments and advice transformed this story.

A special thanks to Stephen Lee Designs for the awesome cover and book trailer. You bring color and visual concept to the story.

To my awesome source for all things SWAT—Matthew Cole, you went above and beyond the call of duty with the fantastic information you gave me. I'm only sorry the scene is so short. Maybe the next novel will make more use of your tactical brilliance.

Thank you to my husband for his patience during all the days and nights when I was writing, editing, or thinking about the story. Your support and love make it all possible.

And to all my family and friends—thank you for being my biggest cheerleaders and for believing in me.

Don't miss out!

Visit the website below and you can sign up to receive emails whenever London Clarke publishes a new book. There's no charge and no obligation.

https://books2read.com/r/B-A-TGRF-KEEAB

Connecting independent readers to independent writers.

Also by London Clarke

Dunmoor
Dunmoor
House of Brutes and Angels

Legacy of Darkness
The Meadows
Whickering Place

Watch for more at https://www.londonclarke.com.

About the Author

London Clarke is the award-winning and Amazon bestselling author of *Wildfell* and the Legacy of Darkness series.

Obsessed with vampires and haunted houses from a young age, London grew up reading gothic tales that featured romantic and tragic heroes. *Wuthering Heights* and *Dracula* are her favorite novels, and although now happily married, she readily confesses that she once moved to England in search of a man who was the perfect amalgamation of Dracula, Hamlet, Heathcliff, and Mr. Rochester. Along with her travels, she's had an eclectic array of jobs including receptionist, legal secretary, literary assistant, high school English teacher, and freelance editor.

London lives in a Washington, DC suburb with her husband and two greyhounds. She's happiest when she's writing novels, reading books, or touring old houses and cemeteries.

Read more at https://www.londonclarke.com.

Milton Keynes UK
Ingram Content Group UK Ltd.
KHW040728161023
697UK00005B/282